ECLIPSED

BY K MURPHY

Copyright © 2025 K. Murphy
All rights reserved.

No part of this book may be reproduced, stored in a retrieval system, or transmitted in any form or by any means electronic, mechanical, photocopying, recording, or otherwise, without the prior written permission of the publisher, except in the case of brief quotations used in reviews, articles, or other critical works.

This is a work of fiction. Names, characters, places, and incidents are the product of the author's imagination or are used fictitiously. Any resemblance to actual persons, living or dead, events, or locales is entirely coincidental.

Cover Design: K. Murphy
Editing: K. Murphy

ISBN: 978-1-969842-00-9

Published by: Butterfly and Bear Books

First, thank you, from the bottom of my heart, for picking up *Eclipsed*, my debut novel and the very first installation in *The Eclipsed Series*. This story has lived in my head and heart for a long time, and it means the world that you've chosen to join me on this journey.

A little about me: I'm K. Murphy, a lifelong dreamer, writer, and now, thanks to you, a published author. I am usually running around with tiny gremlins that can't even read yet, so this is my very first book, which means there were long nights, plenty of coffee, and quite a few "what on earth am I doing?" moments along the way. But here we are. You're holding proof that dreams can make their way onto paper.

Since this book was self-edited, I want to thank you for your patience and understanding if the occasional typo or misspelling snuck past me. If you catch one, feel free to let me know, I welcome the feedback! You can reach me at my TikTok **@i.k.murphy** or by email at **k.murphy.author24@gmail.com**.

Most of all, I hope you enjoy the ride. Let yourself get lost in the magic, the chaos, and the shadows. And when you turn that last page—I'll see you on the other side.

Much love, my little book gremlins and sunlings,
K. Murphy

For every heart that's been caged—

tear the bars apart.

For every fire smothered—

breathe life into the embers.

And when they say you're playing with fire...

tell them you intend to burn,

And take the world with you.

And on a personal note:

When it comes to everyone who persisted in saying that I would never amount to anything in life.

I hope you devour every second of this book,

And

Choke.

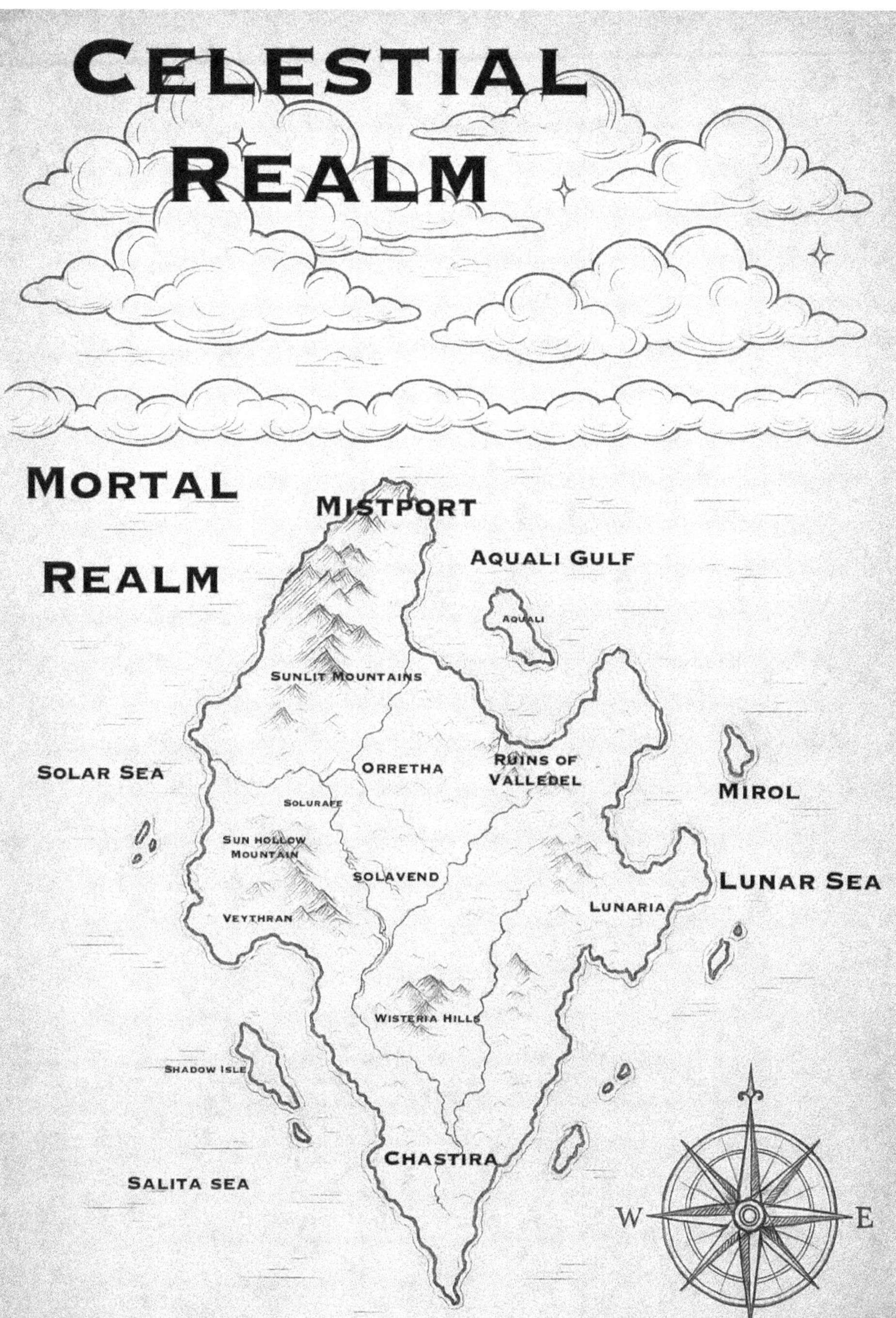

CELESTIAL REALM
MORTAL REALM
MISTPORT
AQUALI GULF
AQUALI
SUNLIT MOUNTAINS
ORRETHA
RUINS OF VALLEDEL
SOLAR SEA
SOLURAFE
MIROL
SUN HOLLOW MOUNTAIN
SOLAVEND
LUNAR SEA
VEYTHRAN
LUNARIA
WISTERIA HILLS
SHADOW ISLE
CHASTIRA
SALITA SEA
W
E
S

Prologue

The night before the festival, Elara could not sleep.

The air of Solia hummed with life, even after dark. From her small window she could see lanterns strung across the village square, glowing like stars caught in nets. Laughter rose and fell outside, tangled with the faint thump of drums that had been beating since morning. Voices sang in half-sloshed chorus, practicing hymns for the Sun God, weaving ribbons, finishing garlands of marigold and fire-bloom. The Eclipse Festival came but once each year, and the villagers meant to wring every joy from it.

But joy was the farthest thing from Elara's mind.

She lay stiff beneath the quilt, her small fists twisting the fabric, her eyes following the firelight dancing across the rafters. She had overheard the older children in the square, whispers about the *chosen*. About how the gods came down to take them away. About how they never came back.

The word *sacrifice* had not left their lips, but Elara was clever enough to know. Clever enough to be afraid.

A soft sound brushed the doorway—her mother's step, familiar as breath.

"Still awake, little flame?" Serinyà's voice carried warmth, though her eyes, pale and ocean-bright, lingered with knowing.

Elara swallowed hard. "Mama... what happens to the *chosen*?"

The question seemed to halt the air itself. Her mother's hand lingered against the doorframe, her body caught between the glow of the hearth and the shadows beyond. At last she crossed to the bed, sitting at its edge. She reached down to brush a curl from Elara's damp brow.

"Why do you ask?"

Elara's lip wobbled. "They say... they go away forever. That the gods take them into the dark. What if—" her voice broke to a whisper—"what if they choose me?"

Serinyà's heart clenched, though her smile did not falter. She drew Elara into her arms, the little girl pressing her face against her gown, curls tickling her chin. "Oh, Elara. The gods are not so simple, no matter what the priests teach in their temples."

Elara sniffled into the fabric. "Then what's true?"

Her mother's voice softened, lowered into that hushed rhythm Elara loved, the one that made words sway like tides. "Once, long ago, the Sun burned too fiercely, and the Moon shone too cold. Their quarrel made the shadows bold. And the shadows rose thick until they smothered the Moon whole, choking the light until nothing remained but silence."

Elara shivered, tilting her face up. "That's scary."

"Yes," Serinyà agreed, her hand smoothing down her daughter's back. "But from that silence, a new light was born. Not Sun, not Moon. Something between. He broke free from the shadows, and they feared him, because they could not unmake him."

Elara's wide eyes glistened. "Did he kill the shadows?"

"No, little flame. Shadows never truly die. And neither does light. They will always chase each other, one rising, the other falling, as the sky turns." Serinyà's fingers traced idle circles against Elara's temple. Then her voice dropped to a secretive hush. "But water..."

Elara blinked. "Water?"

Her mother smiled faintly. "Yes. Water is balance. Both shadow and light are cleansed by it. What others forget, it remembers. When all else breaks, it endures. Washing wounds, feeding roots, wearing down mountains, it restores lost things in the end. Water is the only thing the heavens themselves cannot outlast."

The fire popped, sending sparks spiraling up the chimney. The drums outside slowed, replaced by a far-off chorus, the hymn to the Sun rolling like thunder across the square.

Elara clutched tighter to her mother's sleeve. "Will water... save the chosen?"

Serinyà pressed a kiss to her brow, her lips lingering there. "Yes, my love. Even if they take them, and even if the world falls into shadow, water will always return. Balance will always return."

Her daughter yawned, her small body softening in her arms. "Balance," she murmured, already drifting. "Balance always returns."

Serinyà rocked her gently, and then, as sleep pulled Elara under, she sang—a lullaby so old only the sea itself might remember it.

Drift, my flame, the stars will keep,
Sun may burn and Moon may weep.
Shadows fall, and fade away,
Water flows and finds the way.

Rest, my heart, the tide runs true,
Light and dark will bow to you.
When the skies forget their song,
Water sings and rights the wrong.

Her voice fell to a hum, the melody rippling through the dim room like waves against a shore. Elara's breath steadied, lashes fluttering once, then stilling. Serinyà stayed long after her daughter slept, her hand pressed over the small, steady thrum of Elara's heart. The scent of salt and smoke clung faintly to her skin, though no sea lay near.

At last she rose, careful not to wake the child, and slipped from the room. The hearth had dimmed to embers. Shadows crept along the walls. Yet in Serinyà's eyes, there burned something older, deeper—an echo of waves, an oath of water. Because bedtime stories were never *just* stories.

And one day, her daughter would need to remember every word.

Chapter One

The first breath of morning always carried the scent of smoke and thyme.

Here in Solavend—tucked where the Auren Hills kissed the southern sky—the world stirred slowly under the blush of dawn. The thatched rooftops, soft with moss at the edges, shimmered faintly in the light. Stone chimneys whispered trails of smoke into the pale sky, and somewhere in the distance, a raven cawed—sharp enough to pierce the quiet.

I stood barefoot in the apothecary garden, cool dirt cradling the arches of my feet. The ground was still damp from last night's rain, clinging to my skin with a familiarity that made my stomach ache. I'd already loosened my braid and shoved it back once, but red curls kept escaping—twisting like they had minds of their own, damp and clinging to my cheek. My hands moved methodically through the fire leaf row, fingers grazing the crimson petals with something between reverence and resignation.

The fire blooms had bloomed early again. They weren't supposed to.

I plucked one anyway, brushing my thumb over the velvety underside of the blossom. It pulsed with residual warmth. Sometimes they did that in my grip—like they liked me. I still hadn't decided if that comforted me... or accused me. The petals bled their scent into the air: sharp, almost metallic, chased by something sweet. It smelled like a wound dressed in honey.

"Elara!"

I didn't flinch. Fennah's voice was sharp but never unkind. She leaned out the apothecary window; her face already lined from decades of sun and responsibility, her sleeves rolled up and dusted with dried clover.

"I need that fire bloom tincture," she called. "Ardin's boy's burning up again."

I didn't answer right away. I gave the fire bloom one last glance before tucking it into the satchel at my hip and turning toward the back door. The step creaked beneath my bare foot as I went inside.

The scent of lavender and wormwood hit me instantly, thick in the air and clinging to the walls like memory. Rows of clay jars lined the shelves, each etched with chalk runes to ward against rot or theft, and bundles of drying herbs dangled from the rafters, casting shadows like sleeping bats.

The hearth's warmth wasn't oppressive yet, but it would be by noon, once the sunlight hit the front windows. Fennah didn't look up as she ground feverfew with slow, practiced movements.

"Did you sleep at all?" she asked.

I pulled the fire bloom tincture from the rack, wiping the dust from the glass. "Some."

"Nightmares again?"

My grip tightened faintly around the bottle. "Not this time."

She didn't press. She never did. There were things in Solavend better left untouched. Everyone knew that—even if they pretended otherwise. Especially this week. "The eclipse stirs everything," Fennah said after a moment, her voice quieter now. "The animals get jittery. Bones ache. The gods get... close."

I didn't answer, though my chest ached at the mention of gods. I slid the bottle across the counter, and she took it with careful hands.

"They'll be expecting you at the temple festival," she added gently. "You'll be of age."

"I know."

The weight of it settled between us like an uninvited guest. Twenty-one. The age of full bloom. Of sacred offering. Of divine notice. And the day of the eclipse would return.

Outside, the air had warmed but hadn't yet turned cruel. I moved through the square with my satchel pressed tight to my hip, the clang of hammer against wood echoing from the half-built festival scaffolds. Bright gold and deep red ribbons already fluttered between lantern posts, like tongues of fire in the wind. A merchant called out about candied citrus peels while a child screamed with giddy laughter, his hands sticky with honey.

The statue of Solari dominated the square—sun-forged and looming, arms outstretched toward the sky. In his right hand, fire; in his left, wheat. His face was flawless, untouched by time or rain. Not like the one in the northern quarter—the old statue with the child in his arms. That one had no face left at all. Worn smooth. Forgotten.

I passed it as I always did. Quietly. Without a glance.

A flicker of movement caught my eye—a group of sun-priests in ceremonial robes, the gold thread in their hems catching the morning light like spear points. They moved in perfect formation, blessing villagers with sun-signs traced in the air. One passed me and, without hesitation, carved the sigil in my direction—not to bless me, but to shield himself. The way you'd cross yourself after walking near a grave.

I kept my eyes on the road ahead.

The whispers reached me before I could make out the words—slipping along my spine like smoke under a door. Born during the eclipse... cursed blood... and now she'll be of age. Half-muttered, half-thought, more superstition than sentence, but they clung like burrs. Lirien's voice cut through them—sweet as honey-wine, sharp enough to draw blood. She lounged against her family's stall draped in sugared fruit, her smile all teeth. I never stopped. Slowing down didn't happen. Their giggles and stares fell away behind me like discarded cloaks as I walked past.

They'd always seen me this way—like a shadow masquerading as one of their own.

I turned down the path past the orchard, toward the old ash tree where the stone well waited. Nobody had used the well for years, but it was quiet there. Safe, in a way the rest of Solavend never was. Birds chirped faintly in the boughs above, and the leaves shivered in a breeze I hadn't felt a moment ago.

Stepping to the edge of the well, I set my hand on the weather-worn stone and closed my eyes. Centered me. There was a hum in the earth—quiet, faint, but present. My magic stirred beneath my ribs—not enough to rise, but enough to remind me it was there. Waiting. Waiting always.

The wind brushed the back of my neck.

My eyes snapped open.

The orchard was still unchanged. Stillness characterized the path, the stalls behind me bustled faintly with laughter and clatter, but something had shifted. Something in the air had turned. I didn't know how I knew. Only that I did. I lingered a moment longer at the well, my fingers curled around its rim, straining to listen past the rustle of leaves and the distant chatter of the market. It was nothing. And yet... it wasn't.

Eventually, my feet remembered how to move. I followed the curve of the path back toward the heart of the village, past the orchard's edge and into the sun-warmed streets where everyone still lived like the gods could hear them.

And in Solavend, the gods always could. Every child learned the first thing: Solari watches. Solari judges. Solari blesses.

But not everyone is worth blessing here.

People built the village on a belief so old and deep-rooted that they may as well have carved it into the stones beneath our feet. The sun, giver of life , was sacred. Its warmth, its fire, its rhythm, all part of the divine order. The eclipse was the only time that rhythm faltered, the only moment when darkness bled into daylight. The priests called it an unveiling—when the true balance of the world revealed itself. When the light dimmed, and the old shadows stirred. I'd asked once as a child why they feared the dark if Solari was so strong. The priest had looked at me like I'd spat at the altar.

"Because it is not his dark," he'd said. I hadn't asked again.

The Sun Temple stood at the highest point in the village, its domed roof catching light like a firefly jar. Every morning at the third bell, the priests climbed the spiral steps to light the rooftop brazier, letting its smoke signal the day's start.

Today, the smoke curled straight and clean into the sky. No wind to disrupt it. An omen of stability, they'd say. A good sign.

But it didn't move at all. Not even a flicker. Not natural.

I didn't trust omens. Or signs. Or priests.

I passed a vendor selling eclipse charms—carved disks painted gold and black, strung on crimson thread. Protection from the dark, they claimed. Wards to keep nightmares at bay. One trinket had cracked clean down the center. The vendor didn't notice. Or care.

Farther along, an elder hunched on a stool, her hands trembling as she painted blessings onto prayer scrolls. Children stared wide-eyed as the ink shimmered under her brush, then disappeared entirely. Ink made from sunstone dust, they whispered. Sacred. Holy. Only effective when used by the faithful.

When I was ten, I tried to touch a sunstone shard. It burned my palm.

I still carry the scar—a faint crescent just beneath my thumb.

No one offered to heal it. They said it was a sign. A warning.
Keep your hands where they belong.

I tugged my sleeve down as I passed the old woman.

The temple bells chimed ahead—four low tolls, heavy and deliberate. The hour of offering. Villagers stopped where they were, turning their faces toward the sound. Some pressed the sun-sign over their hearts. Others bowed their heads. I didn't move. I stood still as stone, a single flame refusing to flicker.

A child bumped into my leg and looked up. His eyes widened, and he stepped back without a word. He ran to his mother, who pulled him behind her skirt without so much as a glance in my direction.

I kept walking.

I didn't look at the priests near the temple gates, though I could feel their eyes tracking me—like crows sizing up a carcass. Their gazes slid over my skin like oil.

The eclipse child. The cursed one. *The marked.*

Every year, the festival drew pilgrims from the outer villages. They came to offer gifts to Solari, to bask in the firelight, to pray for thriving crops and protection from lightning and blight. However, this year brought with it a change in the air. This year, the elders brought back the ritual. Not everyone knew what it meant. Not fully. The old traditions weren't spoken aloud anymore, but people remembered. Whispers passed in kitchens, at market stalls, between wine-slick lips in the dark. Eclipses required balance. Darkness taken had to be balanced with light given.

That was the oldest law we had. The last time we had a ritual during the Eclipse Festival was when I was a child. I spent my birthday in fear that they would send me away with the gods, to get rid of the problem before it started. But now that our crops are struggling to grow food for our growing population, the elders will choose one elf, over the age of 21 to burn on the pyre as an offering for Solari, in hopes that he will grace us with his presence and bless our crops. And unfortunately for me I have always been a little too close to the dark for the elders' liking.

I rounded a corner and slipped onto a narrow side path, where the stone walls pressed close and the air cooled. Here, between the buildings, the market noise faded—muffled by distance and stone. This alley led to the back of the weaver's shop—Fennah's sister, old Mirra, who'd never spoken a word to me but still left out scraps of thread and broken needles for me to mend with. Acts of silent kindness were the only ones that lasted in Solavend.

I sat on the low stone bench just beyond the shop and let myself breathe.

It wasn't fair.

Not just the festival, or the staring, or the muttered prayers trailing in my wake. It wasn't fair that my entire life had been shaped by a sky I had no control over. Born under a vanished sun. Branded before my first breath. They didn't see a person when they looked at me. They saw a story. A warning. A necessary offering. And it was getting harder to pretend I didn't feel it closing in.

I leaned my head back against the wall, letting my eyes drift shut. Somewhere above, sunlight pooled on rooftops and caught on gold-threaded tapestries waving from windows. The whole village was dressing itself up as if it didn't already know what was coming. But I did. I didn't need visions or omens or bone-deep magic to tell me something was shifting beneath the surface of Solavend. I could feel it in the way people looked at me. In the way, my magic hummed like a struck chord. In the tightening space between each breath.

But there was nothing I could do. Not yet. Not today.

I pushed myself up from the bench, dusted my hands on my skirt, and started toward the apothecary. Fennah would be waiting. And work, at least, didn't look at me like I was a storm about to break.

The apothecary's door creaked open with its familiar groan, the old brass hinges catching just enough to sing their complaint. The scent of dried herbs wrapped around me like a shawl as I stepped inside—warm, bitter, comforting. The kind of smell that lingered in my hair long after I'd left, clinging like a second skin.

Fennah was already elbow-deep in a basin of crushed yarrow and willow bark, her sleeves rolled up, fingers stained green. She looked up with a grunt and nodded toward the shelf by the back window. "Fever tinctures need bottling. Glass is clean this time—thank the gods." Then, after a beat, more softly, "You alright?"

I gave a single nod as I slipped past the rows of jars and hanging bundles. The shelves were a riot of labeled vials and crooked clay pots, all arranged by Fennah's impossible, arcane system. I'd offered to reorganize once—drawn in by the chaos—and had nearly lost an eyebrow when she barked, "Touch anything without knowing its mood, and we'll both be ghosts by nightfall."

Now, I didn't even think about moving things. I just worked. Quiet. Careful. Reliable.

Villagers were always more comfortable when you were useful.

I pulled the fever tincture from where it rested in a half-filled jug, then began decanting it into small corked bottles with a funnel. The amber liquid slid slowly and thickly into the glass, catching the morning light. My fingers moved with precision—steady hands, sharp eyes. I found a rhythm there, in the work. A kind of peace.

And today, I needed it more than usual.

Fennah passed behind me, muttering as she sorted bundles of nettle and chamomile. "Word is old Marek fell into the irrigation ditch again. His daughter's on her way with a twisted ankle from dragging him out."

I didn't laugh, but the corner of my mouth twitched. "That's the third time this season."

"Fourth, I'm keeping score." Her voice turned dry. "Another fall and I'm charging him a limb."

The door creaked open just then, the bell above it giving a half-hearted jingle. I didn't turn, but I heard the hesitant footsteps before the voice followed.

"Morning, Mistress Fennah."

"Back again, Wren?" she said, not looking up. "What is it this time— did you scratch your elbow and now think you're dying because the wind told you?"

A sheepish laugh. "Sore throat, actually. Swear it's real this time." I glanced up. Wren Telward—barely thirteen, a farmer's son with a heart too soft and a mouth too quick. He shot me a nervous smile as he approached the counter, eyes darting between me and the floor. He always smiled, but it never quite reached his eyes when I was there.

I corked the last tincture bottle and set it on the rack.

Fennah handed Wren a small sachet of dried root. "Boil that with water. Gargle it. If it's still sore tomorrow, come back. And if I find out you're just trying to miss your chores again—"

"I swear I'm not!" he said quickly, then hesitated. "My mum… she told me to ask if Elara made it."

There it was. Fennah's face didn't change, but the silence stretched for a beat too long. "I did," I said quietly, before the pause could grow teeth. I crossed to the shelf, pulled a second pouch, and set it gently on the counter.

Wren took it carefully, like it might bite. "Thanks," he mumbled, and then left with a hasty shuffle of boots on stone.

Fennah let out a slow breath. "Better than last time." Last time, Wren's mother hadn't come back for the remedy at all. Rumor said she'd buried it under the willow tree at the edge of the orchard. Just in case.

There was no open hatred in Solavend. No torches, or stones, or shouted curses. But the distrust ran deep, buried like roots beneath the cobbled roads and sun-kissed rituals. They came to the apothecary because they had to. Because my work helped. Because my hands healed. And then they whispered after they left. Crossed themselves. Prayed for balance.

I couldn't decide which part I hated more—the fear in their eyes, or the need.

The sun climbed higher through the windows, casting long golden beams through the herb-hung rafters. I was labeling the last row of tinctures when Fennah set down a bowl of stewed barley and dried peach slices beside me.

"You didn't eat breakfast."

"I wasn't hungry."

"You're still not, but that's never stopped me before."

I took the bowl, my stomach twisting with quiet gratitude. Fennah wasn't warm—not in the way people usually meant it. But she saw me. And after two decades in this village, I'd learned that being seen was its own kind of miracle.

I ate quickly, quietly, listening to the soft sounds of mortar grinding and the whisper of the breeze through the rafters.

The door didn't open again for a while.

By the time the sun began to lower, the apothecary had returned to its usual rhythm—quiet, herbal-scented, and humming with the low, steady energy of preparation. I spent the rest of the afternoon measuring powders and infusions, wrapping dried herbs into bundles, and bottling the last of the thistle wine extract while Fennah muttered to herself about missing deliveries and unreliable villagers.

We worked without speaking much, and that suited us both. The silence between us was comfortable, productive—better than words, really. It let me lose myself in the repetition, the small acts of purpose that, in moments like these, felt almost sacred. There was something grounding in the work—in the clink of glass and the crinkle of parchment—something that reminded me I was more than what people whispered about behind their hands.

When Fennah finally waved me off, muttering that I'd best go breathe some air before my skin turned gray, I didn't argue.

I slipped through the back garden into the early evening light, the last golden rays stretching long over the village rooftops. The air had softened, cooled. Scents of roasted root vegetables and wood-smoke curled through the breeze, blending with the fading sweetness of late summer flowers clinging to stone windowsills. Children were being called indoors with soft shouts and the occasional bark of a dog. Everything was settling into that dusky rhythm of twilight, where the day exhaled and the night hadn't yet gathered its courage.

I took the long way home, as I often did—past the overgrown vineyard where mint and violet thistle grew wild, past the crumbling stone wall where the elders sat in the mornings to share bread and gossip. Now the spots were empty, bathed in the fading light.

My footsteps echoed softly along the dirt path as I climbed toward the overlook above the sea cliffs—the place where wind met open sky and the entire village lay tucked behind me like something from another life. I sat at the edge of the rise, arms resting on my knees, and let myself fall into the rhythm of the waves crashing against the shore far below.

This was my favorite part of the day. Not because it was peaceful—it rarely was—but because it was honest. No crowds at dusk. No stares. No forced smiles. Just the wind, the salt in the air, and the sky pulling slowly into shades of bruised violet and molten gold.

The temple brazier above the village square flickered faintly now, its fire casting a pale glow that felt less divine and more decorative. Everything shimmered as if it was trying to be more beautiful than it was. And maybe it was working. Maybe the village really did look lovely in this light.

But beauty didn't equal safety. I knew that better than anyone.

I reached into my satchel and pulled out the small, cracked amber charm I kept tucked at the bottom—a thin, worn cord looped through the fossilized stone, smooth and warm from being handled too often. It was the only thing I had from before. No letter. No name. No stories. Just this.

Sometimes I imagined my mother had worn it once, or that my father had tied it into my swaddle before disappearing into myth. But most days, I just held it and imagined it was heavier than it was. That it could anchor me.

The charm caught what little sunlight was left and glowed faintly in my palm. My magic stirred beneath my skin like it always did at dusk—not loud, not insistent, but present. It hummed just below the surface, a low murmur of warmth nestled in my bones, like embers in a hearth that never truly died. I didn't summon it, didn't speak to it, but I acknowledged it. That was all it needed.

A gust of wind brushed over me, soft and cool against my face. For a moment, I closed my eyes and imagined it was a hand—cupping my cheek, brushing back my hair. The thought made something in my chest ache, but I didn't dwell on it.

Then the air shifted. Not just the wind, but the atmosphere. It grew still. Heavy. The kind of stillness that makes you feel like you're not alone. Not quite.

My spine straightened, fingers tightening around the charm. My eyes flicked open, scanning the cliff edge, the path, the horizon.

Nothing moved. Not even the trees behind me.

I waited, heartbeat slow but loud, body alert in the quiet way prey learns to move. I didn't call on my magic—it wasn't necessary. Whatever had passed through had already gone. Or it had chosen not to show itself.

Either way, the moment passed. The breeze returned, rustling through the grass and snapping me back into my body.

I stood and brushed the dust from my skirt, tucking the charm back into my bag. I didn't look behind me as I walked back down the path. Not because I wasn't curious—but because I didn't want to see if the shadows were looking back.

My cottage waited at the edge of the tree line, tucked between two weeping willows whose roots wrapped around the foundation like guardians. The house was small—just a single room with a low-beamed ceiling, a hearth, and a bed pushed under the window—but it was mine. Fennah had insisted on giving me the space when I turned seventeen, claiming I needed my own air and privacy. I suspected it had just been her quiet way of shielding me from the town's expectations.

Inside, the hearth was cold, but the walls were still warm from the sun. On the table sat a plate wrapped in a linen cloth: a small loaf of honey-oat bread and a smear of ashberry jam. Fennah again. She always made sure I had something, even if it wasn't much. Even if she pretended she hadn't.

I ate slowly, the food soft and sweet, though the taste felt far away. I'd barely finished when the first stars began to appear outside, winking between the curling branches of the willows.

I lit the single lamp by the bed and changed into my sleeping tunic, folding my clothes with the kind of care that came from years of needing to make things last.

I lay in bed with the lamp still lit, my eyes tracing the familiar lines in the ceiling wood, following the same grooves I always did before sleep. But sleep didn't come easily tonight. My body was tired, my muscles heavy, my hands sore from hours of work—but my mind felt stretched thin. Something in the air had shifted today, and my bones knew it, even if the rest of me tried to stay numb.

When the lamp finally burned low, I let it die. Outside, the willows swayed. The wind rose again, this time softer.

And I dreamed—of eclipses and blood-bright fire, of masked priests with flame in their eyes, and hands made of shadow reaching through golden light to touch my cheek.

At the center of the dream, a face waited—smiling.

I woke before the sun. The sky outside my window was still draped in that indigo hush of predawn, the stars fading with reluctance as if they, too, wished to linger. A pale thread of moonlight spilled beneath the shutters—soft and spectral. There is not much of it left now. The eclipse was drawing near. Each night the moon seemed to hang heavier above Solavend—too still, too watchful, like it was waiting.

I sat up slowly, the weight of my dream still clinging to me like a veil. Most of the details slipped away the moment my eyes opened, but the feeling remained—thick and heavy in my chest, like a secret not yet spoken. There had been a fire again. And hands. And something else. A presence. Not cruel, not kind. Just aware.

I moved through the dark without lighting the lamp, dressing by memory and moonlight. The quiet felt alive—not threatening, but full.

Charged. When I stepped outside, the air was cool and damp, clinging to my skin with the last breath of night. The grass beneath my boots was slick with dew, and the stones of the village path still held the chill of shadow. Everything was still asleep. No merchants setting up stalls. No bells from the temple. The square lay silent, bathed in soft grays and purples, and for a moment, it almost felt like the village had forgotten to wake. I didn't head toward the apothecary. My body moved on instinct, my steps carrying me past the orchard and the well, past the familiar paths and toward the cliffs.

The sea below churned quietly, waves rolling against stone like a slow heartbeat. The wind had risen by the time I reached the ridge, but it wasn't the usual sea breeze. It was cooler, more deliberate—the kind of wind that felt summoned, not born. It coiled around me like a ribbon, tugging gently at my clothes and hair, and my magic stirred in response—an echo in my ribs, a flicker under my skin.

It wasn't just me. Something else was moving.

I stood there in the half-light, watching the horizon as the sun began to breach it. Orange and rose gold spilled across the sky, but it felt dimmer somehow, like the light was pressing through a veil. My fingers curled around the edge of my tunic as my magic pulsed again—stronger this time, a thrum of recognition. The kind of reaction it gave when it felt something. Someone. Not near, but not far either. I didn't speak. There was nothing to say—just that sense in my blood, ancient and quiet and certain, that I was not alone. Not at this moment. Not in the world. Something had seen me. And it hadn't looked away.

Eventually, the wind softened. The sky brightened. My magic sank back into stillness like a wave returning to the sea. I turned away from the cliffs and made my way back to the village, my steps careful, my pulse steady.

The streets had begun to stir by the time I reached the apothecary, and the illusion of normalcy wrapped itself around Solavend once more like a too-tight scarf. Vendors raised their awnings. Children squealed as they chased one another between baskets of produce. Priests stood near the temple gates in freshly pressed robes, blessing passersby with practiced ease. I noticed how some of those blessings were performed just after someone crossed my path. Little rituals. Small wards. Just in case.

Fennah said nothing, but I could see the tension in her shoulders, the quiet alertness in her eyes. She worked with unusual focus, barely glancing up from her herbs. I joined her without needing to be asked, slipping into the rhythm of bottling and binding, but the silence between us was tighter than usual—thicker. It didn't feel like the quiet we shared when things were calm. This was the kind of quiet that preceded something.

The villagers didn't say anything to me that day. Not directly. But the glances were longer. The smiles were thinner. Conversations stopped when I entered a room and resumed when I left. They were preparing for the festival, yes. But I could feel it in my bones—they were preparing for me, too. They'd always called me cursed. But now, with the eclipse drawing close and my twenty-first birthday nearly upon me, the word tasted different on their tongues. Like a prophecy. Like inevitability.

That night, the wind returned. It crept in just past midnight—no storm, no rain, just a restless current. Steady, cold, threading through the cracks in my shutters and brushing over my skin. I rose in the dark, not afraid, only listening. My breath fogged in the air as though winter itself had slipped through the seams of the cottage. But the longer I waited, the more it felt like the wind was only mocking me—stirring, whispering, then fading into silence. My eyes grew heavy in the stillness, the unease settling into my bones like a lullaby I didn't want to hear. At last, I slipped back beneath the blankets, letting the cold hum of the night carry me into sleep. The charm I kept beneath my pillow was warm to the touch, and my magic surged beneath it like it recognized something just beyond the walls. Gently, I lifted myself out of bed, laying my feet gently on the floor boards so as to not wake Fennah.

I crossed the room barefoot, each step silent, and pressed my hand against the wooden frame of the window. The air outside was still again, but not empty. I pushed open the shutters slowly, my heart ticking in my throat.

Moonlight spilled across the clearing. The willows swayed softly. And there, at the edge of the trees, half-wrapped in shadow, stood a figure.

I couldn't see his face. Could barely make out more than the outline; tall, still, watching. The shape didn't move, didn't waver, like he belonged to the night more than the world. I didn't call out. I didn't move. My magic sparked again beneath my skin—not in warning, but in response.

I couldn't explain how I knew. But I did.

It wasn't a dream.

He wasn't a priest.

And he wasn't afraid of me.

I blinked once. And he was gone.

Chapter Two

I didn't remember falling asleep, but the scent of smoke and mint told me the fire had died sometime in the night. My body ached like I'd been holding tension in my muscles even in sleep—shoulders tight, hands curled, jaw sore. The rest that isn't rest at all.

I sat up slowly, blinking into the faint morning light filtering through the shutters. It wasn't even dawn yet, but the sky had already softened into that pale blue that comes just before sunrise. The birds hadn't started, but the world was stirring. I could feel it.

There had been dreams again—shifting, fragmented, smoke-laced things that clung to my skin even now. I remembered the shape in the woods. The way it hadn't moved. The way I hadn't moved. My heartbeat quickened at the memory, though I told myself—again—that it could've been anything. A trick of moonlight. A shadow. My own fear, conjuring monsters from nothing.

But my magic had stirred. That hadn't been my imagination.

I rose and dressed without lighting the lamp, moving through the room like a ghost. When I splashed water on my face from the basin, the chill of it grounded me for just a moment—but it didn't shake the heaviness that had wrapped itself around my shoulders like a wet cloak.

By the time I stepped outside, the first hints of sunlight had crept across the tops of the trees, casting soft gold over the grass. The village was waking—a baker's chimney puffing smoke in the distance, roosters calling across the fields. The ordinary, familiar rhythm of Solavend returning to itself.

But something felt... misaligned. It was in the way the birds took longer to sing. The way the light didn't quite warm my skin. The way even the wind felt like it was listening too closely.

I took the back path toward the apothecary, walking slower than usual. My thoughts turned to the charm beneath my pillow, the way it had been warm in the night. It had never done that before. And my magic... it had responded to something. I hadn't summoned it. I hadn't needed it. But it had stirred of its own accord.

It felt like recognition. Not a threat. Not quite.

Fennah was already working inside when I arrived, the apothecary's door open to let in the morning breeze. She stood at the hearth, stirring a pot of steeping willow bark with a long wooden spoon. She glanced over her shoulder as I stepped in, then narrowed her eyes.

"You look like you didn't sleep."

I didn't answer. I set my satchel down and moved to the worktable, reaching instinctively for the jars that needed relabeling.

Fennah let the silence stretch before speaking again. "Did you see something?"

Pausing, my hand hovered just above a bottle of dried comfrey. I didn't turn around. "I'm not sure."

Her stirring slowed. "That doesn't sound like a no."

"There was someone in the trees. Or something. It was late. I could've imagined it."

"You don't imagine things like that."

I looked up then, meeting her gaze across the room. Her face was unreadable, but her grip on the spoon had gone tight.

"Do you think it was a god?" I asked quietly.

Her lips pressed into a thin line. "I think we're better off not guessing."

We didn't speak again for a while. The work filled the space—grinding herbs, folding parchment, bottling the day's mixtures. I found some comfort in the familiarity of it, the rhythm of motions I'd repeated a thousand times. But even that comfort felt thinner today. Brittle.

By midmorning, the streets had filled. Festival preparations were in full swing now. The day before the eclipse. Tomorrow, everything would shift.

I stood at the apothecary's front window, watching a group of priests pass through the square. There were more of them now—extra eyes, extra blessings. Gold robes gleamed oddly in the sun, and faces strained with forced piety. One of them stopped to speak with an elder near the statue of Solari, pointing toward the upper district. Whatever they were planning, it had weight.

"Have you noticed the way people are watching?" I asked softly, not turning from the window.

"They've always watched," Fennah replied without looking up from her measuring.

"It's different now. Like they're waiting."

"They are," she said. "They just don't know what to do."

I crossed my arms, leaning my shoulder against the frame. "I think something's coming."

"It's already here."

By midday, Solavend had transformed. The square, once a quiet circle of dust and stone, now bloomed with color. Silk banners in red and gold streamed between rooftops, snapping in the wind like tongues of flame. Lanterns carved from sun fruit husks bobbed in the breeze, strung between posts and stall corners. Every surface seemed gilded. Every vendor is louder. Laughter rang out, bright and forced, just a little too sharp. The whole place buzzed like a hive.

I moved through the chaos like a shadow—unnoticed when people didn't look too closely, but felt when they did. I wasn't wearing anything special, just my work tunic and apron, a strip of linen holding my hair back. I hadn't planned to be out here, but Fennah had run low on eclipse salts and sent me to the crystal vendor before the crowd picked her clean.

People parted slightly as I passed—not cruelly, not obviously. Just enough to say you don't belong here. Conversations quieted until I was gone, then resumed louder than before. One woman gave me a polite nod and quickly crossed herself. Another smiled too tightly and turned away.

The village swelled with color and noise. Streamers fluttered between the cottages, baskets of fruit and bread passed from hand to hand, and laughter spilled into the square like wine. I moved through it all, carrying my share of decorations, trying not to notice the way people's eyes lingered on me—long enough to whisper, quick enough to pretend they hadn't.

I paused to catch my breath, letting the weight of the basket dig into my hip. That was when I saw him.

A hooded figure stood at the far edge of the square, half-shadowed by the archway of a vendor's stall. He didn't move with the rhythm of the crowd, didn't join in the chatter or song. Just watched. Still as stone., eyes red and shining through the shadow of his cloak's hood. For a moment, I thought his face lifted toward mine. My chest tightened, breath stalling—but then a child darted in front of me, tugging at her mother's sleeve, and when I glanced back, the figure was gone.

I told myself it was nothing. Just another villager passing through. But the image clung to me like the ghost of a dream, even as I forced myself to keep walking. I didn't stop. Didn't speak. I kept my gaze ahead and walked like I had somewhere far more important to be. Children darted between stalls, hair wound with ribbons, faces painted with suns and gold streaks. One girl stopped just short of me, wide-eyed. Before I could smile, her mother swept her away with a whispered scold.

I kept walking.

The eclipse salts vendor stood at the far edge of the square. Pale hair, wandering eyes, quick to overcharge strangers. She didn't speak when I approached—just stared, waiting for me to speak first.

"I need three bags," I said quietly, handing her Fennah's written order.

She read it without expression, then turned to measure from a large clay jar. I let myself breathe again. One interaction done. Almost home.

My eyes drifted across the square—and caught on the temple steps. Priests stood in twin rows, golden robes on, pouring pale smoke into the air. At the top, High Priest Carenel is in a deeper shade of gold than the rest, his voice rising in prayer. People gathered, kneeling or clutching charms.

I've seen this every year. It's always the same. But this time his voice was louder, posture straighter, eyes sharper. And when his gaze swept the crowd, it lingered too long on me.

I turned away before he could meet my eyes.

The vendor returned with the bags. I nodded, tucked them into my satchel, and began weaving my way back toward the apothecary.

"Elara!" I froze before turning.

Talia stood at a fruit stall, waving, her red scarf bright against her dark curls. One of the few in Solavend who spoke to me without fear.

"Do you have a minute?" she called. "I know you're working, but I need your eye for something."

"What kind of something?"

"The harvest display booth. I convinced the elders to let us include medicinal herbs, but they want it 'symbolically balanced,' whatever that means."

"That sounds like a priest's way of saying 'do it how we want or we'll burn it.'"

She laughed. "Exactly. Please? Just five minutes?"

Five minutes wouldn't kill me. I nodded.

We walked together past the stalls to the half-finished booth—woven vines and copper rods, baskets of herbs laid out on linen. The smell was wonderful.

"Yarrow next to calendula or valerian?" she asked.

"Calendula. If you want to impress old men in robes."

We worked in a rare calm until a group of festival judges approached. Elder Halven stopped in front of the booth, his eyes narrowing.

"This table looks... unconventional," he said.

Talia smiled brightly. "We're integrating traditional medicine. With blessings, of course."

His gaze slid to me. "Of course."

Silence. Long enough to sting.

"She shouldn't be here," he said coldly. "Not today, not tomorrow. Not when the gods are watching." He walked away without waiting for a reply.

Talia cursed, but I'd already stepped back, folding my arms. "Don't," I whispered. "It's fine."

"It's not," she insisted.

"That's not what they care about," I murmured. "It never has been."

I left with a promise to bring more calendula, taking the orchard path. Cooler air, damp with moss. Quieter.

I hadn't meant to walk this far, but my feet knew the way. Past the well. Past the old orchard slope. I stopped near the ridge that overlooked the valley—unlucky ground, they called it. I'd always found it comforting.

The wind shifted—cooler, deliberate. The orchard was still, but the air carried the wrong weight again. My magic pulsed faintly in warning.

Then I smelled it. Metallic.

I turned—and saw her.

A young doe, limbs folded neatly as if asleep. Eyes open, black, wrong. No wound. No blood. Just stillness. Cold stillness. Not natural.

I crouched, letting my magic reach forward—cautious.

It felt like sinking. Like grief and frost tangled together. And beneath it, something older than the woods. Footsteps behind me.

"Elara?"

I spun to see Ardin Telward, soot streaking his jaw, a hatchet loose in his hand.

"She's not wounded," I said. "Just gone."

He knelt, touched her fur, and frowned. "Cold."

"I did nothing."

"I didn't say you did."

"You didn't have to."

He looked at me, unreadable. "If something did this…"

"It wasn't me."

"I know. But tell Fennah."

"I was going to."

"Good." He hesitated. "Go. I'll take care of it." I left. Fennah didn't blink when I told her.

"Any marks?"

"No, nothing."

"What'd you feel?"

"Cold. Grief. Hunger."

She cursed, pulled sage from the shelf. "Storm vine and ash bark. We'll burn a ward."

"Is it spreading?"

"I think the festival's tomorrow, and too many people are pretending everything's fine." By morning, they found three more animals that were lifeless, with no wounds or blood. A raven in the bell tower, a dog under a merchant's stall, and a mule outside the priests' quarters. No one said the word omen, but it clung to the air. Charms appeared on doors. Salt lines on thresholds. Old prayers muttered like new. Wherever I walked, the world grew quieter.

That night, sleep came hard. When it did, I dreamed—of the orchard without stars, of a perfect, golden well. A voice from its depths: The world remembers you, little flame... soon you will have to choose. What burns... and what remains.

I woke up gasping, the charm beneath my pillow hot to the touch, my magic humming like it remembered too. The morning sky bled red. Not pink. Not gold. Red—thick and low, streaked like a wound across the clouds. The village pretended not to see.

At the apothecary, Fennah had draped salt-lined linen over the doors and was clearing shelves of anything flammable. We worked in silence until the temple bells tolled—three slow pulses. The procession had begun. I pulled my cloak tight and stepped into the crowd, keeping to the back. The villagers didn't speak, but some crossed themselves as I passed. The last circle brought us to the square, to the pyre—built of sacred wood, soaked in sun-blessed oil. This year, its center wasn't a sun figure. It was a pedestal, an empty one. High Priest Carenel stepped forward, voice booming, "Today we honor Solari-" Above us, the sun darkened. The eclipse had begun, the warmth faded, birds went silent. The sky turned gray. Then violet.

And then, the light went out.

Chapter Three

The eclipse had passed. The sun had returned.
And Solavend had lost its damn mind.

The village square was bursting at the seams, every inch of stone and stall drowned in fabric, incense smoke, and shouting. Music surged from copper-stringed lyres stationed near the temple gates—wild and breathless, played too fast to be joyful. Children with sun-painted cheeks chased each other barefoot between the crowds while priests marched in tight formation, chanting blessings and throwing glittering herbs into the air like offerings.

Overhead, the sky stayed brilliant and blue—so cloudless it felt staged. Yet I felt cold.

I lingered near the edge of the crowd, half-shadowed by a bakery stall, fingers clenched around the strap of my satchel until they numbed. Dust clung to my boots, and my cloak felt heavier than it should have, soaked in the weight of something I couldn't name. Magic curled under my skin, restless and sharp, pulsing just beneath the surface like it wanted out.

All around me, the people of Solavend celebrated as if nothing had happened—as if the eclipse hadn't drained the world of light and breath, as if the very air hadn't stilled with something ancient and watchful. They clung to the return of the sun as if it were proof their god still loved them.

I wasn't so sure.

I hadn't felt Solari's warmth during the eclipse.

I had felt nothing but dread.

Talia appeared beside me with a steaming mug of something clove-scented in one hand and a gold ribbon tangled around the other. Her grin was breathless, cheeks flushed from dancing or drinking—or both.

"There you are," she said, shoving the mug into my hands without asking. "You missed the roasted honey root—it's already gone. Apparently Lord Solari brought the sun back, so everyone's pretending they didn't nearly piss themselves an hour ago."

I looked at the drink, then at her. The steam rising from the mug didn't warm me.

"They seem… eager to forget."

"They're scared," she said, her smile faltering. "You know how people get when they're scared."

"Relieved?"

"Stupid."

That almost coaxed a smile out of me. Almost.

Talia's gaze sharpened. "You okay?"

"Fine."

"Don't lie. You twitch when you lie."

"I twitch when I'm surrounded by people who think fire and fruit can undo what just happened."

Talia looked out over the crowd with a small sigh. "They're just trying to make sense of it. Give it meaning. Turn it into something safe."

"There was nothing safe about that eclipse."

"No," she agreed quietly. "There wasn't."

She hesitated, then nudged me with her elbow. "We could leave, you know. Just walk out past the orchard, keep going. No one would stop us."

I glanced toward the temple spires, their gold tips glinting hard under the sun. The light didn't feel warm. It felt watchful. The kind of brightness that burned more than it illuminated.

"No," I said quietly. "I need to see this through."

Talia didn't press. She just nodded and vanished back into the crowd, swept away by music and movement.

I stayed where I was.

By midday, the celebration had taken on a strained kind of euphoria. The music grew louder, the dances more frantic. Every movement in the square felt choreographed, like the villagers had rehearsed it for years and were terrified to get it wrong. The priests' chants had taken on a feverish cadence as they moved from shrine to shrine, spreading sun-charred incense and shouting praise loud enough to keep the dark at bay.

The name Solari hung on every breath.

I drifted along the edges of the square, careful not to draw attention—but it didn't matter. People noticed me now. Not in whispers. Not in avoidance. In expectation. Some smiled too long when their eyes met mine. Some crossed themselves. Some just stared, and that was somehow worse.

I passed a group of children placing garlands on the structure—sun fruit blossoms and cedar branches wrapped around silk-soaked wood. The pyre gleamed in the sunlight, its center adorned with a freshly built pedestal, polished and waiting.

A chill traced down my spine.

The charm beneath my blouse burned against my skin.

When the bells rang, it was like the world exhaled.

Four deep tolls echoed across the square, and in an instant, everything went still. Music cut off mid-note. Dancers froze. The crowd turned as one to face the temple stairs, where the High Priest stood with his arms raised.

The sky shimmered. Not with darkness—no. This time, there was too much light. Blinding, brilliant, unnatural light poured from above like melted gold. The air shimmered with heat. A crackling sound rose through the silence, like fire crawling across silk.

And then he appeared.

Solari.

He descended through the light in a blaze of glory—tall, radiant, wrapped in sun fire and smoke. His eyes burned gold. His hair moved like it had its own will. Every step he took on the temple stairs left a glowing mark behind. The ground beneath him cracked with heat.

The crowd dropped to their knees. I remained standing—not by choice. My body simply wouldn't bend. My bones felt locked in place, my magic coiled tight in my chest.

The weight of him wasn't awe-inspiring.
It was crushing.

He walked through the crowd without looking at anyone. The priests wept openly. Some reached for his robe and drew back burned hands. Children shrank behind their mothers. The heat made it hard to breathe.

When Solari reached the base of the pyre, he finally turned, his gaze sweeping the crowd.
And then it landed on me.

I didn't blink.

He stared for a long moment, unreadable. Then turned away. The moment his gaze left me, something inside me cracked—not loudly, not all at once. It wasn't a shatter. It was the slow fracture of something under pressure too long.

I hadn't expected warmth or welcome from the god of sun, but the dismissal in his golden eyes... That was something different. That was worse.

I wasn't an enemy. No one saw me.

Solari stood tall beside the pyre, radiant and still as a statue carved from living flame. The High Priest approached him with cautious reverence, head bowed low, arms extended to offer a gleaming solar disc—one of the village's most sacred relics. The god took it without acknowledgment, held it in one elegant hand, and crushed it to dust.

The pieces fell like dying stars, gold fragments glittering in the dirt at his feet.

Gasps rippled through the crowd, but no one moved. No one dared.

The High Priest fell to his knees. "Your radiance," he said, voice trembling as he pressed his forehead to the ground, "we offer thanks for your return. For your light. For your mercy."

Solari said nothing.

The High Priest's voice rose with new fervor. "We offer sacrifice so that your warmth may stay with us. That your fire may bless our harvests and burn away the shadow. We hope you are pleased."

And then—he turned.

The square held its breath. The crowd's tension vibrated in the stillness like a taut string.

The priest pointed directly at me.

"She was born during the last eclipse. On the darkest day. She is of age now, untouched, unclaimed. We offer her as your vessel. Your bride. Your flame. Whatever you please."

It felt like something had knocked the air out of the world.

I didn't move. My thoughts scattered, my breath frozen. For a long moment, I stood utterly still, as if stillness might save me. But I felt the shift—subtle and sickening—ripple through the crowd. Heads turned. Faces followed. Some stared in disbelief. Others with hunger. And some—some with relief.

Of course it would be me.

The High Priest's voice echoed again: "The chosen one. Lift her up."

Four guards stepped forward from the temple steps, their movements solemn and practiced, like dancers rehearsing a ritual. Their hands were open, palms up, as they approached. Not charging, not lunging—there was no need.

The crowd did nothing.
	The village did nothing.
		And neither did Solari.

My feet backed away instinctively, bumping into the edge of a fruit cart. My hand gripped my satchel tighter, magic pulsing in my chest like a second heartbeat. I turned to run—but one guard caught my arm. Another grabbed the hem of my cloak.

I kicked, twisted, bit down a scream, but they held fast.

"Don't struggle," one of them said under his breath, his grip bruising. "This is an honor."

To burn? To die? To be nothing more than kindling for a god who wouldn't even speak my name? "Then you do it!" I bit out.

The panic, once sharp, solidified into something bitter. My magic surged—hot, rising—but the square was too full, the walls too tight. There was no space for my power to breathe. Sun-Fire lashed out, hitting nearby buildings, starting a kindling of flame that some adults that weren't focused on restraining me ran to control.

They dragged me forward. The crowd parted—all to a small girl near the edge of the square. Her face showed streaks of gold paint and fear. She clutched a wilting flower in her hands and stared at me with wide, sorrowful eyes.

"I'm sorry," she whispered, just loud enough for me to hear.

Then I was past her. Then I was on the steps. Then, I was standing before the pyre.

It loomed larger than it had from afar, towering above me like the mouth of a waiting beast. The central platform gleamed with fresh polish—golden symbols etched across the wood in a spiral pattern meant to call down divine fire.

A place for a vessel. The guards lifted me onto the pedestal, careful not to bruise me further. Careful not to make me ugly for the fire. I didn't fight anymore. My gaze locked onto Solari, who stood like a statue at the edge of the pyre, unmoved, uninterested. I couldn't feel anything from him—no heat, no divine pulse, not even attention. He looked through me as if I were smoke. Still, I asked, voice hoarse, "Are you going to say anything?"

He turned his head slowly, eyes like molten gold. "Why would I?" My mouth opened—no words came, and above us, the sky cracked open.

It wasn't a sound. It wasn't thunder. It was pressure—wrong and heavy, as if the heavens themselves had bent under a hand no one could see. The light dimmed—violently. It didn't fade; it vanished, ripped away like fabric torn from a window. Heat fled the world in an instant. The air thickened. The sunlight bled out of the village as if something had reached down and swallowed it whole. The wind picked up. Screaming. And this time, it wasn't the moon. It wasn't Solari. It was something older.

Something darker. Something, someone was coming.

The light faded in stages.

Not the way dusk usually fell over Solavend, in soft notes of gold that lulled the village to rest. No—this was wrong. The warmth didn't retreat. Something tore it out of the air, ripping it away like breath stolen from lungs held too long under water. In one heartbeat, amber light illuminated the square. Next, it was brittle and sharp, as though even the sun realized it no longer belonged.

The sky shimmered. Then fractured.

It began at the center of the sun—a pinprick of shadow that didn't just block the light; it devoured it. My eyes snapped upward as a ripple passed across the heavens like warped glass. But it wasn't heat I felt. It was cold, suffocating, seeping into my skin, into my bones, whispering of something ancient clawing its way back. Around me, villagers stirred in panic. Mothers clutched their children. The priests faltered mid-chant. And even Solari, radiant on his pyre, turned toward that unnatural darkness.

The pinprick widened, smooth, deliberate, spreading until the sun looked like a vast eye, lidless and watching. The air thinned. My chest tightened. Then the sky tore—silent, merciless. No thunder. No roar. Just the soundless rending of the world, unveiling endless black.

And from it, something fell.

A spear of darkness hurtled down, trailing silence that smothered everything. It struck the center of the square without a sound, without dust. But the world itself is still. Birds froze mid-flight. A toppled bowl hit the stones and shattered—but no one flinched. My heart hammered in the void. That was all I heard. That was all that moved.

And then he rose.

Not with flame. Not with rage. Just... stood. The dust slid from broad shoulders as if the earth had been waiting to release him. He was tall—taller than any man I had ever seen—his presence bending the air. His cloak wasn't black. It was the absence of all light, a depth that devoured even the sun. Silver thread gleamed along the hem like constellations drowning underwater.

His skin looked carved from pale stone, smooth and cold, the sheen of bone bleached in moonlight. Muscles coiled under it, unmistakable. His tattoos crawled up his arms, stark lines that twisted across his shoulders and throat, glowing faintly with the pulse of something older than gods. His hair—long, black, unbound—shifted with an unnatural weight, as though shadows wove themselves through each strand.

And his eyes, gods, his eyes were the most terrifying beauty I had seen. They weren't eyes. They were ruin. Rings of red fire wrapped in darkness, eclipses caught mid-breath, galaxies dying inward. When they fixed on me, I swore I felt my soul recoil. No one dared to move until Solari did.

The sun god stepped from his pyre, golden fire licking along his skin. Yet even I could see it now—the way the light bent away from the man in shadow. Even the flame didn't want to touch him. They faced each other across the wreckage of the square: Solari, gilded and faltering, and the being I now knew with no need to be told.

Kura.

The Eclipse God.

The air pulsed thick between them, bright and dark clashing in silence. For a breath, it seemed they might tear the square apart with their presence alone. And then... Solari bowed. Not deeply. Not humbly. But he bowed. The priests gasped. One fell to his knees; another dropped his disc of gold, shattering it. Guards shifted uneasily. And I—my fists clenched white at the edge of the pyre. I couldn't move. Couldn't breathe. I watched only the god I had revered bow his head to another.

And Kura smiled.

The smile that promised knives in the dark. His gaze swept across the crowd, then landed on me, on top of the pyre, pinning me in place as surely as shackles. When he spoke, his voice slid through the air like silk hiding steel. "Is this your offering?" His words coiled smoothly, amused. "A gift wrapped in fear and fire?"

The High Priest trembled, stammering. "The rite was meant for Solari—"

"Was it?" Kura cut him off, soft and heavy, pressing the air flat. "Then why does he bow?"

Solari's jaw tightened. Kura's smile widened.

"You light their world, sun god. But every flame exists only because I allow the surrounding dark. Do not forget." Solari flinched, the golden fire wavering. And Kura laughed. Quiet. Knowing.

The High Priest staggered forward, the shards of his disc cutting his palms. "She—she is the chosen vessel. An offering in your name."

"Solari's name," Kura corrected lazily. "Your precious God of the Sun, that bows to another." His eyes narrowed. "The god who let you bind a woman and call it devotion." A chill scraped down my spine. I felt the magic inside me stir, sharp and volatile—the same magic that had already escaped me earlier, burning homes, turning Solavend's festival into a smoldering ruin before anyone could stop me. I saw the wreckage around us now through Kura's gaze: the scorched banners, the ash-stained stone. My loss of control had marked this place before he even arrived. My hands curled tighter.

Kura's gaze swept back to Solari. Without raising his voice, he lifted a hand.

Solari buckled. The golden fire folded against him like dying embers, dragging him down, inch by inch. I watched—horrified—as his knees buckled and the god of the sun, the protector of my people, fell.

And I... couldn't look away.

The High Priest spoke again, but Kura silenced him with a single look. Shadows ebbed out through the priest's nose, blood trailing down over his mouth as his eyes melted into pools of black. The villagers stood in silence for a moment, before the first scream of realization broke out, mothers scrambling to grab their children, fathers ushering their wives and children towards the exit of the square as every single sun elf in Solavend made a break for the streets as I watched the liquid life flow out of the priest on the ground, the same one that ridiculed me, tormented me for being an eclipse born. Now dead on the ground, something inside me shifted.

Kura stood still, unmoving. The storm in the center of everything.

Then he raised his arms, and the world stopped.

No wind. No breath. No sound. Just stillness, as if something commanded the earth itself to wait. His voice slid through the silence, almost tender. "Enough."

The villagers collapsed. Not screaming, just gasping as they met the same fate as the priest, twisting themselves to the ground, eyes a pool of black and red, shadows seeping out of them like smoke. All of them. Every adult. Neighbors. Priests. Elders. Gone.

The children were the only ones remaining.

My lungs froze. Dozens of them, staring wild-eyed, sobbing, clutching at bodies that wouldn't wake. I could barely swallow past the stone in my throat. Solari still knelt, broken, fire dimmed to ash.

And Kura turned to me. His red eyes locked onto mine, tattoos burning faintly under pale skin. The monster in flesh. The man who had toppled gods and silenced my world. He stepped toward the pyre. "Come down," he said.

"Why?" My voice cracked, but it was steady enough.

"Because I asked."

"That's not an answer."

"It wasn't a request." My fear burned, twisted into something else. Anger. Rage. They offered, burned, and abandoned me. Not even Solari had stood for me. And yet—Kura waited. For me.

"You killed them," I spat, disbelief sinking in as I saw the bloodied, lifeless bodies scattered around the square.

"I did." He said as though it was an act of kindness. "They deserved it."

"You left the children."

"I'm not heartless."

"You expect me to thank you?"

"Not yet." He held a hand out—not forcefully, but offered. An invitation. I didn't take it. I leapt down myself, boots striking hard against the stone. I straightened, lifted my chin, and stared into those blood-red eyes without flinching. The fury within me boiled over. Before I could stop myself, my hand flew upward, wild and reckless. I wanted to strike him, to leave some mark on the monster in front of me who had taken everything.

He caught my wrist before it ever landed. His grip was iron, cool and unyielding, locking me in place as though the world itself had paused at his whim. His head tilted, hair falling like a shadow across his face, and he studied me with that unbearable calm. "Defiance suits you," he said, his voice low, a dark amusement curling around each word. "But next time you raise a hand to me—make sure you're ready to lose it."

The square was silent. No one to gasp, no one to scream—only the children watching from the temple steps, their wide eyes fixed on us. My pulse hammered in my throat, but I refused to look away. If he wanted me to cower, he'd have to break more than my bones. His thumb brushed once against the inside of my wrist—not gentle, not kind, more like he was testing how fragile I was beneath the skin. A reminder that with one small flex he could shatter me. Yet he didn't. Instead, he let the moment stretch until I could hear the blood rushing in my ears. Then, with deliberate slowness, he released me, his fingers trailing away as though I wasn't worth the effort of holding.

"You've made your point," I said, breath uneven. "Now what?"

His voice was smooth and deliberate. "Now you stand in the ashes. And you decide what to build from them."

I blinked, startled. "I thought you wanted to destroy us."

"I did." He stepped closer, shadows lapping at his heels. "Then I saw you. Standing above a fire you could not control. And I realized..." His fingers brushed a strand of hair from my cheek. "...you were already burning it down for me."

My heart pounded in my ears. "What are you?"

His red eyes gleamed. His tattoos burned faintly. His smile never came. "I am the one your god forgot to warn you about."

I don't remember deciding to move. My body just did what needed doing. The first child I reached was a girl with soot-streaked cheeks and tangled hair, no older than four. She was crying silently, her little fists clenched tight, eyes locked on the body of a merchant nearby—likely her father, judging by the same wild red curls.

I dropped to one knee, the stone beneath me still hot from the fire, and touched her back gently.

"I'm so sorry." I whispered. My throat felt raw from the smoke. "You're not alone."

Her wide eyes lifted to mine, terrified and searching. Then, without a word, she threw herself into my arms.

And just like that, the others came.

They emerged from the haze like shadows—one by one, stumbling, limping, running, crawling. Some blinked blindly through the smoke, some clutched scraps of cloth, others moved like sleepwalkers through a nightmare. Behind them, roofs collapsed with sharp cracks, flames clawing higher before collapsing into glowing heaps. Smoke curled around their thin shoulders as they drifted toward me, toward the only thing still standing in the square.

Me.

I gathered them beneath the broken arch of the temple, cleared a space where the stones were still warm but solid. I sat them down. Counted heads. Wiped ash from faces. Pressed trembling hands between mine until they stilled. I scavenged water from broken fountains, bitter and smoky on the tongue. Dug through overturned stalls for salves. Tore strips of cloth to bind cuts. Kissed their brows when they whimpered. Wrapped them in cloaks I dragged from the ruins. My hands trembled as I pressed a damp cloth against the boy's bleeding knee. The words slipped out before I realized I had spoken them—my mother's words, long buried. "Water cleanses both light and shadow," I whispered, the sound more for myself than for him. Balance, my mother had said. Balance, when the world was breaking, so I didn't cry, not yet. Because someone had to be the anchor in this storm. Someone had to prove the world hadn't completely shattered, even if it would never look the same again. My movements felt steady, practiced—but it wasn't courage. It was a necessity.

All around us, Solavend burned itself out. Flames licked low along beams until they snapped, showers of sparks scattering like stars before dying against the ash. Banners smoldered to nothing, leaving only their charred poles. The crackle of fire became softer, slower, until it was the whisper of embers breathing their last. Every inhale burned with smoke, every exhale tasted like endings.

Solari did not rise.

By the time the sun had climbed pale and thin above the haze, I had arranged the children into a tight circle of blankets and cloaks, scavenged from the wreckage. The youngest had fallen asleep against my side, their tiny fingers knotted in the hem of my tunic. Behind us, the village was still smoking. Blackened beams jutted like broken bones, and the air hung heavy with the stench of charred wood and flesh.

A boy with freckles and a stubborn jaw sat close, his lips cracked, his eyes wary but unflinching.

"Is he coming back?" he whispered, nodding toward Solari's bowed figure in the square.

I followed his gaze.

The god's back was still bent. His fire—what had once been unshakable—was gone, nothing but ash.

"No," I breathed. My voice nearly broke. "Not today."

The boy didn't argue. He leaned against my leg, and after a moment, his eyes drifted shut.

A warm wind tugged at my hair, carrying with it the last breath of smoke from Solavend's ruins. I tilted my head back, staring up at the sky. The sun hung there—lonely, pale, no longer gold. No gods watching. No chants. No sacrifices.

Just me.

I didn't know what tomorrow would bring. I didn't know how to lead them, or where to take them, or if the silence from the heavens would ever break. But I knew this: I would not leave them. And behind me, the fires of Solavend hissed and sputtered, dying one by one until only embers glowed, weak but stubborn, refusing to fade.

Chapter Four

The morning after the festival felt like waking from a nightmare no one could explain. The sky was too blue.

That's what struck me first as I stood at the edge of the village square, my arms wrapped tight around my waist. The sun had reclaimed its place above the horizon, bold and unflinching, casting light across a world that had been hollowed out. The banners were gone. The laughter silenced. And yet the sky dared to shine as if nothing had happened.

The adults still lay where they had fallen—scattered across the stones like relics of a story no one wanted to tell. Some had been moved to the edges of the square, out of sight of the children, but many remained untouched. No one had the strength or the will to deal with them yet.

I sent the older children to gather what food and clean water they could. I didn't assign tasks—they just saw the look on my face and understood. The need to do something pulsed in all of us like a shared heartbeat.

I crouched beside the well, dipping a clay cup into the bucket with slow, practiced care. My hands shook—not violently, just enough to betray the exhaustion gnawing at my edges. Sleep hadn't come. My eyes burned, gritty and raw. But there was no room for rest. Not while small hands still reached for me, trusting I'd know what to do.

Behind me, the soft crunch of footsteps disturbed the dust. Not a child.

I didn't need to look to know who it was.

"I see you've settled into the role," Solari said, voice cool and distant.

My grip on the cup tightened. "It wasn't a choice."

"No," he agreed. "It was a consequence."

I stood slowly, turning to face him. He looked almost the same—golden robes dulled, glow reduced to a faint shimmer—but his expression was sharper now. Less regret, more calculation. The way I remembered him.

"Why are you here?" I asked.

"I came to say goodbye."

My stomach turned. "You're running."

"I'm leaving," he snapped, jaw clenched. "My presence here serves no one now. The people no longer call my name. They cry for you."

I blinked at him. "So that's it? You lose your power, and you just vanish?"

He stepped forward, his tone hardening. "What would you have me do? Stay and pretend to be what I'm not? Let them worship failure?"

"I don't know. Maybe try."

He laughed—short, humorless. "Try? I tried, Elara. I carried them for a century. Lit their fields, guarded their borders, answered their prayers until they turned them into demands. And the moment I hesitated—" His eyes narrowed. "They turned on you."

Fire rose in my chest. "They turned on me because you let them."

He flinched. Just barely.

"I knelt to spare what I could," he said, quieter now. "But you don't see it that way."

"No," I said. "I see a god who watched his people burn and did nothing."

His jaw clenched. "And yet here you are, pretending you're any different."

I stepped closer, staring up at him without flinching. "I am different. I stayed."

We stood like that for a moment—him, glowing faintly beneath a sun that no longer felt warm; me, steady despite the weight on my shoulders. Finally, Solari exhaled.

"He will come again. Or others like him. This world does not offer mercy."

"I'm not asking for mercy."

"Good," he said. "Because you won't get it."

I turned back to the well.

His voice followed me like a shadow. "They'll break you, Elara. All those wide-eyed children clinging to your skirts? One day, they'll turn on you too."

I didn't look at him. "Then I'll face them when they do."

Silence stretched behind me, and when I turned again, the Sun God was gone.

Not burned away. Not vanquished.

Just... gone.

The sky was still bright, but the warmth was thin. For the first time, I wondered if maybe that was how it was. The ache in my fingers. The scrape of stone under my boots. The silence left behind in the space where a god used to be.

There was no time to dwell on what he hadn't said.

The sun had climbed higher while we spoke, and the square was stirring again with soft voices and small footsteps. The children would be hungry. Thirsty. Scared. I could feel their need pressing against me already, like waves lapping at a crumbling shore. There was no time to mourn him. No room left to bleed.

The sun crept higher as I moved through the square, and the village stirred with it. Children peeked from doorways, squinting at the light, still unsure whether the nightmare had passed or simply changed shape. Their eyes followed me as if I were the last page of a story none of them had learned to read.

I didn't speak unless I had to. My throat still felt raw. The ache hadn't left—it had simply shifted, settling somewhere deeper, under my ribs. Each moment carried a thousand decisions: who needed water, who needed rest, what to ration, what to let go of. I worked without thinking. Without stopping. Not because it made me brave, but because stopping meant feeling—and there was no space for that yet.

We slept in the temple now, what remained of it. The broken arch still stood, half-collapsed, casting crooked shadows across the cold stone floor.

We'd piled cushions and blankets beneath the altar and tucked the youngest into nests of fabric where the wind couldn't reach. No one prayed anymore. The names of the gods tasted like ash.

By midday, I stood over a simmering pot, coaxing warmth from a fire that hissed against damp wood. The broth was watery, with overcooked vegetables and bread crumbs, but it was warm and edible. That counted for something. Cas sat nearby, idly worrying a tear in the hem of his blanket. He had spoken little since the first morning, though he never strayed far from my side. I didn't ask why. We both knew what the silence covered.

"You know how to cook?" he asked after a while, voice small but steady.

I glanced at him, then back at the pot. "Enough to keep you alive."

He snorted softly. "My mum used to burn everything. Even soup."

I gave the broth a slow stir. "Did that bother you?"

"Nah. It meant we got to go to the market more. The baker always gave me extra bread if I smiled nicely."

The edge of my mouth twitched upward. "Does that still work?"

He peeked up at me, expression testing. "Only on old ladies."

I arched my eyebrow without looking at him. "Old ladies are gullible like that."

Cas let out a stifled laugh and looked away quickly, cheeks coloring. I ladled the broth into a wooden bowl and handed it over without ceremony. He accepted it with both hands, suddenly quiet again.

The rest of the day passed in fragments—tending to the sick, organizing scavenged supplies, listening when the older girls whispered about missing parents after they thought the little ones were asleep. I gave them tasks to keep their hands busy. When they worked, they didn't cry. Neither did I.

That night, I pulled a tattered curtain across the altar space and helped Alin settle onto a bedroll layered with cloaks. The girl had started her first blood the night before, terrified and alone. I sat beside her for nearly an hour, combing out her hair with gentle fingers, explaining what it meant to grow up in a world where no one warned you when it would begin.

I didn't offer false comfort. I didn't promise safety. But I stayed.

Later, I lay down with a child curled on each side, their small bodies clinging to me like roots searching for soil. Outside, the wind whispered across the temple stones, too warm for night. The sun was long gone, but its heat lingered—stripped of holiness, stripped of hope. I stared up at the ceiling, where cracks spider-webbed through once-hallowed carvings. The old gods stared back, faceless and distant.

I didn't close my eyes. I just listened—to the breathing, the rustling, the murmured dreams of children who didn't know how to mourn. The rhythm filled the space where thought would have been.

Somewhere in the stillness, morning arrived. Not in gold or song, but in the sharp ache of a spine pressed too long against stone, in the muted gray that bled through cracked temple windows, and in the chill that crept under blankets as the fire burned itself to embers.

I didn't remember falling asleep, only the weight of little limbs tangled around mine and the faint soreness in my jaw from clenching it all night. I slid out from beneath the blankets as quietly as I could. Cas shifted in his sleep, one hand reaching toward where I'd been, but he didn't wake.

I pulled my shawl tighter around my shoulders and crossed the stone floor barefoot.

The village was quieter than the day before. Not peaceful. Just tired.

The tired that sinks into the bones of buildings, into the soft thud of children's steps as they wake, into the sound of a cough echoing from behind one of the curtained corners of the temple.

Alin. Again.

I made a note to check on her after breakfast.

There wasn't much food left. I gathered what remained—two wrinkled apples, a heel of stale bread, and a bundle of herbs that had dried out during the eclipse. It would have to stretch. Again. I brewed tea from crushed chamomile and firegrass, doling it out in chipped clay cups with a warning not to spill. The youngest barely held theirs steady, fingers curled tight around the warmth like it might keep the world from slipping away again.

It was the third morning since the eclipse. The third day of pretending I knew what came next.

By midmorning, the coughing had worsened.

Alin was pale beneath her freckles, her skin hot to the touch and slick with sweat. I pressed the back of my hand to her brow and didn't need an apothecary's training to know it was bad. The fever had sunk deep, and there was no one left with the right knowledge to treat it.

Except me.

Maybe.

I found the remaining supplies in the apothecary's corner of the temple, which were scattered across a splintered shelf and a half-open crate. Most of the tinctures had shattered. The damp caused the dried herbs to be mislabeled or mold-slick. I sorted through them anyway, slowly and methodically, pretending I wasn't terrified of choosing wrong.

I chewed my lower lip and grabbed the feverfew and elderflower, hoping instinct would carry me where wisdom had no footing. I'd watched the old healer make teas like this a dozen times, but I'd never had to do it with someone's life hanging in the balance.

Especially not a child's.

I boiled the water twice, added the herbs, and said nothing as I carried the cup to Alin's corner. The girl blinked up at me, eyes glassy and confused, her breath a soft rattle.

"This will help," I murmured.

I didn't know whether it was true.

But she drank.

The other children stayed quiet that day. They watched me work, followed me with wide eyes, carried bowls and fetched water and tried not to get in the way. Not because they were afraid of me—but because something in the air had shifted.

They knew I was all they had.

By evening, the fever hadn't broken.

I sat beside Alin, my back against the stone wall, eyelids heavy but refusing to close. I held the girl's hand loosely in mine, feeling the shallow twitch of her pulse beneath my thumb. Her skin was still too hot. Her breathing—ragged. Uneven. Every inhale sounded like it might be the last.

Around us, the temple had dimmed into near-darkness. The fire had burned low again. No one had relit it. The children were curled together in their makeshift nests, quiet, still, as if afraid that too much movement might shift the balance of things. Might shatter what little held us together.

I didn't speak. There were no words that meant anything anymore.

The weight pressed in—not like a sudden blow, but like drowning in silence. Like waking every day to the same nightmare with no end in sight. I felt it in my shoulders, in the way my breath caught in my chest, in the sharp sting behind my eyes that never quite spilled over.

I should've known what to do. I should've known. I was the one they looked to, the one they reached for when they cried in the night, the one who answered their questions without letting my voice tremble. The one who stayed.

And right now, that meant I was the one who had to sit and wait... not knowing if Alin would wake again.

My hand clenched tighter around hers—not for her sake, but for my own. Because letting go felt like admitting defeat. Like saying aloud what I couldn't bear to think.

I lowered my head slowly until my forehead touched her shoulder, closing my eyes against the dark.

I stayed like that longer than I meant to, my body locked in place by exhaustion and the quiet terror of helplessness. Eventually, I peeled myself away. My joints ached. My hands felt like stone. But I moved anyway because the morning demanded it.

Outside, the square was empty, still wrapped in the eerie hush that had taken hold since the eclipse. I walked to the well with stiff, dragging steps of someone who hadn't truly slept in days. The bucket creaked as I lowered it, and the splash of cold water against clay sounded too loud in the silence. I drank deeply twice, maybe three times, barely tasting it. The chill helped—if only to remind me I was still here.

That's when I noticed it.

Not a noise—but the absence of one. A stillness that wasn't just silence, but wrongness. Like the moment before a glass tips from the table.

My spine tensed. My fingers curled tighter around the cup.

Across the square, at the tree line where the forest met the crumbled edge of the village, a figure stood. Cloaked still, and watching. Not one child. Not someone from Solavend. I was sure of that.

My pulse kicked up, but I didn't back away. Instead, my hand drifted down to the knife I kept tied at my hip—a pathetic little thing that wouldn't do much against a god or a monster, but it made me feel less naked. The stranger's presence was a weight of shadow, heavy and watchful. Elara swallowed hard, a single word rising unbidden in her mind—*balance.*

Her mother had once said it like a secret, a truth too fragile for the world to hold. But staring at him now, she felt only the tilt, the wrongness of everything. I squared my shoulders and stepped forward. "You're not from here," I said, my voice low but firm in a way I didn't quite feel.

The figure didn't respond. Only tilted their head slightly to the side, as if acknowledging me without confirming a damn thing. Then they took a single step forward—measured, slow, not threatening, but not exactly welcome either.

I waited, watching, heart thudding in my throat. Now, the air smelled wrong: damp earth, singed herbs. The scent that lingered in dreams and funerals. The scent that followed gods who didn't belong.

"Say something," I demanded, my voice sharper this time, cutting into the stillness like a blade.

The figure lifted a hand—not threatening, not fast—and pointed.

Straight toward the temple.

My blood turned cold.

"You don't get to point and act cryptic," I snapped, all the exhaustion slipping sideways into fury. "If you're here to finish what he started—"

"I'm not here for them." The voice was smooth, but it cut through me like frost. Not cruel, not warm. Just... clean. Like a slate wiped bare.

My stomach clenched. "Then what the hell are you here for?"

He didn't answer.

I watched him from across the square, my fingers tightening around the hilt of my knife, though I already knew it would be useless if he turned violent. Still, I stood my ground. I'd stood through worse.

The stranger slowed near the edge of the ruined fountain, his steps soft, too deliberate to be casual. I could feel the tension building in my limbs, in the air—thick and waiting, like a held breath.

"You're trespassing," I said evenly. "And I'm not in the mood to deal with another cloaked threat acting like silence makes them clever."

The figure didn't flinch, but his head turned slightly toward me, as though considering whether I was worth the trouble. He reached up and pulled back his hood.

He wasn't what I expected. Dark-haired, sharp-featured, not unkind in appearance—but not gentle either. There was something closed off in the way he held himself, like every part of him was locked behind a door I didn't have the key to. His eyes—steel gray, unreadable—swept over my face. A Moon Elf.

Then he said, calmly, "The Eclipse God sent me." My stomach turned cold.

I didn't drop my stance. "You're a little late for a massacre."

He replied without hesitation, "I wasn't sent to kill."

"And that's supposed to make you welcome?" My voice sharpened. "The Eclipse God slaughtered our elders. Our families. If he's sending you, I'm not interested."

"I'm not here to convince you otherwise," the man said. "Only to deliver a message... and observe."

I didn't like how easily those words fell from his tongue. Like he'd rehearsed them. Like he'd had time to.

"Observe what?" I demanded.

His gaze shifted past me, toward the temple. "Survivors. Resistance. The shape of what remains."

I stepped closer, slowly. "And what name does the Eclipse God give to his messenger?"

There was a flicker of pause. Just long enough to make me notice it. "Kael."

I repeated it in my mind. Tested it on my tongue. It sounded like a lie dressed in truth. "You have proof of who sent you?" Kael—if that was really his name—tilted his head, a faint smirk ghosting at the corner of his mouth. "If I wanted to harm you, I would have already."

"Not the answer I asked for."

"It's the one you'll get."

For a moment, we just stood there—me with my knife, him with his steady, unreadable gaze, and the unspoken truth hanging between us like a shadow neither of us wanted to touch.

Finally, I exhaled and lowered the knife a fraction. Not because I trusted him. Because I needed to know why he was here.

"Fine," I said. "You can stay. But you'll work for your place. And you'll answer when I ask."

His expression didn't change, but I thought I saw something shift in his eyes—a spark, quick, before vanishing again. "Agreed," he said simply.

I didn't believe him. But for now, it would do.

The sound of her laughter pulled me from sleep.

"Kael! You're going to miss the morning bread again!"

Her voice drifted in through the open window, carried on warm air that smelled of wood-smoke and crushed thyme. The sun hadn't yet climbed high enough to cut through the shadows on my floor, but the scent of baking—and the stubborn cheer in my sister's voice—was enough to drag me upright. I sat on the edge of my straw mattress, rubbing grit from my eyes, dragging a hand through hair that had no interest in being tamed.

The room was small: cot, shelf of worn books, the crude bow I'd carved myself leaning against the wall. A bowl of cooled water waited by the door. I splashed my face and flinched at the cold.

Outside, the village stirred. Birds called lazily from the trees beyond the stone path. I heard the familiar clatter of the baker's crates and the murmur of neighbors greeting each other. Peace clung to this place like ivy to old stone.

I stepped out barefoot, the stone porch cool beneath my feet. Mayli stood in the middle of the path, a crooked braid down her back and flour smudged across her cheek, holding a woven basket half-filled with fresh loaves.

"You're hopeless," she teased, pressing a warm roll into my hand before I could speak. "That's the third time this week you've slept through breakfast."

"I was dreaming," I said around a bite, my voice rough. "Important business."

"Saving the world again?"

"No. Trying to sleep through your voice."

She threw a crumb at me, grinning wide enough to squint her eyes. I dodged and fell into step beside her toward the village square.

The sun crept over the rooftops, spilling gold across the cobblestones. Children ran past us with sticks shaped like swords, yelling about dragons. Elders sat on porches weaving rope or whittling stories into wood. It was the kind of morning that made you forget the world could be cruel.

By the time we reached the square, it was alive—market boys hauling crates, women bartering over fish with good-natured sharpness, the blacksmith's hammer keeping its steady rhythm. Mayli peeled off toward the baker's stall, calling over her shoulder, "Tell Alen if he burns the nut bread again, I'm stealing his shoes."

"He wouldn't notice until winter," I muttered, tearing off another bite of bread.

I drifted toward the stables, nodding at familiar faces. Here, I wasn't anyone important—just Kael, the boy who fixed fences, taught the little ones how to string a bow, and managed to annoy half the elders weekly.

Elder Meren was near the grain sheds, wrestling a sack onto a cart. I stepped in, hefting it for him.

"You're late," Meren grunted, though the corners of his mouth twitched. "Your sister already brought the morning bread."

"She bribed me with it to get me out of bed," I said, tossing the sack into place.

Meren chuckled. "Your mother had that charm. Your father had the spine to match. Dangerous mix."

I looked away at that, brushing it off like dust. "Maybe that's why they left us with yours."

He snorted. "Go on, boy. Your sister said you've got traps to check."

I followed the winding path past the apothecary into the woods. My snares were small, enough for rabbits or birds, just to pad out the village's winter stores. Two rabbits, one empty snare, one rope chewed through. I reset it, sat for a moment on a mossy log, and let the hush settle over me.

Out here, I could almost believe the world wasn't full of gods and blades. Almost.

By the time I got back, the square was quiet—between lunch and supper. The wind had shifted, carrying something faint, something I didn't recognize.

Mayli was on the porch, arms crossed, brow arched. "You missed lunch."

"I brought rabbits," I said, raising the satchel.

"Then you missed stew and dumplings."

"That's cruel."

She rolled her eyes and stepped aside. The house was warm, the hearth crackling. She'd kept the pot simmering for me. I kissed the top of her head on my way in.

"You're too good to me."

"I know," she said, voice softer than her smirk. "Now sit down before I test that new knife on you."

I ate while she worked herbs into jars, muttering about lavender shortages. I watched her in the quiet—the way her braid slipped down her back, the way she hummed when she thought no one was listening. I didn't know it then, but those little things would matter more than anything else.

The knock came sharp and sudden.

"That's not—" she began.

"I've got it."

I opened the door.

The man on the porch wasn't from Valedell. Too tall. Too pale. His face hollow, his eyes like polished stone. No horse. No trail. No wind.

"Can I help you?" I asked.

The smile he gave me didn't belong on a human face. "You can try."

His gaze slid past me, landing on Mayli. She froze. My body moved before I thought, stepping between them.

"I asked you a question."

"So you did."

Then he turned and walked away. No reason. No warning.

We didn't talk about it, but the air felt colder when I shut the door.

The next morning came without clouds or omens. But I rose early, restless. Mayli had been quiet the night before, carrying her worry the way she always did—tight shoulders, a careful smile.

I told myself I was checking the traps again. In truth, I just needed space.

The woods were still. My snares untouched. Everything looked normal. That, somehow, felt worse.

I crouched by a stream, refilled my flask, stared at my warped reflection. Why had he come? Why had I let him leave?

I stood, turning toward home—

And saw it. Smoke.

Thin at first. Then thick. Rising in a black column from the east.

From Valedell.

I didn't think. I ran.

Chapter Six

The temple lay in that soft, gray light that made everything look suspended—like even time was too tired to start again. My limbs ached, though I had moved little in the night, curled protectively around two small, restless bodies. The stone floor stopped bothering me days ago. It was the silence pressing against me now, heavier than any cold.

I didn't get up right away. Instead, I stared at the old carvings on the ceiling while the dull glow of morning crept down the walls. The air was thick—full of breath, grief, and the stubborn scent of ash that refused to leave. Somewhere near my feet, a child murmured in their sleep. I reached out, brushing my fingers over their tangled hair until they settled back into whatever dream they'd found.

I hadn't dreamed. Not really. Just scraps of memory—heat, light, screams trapped between stone walls. Solari's face burning gold in the sky. Kura's voice is still echoing in my bones. And then... Kael.

His name tasted bitter in my mind, like bark steeped too long in boiled water. I hadn't seen him again after our tense exchange last night, but I could feel him out there—hovering at the edge, testing how close he could come without crossing whatever line I'd drawn.

Slowly, I untangled myself from the knot of limbs beside me and pulled the worn wool blanket higher over the children's shoulders. Their breaths were shallow and warm. Still dreaming. Still whole. That was enough for now.

I rolled my neck until it popped and padded toward the temple doors on bare feet. The great doors gave a low groan as I pushed one open just enough to slip outside.

The air was cool, the morning wind brushing my skin like a warning. The village was still. Empty in a way that had only started to feel wrong recently. Birds didn't sing here anymore. My eyes scanned the square automatically—looking for movement, damage, the small shapes of children who sometimes wandered out too early.

And then I saw him.

Kael stood near the edge of the village, where stone gave way to tree. Half-shadowed beneath the charred branches of an elder woo, arms crossed, cloak drawn close. Still as carved stone. Still watching.

I didn't acknowledge him. Not with a glance, not with a twitch. My gaze moved instead to the well, the broken market stalls, the sweep of ash across the square. I felt his weight behind me the whole time while I tidied and cleared what little I could clear.

He didn't speak. He didn't approach. And I didn't invite him.

When I stepped back inside, the air was warmer from too many bodies and too little space. The children were stirring, stretching under threadbare blankets, blinking against the pale morning light leaking through cracks in the stone. I moved among them quietly, smoothing hair, adjusting blankets, murmuring reassurances I didn't quite believe.

No one cried. That unsettled me more than wailing ever could. Their grief had sunk deep—thick and quiet as fog.

Ferin was already upright in the back, arms looped around his knees, watching me like he was waiting for orders. The second our eyes met, he stood. "I can help," he said. No preamble, no hesitation. Just a boy trying to keep fear from swallowing him.

I nodded. "We'll need water. And someone to check the storerooms."

"I'll take Orren and Neira," he replied, already scanning for them. His voice was steady in the way only grief can forge—too young for that kind of bravery.

By the time the sun was fully up, the temple hummed with small motions. I gave out simple tasks—pairing younger ones with older, sending them to collect herbs, sweep steps, sort whatever goods they'd salvaged. It wasn't much, but structure was something.

I'd been avoiding the apothecary. But when I finally stepped through its shattered doorway, something in my chest twisted hard.

The shelves I'd so carefully stocked were broken, buried under fallen beams, scorched beyond use. My hand-copied scrolls were ash. Mortar and pestles—split down the middle, as though they'd tried to hold the weight of the world and cracked.

I picked through the rubble, lifting a half-burned jar still faintly smelling of rosemary. I held it to my chest for a breath before tucking it into my satchel. No time for mourning books or bottles. Not now.

When I returned, Lani was waiting at the temple steps, twisting her tunic in small hands.
"I cut my hand," she whispered, holding it out.

I crouched to take it gently. A shallow slice—enough to sting, not enough to matter.
"Let me see."

Inside, I rinsed it with water that still smelled faintly of charcoal and wrapped it in clean linen I couldn't afford to waste. She didn't cry—just sniffled once, leaning her head on my shoulder until I tied the last knot.
"Thank you," she murmured.

I kissed her hair. "You're braver than most warriors I know."

Her smile was small, tired. Then she padded off without another word.

Evening dragged in with exhaustion, not sunlight. Supper was root vegetables in thin broth and half a loaf of bread salvaged from someone's ruins. No one complained. The silence didn't need filling.

Ferin sat beside me, staring into the cold hearth. "Do we bury them?"

I didn't ask who he meant. The village still held its dead—parents, siblings—bodies untouched.

"They deserve more than this," I said after a moment. My voice barely held.

"We'll need firewood," he replied.

"I'll help tomorrow."

"You don't have to."

"I do."

We left it there.

Later, I found myself outside again. The wind had shifted. Somewhere beyond the trees, I felt it—eyes on me. Kael was still there.

The next morning broke colder than it should have. I stirred beneath blankets, chilled despite the bodies curled around me. Ferin was already awake by the door, satchel on his shoulder. He nodded once—he hadn't forgotten our plan.

As I rinsed a cracked bowl at the basin, I heard a small cough. It came again—sharp, dry. Lina sat up, rubbing her eyes, a blanket slipping from her shoulders. I crossed to her, pressing my hand to her forehead. Warm. Not a fever, but warmer than I liked.

"You don't need to be sorry for breathing, little moon," I told her when she mumbled an apology. She smiled faintly and lay back down.

By evening, the cough had returned, sharper. Lina curled in a corner under her blanket, trying to hide it. The others glanced her way, eyes edged with fear they didn't name.

That's when I saw it—near the well, tucked in shadow. A bundle wrapped in clean cloth.

I approached carefully, loosening the knot. Herbs. Feverfew, chamomile, licorice root. All medicinal. All useful. All from him.

I dropped them into the fire.

Neira came up beside me, watching the smoke curl. "What was that?"

"Rotten," I said evenly. "Not safe."

Night fell without comfort. I sat by the low fire outside the temple, arms around my knees, too wired to rest. Lina's cough still cuts the silence every so often.

And then—I felt him. No footsteps. No sound. Just a shift in the air.

"I told you not to come close," I said without looking up.

"I didn't," Kael answered from the edge of the firelight. "You came out."

I laughed once, humorless. "Convenient."

He crouched, still keeping a distance. "I left you medicine."

"I burned it."

"I noticed." No anger. No surprise.

"I don't want your help."

"That's not entirely true."

My gaze snapped to him.

"You didn't tell the others," he went on. "About the herbs."

"They're children. They don't need to know there's another stranger circling us."

"I'm not creeping."

"Oh? What would you call it?" I stood, my voice rising. "You hover. You leave things. You watch. Like I'm an animal in a cage waiting to break."

"I'm making sure you survive."

"We're not your concern."

"Tell that to the Eclipse God."

The words landed like a blade.

"If you're here to preach to some unseen god, do it elsewhere."

"He watches over the remnants. You should be grateful he didn't take everything."

"Oh, how merciful—He only murdered the adults and burned the village. I should kneel." I tilted my head at him in a way that could only be described as radiating pure sarcasm.

Something flickered in his face, gone too fast to name. "Your gods failed you long before he arrived," he said softly.

I looked away. "Stay away from the children. God-sent or not."

He nodded once. "Noted." And then he was gone.

By the following day, Lina's cough had worsened—thin wheezes that made my stomach knot. Tea hadn't worked. Herbs hadn't helped. And the others were starting to keep their distance. Fear spreads faster than illness.

That night, the cough turned violent. Fever burned through her skin. The others woke, their eyes wide, already knowing what I refused to say.

And then—one soft knock at the temple door.

Kael stood there, no cloak this time. "She's dying," he said flatly.

"I don't trust you."

"I know."

"I don't want your help."

"Then let her die." The words hit like a slap.

"You want to hate me, fine," he went on. "But your pride isn't worth her lungs." I stared at the bundle he held—neat folds, sharp herbal scent. Every instinct screamed no. But Lina's coughing was in my ears.

I took it. "Thank you," I said, stiff.

"I'll stay out of sight," he promised. "But if you need more—"

"I won't."

Inside, I unwrapped the bundle. Feverleaf. Gold root. A salve I didn't recognize.

"Is it safe?" Neira asked.

"I don't know." But I used it anyway.

And when Lina's cough eased, just a little, I let out a breath I hadn't realized I'd been holding.

I didn't look at the door again. But I didn't throw the bundle away either.

Chapter Seven

They made the throne to remind the world that the sun did not forgive. Shards of molten gold, veins of white fire—solid sunlight forged into a seat of judgment. It burned even when I sat perfectly still, back straight, face composed into the serene mask expected of a god. The heat licked at my spine, pressed behind my ribs, coiled in my thoughts.

I could silence storms with a thought. Boil oceans. Wilt forests. And yet... I could not silence the ache that had been growing since the eclipse. Since the massacre.

Since her.

"My lord Solari," a voice trembled from below the dais. "The mortal realm is stabilizing, but... the eclipse has not faded from the sky. It lingers. Unnatural."

I didn't move.

The Council of Celestials stood in neat rows beneath the dome of the court, robed in starlight and sun-woven silk. None dared meet my gaze. Fear still clung to them like smoke. Kura had made sure of that.

"The eclipse has not faded," I said at last, my voice smooth, cold. "Because it was not natural."

Silence followed—cowardly and tight. A minor god cleared his throat. "There are... rumors, my lord. That the Eclipse God—"

I interrupted, sharper than intended, and said, "is contained. Bound by ancient law. What he did in Solavend was not a declaration of war. It was a performance."

I rose. The light in the chamber bent with me, bowing instinctively. The council dropped to their knees without being told. Reflex. Reverence. Or guilt.

"The eclipse will fade," I said, my tone as calm as my hands were not. "When it does, the sun will shine brighter than before."

One elder—a silver-haired elf with eyes like broken glass—leaned forward. "Genesis would have handled this quicker."

The name landed like a blade under my ribs. My jaw tightened, but I didn't give them the flinch they wanted. Genesis. My father in title, never in mercy. The god who had plucked me from nothing, crowned me in fire, and burned me just as often as he praised me. The one who ruled the sun for centuries before deciding I was ready—not because I was, but because he'd finished molding me into something he could use.

"My father is gone," I said evenly, steel under every word. "And I am not him."

Another councilor opened their mouth. My gaze cut across the chamber like a blade. Silence fell again. "Be grateful I'm not," I added quietly, the warning coiled in my tone.

I descended the dais, the gold-threaded hem of my robe sweeping heat across the marble. At the door, sunlight caught the carvings of creation. At the very top—Genesis, immortalized in merciless detail. Hands raised, not in blessing, but command.

My throat tightened. I turned away before the old light could burn me again.

The inner halls were polished mirrors of light, every flare of gold following me like an accusation. I passed through the wards of the Solarium— my father's sanctum, now mine. The heat inside was suffocating; the air thick with old power. Mirrors lined the walls in a perfect ring, each one holding a different reflection of my past: kneeling, bleeding, obeying.

The solar disk floated at the center, still pulsing faintly with Genesis's magic. I laid my palm against it. The burn came instantly—memory more than heat.

"You are light, boy. You do not cast a shadow. You burn what needs to be burned. That is what it means to rule the sky."

I remembered the first time I'd refused him, begging mercy for a mortal city. His silence had been worse than rage. The punishment had come later—scars still hidden under the illusion of flawless skin. My ascension had been no gift. It had been a sentence.

I pulled back, breath sharp, the shame, and anger knotted too tightly to separate. They dared to give me this throne and this crown, but not in trust.

I left the solarium and turned toward the quieter halls. The Chamber of Reflections waited in its solitude. No guards. No Council. Just the Celestial Mirror hanging over its pool of light.

I didn't need to close my eyes. At my unspoken command, its surface shifted—Solavend bloomed in perfect clarity. Torchlight. Music. The smell of garlands even through the vision. And there—Elara. She didn't take part in the celebration. Her eyes were sharp, and her spine rigid as she stood apart. She'd known. Somehow.

I should have signaled. I should have intervened. Instead, I stood still. The law explicitly prohibited divine interference following a blood sacrifice. Kura showed no care for laws.

The sky darkened in the vision; the sun ringed in shadow. Kura descended with the elegance of a predator, his voice all velvet and steel. The massacre began—silent, deliberate. Adults fell one by one. Kura marked the children but spared them.

And I stood there. Watching. Doing nothing.

Kura hadn't just killed. He'd crafted a message. This is your god. See how he lets you die.

Shame had burned hotter than any fire I could summon. I felt it again now, seeing her drop to her knees beside a fallen child, brushing ash from their cheek without breaking. She didn't burn. She glowed. I shut the vision away, but it stayed with me.

I left the Mirror and descended deeper, into the halls that few walked. The Archive of Threads. The Loom of Destiny pulsed in the dark, holding every mortal life in its weave.

I thought of her name. Elara.

Her thread pulsed in answer, gold laced with black, silver and blue—Kura's magic and another magic unfamiliar to me. Strong magic, fused into hers so tightly it was impossible to tell where one ended and the other began. That bond wasn't chance. It was deliberate.

I traced it back—through her parents' deaths, her childhood, her defiance. Kura had been there, unseen, at every turning point. But further back... the thread vanished. Not frayed. Not obscured. Cut.

No beginning.

No mortal life simply appeared in the loom. Someone had torn out another fate to make space for her. Someone older, and far beyond me.

The thought lodged under my ribs like glass. No wonder Kura had spared her. No wonder she haunted me. I left the loom untouched, but the gold-and-silver pulse followed me out of the chamber, steady and alive.

I didn't look back.

The morning mist clung stubbornly to Solavend, curling through the narrow alleys like it was staking its claim over the village. It gathered thick in the hollows between sagging rooftops, softening the jagged lines of the broken square until the ruins almost looked harmless—if you didn't know better. But I did. I could still see the splintered bones of beams and the blackened teeth of stone beneath that gauzy veil. And I could still smell the damp ash under the river's cold breath, a ghost that hadn't stopped haunting us since the festival.

I pulled my cloak tight at the neck, the wool rough against my skin, and called names into the haze. My voice broke the stillness in steady bursts, coaxing figures from doorways and shadows. Bare feet whispered over stone, and small shoulders hunched against the morning chill. The littlest ones clung together like they could share warmth just by holding on; the older ones straightened when they saw me, blinking away sleep as though pretending to be ready for the day might make it true.

"Jory—water from the well. Lera, check the jars in the storehouse. Corin, with me. We'll sort the fish racks."

The words fell easily. I'd carved this routine into the bones of my days since the festival, each task meant to keep their hands busy and their eyes forward. Work was the closest thing we had to safety now.

I was halfway through my list when a voice—low, steady—threaded through the mist like it belonged there.

My gaze found him instantly.

Kael sat on the low stone wall beside the fish racks, one boot hooked over the edge, the other grounded. The fog had caught in his dark hair, dampening it until faint curls framed his temples. A net stretched between his knees, and his hands moved with patient precision, knotting frayed cords like the motion was written into his bones.

Bram and Corin flanked him, chins almost resting on the net. They watched the shift of his fingers with the same wide-eyed attention they'd give a conjurer pulling coins from the air. Every few knots, Kael spoke—too low for me to hear—but whatever he said made Bram grin.

My jaw tightened before the thought to check it.

"Bram," I called, sharper than I meant to. He turned, blinking like I'd dragged him back from somewhere warm. "You're with Etta today. Wood duty."

He hesitated, eyes sliding back to Kael.

"Go on," Kael murmured, not even looking up. Just a quiet flicker of sound, but Bram moved at once, dragging his feet toward Etta.

I turned on Corin. "With me. Now."

His mouth opened, but my look shut it again. He slid off the wall, boots scuffing the ground, his gaze still hooked on the net.

Kael didn't pause. The only sign he'd registered my interference was the faint stilling of his fingers before he drew the cord taut again.

I pushed the children toward their tasks, guiding them into the thinning mist. The sun was rising now, stripping the haze away to reveal the ribs of our village—buildings gutted and charred, shadows pooled in the hollows where doors had once stood. My boots struck hard against the stone when I passed him. I didn't look his way.

A stranger threading himself into our world was a risk I couldn't afford. And Kael... Kael was all threads, all deliberate knots.

Still, I could hear the slow scrape of cord on cord behind me until the river swallowed the sound.

By midday, the square had settled into its rhythm. Children darted between chores, bursts of chatter falling into the quiet scrape and thump of work. Somewhere nearby, wood stacked in a steady heartbeat.

I'd spent the morning in the storehouse, sorting dried fish from brittle scraps that would break a tooth. The brine clung thick in my mouth and stepping into the pale sunlight felt like surfacing for air.

And there he was again.

Kael crouched at the well, cloak folded neatly beside him. His sleeves were rolled high, revealing forearms faintly streaked with green from the moss he was cutting away. The knife in his hand worked between the stones with the same quiet focus as before, every movement precise, patient.

"You don't need to do that," I said, my voice carrying across the square.

"The moss holds water," he answered, still working. Steel scraped stone in a slow rhythm. "It seeps into the cracks. Then the stone crumbles."

"I can handle it," I replied—too sharp, too quick.

"You didn't."

It wasn't a jab. Just truth, spoken in that steady way of his that left no room for argument.

"The well's stood for decades," I countered.

That made him look up.

No smirk. No challenge. Just a quiet, measured distance, like he was standing on the far bank of a river he had no intention of crossing.

"It'll last longer now," he said, then bent to his work again.

The sun slid over him, catching in his hair and teasing out threads of silver I hadn't noticed before. I should've walked away, but the bucket still needed filling. That was an excuse enough to step closer.A drop of condensation slipped from the bucket's rim, tracing a path across my fingers before vanishing into the dirt. I thought of her mother's voice, soft as waves against a shore. Then it was gone, carried away by the scrape of Kael's blade against stone. I lowered the rope slowly, letting the groan of the pulley fill the space between us. The bucket hit the water with a hollow splash, and I wrapped the rope around my wrist to haul it up.

"You always fix things that aren't yours?" I asked without looking at him.

He didn't glance my way, but his mouth ticked faintly at one corner. "You'd rather I leave them broken?"

"I'd rather know why you're fixing them."

"That's not much of an answer."

I set the brimming bucket on the wall and let the water lap against the rim. "It wasn't a question."

This time, he did look at me. Brief, steady. Long enough to make my skin prickle, like he was weighing whether I'd actually listen if he told me. "Some things," he said finally, "don't wait until you're ready to fix them." I didn't know if he meant well. Or the moss. Or something else entirely. Before I could decide whether to push, he turned back to his work, knife sliding between stone and green with that same unhurried precision. I lifted the bucket, the weight biting into my palms, and walked away.

The surface of the Celestial Mirror rippled like disturbed water, bending the image of the mortal realm below. I stood before it with my hands clasped loosely behind my back, pale firelight from the glass painting its glow across my face.

The Mirror could show me anywhere—its reach as wide as thought—but my focus kept circling back to the same place. A small, dim settlement clinging stubbornly to the river's edge. On the surface, it was unremarkable. But the air there... it moved differently. Still. Waiting.

"You've been staring at the same patch of dirt for some time," came a voice from behind me.

I didn't turn. "Observing patterns."

Measured footsteps drew closer until Hima took his place beside me. The Moon God never arrived without intent—tall, robed in silver and deep blue, moonlight threaded through his dark hair like spun metal. Where my gaze burned, his reflected.

"That is Solavend," he said, tasting the name as if testing it for cracks. His eyes lingered on the image in the Mirror. "Curious place to devote your attention. It is... small."

"Small things can grow," I answered. "Or spread."

A faint curve touched his lips, but it never reached his eyes. "Ah. So it is the Eclipse God's little shadow you're watching for."

The title landed between us like a pebble in still water, ripples of challenge spreading in the silence. I didn't bother denying it.

"I've heard whispers," Hima went on, his voice smooth as polished stone. "Not from the council—they speak too loudly to hear anything worth knowing. From other places." His silver gaze cut toward me, assessing. "You're hesitating."

My jaw tightened. "I'm weighing the cost of striking too soon."

"Or perhaps," he said mildly, though the glint in his eyes sharpened, "the cost of striking at all. Genesis would not have paused to count the cost."

That drew my eyes to him at last. "Genesis had the luxury of being feared enough not to need caution."

"And yet," Hima murmured, "here you are. Cautious." He stepped closer to the Mirror, our reflections crossing in the shifting glass. "Be careful, Solari. Kura does not leave things untouched. He leaves marks. On places. On people." His voice dropped, so low it brushed the edge of sound. "Some of them never fade."

The stillness between us was knife-sharp. Even the Mirror seemed to hold its breath.

"I will act," I said at last. "When the time is right."

Hima studied me for a heartbeat longer, some shadow of thought moving behind his eyes. Then he inclined his head. "May the right time find you before the wrong one does."

His footsteps faded into the long corridors of the celestial hall, leaving me alone with my reflection—distorted by the rippling image of Solavend below. The village lights flickered faintly, shadows threading between them.

The quiet there pressed against me like a warning.

It was too quiet.

The cold woke me before the light did.

It had crept in through the seams of the patched window and the gaps in the old timbers, sliding under my blankets and curling against my skin until the warmth was gone. I blinked in the gray dimness, listening to the soft rhythm of the children's breathing around me. The common hall still smelled faintly of the stew Kael had made, the scent soaked deep into the wood of the walls.

I pushed myself up quietly, pulling my cloak over my shoulders. The fire had burned down to a few stubborn coals, their glow pulsing faintly in the ash. It was too early for the day's noise—no scraping of chairs, no chatter, no footsteps in the square.

Stepping outside was like crossing into a different world. The village lay hushed beneath a thin veil of frost, every roof edged in pale white. My breath rose in front of me in slow clouds as I crossed the square, the sound of my boots muffled by the frozen earth.

The quiet felt heavier than it should have.

It wasn't just the absence of noise—it was the way the air seemed to hold itself still, as if waiting. I'd felt it before, on mornings when storms gathered out of sight beyond the hills, or in the moments before an arrow was loosed. My eyes drifted to the repaired section of the eastern fence. The pale wood stood out against the dark rails, rope wound tight and clean. No movement beyond it. No sign of anyone else awake.

No sign of him.

That should have been a relief—Kael being elsewhere meant the day could start without the prickling unease he always seemed to bring with him. But as I turned back toward the hall, I caught myself glancing again toward the fence, scanning the tree line beyond.

The air still felt like it was holding its breath.

I threw myself into the morning tasks, the same rhythm I knew by heart—checking the storage jars, dividing what was left of the bread, sending the older children to fetch water. But even with my hands busy, my mind kept circling back to the stillness outside. It clung to me as I worked, making me strain for sounds that never came. No birdsong in the trees. No creak from the old docks. Not even the lap of water against the posts.

When a chair leg scraped suddenly against the floorboards, I flinched harder than I should have.

Kael appeared in the doorway, the cold clinging to him like an extra layer. Frost dusted the hem of his cloak, and his dark hair had caught a faint silver sheen in the weak light. He crossed the room without a word and placed a bundle wrapped in cloth on the table.

"What's that?" I asked, not moving closer.

"Dried fish. And salt," he said simply. "From upriver."

My brow knit. "You went to the river this morning?"

"Farther." He unwrapped the bundle, and the sharp, clean scent of brine filled the air. "The trading post there is abandoned. No one's touched it in months."

He began dividing the food into smaller portions, quiet and deliberate. I noticed the faint scrape along the side of his hand, the skin reddened like rope burn.

"You could have told me," I said before I could soften the edge in my voice.

His eyes lifted briefly. "Would you have let me go?"

I didn't answer.

The corner of his mouth shifted—too slight to call a smile. "That's what I thought."

He finished, leaving the portions neatly wrapped and tied. "The cold's going to stay awhile. This will stretch what you have."

And then he turned, stepping back into the frost-hushed morning, the door closing softly behind him.

The silence rushed in after him, heavier than before.

I stared at the neat little bundles on the table. The smell of salt lingered, mingling with faint hearth smoke. I hated that part of me wanted to check the portions—not because I doubted his work, but to make sure he hadn't given away more than we could spare.

I unwrapped one. The fish had been cleaned and trimmed with surgical precision, the salt packed evenly into the folds. No corners cut. If anything, he'd been more careful than most traders I'd known before the festival.

The doorframe still held a trace of the cold where he'd passed through. I caught myself glancing toward it, as if I might see him come back. Foolish. I pulled the cloth back over the fish and forced myself to keep moving.

Outside, frost had begun to break under the pale sunlight, dripping from the eaves in thin threads. The children's voices rose slowly in the square—soft at first, then louder as the day warmed. I moved among them, checking chores, answering questions... and finding my eyes drawn, without meaning them too, to the far side of the square.

It was just after midday when I saw him again. Kael was crouched beside one of the older boys, showing him how to lash two broken crate slats into a sled for hauling firewood. His hands moved with unhurried precision, his head bent as he explained each step.

The boy laughed at something he said, and for a moment—just a flicker—the tension in Kael's shoulders eased. A softness touched his expression that didn't belong to the man I'd been guarding against since the moment he arrived. My steps slowed without my permission. Watching him like that felt... intrusive, like glimpsing something he wouldn't want me to see.

Then his eyes lifted and found mine across the square. The moment shattered. His expression hardened back to the stillness I knew. He said something to the boy, handed him the rope, and straightened.

I turned away before he could start toward me. I told myself it was because I had work to do, but the truth was simpler—I didn't know what I'd say if he came closer.

The rest of the afternoon passed in a steady rhythm. Children hauling firewood on their new sled. Older ones mending baskets by the hall. Me moving between them, keeping the work from unraveling into play. The quiet from the morning had loosened, replaced by the low hum of the square—but it hadn't left entirely.

I felt it most when Kael was near. He never hovered, but his presence shifted the air—just enough to mute the chatter, just enough to pull my attention no matter how hard I tried to keep it elsewhere. He spoke little, his voice low and even, never staying in one place for long. One moment repairing the hall latch. The next stacking kindling by the hearth without being asked.

By late day, the light had thinned toward dusk, shadows stretching long across the square. I stood by the well, hauling the last bucket of water for the evening, when I saw him again. He was leaning against one of the repaired fence posts, arms crossed loosely, watching the horizon beyond the trees.

It wasn't his usual assessing stare—it was quieter, distant, as if he were seeing something I couldn't.

For a moment, I thought about walking over, asking what he was looking for.

Instead, I turned toward the hall, the weight of the water dragging at my arms. I told myself it was because the children needed me inside before nightfall.

But the truth was... I wasn't sure I wanted to know the answer.

Chapter Nine

I was already elbow-deep in grain sacks when I heard the soft thud of boots behind me. I didn't need to turn. Kael moved differently than the rest—measured steps, the kind of steady tread that came from a man who never forgot the ground beneath him.

He stopped just inside the doorway, setting a bucket of water down beside me. "You're short on barley," he said, his gaze sliding to the open sack at my side.

I brushed the dust from my hands onto my skirt. "I know."

He crouched without another word, testing the seams of a second sack as if checking its worth. A loose corner had frayed halfway through, and before I could stop him, he was threading a strip of leather through it, pulling it tight with the sure, practiced grip of someone who'd mended more than grain bags in his life.

"You could've left that for later," I said, keeping my tone flat.

"It would split before the week's over," he answered, eyes still on his work. "No point in letting it pile up."

I didn't have an argument ready for that, so I turned back to the tally marks I'd been scratching into a piece of wood. He finished the knot, gave it a quick tug to test the hold, and stood, brushing dust from his palms. Without being told, he lifted the bucket again.

"I'll top this off," he said, heading for the door. "You'll need more once the children are up."

It was a small thing—practical, ordinary—but I caught myself watching him go, noting the way he moved like he'd been walking through this hall for years, like he already knew where everything belonged. The thought unsettled me more than I cared to admit.

The door opened again before I could dwell on it, and two of the older boys came in, gathering baskets hooked over their arms. They grinned when I told them to bring back reeds from the river, nodding before trotting off into the pale mist. Kael passed them on his way out, the bucket swinging from his hand. He didn't speak, but his eyes followed them a shade too long.

By the time he came back, the hall was waking. Younger children padded in from their sleeping mats, rubbing their eyes, stretching against the chill. I set the water near the hearth while Kael moved through the room without a sound—stacking kindling, pressing his palm along the patched window frame to check for drafts.

The boys weren't back yet.

It wasn't unusual for them to dawdle along the river, stretching those last few minutes of freedom before the weaving work began, but by midmorning they were always back—reed bundles heavy on their shoulders, damp hair curling from the river air.

I stepped outside, scanning toward the mist-shrouded bank. No movement. No voices.

I sent one of the older girls to find them. "Follow the path to the bend," I told her. "Call out if you see them. Don't go farther than that."

She was gone for less than fifteen minutes. When she came back alone, her cheeks were flushed from the cold, breath puffing in quick clouds.

"They're not there," she said. "I went all the way to the bend. I think... I think I saw their footprints going into the trees."

My stomach pulled tight. "You're sure?"

She nodded. "I didn't go after them. You said not to."

From behind me, Kael's voice cut in. "Which way?"

The girl turned, pointing downriver. Kael followed the line of her finger to the dark fringe of trees.

"I'll come with you," he said to me. Not an offer.

I opened my mouth to tell him I didn't need help, but the cold in the air and the sharper cold crawling along my spine made me shut it again. "Fine. But we move quickly."

He didn't answer, already reaching for the spear leaning by the wall. His hand wrapped around the leather grip like it had been waiting for him, his thumb brushing the head to test its point before settling it against his shoulder.

We left the square together, boots crunching over the frost-hardened path. The mist hung low, swallowing sound, until even our steps felt muffled. I kept my eyes on the narrowing trail. The cold air stung my lungs. "They know better than to wander off," I muttered.

"Knowing better doesn't keep people from doing it," he said, his voice unreadable.

When we reached the bend, the river lay gray and sluggish. No ripple of waterbirds, no reeds shifting in the wind. Then I saw it—a narrow break in the frost, small boots pressed into the mud, tracks angling toward the treeline.

I crouched, brushing my fingers along the edge of one print. "These are fresh."

Kael's gaze was already fixed past me. "They're not alone out here."

I looked up sharply. "What do you mean?"

He didn't answer, just stepped past me, spear angled low. I hesitated only long enough to curse under my breath before following him. The trees swallowed us in a damp, metallic tang that clung to the back of my tongue.

The boys' prints wavered as we went, sometimes doubled back on themselves. A few yards in, a bundle of reeds lay crushed into the leaves.

I picked it up, heart thudding. "They were here."

Kael studied the ground, his eyes catching on something invisible to me. His jaw tightened before he straightened. "Keep moving."

The forest thickened, shadows pooling like water around us. A branch shifted ahead, slow and weighted. Kael stepped in front of me, the spear tilting toward the sound. We waited, breath shallow, until the silence became its own kind of pressure.

"Stay close," he murmured.

I did. The ground softened under our boots, the air heavier now, like the mist had sunk into the roots. A strip of wool snagged on a thorn caught my eye—deep green, one of the boys' scarves. Cold, damp, frayed at the edges.

Kael's gaze swept the ground, and whatever he saw made his mouth press thin.

"You know what did this," I said.

His eyes met mine only briefly. "I know it's not the boys."

"You think something took them?"

"I think we're not alone. And whatever else is out here knows we're looking."

The wind shifted, bringing a rustle from up ahead—not footsteps, but something dragging across the leaves. His grip on the spear tightened. He motioned me forward, slower now, every step deliberate.

The trail thinned. A half-print here, a scatter of disturbed leaves there. Each sign felt fainter, as if whatever we were following had decided it no longer wanted to be found. The metallic scent sharpened. A crow called once behind us, the sound too loud, too close.

Kael crouched by a patch of moss, his fingers tracing over it. "Not them," he murmured. "Something heavier. Dragging."

My grip tightened on my cloak. "Dragging what?"

He stood, scanning the trees. "We turn back."

"That's it? Now?"

"The light's going." He tilted his head toward the canopy—already dimming, sky cut into thin strips overhead. "If they're alive, we help them better in daylight."

The words *if they're alive* sat in my chest like a stone. "Five minutes," I said, before I could stop myself. "Five more. If the trail dies, we turn."

He studied me—one long, even breath—then nodded once. "Five."

We moved deeper, the trees knitting tighter above us. The hush changed—no birds, no insect-buzz, just the soft hiss of mist rolling between trunks. My boot nudged a loop of vine near a fallen log, and Kael's hand snapped out to catch my wrist. He didn't yank—just set it back a span to the left.

I followed his gaze. Not a vine. A snare—thin cord, bark-dyed, tight as a bowstring. The noose was small. Child-small.

My stomach turned. "Who sets something like that here?"

His answer was a flat look at the ground beyond the log, where the leaves bore the scuffed signature of something thrashing. He cut the snare with a quiet flick of his knife and pushed the coil under the log with the spear butt. "Keep your feet where mine go."

We did. A few paces later, we found another sign: a little plait of reeds hung from a twig at eye level, woven into a tidy knot I recognized—Bram's restless fingers made that same pattern when he waited for stew to boil. Only this knot was wrong. The tail ends had been spit-slicked and pulled too tight, each reed trimmed square with a blade. A child would leave ends ragged.

"It's a lure," I said, throat dry.

"It's a message," Kael corrected. "For us."

The path ahead narrowed into a shallow dell. An old stump sat at its center, furred with gray-green lichen. Atop it, laid carefully as an offering, was a small strip of leather with a bone bead threaded through. I knew that bead—the boys had traded half a bundle of cattails for it at midsummer.

I stepped forward and felt Kael's spear shaft lift across my middle—gentle, but firm enough to stop me. He pointed—there, and there. The ground's color changed in four neat squares around the stump, just a shade darker where the leaf-litter was too even. Pits. Covered.

"Someone wants you to walk to the center," he said.

"Someone," I echoed. Not an animal. Not the wind. Someone.

A sound curled through the trees then—a thin, breathy whistle, four notes rising and falling. It could've been a boy trying to learn a tune. It could've been. My heart leapt before my head caught up. The last note hung too perfect, like it had been held in a fist.

Kael didn't move. "Don't answer."

"I wasn't going to," I lied.

He slid the spear-tip beneath the leather strip and flicked it off the stump. It landed safely beyond the pits with a soft pat. The ground didn't move. Nothing sprang. Whoever set this preferred patience to surprises.

"Five minutes are done," he said.

"Not yet." I swallowed. "We mark it. So we can find it again."

He glanced at me, then knelt and pressed his palm into the damp soil, drawing a quick, clean symbol with the point of his knife—three short lines and a longer slash beneath, tucked low where a careless foot wouldn't kick it. Not a ward. A memory.

We eased backward the way we'd come, placing our feet into our own prints, stepping over the cut snare, past the lure-knot. The whistle came again behind us, the last note bending too smoothly, and then stopped. As if it had learned how long we'd listen.

Near the treeline, a pale scrap fluttered from a birch branch, catching at the edge of my vision. Another strip of wool, this one a different shade—Corin's, not Bram's. It was tied with a careful square knot, the ends trimmed neat. My hands wanted to reach for it; my feet stayed where Kael's shadow fell. He cut it loose and tucked it into my palm. Cold. Damp. The bead mark in the leather from the stump still pressed against my skin, as if both pieces had been waiting for me specifically.

We broke from the trees as the mist thickened over the river, the village a blurred shape across the gray.

Inside the hall, faces lifted—hope first, then the stillness that follows when hope lets go.

"They're still out there," I told them, keeping my voice level. "We look again at first light."

They settled back, but the quiet that followed felt brittle.

Kael set the spear by the door and went to the hearth, adding wood until the flames climbed high. The warmth pushed at the shadows, but it didn't touch the knot in my stomach.

I sat near the patched window, watching the light drain from the sky. Somewhere in that black tangle of forest, the boys were either waiting for us— or not waiting at all.

Kael hadn't moved from his place near the fire. His stillness wasn't rest; it was something sharper, a kind of waiting I didn't understand. When I finally crossed to him, the firelight caught a thin scar along his neck I hadn't noticed before. It made me wonder if he'd earned it in woods like the ones we'd just left—or from something worse.

"We'll start at the bend," I said quietly. "Follow the trail deeper."

His gaze lifted to mine. "You're assuming it'll still be there."

"You think it won't?"

"I think it will be watching to see if we come back."

Before I could answer, a soft thud tapped the patched window behind me. Not wind. A single, deliberate knock. I turned, heart in my throat. Nothing waited outside but fog and the faint ghost of my own face on the glass. Then I saw it—caught in the warped frame of the latch, a narrow twist of reed tied in a tiny square knot. Trimmed ends. Too neat. The same knot as in the trees.

I pulled it free with numb fingers and turned back to the fire.

"Get some rest," Kael said, his voice low. "Tomorrow might be longer than you expect." I almost told him I'd sleep when the boys were safe. But something in his eyes kept me quiet. It wasn't reassurance. It was a warning.

The Celestial Hall was quieter than it should have been. Not silent— never silent—but the kind of quiet that meant every word spoken was meant to be overheard. Gold light pooled along the marble floor, refracted from the vast mirror at the far end of the chamber. The light shifted uneasily, breaking into fractured shards that slid over the pillars and across the faces of those gathered. I stood at the center dais, hands clasped loosely behind my back. My reflection in the mirror was split into a dozen distorted copies, each warped by the mirror's shifting surface. The realm itself felt unsettled, the light never quite steady.

The council lingered in their semicircle, positioned as if their proximity to the dais marked their importance. They never stood still, those gilded creatures—robes whispering over the floor, heads bending toward each other. They thought they could keep their voices low enough that I'd only hear what they wanted me to.

"Genesis would have acted already," one of them murmured.

"He never let mortal matters linger this long," said another.

My father's name—dropped like a coin into a shallow bowl—rang just loud enough for the echo to sting.

I flexed my fingers once at my sides, the motion small but enough to make the gold thread at my cuffs catch the light. Whenever they wanted to measure me, they always used his name and found me lacking. Genesis, the paragon of decisive action. The perfect Sun God in their eyes.

None of them had stood in his shadow. None of them had seen how easily glory could mask cruelty.

"I see some of you are eager to rewrite the laws of patience," I said, without turning to face them. My voice carried easily to the edges of the chamber, smooth enough to pass for amusement.

A few stilled; others shifted like they'd been caught mid-step.

I turned toward the great mirror. Threads of light wove over its surface, each one a place under my watch. Most glowed with steady warmth, deep and sure. But one—one flickered faintly, caught in the lingering shadow of the last eclipse.

Solavend.

I stepped closer. The flicker pulsed and stuttered, dimming as though something unseen pressed against it from the other side. Not a chance. Not the ebb and flow of mortal misfortune. This was interference—shadow-born and deliberate.

"You see it too, don't you?"

The voice came from my left, smooth as silver over glass.

Hima stood half in shadow, the faint sheen of moonlight catching at the edges of his hair. His expression was calm, his eyes sharper than I liked.

"I see enough," I said.

"And you'll do nothing?"

Not accusation—too controlled for that. But there was an edge to it, the kind that slides under the skin.

I kept my gaze on the mirror, on the way that flicker seemed to breathe. "Mortals have their own battles to fight. If I step in every time the dark stirs, they'll never learn to stand."

"The moon has moved on," Hima said, voice still even. "Yet the darkness has not."

My eyes narrowed slightly. "You think this is unnatural?"

"I think the last eclipse ended weeks ago. And I think you know no one has seen Kura since." The name rolled into the room like a shadow, heavy enough that the council's murmur rose instantly.

"If Kura were here, we would know it," I said.

"Would we?" Hima asked. "He's vanished before."

And returned. I didn't need him to finish the thought.

I turned toward the council, letting the gold light catch along the edges of my voice. "Do you think repeating my father's name will burn this shadow away? Do you think pointing at a flicker will make it vanish? You stand here draped in authority, yet you wait for me to act as if your own hands are useless."

Their murmurs died. Not agreement—just the careful quiet of predators unwilling to bare their teeth first.

"Bring me facts, or bring me silence," I said, and let the dismissal cut sharper than a blade.

The chamber emptied slowly, silk and gold thread brushing over marble. None of them bowed lower than they had to.

When the doors closed, only Hima remained, his shadow still anchored in the far side of the hall.

"You linger," I said.

"I thought you might prefer honesty without an audience," he replied.

"An unusual choice for you," I said.

His lips curved faintly. "You've grown fond of that tongue since Genesis left."

"And you've grown fond of watching me," I said, starting toward the upper gallery stairs. He followed without invitation, his footsteps soundless.

The gallery was quieter, the light thinner. The mirror's reflection here was smaller, more fractured—every thread of light a narrow line stretched across glass. Solavend's was still dim.

Hima leaned against the railing, looking down at the hall below. "It's not a prophecy, Solari. I won't insult you with that. This was not foretold. The eclipse was meant to pass."

I studied him. "And yet it hasn't."

"And yet Kura hasn't been seen," he said.

The name again, placed with the care of a man setting a knife on the table between us.

"You think this is him?"

"I think," Hima said, "that I don't believe in coincidence. And if it isn't him... it is something worse."

His voice carried no dramatics, no thunder, just the steady confidence of someone who had survived Kura once already.

I turned back to the mirror. Solavend's flicker seemed almost deliberate now, as if whatever caused it knew I was watching.

"What would you have me do?" I asked finally.

"Watch more closely," he said. "And perhaps—consider that the mortals aren't the only ones unprepared for what's coming."

I didn't give him the satisfaction of answering.

When Hima finally left—no bow, no parting shot, just his absence settling like cooled metal—I stayed in the gallery with the mirror's fractured light stuttering against my hands.

I've pushed light through this glass since the day Genesis forced it on me—training until my vision burned, until my lungs felt scraped clean. The mirror answers to the sun's will; that's the law written into its making. It has limits, yes, but they are mine to set.

I placed my palm to the rail and focused. The threads across the mirror tightened, brightened. Most offered easily, like reeds flexing in a current. Solavend did not.

I closed my eyes and reached the way I was taught: not with muscle, not with anger, but with the disciplined pressure that bends heat into a blade. Light draws light. I gathered a thin band from the surrounding threads— warmth skinned down to its most obedient edge—and eased it toward the dim place on the glass.

It hit resistance before it even touched.

Not a simple absence. Not the soft give of cloud or mortal grief or winter famine. This felt like a woven thing—fine, cold, and patient. A mesh set just beneath the surface.

I pressed again. The band of light thinned, brightened, hissed along the boundary. The mirror's surface didn't ripple; it held. My teeth locked on reflex. I adjusted the angle—lower, then higher—probing, seeking a seam.

There. A hair's-breadth laxity along the southern edge of the village thread, as if whoever placed the mesh had not woven it in one sitting. I slid the light along that weakness and pushed.

The mirror gave an inch.

Cold surged back through the narrow opening—thin as breath, sharp as iron. The sensation wasn't pain so much as refusal. Not a wall, but a will.

I reined the light hard before it could snap, let it settle, then widened my stance and drew from higher—past the hall's ceiling, past the realm's bright canopy, from the steady core that answers when I call it by name. Heat gathered in my bones like a storm taking shape.

"Yield," I said—to the mirror, to the mesh, to the thing that presumed to fence my light.

The glass did not crack. The chamber did not tremble. The resistance... thickened, as if it had understood me and chosen its reply.

I hate repeating my father's methods, but I learned the geometry of siege at his hand. If a gate won't open to a blade, drown it in river water first.

I split the beam, fanned it into a lattice of narrow strands instead of a single strike, and sent them in sequence—one-two-three—testing the weave for pattern. The mirror flared, the gallery's pillars throwing back sun in quick pulses. The mesh answered in kind: a counter-pulse that met each strand half a heartbeat late, as though it had to feel the first before it could smother the next.

Not instinct, then. Design.

"Who taught you to breathe like that?" I murmured, and pushed the fourth strand on an off-beat, slipping it through the half-breath between their answers.

It went in.

A flash—brief, jagged—cut across my vision. The scent of river silt and cold ash, a square of broken stone, small footprints pressed into frost—then the opening clamped, and my strand sheared away so cleanly the recoil stung my knuckles though I hadn't moved them.

I pulled the remaining light back, steadying it in my chest until the urge to lash out passed. Feeling for frayed edges, for damage. None. The mirror's surface smoothed, innocent as water.

I've fought storms that accused me. I've burned mountains that begged. I have never been told no by something that refused to admit it exists.

Below, in the shadowed hall, the last of the council's footfalls faded behind the great doors. I listened to the quiet, to the tick of cooled heat along the railing, and let my voice find the glass again—low, even, the way Genesis taught me to speak to frightened horses.

"I am not taking Solavend," I said. "I am not claiming it. I am warding it. There are children in that light. Step aside."

Nothing. Then—so faint I almost doubted it—a drag across the glass like a knuckle drawn over frost. Deliberate. Petty.

Not Kura's signature. Kura's shadow moves with appetite; it darkens, and it devours. This was different. Drawn tight, careful, covetous. It wanted not to swallow the place—but to keep it.

"Who are you?" I asked and felt ridiculous for it. The hall did not answer. The mirror never does. But somewhere in the weave, the counter-pulse steadied, as if it had moved from learning me to memorizing me.

I cupped both hands before me and shaped something smaller: a watcher's spark. A mote no bigger than a seed, wrapped in a sheath of my heat, its only purpose is to sit in the eaves of Solavend and show me what the mirror would not. Genesis used to pepper the mortal realm with them until the sky felt like a net. I hate the taste of his tricks, but today I need eyes.

I sent the spark along the same southern laxity, riding the breath between pulses. It slipped through—and guttered the instant it crossed, snuffed without smoke, like a candle pinched between fingers you cannot see.

My mouth went dry. "Enough," I said, to nobody, to the mesh, to my own rising heat. I banked the light, layered it back into the chamber until the gold steadied and the fractures along the mirror resolved into their restless normal.

When I looked again, Solavend's thread still flickered—fainter now, only because my eyes had learned the rhythm of its stutter. If I stared long enough, I could almost pretend the dim was ordinary dusk.

I stepped away from the rail and let the sound of my boots remind me what is still under my command.

If I name this a siege, the council will demand spectacle—banners, proclamations, a cleansing sun that burns until even our allies choke. If I pretend nothing is wrong, the mesh tightens and whatever sits in those trees graduates from lures to graves.

Kura would break the mirror. He would step through shadow and take the thing in his hands until it stopped moving. He would make a lesson of it. He is not here.

I am. And I will not let some cautious little net tell me where my light may fall.

I turned from the gallery and descended to the dais. Alone, the hall felt bigger than it needed to be, an inheritance built to fit a man I refuse to become.

"Send no summons," I told the empty air, because there are always ears in these walls. "There will be no council theatre." If the mirror would not show me what I need, then I will find my own way to see it. Come dusk I will find a new way to gather the information I need.

I left the hall with the sun banked low inside my ribs, not quenched, just narrowed to a blade's width. If the mesh wants to learn my rhythm, it can. Tomorrow, I will change it.

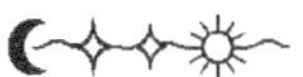

Chapter Ten

Morning should have shape—smoke lifting, voices finding their edges, the particular rhythm of bowls and bare feet and somebody laughing too loudly because they're glad they woke up again. This had none of that. The common hall breathed slowly around me—blankets shifting, a cough swallowed into cloth, the scrape of a heel against the floor—and all of it felt like a pause that had gone on too long.

I counted heads. I counted bowls. I counted the things I could still control because counting stopped the other kind of math, the kind with names. Two bowls untouched. Four children pretending the bread was enough. The littlest girl clutched her rag doll by the leg and stared at the patched window like she could conjure the boys with wanting alone. No one asked when they were coming back. That was new. That was worse.

I crossed to the door. Frost scratched faint white along the inner sill. I lifted the latch. The wood stuck, then gave, groaning like it resented the effort, and cold pressed against my face like a flat palm.

I stepped out—and stopped.

Mud streaked the lower plank, thin and crooked, as if a dirty hand had dragged across it looking for purchase. A floorboard creaked behind me. Kael's shadow slid over my shoulder in the doorway before he did. He didn't ask; he knelt. He traced the edge of the mud without touching, eyes narrowed like they'd been in the woods when he was listening with more than his ears.

"Night visitor?" I kept my voice level.

His mouth twitched—not a smile, just a shift that said he'd heard me and didn't like the words. "Visitor implies manners."

I waited for more. He offered none. He stood and checked the hinge, the latch, the gap below the door with brisk, spare movements, not because he doubted my work but because he catalogued every opening like a soldier learning a stranger's outpost. When his gaze slid toward the fence, I felt the petty, human urge to step into his line of sight—to make him look at me and not the danger I could not name. I didn't.

"We're not feeding fear," I said, and pitched it for the little ears behind us. "We eat, we work, and then we go."

"Eat first," he agreed, already turning for the hearth. "And hot for once."

The streak on the plank had dried to a dull crust that didn't flake when I rubbed it with my thumb. Not river mud. Something heavier, oil in the grain. It clung to my skin like it wanted to seep in and call it home. I wiped my hand on my cloak and shut the door with more care than I needed; the wood thudded soft into the jamb like it, too, was trying to pretend.

By the time I crossed back to the hearth, Kael had coaxed a brighter flame from the coals. He'd set a pot and filled it without asking, moving sparely through the hall like he belonged to its angles. The children watched him the way you watch a large animal—quiet, intent, ready to startle. He tipped oats into the boiling water and—unexpectedly—a pinch of salt, careful enough it felt like a spell. The littlest girl's shoulders loosened by the width of a finger.

"Boys first," I said, letting the lie sit where they could hear it. "If they smell porridge, they'll come in for a bowl."

Kael flicked me a look. Not mockery. Acknowledgment. The lie was the right size for the room.

I spread my hands on the table and did the morning math: light-to-distance, bodies-to-work, which teens could carry fear without dropping their wits. I could have done it with my eyes closed. I didn't, because the room had too many eyes of its own.

When the bowls were ready, I passed them out. Count. Nod. Correct the ones who forgot "thank you" with a look and not a word. Kael ate last, standing, one shoulder against the post like he needed the wood to keep him from drifting into some thinking I couldn't reach.

When the air lost its bite and conversation rose a little from the floor, I stood. "Toma. Leren. With me." I turned to the rest. "The bar stays down unless you hear my voice. No games by the river. If you need wood, you take someone with you. Clear?" Nods. A few thin yeses.

I stepped to him. "Fence line first," I said. "Then the bend. We pick up the trail where we lost it."

"We won't find the same trail," he said.

"Then we find a new one."

He lifted the spear from its place by the wall and checked the binding at the head with his thumb, like a man who had learned the cost of trusting shoddy work. "Keep your pace behind me," he said softly. "If something swings wide, I want it swung toward me."

I hated that it made sense. I hated that my body answered yes before I did.

Before we left, I took a bit of charcoal and marked the inside of the doorframe where only the children would see: three short lines with a longer one beneath. *All-in. All-safe.* We'd made the signal together after the first week. Kael's brow lifted in question. I did not explain. Some things in this village were mine.

We stepped into the square. The day had gathered itself into a dim, even light without warmth, like a bowl of water left in the shade. Toma and Leren fell in behind us, quiet, faces set in the careful blankness of boys who know fear and won't let it see itself reflected. Beyond the fence, the river fog lay in low bands, the kind that clings if you let it. I tugged my cloak close at the throat and set for the eastern posts.

At the repaired section, the timber still breathed sap. Something had brushed along the outside rail in the night, leaving a thin scuff parallel to the ground, like a damp cloth dragged and lifted away. No prints to match it. No story pressed into the dirt to flatter me with clarity. Toma swallowed hard. Leren glanced at Kael and then disciplined his eyes back to the ground.

"Eyes up," I said. "Mouths shut unless it's useful."

Kael angled toward the bend without being told. I let him lead until the path pinched to a squeeze between thorn and alder. Then I stepped past him into the narrow and made the choice with my own boots. At the riverbank, the reeds stood heavy with dew and bent under their own weight. The place where the boys had cut them yesterday looked older than a single night should make it—edges darkened, water pooled where none had been. A gull wheeled once and didn't cry.

"Split," I said. "Ten paces apart, keep the line. We don't get clever. We don't get brave."

We slid into the fog like thread into cloth. It took the shape of us because everything takes the shape of what presses it, but it never became ours. Cold nosed my wrists and throat where the cloak gapped. Sounds arrived thin and late: the hiss of water on stone, a shy plunk from a branch, the whisper of something small that wanted to be a name and wasn't.

My boot touched a half-braided reed cord and nearly missed it. Half-buried in silt a hand's span from the path, braid neat where it started, ragged where small fingers had stopped. I held it up. Kael didn't touch it. He looked past it into the trees, his jaw a line.

Along the bank, a second sign: a drag mark that interrupted the delicate veining the ebb had left. Not long. Not heavy. Just enough to say *See?* When I crouched to gauge its bite, the smell found me—thin and metallic, a winter-blood scent without warmth.

"Same as yesterday," I said.

"Stronger," he answered.

The river wore the fog like a shawl pulled tight, surface smooth as a blade. No ripple, no ring from fish or frog, no careless splash from a creature that hadn't learned the new rules. The silence had a top and a bottom. You feel that more than hearing it—the box of it, the lid. I did not like being inside.

"Forward," I said, because the only other choice was backward and I am too stubborn to let fear teach me.

Reeds given to young willow, willow to alder and birch. The ground lifted, and the brush closed in. The boys' marks thinned to suggestions: a sapling bowed the wrong way; a scuff that might have been heel or hoof or a trick of water; dew wiped from a leaf at a child's height. Twice I raised a hand to halt us for sounds that died before they earned names—once a breathy chuckle like river under rock, once a tight clicking like teeth worrying wood. Toma went a shade gray. Leren white-knuckled his knife, and I didn't tell him to put it away because lies only work when you can offer a better one.

Kael stopped us with a palm lifted to the height of my waist. He didn't look at us; he looked through the trees with his whole body, the spear angled low like a promise made without words. When he spoke, it was so soft the fog tried to keep it. "Left."

I didn't ask why. I signaled the boys and angled left, my heart keeping time against my ribs. A low branch caught my cloak, and I freed it without swearing, which felt like a triumph. Ten paces. The fog unrolled enough to reveal a stump slick with damp and—on top of it—clean and alone, a neatly folded scrap of green wool.

One of the boys' scarf-ends. Folded, not dropped. Placed.

"We're being led," I said, and the words came out flat enough to be rock.

Kael's eyes didn't leave the trees. "We were the moment we left the door."

The deeper we went, the more the forest felt intentional. Not wild—shaped. The fog funneled us down narrow corridors where branches leaned like ribs around a cage. The air had weight that climbed into clothes and settled against skin, making each motion a little slower than it had any right to be. Toma kept glancing back despite my earlier order. Leren moved too stiffly, as if the knife could hold him up if he let it. Fear makes a person noisy to themselves. Nothing I said would have been louder than their own pulse.

Kael walked just to my right, close enough that I could hear the leather wrap on his spear grip creak when he shifted. His eyes didn't linger anywhere long, and the set of his jaw spoke a language I couldn't yet translate but understood well enough: ready, ready, ready.

The trail—if it still deserved the name—splintered. Damp ground too soft to hold a clean print, but firm enough to carry a different mark: long, thin, too narrow for boot and too regular for random. It ran parallel to itself for a while, then cut east and vanished under brush like a drawn line someone got bored with.

"Animal?" Leren asked before he could stop himself.

Kael crouched and laid his fingers close to the mark without touching. "No animal you want to meet."

"We stay on the boys' sign," I said. "No detours."

That would have been easier if the lines hadn't tugged at the eye like a thread snagged in cloth asking your fingers to pull. I pushed my gaze back to smaller truths: the bent stem, the brushed leaf, the place where bark grazed at child-height. You can follow big stories into pits. Small ones keep you alive.

The sound came like a kindness at first. A chuckle with no echo. It hung in the air as if it could hang by itself. Close enough to a child's laugh to tip my stomach, wrong enough to stop me cold. The pitch is too steady. The breath is too even.

Toma breathed, "That's—"

"Quiet," Kael cut, low and edged enough to slice the fog.

We held still. The chuckle stopped. When it came again, it was farther. Or deeper. I couldn't tell which, and that was worse.

"It's not them," Kael said, and he didn't need to add *I know,* because certainty like that is its own weight.

We pushed on. Branches knitted tighter overhead until the light thinned to green glass. The ground sloped and I let us slow because pretending strength doesn't earn you any. A strip of green scarf hung snagged on a bare branch too high for a child, tied in a single, deliberate knot. No broken supports beneath. No smear where someone climbed.

"Someone's playing," Leren whispered.

"Not playing," Kael said, jaw tight.

The wind shifted. Fog thinned just enough that the darkness ahead seemed to have more shape than it should. A suggestion of movement between trunks where nothing should move. By the time I looked twice, it had become a certainty that I had imagined it.

"Slow," I said, and Kael didn't argue. The not-arguing, more than anything, made me want to turn back.

A snap like a twig underfoot cracked the quiet. Neither boy moved. Neither of us had, either. The fog seemed to breathe closer. Kael adjusted his grip; his knuckles blanched.

"It's following," he said.

"How close?"

"Close enough."

The silence after said, *Don't make me measure it for you.*

The smell reached us faint as a warning and then coiled thick: metal and sour, like iron left to steep in water. It slid into my lungs and settled there. Kael's nose wrinkled. Mine wanted to do more and I wouldn't let it.

"We turn back," he said, with no room left for bravado.

"The boys—" It came out because it always comes out.

"—will be names if you keep going," he cut in, and it was the steadiness more than the words that stopped my mouth. Not lack of heart. Discipline.

The fog resisted like wet cloth—heavier when you push, lighter when you surrender. It thinned behind us in ways that made the back of my neck feel watched. Toma murmured an old prayer that probably had more dust than power on it. Leren kept glancing over his shoulder, knife lifted pointlessly high, and I didn't correct him because sometimes the ritual matters more than the outcome.

When the trees finally let us go, the cold slapped so hard my lungs did that ugly first-breath stutter. Fence. Roof. The shape of home where we had left it.

Relief cracked like thin ice under a boot.

A shoe lay against the hall door, perfectly straight. One of the boys'. Wet with mud, and darker streaks clung stubbornly to the leather where no rain had any business leaving them.

I went down into a crouch before my body could ask why. My hand reached—habit, hope, hunger—because what if? What if this was the cheap miracle we'd spent all morning trying not to beg for?

"Don't—!"

Kael's voice broke the air clean as a blade. Everyone stopped like a hand had closed around their throats. Toma flinched. Leren froze mid-step.

"It's a shoe, Kael," I said, because the part of me that refuses to be ordered enjoys hearing itself.

He was nearer than I'd realized, spear angled away, his free hand half-raised like he'd grab my wrist if I didn't listen. His breath wasn't steady.

"It's not just a shoe," he said, quieter but no less strained. "You don't know what's on it. Or who put it there? Or what's waiting for you to touch it."

Not a command. Fear. For me. It rooted my hand more effectively than orders ever do.

"And you do?" I asked, softer than I meant. "You've been telling me where to step and where to stop since we left, but you haven't said what you actually know."

His jaw worked before words did. "I know what bait looks like."

The ripples from that landed sentence traveled a long way and came back to hit the bank behind my ribs.

"You think they're gone already," I said, not as a question because I didn't want the gift of his answer.

He didn't look away. "I think I've watched too many people walk into traps because hope blinded them to the teeth waiting in the dark. And I think if you pick that up, something out there will know it worked."

My throat tightened around something too big to swallow. "You think I can't tell the difference between hope and foolishness?"

"I think you've got too much heart to care about the difference," he said, the edge sanded by a weight I recognized from cemeteries. "And that's the kind of thing that gets people killed."

The first retort in my mouth tasted like metal. I kept it where it was because the way he said it—like he'd dug graves with his hands—made temper feel smaller than it should.

"And you?" I said instead. "No heart at all?"

His mouth moved, almost a smile, but there was not a single bright thing in his eyes. "Not for lack of trying."

We looked at each other too long for strangers. The air between us felt raw, edges still sharp but no longer cutting.

I stood and stepped back. "We leave it there," I said. "But it stays by the door."

He nodded once, short, reluctant, and eased aside so I could pass. I brushed his shoulder in the doorway. He didn't shift. The weight of his gaze stayed with me past the threshold and into the hall like the tail of a comet.

I set the bar. I turned toward the children, their eyes wide over the rims of bowls, small bodies stiff with the effort of being quiet. I opened my mouth to start the next round of necessary lies—and the light in the doorway changed.

Not brighter. Just... truer. That's the only word I have for it. As if the color had been turned down on the world and someone nudged the dial with two fingers. I looked back.

A man walked across the square from the far fence line. Tall. Shoulders squared. He wore travel leathers cut like someone had made them for him and then decided to pretend they'd been bought at a market. He moved the way heat moves through a room on the first good day after winter—nothing dramatic, just a fact other facts cling to.

Kael felt him before he saw him. I know that because I felt Kael change. A stillness came into him that I hadn't yet seen, like a lake going flat under a held breath.

The man stopped at the foot of the steps. His hair held gold where this morning had refused to hold anything. His eyes found mine like they'd known where I would be. There was no question in them.

"Elara," he said, and my name in his mouth sounded like it had been spoken in rooms I'll never see. The word went through the hall like a draft under a door. I heard the children's inhale. I heard my own. Behind me, Kael did not move. I didn't either.

The shoe sat where we'd left it, a dark comma against the wood. The smear on the latch had not dried any lighter. The morning leaned toward us, expectant and unkind. "May I come in?" Solari asked, not because he needed permission, but because manners in a small room are a different kind of power. I let the silence hold one heartbeat too long.

Then I stepped aside.

Chapter Eleven

The sun barely skimmed the horizon as Solavend stirred to life. I watched from a distance as Solari stood in the middle of the village square, completely out of place in a way that was almost painful to witness. His usual celestial grandeur was gone. No golden armor. No shimmering aura. Just the plain tunic and the awkward way he held himself like he was trying to blend in, but couldn't quite get it right.

He looked like a god trying to be human. A god failing at being human.

He shifted on his feet, glancing down at the ground with uncertainty, as if the earth beneath him were something alien he couldn't quite trust. His gaze moved over the children who had begun to gather around him, their eyes wide with curiosity and mischief. They knew he wasn't like them, knew he was someone important—but here, in this village, that didn't mean much.

"Try sitting like this," Aric, one of the younger boys, piped up, crossing his legs on the ground with an easy grace. He patted the dirt beside him and shot Solari an expectant look. "Come on. You'll be more comfortable."

Solari hesitated, glancing at the ground like it might swallow him whole. He tried to mimic the gesture, but his limbs were too stiff, his legs too long. He planted himself awkwardly on the dirt, looking less like a celestial being and more like a giant who didn't understand the rules of the world.

I tried not to stare, but I couldn't help it. There was something almost... heartbreaking about watching him struggle with something as simple as sitting down.

"Maybe you should just leave him to it," Kael muttered beside me, his arms crossed as he leaned against the stone wall of the nearby building. I glanced over at him, catching the faintest smirk tugging at the corner of his mouth.

"I'm not leaving him here to make a fool of himself," I replied under my breath, but the way Solari was fumbling his way through everything did make it hard to keep a straight face.

"I can do this," Solari muttered to no one in particular. He reached down, trying to bend his legs the way Aric had, but ended up with them sprawled awkwardly in front of him. His tunic didn't help—its hem kept catching, pulling awkwardly at the fabric as he shifted again.

"I'm supposed to be a god," he muttered with frustration, glancing up at Kael as if seeking some kind of reassurance. "I'm not supposed to struggle with something as simple as sitting on the ground."

"You're not a god right now," Kael shot back without hesitation. "You're just like the rest of us."

"I *was* a god," Solari said, his voice almost bitter, though there was something soft in it—an edge that didn't belong in a god's tone. "And now, I'm just... trying to be normal."

The words hung in the air, and for a brief moment, I found myself looking at him differently. Not as the Sun God, not as the force that had devastated everything I knew, but as someone who was *trying*—and failing—to understand what it meant to be human.

I crossed my arms, torn between discomfort and curiosity. "What's *normal* to you, Solari?" I asked before I could stop myself. My voice sounded too sharp, too accusing.

Solari looked up at me, but there was no fire in his gaze, just... resignation. "I don't know. I've spent centuries *above everyone*. I don't know what it's like to be *here*." He gestured to the village, the people, the simple earth beneath us. "This is all new."

Kael's expression softened, his usual sharp edges dulling in the face of Solari's rawness. "No one's going to pity you for being *normal*," he said quietly. "But you're here now. Might as well get used to it."

Solari exhaled slowly, as though the weight of his situation had just hit him. He straightened up and attempted to re-cross his legs, trying again to find a semblance of comfort. It was awkward—his movements jerky, as if he were still trying to figure out the mechanics of being human.

I watched him for a long moment before I couldn't help myself. The sight was just too strange, too raw. "You've never had to just *sit* before, have you?"

Solari didn't look at me, but I saw the way his shoulders slumped in defeat. "No. I was never allowed to be *normal*." The words were quiet, vulnerable in a way that unsettled me.

"I was trained for... everything else. But never this. Never how to live as a person."

I took a breath, holding back a sigh. The discomfort I'd been feeling all morning suddenly shifted—just enough for me to realize that I was watching someone who had always been *more* than a person, who had never had to struggle in the same way we did. He had never known this part of the world— this humble, messy, confusing part.

It felt strange. Not pity, but... understanding? I wasn't sure. Solari had never been someone I'd thought I would *relate* to. Yet here he was, fumbling through the basics, and I couldn't deny the twisted sense of connection that had formed between us.

"Do you want some help?" I asked, and before he could respond, Kael's voice interrupted.

"We *could* just leave him to figure it out," Kael said, amusement clear in his tone.

Solari shot him a glance, his patience running thin. "If you want to *help* me, you can show me how to do this properly."

Kael didn't even try to hide his grin. "You're on your own for this one. But it is cute watching you try."

Solari let out a frustrated breath, sinking a little lower. "I can't *be* normal, can I?" His voice was soft, like he was asking himself as much as anyone else.

I stood there, still unsure of what to feel. Watching him struggle with something so simple, something I had taken for granted my whole life, left me feeling uneasy in ways I couldn't describe. He was a god, and yet he was so far removed from what I had imagined.

He was, in some ways, more like me than I ever expected.

Solari was still sitting on the ground, his legs crossed uncomfortably in front of him. He had finally gotten the position right, though it took far too long. His tunic, though simple, still looked out of place on him. He was trying—too hard, maybe—but I couldn't bring myself to pity him. Not yet.

There was something about watching him struggle that gnawed at me, but it wasn't a soft, sympathetic feeling. It felt like a sharp annoyance, the kind you get when someone refuses to acknowledge how far they've fallen. I couldn't help but feel irritated every time he fumbled with something so simple. Like it was his *choice* to be human now, and that should come with some responsibility.

I crossed my arms, trying to keep my thoughts in check. This was the god who had destroyed my family, taken everything I'd ever known, and yet here I was, standing in front of him, watching him *try* to learn the basics of being a person. He looked... *pathetic.* There was no other word for it.

Kael's voice broke through my thoughts. "You're not buying it, right?" he asked, his gaze flicking from Solari to me.

"What?" I snapped, too quickly. I was still too angry. *Too* much.

Kael raised an eyebrow, his lips curling slightly. "This whole... being mortal thing. Not buying it, are you?"

"I don't know what you mean," I muttered, my eyes narrowing at Solari, who was still fiddling with the hem of his tunic, trying to get comfortable.

"I think you know exactly what I mean." Kael's voice was steady, almost amused. "You're pissed off, aren't you? Watching him struggle like that."

I clenched my jaw. "I'm not pissed off. I'm *irritated*. There's a difference."

"Sure there is," Kael said, barely containing a grin. "You're irritated because you don't know how to deal with him trying to be *human*. And you don't want to pity him."

"No, I don't want to *feel* anything for him," I shot back. "He doesn't deserve that."

Kael gave me a pointed look. "Not *pity*," he corrected, "but maybe *empathy*."

I exhaled sharply, unwilling to meet his eyes. "Empathy for a god who watched that—that *monster* kill an entire village?" I glanced at Solari again. "Not likely."

I swear I could have seen him flinch. "I'm not saying forgive him, Elara." Kael stepped closer, his voice quieter now. "But... *seeing* him, *really* seeing him, doesn't mean you're letting him off the hook. There are some things that may be out of his control."

I didn't respond. My heart was still pounding too loudly in my chest. Seeing Solari like this was messing with my head in a way I didn't know how to handle.

Solari looked over at me, catching my gaze for the first time in a while. His face was still distant, but there was a flicker of something in his eyes. What was it? Regret? Frustration?

I quickly turned my gaze away. The last thing I wanted was to *feel* bad for him. I hated him for what he had let happen to me, to my home, to my people. But here he was, sitting in the dirt, like a child who had never been taught how to live. And that made my skin crawl. He was the one we were taught to worship, that if we worshipped him he would protect us. Yet he watched on his knees as they were all massacred.

"You're still not making it easy, are you?" I muttered to myself, though Kael heard me.

"I don't think he's trying to make it easy," Kael said, his tone slightly softer now. "But you don't get to control *how* he learns this. You just have to decide if you want to watch him learn."

I bit my lip, fighting the surge of irritation that bubbled up at the thought of him learning anything at all. I didn't want him to learn. Not from me. Not from anyone. He wasn't entitled to be human. He wasn't entitled to feel these things now.

"I don't care how he learns," I said through clenched teeth. "I care that he's *still* here. And I hate that I'm forced to even watch him *try* to be something he's not. It's irritating, Kael. It's frustrating."

I glanced back at Solari. He hadn't noticed. He was still trying to sit properly, his attention fixed on the ground in front of him. A small, strange sigh escaped him as he seemed to give up on adjusting his legs and instead just leaned back slightly, propping himself up with his hands.

I couldn't help but watch for a second longer. He seemed so... small at that moment. So human. And I hated it. I hated feeling the pull of something in me that wanted to... help him. Feel something for him. Anything but hate.

"Don't pity him," Kael said, his voice cutting through the tension. "That's the trap."

I snapped my gaze to him. "What?"

"If you pity him," Kael said, his eyes locking with mine, "you'll end up giving him something he doesn't deserve."

I looked back at Solari. He hadn't moved, and a cold knot twisted in my stomach. He wasn't looking for pity. I knew that much. But *I* wasn't looking to feel it, either.

"Are you sure about that?" I muttered, more to myself than Kael.

"I'm sure," Kael said firmly. "I know it's hard. But he has to live with what he's done. And you have to live with him trying to make it right—whether you like it or not."

I didn't answer Kael right away. I didn't even know what to say. His words had cut deeper than I was willing to admit. *Seeing* him wasn't the problem. It was feeling anything for him that was the issue. I hated him. He didn't deserve my sympathy, and yet, there I was, watching him try to fit into a world he had destroyed. And it felt... wrong.

I didn't want to pity him. But that didn't mean it wasn't *there*, lurking beneath the surface, like a quiet storm just waiting to break.

I turned my back to Kael, walking a few steps away, needing space from everything—Solari's awkwardness, the kids' teasing, the pull I felt to feel something I shouldn't.

That's when the laughter started again.

The children had completely surrounded Solari. What started as curious glances and quiet giggles quickly grew bolder. They weren't content just to watch anymore—they wanted to test him, to see how far they could push before he snapped. And for some reason, I couldn't stop watching.

Aric was the first to make a real challenge. He stood directly in front of Solari, an amused grin spreading across his face. "Hey, you," he said, tapping Solari's shoulder. "Can you do this?"

Before Solari could respond, Aric dropped down into a squat, his small legs bending easily beneath him as he balanced himself effortlessly. "Come on, do a squat like this. You're strong, right?"

Solari hesitated. He didn't know what Aric meant, and I could see the discomfort flicker across his face. He tried to mimic the movement, bending his legs, but he wasn't used to this kind of flexibility. His body didn't work the way Aric's did—too stiff, too rigid. He made it halfway down before his knees buckled, and he stopped, grunting in frustration.

"I—" Solari started, his voice faltering. "I do not squat. Gods do not squat"

The children burst into laughter. Some of them were genuinely amused, but I could tell it was beginning to feel a bit too much. Too easy. They weren't being cruel—at least not at first—but they were pushing him, seeing how much they could get away with. Testing his limits.

"Can't squat?" Aric repeated, his voice rising in mock disbelief. "Seriously? What kind of god can't squat?"

I felt a jolt of irritation twist in my chest. I didn't know who I was angrier at—Solari, for being so helpless, or the kids, for treating him like a joke. The more I watched, the more my frustration grew. This wasn't just curiosity anymore. This was *mocking*.

"Gods do not squat," Solari muttered, his tone defensive but weak. "I wasn't trained for this."

The kids snickered louder, clearly enjoying the show. They didn't understand what it meant for him to struggle like this. They didn't care. And the more they pushed, the more I felt my own resentment rising, like a bubble threatening to burst.

I turned away, needing space, but Kael's voice cut through the tension, sharp and dry.

"Maybe you should let him struggle on his own," Kael muttered, his eyes flicking from Solari to me. "It's not like we *need* him here, anyway."

My heart skipped a beat. I shot him a sharp look. "What's that supposed to mean?"

Kael didn't look at me, but his words were laced with something I couldn't ignore. "I mean, we were fine without him," he said, the bitterness in his voice unmistakable. "We survived without the Sun God gracing us with his presence. What's he really doing here, anyway?"

I stood there, taken aback. Kael wasn't hiding his resentment anymore—not even a little. I could feel it in his words, in the way he looked at Solari. It wasn't just irritation. It was deeper. It was personal. And something in me couldn't help but wonder if it was about more than just Solari's awkwardness. Maybe it had something to do with the history between Solari and the moon elves. With Kael's own people.

I tried to push the thought away, but it lingered. Kael's unease had been obvious from the start, but now it felt like it was more than just discomfort with Solari being here. It felt like *resentment*.

"Is that why you're upset?" I asked, my voice colder than I intended. "Because he's a god?"

Kael glanced at me, his gaze hard and unreadable. "It's not about that," he said quickly, almost too quickly. "It's about him barging in here and making everything worse. We were fine without him, Elara. We didn't need him to come in and remind us of all the things we couldn't change."

I didn't know how to respond. He was right about one thing—we had survived without Solari. But now that he was here, now that he was trying to be *human*, I wasn't sure if I should feel pity for him—or frustration. My thoughts were tangled, and Kael's words weren't helping. They were only making me feel more conflicted, more *irritated* with Solari.

I glanced back at him. He was still sitting there, trying to bend his legs into a comfortable position, his posture still too stiff. The children had scattered, leaving him alone again. He looked... defeated.

He wasn't the god who had destroyed everything. He wasn't even a god anymore, not in this world. He was just a man—someone who didn't know how to belong.

And I couldn't decide if I hated him more for it, or if I felt… sorry for him.

"Maybe you should cut him some slack," I muttered, more to myself than to Kael, echoing his advice from earlier.

Kael didn't meet my eyes. He was watching Solari, his voice sharp but quieter now. "Cut him slack? Why? He doesn't need it. He wants to be here, let him figure it out. It's not like he's offering any help other than entertainment for the children."

I clenched my jaw, frustration rising in my chest. "Maybe he's trying. Isn't that what you told me, not even 5 minutes ago? To try and see him?"

Kael shrugged, a faint smirk curling at the corners of his lips. "Trying? Sun Gods can't try anything, they take and destroy." The words hit me like a slap, but I didn't let it show. I turned my back to him, walking away before the anger could slip out in words I might regret. Solari was still sitting there, looking small and *human*, and it made something twist uncomfortably in my gut. Kael was right about one thing—we had been fine without him. But now he was here, trying to be part of something, and I couldn't decide if that made him weaker… or just more *real*.

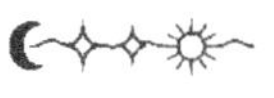

The sun had dipped below the hills, and the village square had grown quiet. Most of the children were asleep now, wrapped in blankets around the fire, the warmth from the embers flickering against the darkening sky. But not Aric.

I had been standing on the outskirts of the village, staring into the fire, my thoughts still heavy with the weight of the day and the growing unease in my chest. Kura's absence weighed on me, but it wasn't something I could afford to dwell on here. Not yet. The village, these children, were the only things I could focus on—at least for now.

I glanced around and noticed Aric, still awake, crouched by the embers of the fire with a spear in his hands. His movements were jerky, awkward, as he swung it through the air, mimicking what I could only assume was Kael's fighting style. The way the spear cut through the air looked too familiar, too practiced for a child like Aric. He had clearly seen *someone*—Kael, no doubt—move like this, and now he was attempting to replicate it.

I watched quietly for a moment. His form was clumsy, the movements too sharp, but there was a determination in his eyes. Aric was trying to do something that he didn't fully understand yet, something that came from a place he couldn't quite grasp.

Finally, I stepped forward, my boots barely making a sound on the ground. The sharp scent of the smoke from the fire filled the air as I approached him.

"Aric," I said, my voice carrying through the quiet night.

He stopped, frozen with the spear raised in mid-air, and glanced over at me. His eyes were wide, his expression a mix of surprise and uncertainty. "I... I was just practicing," he muttered, lowering the spear to the ground.

I nodded, observing his stance, the way he held the spear too tightly in his small hands. "I see that. But you're trying to do more than just practice," I said softly, stepping closer. "You're trying to be someone else."

Aric looked at the ground, clearly embarrassed. "I just... I saw Kael do it. I thought if I could do what he does, I could... be strong like him." I studied Aric for a moment, seeing the rawness in his eyes—the same desire to prove something that I'd seen in many before him. But what Aric didn't understand was that strength wasn't about copying another person's movements. It was about understanding what made you strong, what you could bring to the fight. I knelt beside him, my movements slow and deliberate. I couldn't help but notice how small he looked, how young he was, trying so hard to be something more than what he was. The spear was too big for him, just as his desire to emulate someone he admired was too big for his current understanding.

"Let me show you," I said, my voice steady, yet softer than before. "The spear is not just an extension of your arm, Aric. It is an extension of your mind. You cannot simply mimic Kael's movements. You must learn the purpose behind each one."

Aric stared at me, his confusion clear. "The purpose?"

I nodded, holding my hand out for the spear. He hesitated before placing it in my hand, but when he did, I gripped it carefully, feeling its weight. The sensation was familiar—muscle memory from centuries past, though now strange in a world that wasn't mine to command. The spear felt both alien and intimate in my grasp, like something I should have let go of long ago. "Watch closely," I said, lifting the spear. "It's not about strength. It's about balance. The spear is an extension of your body. Each movement you make, each breath you take, should be in tune with the weapon. It should be fluid—not forced, like the flow of the river, washing away any imperfections and impurities. Balance."

I swung the spear through the air slowly, deliberately, allowing the weight to guide my movements. The fluidity of it was instinctual, but I didn't rush. I didn't *show* Aric the speed. I showed him grace and control. Each swing, each shift of weight, was done with purpose—not power.

I lowered the spear, holding it gently in my hands. Aric had been watching intently, his eyes focused and wide. He hadn't said anything, but I could see the gears turning in his mind. The spark of understanding was there—just barely, but it was there.

"Now you try," I said, passing the spear back to him, careful to let him hold it the way he felt comfortable. "But don't rush it. Don't focus on *how fast* you can do it. Focus on how it feels."

Aric took the spear, gripping it more loosely than before. His movements were still a bit stiff, still unsure, but I could see him trying to let go of the rigidity in his body, the need to force the motion. He took a slow swing, trying to replicate what he had seen me do. It wasn't perfect—far from it—but there was something in the way he held the spear, something that felt more confident.

"Better," I said, nodding slightly. "But remember, Aric: strength without control is nothing. You must master *yourself* before you can master anything else."

Aric nodded, his face serious. I saw the small flicker of understanding in his eyes. He wasn't there yet, but he was on the path. And that was more than I could have hoped for.

He set the spear down beside him, looking up at me with a quiet expression. "Thank you," he said, his voice small but earnest.

I stood up, offering him a nod. "You're welcome. Rest now. Tomorrow, we will try again."

As I turned away, I felt a strange sense of... pride? It wasn't that Aric had learned everything in that moment. But I had taught him something, something more than just the motion of the spear. I had taught him *control*.

The fire crackled softly in the background as I stood alone, watching the embers flicker beneath the darkening sky. The village was quiet now—most of the children had settled into sleep, the day's activities slowly fading into a heavy silence. But I couldn't shake the feeling that something was still unresolved. Something I couldn't quite touch.

Aric had gone to bed after our brief lesson, his small form curled up beside the others, still gripping the spear as if it had become a part of him. I had watched him for a moment before he fell asleep—his brow furrowed in thought as if he were still processing what I had taught him. That was a good sign, I thought. I had done what I had set out to do.

Or so I told myself.

But as the night grew darker, I felt the weight of the day press down on me in a way I hadn't expected. I wasn't used to this—the stillness of it all. The absence of divine energy, the absence of certainty. My thoughts drifted back to the celestial realm, to the lingering unease surrounding Kura, and the sense of unfinished business I had left behind. The feeling gnawed at me, but I couldn't act on it. Not yet.

I leaned against a tree, letting the cool evening breeze brush through my hair, and closed my eyes for a brief moment. I had hoped for clarity, but all I had found here was *more* questions.

"Solari," came a voice, cutting through the quiet night.

I opened my eyes to see Elara standing a few paces away, her arms crossed over her chest, her expression unreadable. She had been watching me for a while, I realized—quietly observing, as she always did. It seemed she never left me alone for long.

I pushed off the tree, straightening my posture, suddenly aware of how tired I felt. "Elara," I said, my voice steady. "You're awake later than usual."

She didn't smile. She rarely did. But her gaze softened just enough for me to notice. "I was... watching," she said, her eyes flicking briefly to where Aric slept. "With the spear."

I nodded, feeling the weight of her gaze as it lingered on me. "He was trying. I showed him what I could. The discipline he needs."

Elara said nothing for a moment, her gaze steady. Her lips pressed into a thin line, like she was trying to sort through something. "You really believe in this, don't you?" she asked, her voice a little softer now, though still tinged with the edge of frustration. "All of it. The balance. The control."

"I believe it because it is true," I replied. The words came easily, as they always did, but there was an unease beneath my conviction. I wasn't just teaching Aric. I was trying to teach myself something, too. But that was a truth I didn't want to confront.

"I think it's easy for you to believe," she said, her tone growing sharper again. "You've been a god for so long, Solari. Everything comes *easy* for you, doesn't it? Control. Power. Strength. You've never had to struggle for any of it."

I clenched my jaw, the sting of her words cutting through the air between us. "You don't know what it's like to be in my place, Elara. To carry the weight of an entire realm. Of an entire *people*."

Her eyes flashed. "You don't know what it's like to lose everything. To see your home burn. To watch the people you love—*gone* in an instant."

My chest tightened at the rawness in her voice. The weight of her words pressed against me, though I didn't allow myself to show it. "You think I don't understand loss?" I asked quietly, my voice steady, but the edges of it betraying me. "You think I haven't *lost* everything? My home... my family..."

I stopped myself, realizing I had said more than I had intended. The words felt too heavy on my tongue, too close to something I wasn't ready to share. But Elara didn't flinch. She didn't take pity on me. She just stood there, waiting for me to continue.

I exhaled sharply, stepping back from the weight of the silence. "I didn't come here for pity, Elara. I came because I *have to* be here. To understand. To find out... what Kura is doing."

The mention of Kura caught her off guard. Her brows furrowed, and I saw the flicker of confusion in her eyes. She took a step forward, the distance between us narrowing.

"*Kura?*" she asked, the word falling from her lips with uncertainty. "What does Kura have to do with any of this? With you teaching the children?"

I hesitated, unsure of how to explain what I could not yet understand myself. Kura's absence, his growing influence, it all felt like a storm on the horizon—a storm I could sense, but couldn't yet see clearly. But I couldn't tell her that. Not yet.

I met her gaze, my voice quiet but firm. "Kura's actions have disrupted everything. I don't know what he's planning, but I must be here, to find out. To stop him if necessary."

Elara stepped closer, her eyes narrowing as she studied me. "And that's why you're trying to fit in? You think playing teacher to these kids will help you *understand* what's happening?"

I didn't answer immediately. Her skepticism was clear, but there was no denying that part of me had hoped teaching them, connecting with them, might bring me some clarity. But I couldn't admit that to her. Not yet.

"I'm doing what I can," I said, my voice low. "I'm trying to be more than just a god. To understand... what it means to be something else."

She tilted her head, her eyes softening just slightly, though the wariness never left her expression. "And what exactly do you think that will get you, Solari? What will being 'something else' do for you?"

I met her gaze, my heart heavier than I'd expected it to be. I didn't have an answer. Not one I could give her, not without revealing things I wasn't ready to admit.

"Maybe it's the only way to *learn* something," I said quietly. "Maybe it's the only way to stop Kura."

Elara didn't respond right away. Instead, she just stood there, watching me, her arms still crossed, a frown playing at the edge of her lips. She wasn't ready to forgive me. Not yet. But there was something in the way she looked at me now—something that felt... different.

For a moment, I felt a flicker of understanding. Maybe she didn't pity me. Maybe she didn't need to. But I wasn't ready to leave, either.

I turned away, letting the weight of the evening settle over us both. "Rest, Elara. Tomorrow will come, and we'll see where this goes."

She didn't say anything more, but I knew she wasn't finished with me. Neither was I with her.

Chapter Twelve

The morning broke colder than it should be, the kind that sank straight through wool and skin to settle in the bones. I woke to the faint snap of wood in the hearth, the smell of smoke lingering like a warning, and the faint rustle of blankets as the children shifted in their sleep.

Most were still curled together on the far side of the common hall, faces half-buried in makeshift pillows, but Aric lay apart from them. The spear he'd been gripping last night was gone—tucked back near the door where we kept the tools—but he still had that pinched look in his brow. Even in sleep, he was holding on to something too heavy for his small shoulders.

I tried not to think about Solari. About the way he'd moved last night, fluid and precise, like the spear was more a memory than a weapon. I'd told myself I didn't care how easily the god could slip into our lives, into the children's trust. But the truth was, there had been something in Aric's expression when he'd been watching that lesson... something I hadn't seen since before the raids.

The wind slipped through a crack in the wall and found my neck, dragging me back to the present. There was work to do—breakfast to scrape together, the little ones to herd outside to wash. I moved quietly, not wanting to wake them yet, and reached for the basket by the door when a shadow crossed the threshold.

"Up early." His voice was low, smooth, and I didn't need to look to know it was him. Kael leaned against the doorframe, the early light catching in his eyes in a way that made them look like a storm waiting for somewhere to break.

"I could say the same," I said, straightening and brushing the dust from my hands. "Or do you just lurk in doorways for sport?"

His mouth curved, not quite a smile. "Only when I have something worth sharing." He stepped inside without waiting for an invitation, bringing the cold with him. "I found something. Out past the riverbank."

I narrowed my eyes. "Something... or someone?"

"Not someone," he said, his gaze holding mine a beat too long. "But close enough."

From the inner pocket of his coat, he pulled a scrap of worn cloth—mud-caked and frayed at the edges. I knew that shade of green, the uneven stitch along one corner. My stomach turned.

"That's Daren's," I said quietly.

Kael nodded once. "The trail is faint, but still there. Whoever took them... they're not far. I thought you'd want to see for yourself."

There was no reason to hesitate, but I did. He noticed—of course he noticed—and his expression shifted, almost imperceptibly, from the cool mask he wore to something sharper.

"I can go alone," he said softly. "But I doubt you'd like what I'd do if I caught up to them first."

The words hung between us like bait and a threat all at once. I pulled my cloak tighter around my shoulders. "Fine. Show me."

He didn't smile, but the corner of his mouth twitched, like he'd just won a small game I hadn't realized we were playing.

The air outside hit harder than I expected—sharp, wet, the kind of cold that made the inside of your nose ache. Kael didn't seem to notice. His stride was long, unhurried, as if he'd been waiting all morning for me to catch up.

We cut past the frost-stiff grass and out toward the narrow deer trail that led to the river. The forest swallowed us quickly, the village sounds fading into the slow drip of melting frost and the muted crunch of our boots.

Kael didn't speak for the first stretch, which should have been a relief, but the silence between us felt taut. When he finally glanced over his shoulder, it wasn't to check if I was keeping pace—it was to watch me, like he was measuring how much I really wanted to be here.

"You're quiet," he said at last.

"I'm thinking," I replied, stepping over a fallen branch.

"About?"

"About what kind of trail we're following," I said. "And how much of it you're not telling me."

That earned the faintest smirk. "You think I'm lying to you?"

"I think you tell the truth the same way you breathe—when it suits you."

He didn't deny it. Just kept walking until we reached the riverbank, the water running slow and black under the thin veil of mist. He crouched low near a patch of mud, brushing his gloved fingers along a shallow indentation.

"Boot print," he said. "Small. Matches the boy's size."

I stepped closer, squinting at it. The edges had already begun to soften with moisture, but the shape was still there.

"More than one?" I asked.

"Two," Kael said. "But the second is heavier. Adult. Likely the one leading him."

A muscle in my jaw tightened. "Leading," I repeated. "Not dragging?"

He glanced up at me, and for the briefest heartbeat, something dangerous flickered in his eyes—like he'd thought of exactly what he'd do to whoever left that print. "No. Leading," he said finally. "Which means the boy's still alive."

I let out a slow breath I hadn't realized I was holding.

Kael rose, brushing the mud from his hand, then gestured for me to follow. We trailed along the bank until the path veered into the trees, narrowing into something only a child—or someone tracking one—would bother to take.

The forest felt closer here, the air thicker. I caught a faint sound ahead—branches shifting, maybe, or water dripping through the leaves—but Kael lifted a hand without looking back, signaling me to stop.

He tilted his head, listening. Then, in a voice barely above a whisper, he said, "We're not alone."

The words hadn't fully settled before two figures slipped from the shadows between the pines—tall, lean, their pale hair braided tight against their skulls. The curved blades at their sides caught the light like water over ice, and the way they moved... it was too fluid, too silent. Moon-elves.

My pulse kicked hard. I'd seen raiders before—Solavend had bled for it—but there was something more deliberate in these two. No blood-mad chaos, no ragged scavenger's look. They stood like soldiers on assignment.

One of them smiled, a slow curl of the mouth that didn't reach his eyes. "We didn't expect competition." His voice was lilting, cold, as though the words were meant for Kael alone.

Kael's posture didn't shift, but the surrounding air seemed to tighten. "You're far from home."

The elf shrugged, the motion lazy, but his gaze flicked to the cloth in my hand. "We follow where the trail leads. Orders are orders."

Something in Kael's jaw flexed—barely there, but sharp enough that I caught it. "Whose orders?"

That earned a thin, knowing smile. "The kind you don't refuse."

The exchange lasted only seconds, but the tension in it wrapped around my ribs. They were talking in a language I couldn't quite hear, each word weighted with something unsaid. And for the first time, Kael didn't look like the predator in the clearing. He looked like someone facing a shadow he'd thought he'd left behind.

The silence stretched until it felt brittle, like the wrong word might shatter it. I shifted my grip on the cloth, the frayed edges biting against my palm.

"You have something that belongs to us," the second elf said, his tone almost conversational, but his eyes... his eyes were cataloguing everything. My stance. Kael's position in front of me. The way his hand hovered near his coat, where I knew a blade sat hidden.

"They're not yours," I said before Kael could speak. My voice was steadier than I expected.

The first elf's attention slid to me, and it was like being pinned under frost. "Everything taken becomes ours, sun-girl. Even the children."

The word *sun-girl* landed like a sneer. Kael stepped half a pace forward, his shadow folding over mine. "Careful," he said softly, and it wasn't a warning—it was a promise.

The elf tilted his head, studying him. "Still playing guardian? That's almost funny."

Kael's jaw tightened, but his voice stayed even. "Let them go."

"Not possible," the elf replied. "We were sent for them."

There it was again—*sent*. Not wandering raiders, not scavengers. Someone had pointed them here.

Kael's expression didn't change, but I caught the faintest breath of something sharp in the air between us—like the way the air shifts before lightning strikes.

"Who?" I asked, because Kael clearly wasn't going to.

The elf's mouth curved, not quite a smile, but something sharper. "The kind of name you don't speak in the daylight."

That got Kael's full attention. His gaze locked on the elf, and for a heartbeat, the stillness in him was almost worse than any movement. Whatever name had gone unsaid, I could feel the weight of it pressing against him.

"You shouldn't be here," Kael said finally, his voice low enough that I almost didn't catch it.

"And yet we are," the elf answered, tone light, as though this meeting were nothing more than a passing amusement. "So, will you move aside, or will we make you?"

Kael's hand slid from his coat, fingers curling with deliberate slowness. I felt the pull of the moment, the inevitability of it. Kael didn't look at me, but the weight of his presence pressed me backward all the same. His voice was almost calm when he spoke, which made it worse.

"Go back to the village, Elara."

I narrowed my eyes. "Not a chance."

"Not asking," he said, and there was a glint in his eyes—cold, calculated—that made the air between us feel suddenly thinner.

The first elf chuckled under his breath. "Touching. She follows you like a tethered hound."

Kael's jaw flexed. "Say that again."

I put a hand to his arm, but he stepped forward, drawing the elf's attention entirely to himself. It was so deliberate I almost didn't catch it—he was baiting them, shifting their focus until they seemed to forget I was even there.

"You want the children?" Kael said, his tone light in a way that didn't match the sharp stillness in his body. "You'll have to take them from me."

The first elf came at Kael in a blur of steel and leather, but he didn't so much dodge as *flow*. A shift of weight, a twist of his wrist, and the raider's blade glanced harmlessly off the curve of his coat. He stepped into the elf's space, catching the man's arm and wrenching it until the joint popped with a sickening sound. The sword clattered to the dirt.

Before the first could recover, the second was already moving—faster, lower, trying to sweep Kael's legs. Kael spun, catching the kick with his shin and driving an elbow hard into the elf's temple. The man went sprawling, groaning into the mud.

I should have stepped back. I should have listened when Kael told me to stay behind him. But I was too focused on the flash of movement in the corner of my vision—another figure breaking from the shadows.

The third elf wasn't aiming for Kael. He was aiming for me.

My body locked, too slow to react. The blade caught the moonlight as it swung for my side—deadly, certain.

Shadows lashed out before I could scream. They wrapped around my waist, dragging me off balance and straight into Kael's chest. His arm caged me against him for the briefest heartbeat before he shoved me aside, snarling—

"Damn it, Elara, I can't fight with you here!"

I stumbled back, breath knocked from my lungs. And in that split second of distraction, Kael turned too late. The raider's sword cut deep, slipping past his guard and biting into his ribs. His hiss of pain tore through the clearing, sharper than the steel itself.

Blood spread across the black fabric of his coat, dark and merciless. I froze, a raw panic clawing up my throat. The raider lifted his blade again, this time angling past Kael's staggering form—straight for his unprotected back.

Heat ripped through my veins, white-hot, searing. My vision tunneled, the edges sparking like fire. I didn't move—I didn't have to. Light flared from my skin, a sudden, violent pulse that exploded against the raider. His scream cut the night as flames licked up his arm, racing across leather and flesh alike.

I gasped, the air burning in my lungs, hints of blue and red tinted my vision. The smell of smoke and charred cloth curled around me, and when the light faded, the raider was writhing on the ground, his weapon forgotten.

Kael turned his head, blood dripping from his lips, eyes wide—not at his wound, but at me.

The world narrowed to that sight—the bright smear of red, the way his jaw clenched as he ripped the blade from the elf's grip and drove the man back with a brutal kick. The raider slammed into a tree so hard the bark splintered.

The second elf lunged for Kael's wounded side. He pivoted, shadows snapping around his arms as he twisted the attacker's wrist and wrenched the blade free. "If you've still got that fire in you, Sunling," he bit out between blows, "now would be the time to use it."

Heat rushed to my face. I threw up a hand, willing the spark that had erupted before—but nothing came. Only the air itself seemed to shift, drying and tightening in my lungs as though the night were holding its breath.

Kael slammed the heel of his palm into the raider's skull, dropping him like a sack of grain. The last one hesitated just long enough for Kael to seize him by the front of his armor and hurl him toward the treeline.

"Run," Kael growled, low and lethal. "And tell him he's out of chances."

The elf fled into the dark without looking back.

Something in the way Kael said *him* made the hairs on my arms rise, but the elf didn't need telling twice. He vanished into the dark, dragging his unconscious comrade by the collar.

The moment they were gone, I moved toward Kael, reaching for the wound at his side. He caught my wrist—not gently.

"I'm fine," he bit out, though his breath was rougher now, each inhale pulling at the cut.

"You're bleeding," I said, pulling free from his grip. My fingers came away slick, warm. "Fine isn't bleeding through your shirt."

His gaze held mine, hard and unyielding. "If you'd listened to me, I wouldn't be. Now—keep up, or go back. But don't get in my way again."

The words should have sent me stalking back to the village. Instead, I pulled my cloak tighter and stepped in behind him. He didn't turn, didn't slow, but I didn't miss the faint hitch in his stride as we moved into the trees.

We followed the trail into the trees, the air colder here, the canopy trapping the night like it didn't want to let morning in. The ground was uneven, damp from the river's edge, and every so often I caught the faint scuff of a boot print, the drag of something heavy being pulled along.

Kael moved ahead, silent as a shadow, but I noticed it—the way his pace had shifted. He was still quick, still precise in where he stepped, but the rhythm was off. His left side lagged just slightly.

He was hurt worse than he wanted to admit.

"Kael," I said, low enough not to echo. He didn't slow.

"You're losing blood," I tried again.

"I'm fine."

It was the same clipped answer as before, but his shoulders were tighter now, like even speaking cost him. I lengthened my stride until I was beside him. "You're not fine. You're slowing down."

His jaw worked, but he kept his eyes on the path. "We don't have time to stop."

"We do if you collapse before we get there," I shot back. "You can't help them if you're bleeding out in the dirt."

That made him pause—not long, just a hitch in his step before he muttered, "You think I can't handle a scratch?"

I stepped in front of him, blocking the trail. "I think you're bleeding through your shirt, and if you keep pretending you're invincible, we're going to lose both the boys *and* you."

His gaze lifted to mine, cold at first... but under it, I caught something else. Tired. Worn thin.

The silence stretched until I thought he'd push past me, anyway. But finally, he exhaled, a sharp, begrudging sound.

"Two minutes," he said. "No more."

I led him to a fallen log off the path. He sat stiffly, like even the act of resting was an admission of defeat. When I reached for the edge of his coat, his hand shot out, catching mine.

"Don't," he said. The word was low, almost rough.

"I'm not asking," I replied, my voice softer but firm. "Let me see."

Something flickered in his eyes—resistance, pride, maybe even a little warning—but after a long beat, he let his hand fall away.

The fabric at his side was slick and dark, the wound beneath it deep enough that I hissed through my teeth. "This isn't a scratch, Kael."

He didn't flinch. "It's enough to keep me from stopping."

I tore a strip from the inside hem of my cloak and pressed it to the wound, feeling the heat of his skin under my fingers. His breath caught—quiet, but enough that I knew the pressure hurt.

"Hold still," I murmured.

His gaze stayed on me, unblinking, until I finally looked up and met it. There was something unreadable there, sharp and heavy all at once, like he was weighing whether to say what was in his head.

Finally, he said it. "I didn't know you had elf magic."

The words lodged in my throat. For a heartbeat, I didn't even breathe.

"Neither did I," I admitted, softer than I meant to. My hands stilled, the cloth darkening beneath them. "It just... happened."

Kael's gaze lingered, unreadable in the low light. Then he leaned back against the tree, shadows curling faintly at his fingertips. "Then you'd better hope you learn to control it. Surprises like that will get you killed."

When I tied the makeshift bandage in place, I straightened and stepped back. "Better?" Completely ignoring the training statement. No need to train something that won't stick around.

He rose without answering, only giving me a look that was half warning, half something else I couldn't name. Then he turned back toward the trail.

"Two minutes are up," he said.

The trail grew sharper the farther we went, as if whoever we were chasing had stopped caring about being followed. Broken branches leaned across the path like warning signs, and the air carried the faint, metallic tang of a camp not far ahead—cooked meat, oiled leather, steel.

Kael slowed at the edge of a ridge, his gaze cutting down through the pines below. From where I stood, I could just make out movement—dark shapes between the trees, glints of silver catching the weak daylight. Moon-elf raiders.

The sight of them sent a cold knot twisting in my gut. I'd seen raiders before—chaotic, disorganized scavengers picking over whatever scraps they could find. But these weren't that. They moved with precision, their formation tight, their armor carrying the same crescent-marked etching on the pauldrons.

That was no accident.

Kael's voice was low, barely stirring the air. "They're not here for coin."

I glanced at him. "Then what?"

His jaw shifted, but he didn't look at me. "Orders."

Something about the way he said it made my skin prickle. "From who?"

He didn't answer—not exactly. "You've seen that mark before, haven't you?"

I had, though not up close. I'd heard stories from the traders who came through Solavend—stories of moon-elf captains who took orders from a voice no one saw. Whispers of raids carried out not for gold, but for leverage.

Kael started forward again, crouching low as we descended the ridge. "Stay close. If they see you before I'm ready, they'll scatter... or worse."

I kept my eyes on the group below as we moved, trying to track their numbers. Four at the outer edge. Two near the fire. One—taller than the rest, silver-braided hair catching the light—was giving orders in a language I didn't know. The sound of it felt deliberate, each word edged like a blade.

When we were close enough to hear the scrape of their boots over dirt, Kael stopped and glanced at me. "I'll draw them out. You wait for my signal."

"And if you get yourself killed?"

One corner of his mouth twitched, humorless. "Then you'll have to do better than that spear-boy imitation you've been watching."

Before I could answer, he stepped into the open, his presence cutting through the camp like a shadow swallowing the light.

The raiders stilled, hands going to their weapons. One of them spoke sharply, the words quick, clipped—and the tall one with the silver braid turned to face him fully.

There was recognition there. Not surprise—recognition.

"You shouldn't be here," the silver-braid said in accented Common.

Kael's expression didn't change. "And yet."

The other elf's gaze flicked toward the woods—toward me. I knew they couldn't see me from here, but the way Kael's posture shifted told me they suspected more than they should.

"What do you want?" the tall one asked.

Kael's voice was calm, but under it I could hear the pull of something tighter. "You've taken children. You'll give them back."

A slow, deliberate shake of the head. "Not mine to return." The tall moon-elf didn't move, but the others tightened their formation, blades sliding free in soft, deliberate whispers of steel. Kael stayed loose, balanced, one hand resting at his side like he had all the time in the world.

"You have something that doesn't belong to you," he said again, tone almost conversational. "Return them, and I'll let you walk away."

The silver-braid gave a humorless laugh. "Walk away? You speak as if this forest belongs to you." His eyes flickered—again—toward the tree line where I crouched. "Or perhaps to her."

I felt the weight of Kael's gaze flicker toward me for the briefest moment before he turned back, voice edged now. "Careful where you point your curiosity."

The tall moon-elf's smirk lingered just a moment too long. "You've gone soft, Kael. Fighting for sun-elf scraps now?"

Kael's expression didn't shift, but the surrounding air seemed to change—cooling, pressing inward, as if the shadows themselves were paying attention.

"They're mine," he said evenly. "Give me my boys, and you get to keep breathing."

The silver-braid laughed low in his throat. "Listen to yourself. The Kael I heard of wouldn't have wasted his breath on beggar children."

Kael stepped forward, and for a moment his silhouette seemed to stretch—shadows peeling away from the tree trunks to curl faintly at his heels. "Then you've been hearing old stories," he murmured.

The silver-braid's amusement faltered just enough for me to notice.

He barked an order in their tongue, and two of his raiders surged forward, blades high. Kael moved to meet them, his hand lifting—not toward his sword, but palm open.

The shadows behind the raiders shivered, then lashed forward like living things, catching one by the ankle and yanking him off his feet. The other hesitated, and that was all Kael needed—he slid in close, blade flashing, the edge stopping just shy of the elf's throat before driving the hilt into his jaw with a crack.

Another raider came from his blind side, but Kael's hand swept through the air, and the shadow of a branch above seemed to twist unnaturally, whipping down and tangling the attacker's arm long enough for Kael's blade to finish the movement.

It was the first time I'd seen him truly fight without restraint. There was a rhythm to it—predatory, precise—but the magic moved with the same intent as his blade, neither one secondary to the other.

And yet, through it all, his eyes never left the silver-braid.

The tall elf tilted his head, mocking. "Look at you. Pretending you're something more than a knife in the dark. Pretending you care."

Kael's voice was low, but it carried, dangerous in the way winter rivers are dangerous—still on the surface, deadly underneath. "I don't pretend."

A sharp whistle from the silver-braid, and two more raiders broke formation—one slipping behind Kael, the other moving toward the trees. Toward me.

I'd barely drawn my knife before Kael was there, intercepting the blow meant for me. Steel met steel with a jolt that rang in my teeth. The raider's blade slid past Kael's parry just enough to bite into his ribs.

The sound he made was not a groan, not a cry—more like the snarl of a cornered animal. He shoved the attacker back hard enough to send him stumbling, then rounded on me, eyes sharp with pain.

"I told you to go back," he snapped, each word tight.

"I'm not—"

"Go!" The bark of it startled even the raiders.

The silver-braid called something sharp in their tongue, and just like that, the tension broke. The raiders withdrew, slipping back into the trees with the swiftness of predators who'd already fed.

Kael stood there a moment, breathing hard, his free hand pressed to his side. When he lowered it, blood gleamed dark across his fingers. "They'll be back," he said finally, voice low. "And next time, they won't leave anyone breathing."

The trek home was taking longer than planned.

At first, I thought it was just the terrain—thick undergrowth, tangled roots, the kind of uneven forest floor that slowed even the sure-footed. But as the sun dipped lower, I noticed the real reason.

Kael was slowing.

Not enough to make it obvious to anyone else—if anyone else had been with us—but I'd spent enough hours watching the way he moved to see the difference. The easy prowl in his stride had dulled, his left shoulder dropped slightly, and every so often, his hand ghosted toward his ribs like he thought I wouldn't notice.

He was still bleeding.

"You're not going to make it back to the village like this," I said finally, breaking the silence that had stretched between us since the fight.

"I've had worse," he muttered, not looking at me.

"Congratulations. You'll have had worse again if you keep walking until you fall over."

His jaw tightened, but he didn't answer.

I stepped ahead of him, planting myself in his path. "We make camp here. Solari's with the children—they'll be fine for one night."

Kael's gaze flicked past me, scanning the treeline as if he could find a path that didn't involve stopping. "We're close enough to—"

"Camp. Here." I didn't raise my voice, but I didn't move either.

The muscle in his cheek twitched. "You're infuriating."

"You're bleeding."

That earned me a look—one of those dangerous, half-lidded stares that could have been meant to intimidate if it wasn't for the fact that he swayed just slightly before catching himself.

I set my jaw. "Sit down before you fall down."

For a moment, I thought he'd refuse just to spite me. Then he sank onto a moss-covered log with a quiet exhale, his hand pressing harder against his ribs.

I knelt in front of him, pulling my cloak tighter to block the wind. "Let me see."

"Elara—"

"Don't make me argue with you. It won't end in your favor."

His mouth curved faintly at that, but he didn't stop me when I reached for the hem of his shirt. The fabric was stiff with blood, sticking to the wound. When I peeled it back, he drew in a sharp breath through his teeth.

The cut wasn't deep enough to kill him, but it was long and ugly, the kind that would keep tearing if he moved wrong.

"You're lucky," I murmured, brushing the edges clean. "An inch higher and you'd be—"

"Dead?" He smirked faintly, though it didn't reach his eyes. "You underestimate me."

I didn't answer, already shifting my focus to the familiar hum in my palms. Sunlight wasn't easy to call in the fading dark, but I closed my eyes, searching for the warmth still stored deep in my magic. It rose slowly, burning through me as I pressed my hands over the wound.

The light pooled between my fingers, soft and gold, sinking into torn flesh. I felt it pull at me, the effort heavier than I wanted to admit, my heartbeat quickening with the strain.

Kael watched me silently, his gaze steady on my face. When the glow faded, I pulled back, my hands trembling slightly from the exertion.

His wound was closed—not perfect, but enough.

"You didn't have to," he said quietly.

"Yes, I did."

Something passed between us in that moment—wordless, taut, as if the shadows had drawn in closer just to listen.

I shifted back, but the cold had already started creeping in. The fire I managed to coax from the damp wood was small, barely enough for warmth, so when Kael stretched out beside it, I found myself settling down next to him without thinking.

"Don't read into this," I muttered, tugging my cloak tighter than our shoulders brushed.

"Too late," he said, the faintest thread of amusement in his voice.

It was quiet after that, just the crackle of the fire and the slow, even rhythm of his breathing. I told myself I wasn't paying attention to the way the heat from his body bled into mine. I told myself it didn't matter that, for the first time since this started, I didn't feel cold.

The fire burned low, its light a wavering gold that seemed to breathe with the wind. I stayed on my side, facing the embers, telling myself I'd fall asleep soon. I didn't.

Kael had gone quiet not long after lying down, his breathing slow and steady in that way people only manage when they're pretending to rest at first, then giving in. I should have taken the peace while it lasted, but my mind refused to still, he slept like someone bracing for a blow. His jaw was tight, his hands curled loosely near his chest as though he was gripping something in a dream, and his breath came uneven—too shallow for comfort. Even in the dim light, I could see the tension in the line of his shoulders, the way his body refused to give itself fully over to rest.

I thought he'd finally gone still when a faint sound broke the quiet—low, almost too soft to catch. I leaned forward without realizing it, my elbow brushing the rough wool of his blanket.

"... Mayli..."

The name slipped out like it had been torn from him, hoarse and frayed at the edges. It caught in the space between us, heavy enough to pull at me. Whoever she was, the syllables carried more than just memory—they carried ache.

His brow furrowed as if the dream had turned, the muscle in his jaw flexing. A faint tremor ran through him, and his fingers twitched, curling tighter around whatever phantom object he held in his mind. I stayed where I was for a moment, just watching, telling myself I didn't care. That it wasn't my place to care.

But the lie sat bitter in my throat.

Without thinking, I reached out, brushing a damp strand of hair away from his temple. His skin was warmer than it should've been—not fevered, but warmer than the cold night warranted. He flinched under my touch, not waking, his breathing hitching as if my hand had brushed against the dream itself.

I let my fingers linger for a heartbeat longer before pulling back. The fire crackled softly, shadows dancing across the sharp lines of his face, and I wondered how long it had been since anyone had touched him without a blade in hand.

"Mayli," I murmured under my breath, tasting the name like it might give me answers. It didn't.

Instead, it lodged in my chest like a splinter, sharp and impossible to ignore. Whoever she was, I wasn't supposed to know. But that didn't stop me from wanting to. By the time the sky began to pale, my eyes burned from lack of sleep. I'd stayed near him all night, telling myself it was just to make sure the wound didn't worsen, that if his breathing faltered, I'd be ready.

But when Kael stirred, it was the shift of his weight against mine that jolted me from the haze. At some point during the night, he'd ended up closer—our shoulders brushing beneath the shared blanket, his arm draped loosely where it must have fallen in sleep. The heat radiating off him had been enough to keep the cold at bay.

His lashes flickered before he opened his eyes, and for a brief, unguarded moment, they were softer than I'd ever seen them. Confused. Almost... human.

Then the mask slid back into place.

"You didn't sleep," he said, voice still rough from dreams.

"I was keeping watch," I replied, pulling back slightly. "And someone had to make sure you didn't bleed out in your sleep."

He pushed himself upright with a faint wince, his hand brushing absently at the side where I'd closed the wound. "You didn't have to."

"Maybe not," I said, meeting his gaze. "But I did."

For a moment, he held my stare, like he was searching for something in it. His eyes drifted—just briefly—to the space between us where the blanket still touched both of us, then back up to my face. He didn't comment on it, but he didn't move away, either.

Instead, he looked toward the horizon, the faint gold of sunrise brushing the edges of his features. "We'll move when the sun's fully up," he said. "Solari's good with the children, but I don't like leaving them too long." I heard the faintest echo of his voice from last night—*Give me my boys*—and the thought settled in my chest like a weight.

"Fine," I said quietly, pulling the blanket from my shoulders and standing. "But you're letting me check that wound again before we go."

One corner of his mouth lifted, though it was more wry than amused. "Bossy."

"Alive," I corrected, stepping past him toward the embers. "You should try it sometime."

The fire had burned low, the faintest orange glow just enough to outline the stubborn set of his jaw as I crouched to stir the ashes. I didn't have to look to know he was still standing there, arms folded, pretending he hadn't heard me.

"Sit," I said, my voice sharper now.

"Elara—"

"Sit," I repeated, glancing back. "Or I'll drag you down myself."

His sigh was long and deliberate, the sound of a man weighing whether my threat was worth testing. Finally, he lowered himself to the ground, coat shifting open just enough to show the dark stain creeping through his shirt. I knelt beside him, catching the way his eyes followed my hands. "You're still bleeding," I murmured.

"It's nothing."

"It's stupid," I corrected, tugging at the edge of his coat until he let me push it back. The bandage was worse than I'd hoped—darker along the edges, the copper tang of dried blood cutting through the pine-scented air. "You pushed it- this is supposed to be a rescue mission for the boys- not some chance for you to hash out old vendettas." I said, keeping my tone flat but not softening the accusation.

"It needed to be done, they had our boys. No further justification was needed." The words came quickly, clipped, like the argument was over before it started.

I hesitated the echo of what he just said, *Our* boys ringing through my ears like a sharp tone. A slight falter in the hesitation allowed for me to remember last night, my fingers brushing against the edge of the cloth. "They are important to you- like Mayli was-"

His entire frame went still. The cold seemed to sharpen, the air suddenly thinner.

"That's not a road you want to walk down."

"Why? Clearly it's bothersome enough to disrupt your sleep." I held his gaze now, unwilling to give him the easy way out.

"Because it's not your fight." His voice was low, steady, but there was a tightness there—an almost imperceptible catch that made me wonder if the wound I was tending was the lesser of the ones he carried. "And you already have enough of those."

I leaned in a fraction closer, not in challenge but in search. "Maybe I can decide what fights are mine."

The corner of his mouth twitched—not quite amusement, not quite anger—but he looked away first. His eyes fixed on the far wall, somewhere beyond it.

"You're wasting time," he said finally, the words soft but dismissive.

"Then let me waste it making sure you don't tear this open again." I pressed a fresh strip of cloth against the wound. He flinched—not from the pain, I thought, but from the nearness—and then forced himself to still.

For a moment, there was nothing but the sound of my breathing and the faint crackle of the embers. His jaw stayed tight, eyes fixed on the shadows beyond the door. And yet, when I tied off the bandage, his hand brushed mine—not enough to be deliberate, but not entirely by accident either.

By the time I sat back, he was already on his feet, coat falling back into place as if it had never been moved. He didn't look at me when he said, "We should go," but there was something in the way he avoided my eyes that told me the conversation had cut closer than he'd intended.

We continued on for another few hours, the sun raising well above the tree-line at this point. It must be around noon. I wanted to bring up Mayli, tell him it was my choice whether I went down that path or not, but when I looked up to speak, Kael had frozen in place.

Chapter Thirteen

The path wound narrow and uneven beneath our boots, the frost still clinging in stubborn patches where the sun hadn't yet reached. My leg throbbed with every step, but I kept my pace steady, refusing to let her see me falter. The forest was quiet—too quiet, save for the brittle crackle of ice underfoot.

I'd been counting the minutes, letting the rhythm of walking and the bite of cold air keep my mind in the present. But when we crested the low ridge above the river bend, the wind shifted. Smoke.

Not the distant curl of hearth fires. This was heavier, darker.

My gaze followed the direction of the wind until it landed on a smear of black smudging the horizon. The surrounding air seemed to thin, the sound of the river below flattening into silence. The shape of that smoke was wrong—familiar in a way my chest refused to accept.

It was rising from the direction of Solavend.

My feet stopped moving before I'd even realized it.

"Elara." My voice came out low, but she didn't hear—or maybe she ignored it. She kept walking until she realized I wasn't beside her.

The crunch of her boots stopped. "Kael?" She turned, eyes narrowing at the way I stood rooted in place, my jaw locked and my hands clenched so tightly my nails bit my palms. "What—what the hell are you doing? We don't have time to stand around."

The smoke pulled at me like a hand around my ribs, dragging me backward through years I didn't want to remember.

"Kael." Her tone sharpened as she finally spotted the smoke. "Move."

I didn't. Couldn't. My legs felt carved from stone, my chest tight, the cold seeping deeper even though the air hadn't changed.

"Gods, what is wrong with you?" She stomped toward me, the sound hard and angry. "If there's trouble, we *run toward it,* remember? Or are you suddenly the type to stand here gawking while the people you swore to protect—"

I was running.

Not just moving—running as if the cold could flay me alive if I slowed, as if the breath in my lungs might turn to ice and shatter.

Branches clawed at my face and arms, snapping under my hands when I tore them out of the way. Frost cracked beneath my boots, scattering into glitter in my wake. My breath came in sharp bursts, each one burning like ground glass in my chest. The winter air was sharp enough to cut, but I barely felt it. All I felt was the pull—tight, unrelenting—dragging me faster. The pull toward home.

Somewhere ahead, a crow screamed. The sound echoed across the barren fields, too sharp, too knowing.

Then the trees thinned, and Valedell's rooftops broke through the skeletal line of the forest, and my stomach turned to stone.

Fire.

It moved like a living thing, swallowing thatch and timber with greedy, snapping jaws. Red and gold bled into the pale sky, smoke curling upward in thick, choking ribbons. Sparks spat into the wind, riding it higher. The air was heavy with the smell of scorched wood and something worse—burning flesh—sour, sickening, and final.

I faltered for a step, the instinct to turn back hitting hard and fast. But Mayli's face—small, stubborn, smiling—rose up in my mind, and my legs moved before I told them to.

I tore down the path, boots skidding on churned mud where hooves and boots had trampled the earth. The market lane came into view—a chaos of overturned baskets spilling grain into the dirt, half-crushed barrels leaking sour ale, stalls splintered and gutted.

A boy I knew from the tannery lay face-down in the mud, his limbs twisted at wrong angles, eyes open but seeing nothing.

My stomach lurched. I swallowed hard and forced my gaze forward.

"Mayli!" My voice cracked, raw from the cold. "Mayli!"

No answer.

I cut through the side street, shoving past a toppled cart, and reached our garden fence—splintered, one post sagging toward the earth as though it had been kicked in. The patch where Mayli kept her herbs was nothing but blackened stems and ash.

The front door hung from one hinge, groaning with every gust of wind. I pushed inside.

The heat hit first—molten and heavy, the air thick enough to choke on.

The table lay overturned, dishes shattered in jagged heaps beneath it. My mother's woven wall hanging—hours and hours of her life in dyed thread— was blackened, half-eaten by flame.

Near the hearth, a scrap of green caught my eye. Her scarf. The stitching is still uneven from where she'd mended it last summer.

"Mayli?" I took a step toward the hallway—and froze as three figures stepped through the broken doorway.

Moon-elves.

Their armor gleamed silver white, moonstones catching the dim light, pale runes etched along the curve of their pauldrons. The one in front wore his hair in a long silver braid that swung over one shoulder, his expression too calm— as if he'd been waiting for me.

"Kael," he said, drawing out my name like a taunt. "You're late."

My pulse pounded in my ears, drowning out the crackle of the fire. "Where is she?"

He tilted his head, studying me as though he could pull the answer to some unspoken question from my face. "The little sister?" His voice was smooth, almost bored. "She's with us now."

I took a step forward. My fists clenched until my nails bit into my palms. "Give her back."

That faint smile again, just enough to bare teeth. "You'll have to ask Mēnô yourself." His tone carried no reverence for the god's name—only certainty, like it was supposed to frighten me. "He likes to choose his gifts."

Mēnô. The Moon God. The architect of every raid, the shadow that bled into villages and left only ruin.

Something moved behind them.

"Kael!"

Her voice was high and thin, choked with smoke, but I'd have known it anywhere.

Mayli.

She was struggling in the grip of one of the other raiders, her arms flailing, nails raking over steel, leaving no mark. Her cheeks were streaked with ash, eyes wild. She kicked, screamed my name again, and for a heartbeat, I believed I could get to her.

The braid moved like a striking snake. His sword flashed, silver catching the firelight, and the blade buried itself in my father's chest.

The man's breath left him in a wet gasp. He staggered, his gaze catching mine for a fraction of a second—blank, empty—and then he crumpled.

My mother's scream cut through me, raw and jagged until the braid's dagger swept across her throat. The sound stopped. She folded at my father's side, their blood pooling together in the dirt, running in thin streams toward the hearth.

Something inside me broke.

I roared, the sound tearing my throat, and charged. But pain speared through my ribs before I'd taken three steps—an arrow buried deep in my side, the shaft vibrating with the impact. My knees buckled, the world tilting as the firelight swam in my vision.

I tried to stand. My legs refused.

The braid's shadow fell over me. "Pathetic," he murmured, crouching until we were eye-level. His eyes were pale silver, reflecting the flames. "You can't even protect them."

Behind him, Mayli's voice broke again, her sobs fracturing into syllables of my name. The sound was desperate, clawing.

I reached for her, arm trembling with the effort- but the braid's gauntleted fist crashed into my temple. White burst behind my eyes, the last thing I saw was her small figure, thrashing, being dragged into the dark and then nothing.

When I woke, the world was silent.

Not the peaceful kind of silence, the kind you find in snowdrifts or still mornings.

This was the silence that comes after something ends.

I was flat on my back, the ground cold and damp beneath me. My head throbbed in time with my heartbeat, the side of my face caked with half-dried blood. The air stank—burnt timber, scorched meat, coppery and thick. My ribs screamed when I rolled onto my side, the arrow gone but the wound raw and aching.

Valedell was unrecognizable.

The houses were black skeletons, beams twisted and half-collapsed, their bones still smoldering. Ash drifted lazily through the air, clinging to my hair, my skin. Where the market square had been, there was only a heap of splintered wood and the charred outlines of stalls.

And bodies.

Dozens of them, some face-down in the mud, others curled in on themselves, mouths open in silent screams. Neighbors. Friends. People I'd spoken to just that morning. I climbed to my feet, my boots crunched over debris as I stumbled toward my home. The garden fence was gone entirely. Inside, there was nothing left but the scorched husk of what had been my life.

They were still there. My parents.

Lying together near the hearth, just where they'd fallen. My father's eyes were half-open, clouded and distant. My mother's hair was matted to her cheek with dried blood, her hand curled near his as if she'd tried to reach him in the end.

I hated him. Gods, I hated him. His words had been sharper than any blade, his indifference colder than any winter. But now... now all I felt was hollow.

A different kind of pain took root. It wasn't grief—not fully. It was heavier, darker.

It was rage.

It swelled in my chest, tightening my throat until I could barely breathe. My vision tunneled, heat crawling beneath my skin, my fingers curling into fists so tight they ached. Every breath tasted like ash and blood and failure.

Somewhere in the distance, I could still hear her.

Mayli.

Not her voice now, but the memory of it—thin, trembling, calling my name. And I hadn't saved her. I hadn't even gotten close.

I sank to my knees. The ash stirred around me, clinging to my cloak. My hands pressed into the dirt, into the soot and the blood, nails digging in until they split. The heat from the fires had died, but the one inside me roared hotter— gnawing, clawing, demanding something I couldn't name.

It built with every heartbeat, with every breath that rasped past my teeth. My chest felt too small to hold it. My skin felt too tight. The pounding in my skull merged with the sound of Mayli's voice echoing in my head—calling my name again and again, fading into the darkness I'd woken from.

And then I heard the silver braid's voice, soft and cruel, telling me I couldn't protect them.

Something inside me snapped.

The sound that tore out of my throat didn't feel human. It was raw, primal—dragged up from somewhere deep, from a place made of grief and hatred and failure. It ripped the air apart, sent the crows shrieking from their perches in the burned timbers. My vision blurred, edges going molten, the world narrowing until all that remained was the need to destroy.

The scream bled into a ragged gasp, my lungs burning, my hands shaking with the force of it. Ash rained down, slow and silent, as if the world itself had paused to watch. And in that silence, I made a promise, not to the gods, not to the dead, but to myself.

Elara's voice cut through the haze like a blade.

"Kael!"

The fires of Valedell still burned in my head, the smell of blood still sharp in my nose, but the world around me had shifted. Cold air, the steady rush of the river, the weight of the pack on my shoulders—none of it matched the memory. I blinked, and she was right there in front of me, her hands gripping my arms hard enough to hurt. Her eyes were wide, searching my face like she was trying to find me in whatever abyss I'd just fallen into.

"You stopped walking," she said, her voice low but tight. "You just—froze. What's wrong?"

My throat was dry. The words wouldn't come, not the ones that mattered. The promise I'd made in the ash still clawed at me, too fresh, too raw to be spoken.

"Nothing," I said, but it came out rough, strained. I pulled from her grip and started forward again, faster now. "We need to get back." She didn't follow right away. I could feel her eyes on my back, heavy with questions I had no intention of answering.

Because if I did... she'd never look at me the same way again.

The path back felt longer than it had any right to be.
Elara trailed just behind me at first, silent except for the crunch of frost beneath her boots. I kept my pace clipped, not trusting myself to slow down. My chest

was tight, my ribs still aching where the arrow had been in another lifetime, and the ghost of Mayli's voice lingered like a hook in the back of my mind.

I could feel her wanting to ask—every so often she'd quicken her stride, like she might, and then think better of it. The air between us was too sharp, full of things neither of us would say.

When she finally spoke, it was simple. "You're bleeding again."

I didn't look at her. "It'll keep."

"That's not an answer."

"It's the one you're getting." My voice came out harsher than I meant, but I didn't take it back.

After that, the silence was heavier. Even the trees seemed to crowd closer over the trail, cutting the light down to a dim gray. The only warmth was from the faint coil of anger building low in my gut—the kind that made me welcome the ache in my side because it kept me steady.

The village walls came into sight just as the sun dipped low enough to bleed gold across the treetops. For a breath, I thought I'd imagined it—music, faint and lilting, spilling from the square.

Then we rounded the last bend and stepped into something that made my stomach twist.

Solari stood in the middle of the common, a ridiculous smile on his too-perfect face, surrounded by children darting back and forth with streamers and baskets. The cracked stones had been scrubbed clean, new planks replaced the splintered benches, and fresh garlands hung from every post. In the center of it all, a massive hay pyre towered over the square, bound tight and crowned with flowers.

The Autumn Solstice. I'd forgotten.

I heard Elara's breath catch beside me. For a moment, the hard line of her shoulders eased. She even smiled—a small, tired thing—but there was a shadow in her eyes I couldn't place. Relief, yes, but threaded with something else.

I didn't smile. My hands curled into fists at my sides. The sight of that hay pyre felt like a slap—one errant spark and the whole square would go up. And with raiders still out there, with two boys still missing, the sheer stupidity of it made my teeth grind.

Solari turned at last, catching sight of us. His grin widened like this was all some kind of gift. "You're just in time—"

"What the fuck is wrong with you?" I cut in, my voice carrying over the music and chatter.

The square went quiet.

Chapter Fourteen

Children froze mid-game, small fists still clutching garlands and scraps of ribbon. Even the oldest boy who was rustily playing the fiddle slowed his bow over the strings, stopping to watch.

Solari's head tilted, his smile sharpening like a blade sliding free of a sheath. "Excuse me?"

"You heard me," I said, stepping forward. "With threats still out there, with *two missing boys*—you thought this was the time to stack a pyre taller than the old tavern?"

His golden eyes caught the firelight, bright and infuriating. "It's called *morale*, Kael. A village can't live on fear alone."

"And it can't live if it's in flames because you wanted to play festival god," I shot back. "You've been here all of three days and think you know what these people need? What the hell would you know about not living off fear?"

"I know exactly what they need." His voice stayed maddeningly smooth, but there was an edge under it now. "They've been living under shadows and silence. Tonight is about light. About reminding them they're alive."

"Alive?" I stepped in close enough to see the reflection of the pyre in his eyes. "You think piling kindling in the center of town while raiders are still out there is *keeping them alive*? You're either arrogant or reckless—"

"—And you're predictable," he cut in, his smile not reaching his eyes now. "Always the brooding watchdog, waiting for the sky to fall. I wonder if you even know what it's like to let people breathe, let people live and enjoy the sun while they have the chance. The children are sleeping on a rocky floor in a decrepit hall- the least we could do for them is let them be comfortable for one night."

My jaw locked. "I know what happens when you get too comfortable."

He arched a brow, leaning in slightly, voice low enough that only I caught it. "Or maybe you just don't know how to stop being angry long enough to see what's in front of you."

Heat flared in my chest, sharp and familiar. The square felt smaller, tighter.

A hand brushed my arm, and a cold wave flowed through me.

"Kael," Elara's voice came quiet but steady, cutting through the taut air between us. I didn't look at her, but she didn't move away. "They've been scared for days," she said, louder now so the children heard her instead of us. "Let them have one night." Her tone wasn't pleading—it was anchored. Certain. She shifted just enough to stand between us, the firelight painting her in gold. My breathing was still hard, the need to tear into Solari clawing at my ribs, but the sound of the children's laughter, tentative as it was, seeped back into the edges of the night.

Her gaze flicked toward me, and her voice dropped again. "One night, Kael. You can stand guard from the bench if you want, but let them dance without looking over their shoulders." The muscle in my jaw ached, but I stepped back. Not because I wanted to, but because her eyes told me this was a battle I didn't get to win without taking something from them.

I moved toward the far bench, the wood cold beneath me. The square returned to life—music picking up again, children darting in and out of the firelight, the air tasting faintly of roasted apples. Elara's laugh carried over the music, bright enough to thread through the cold. It wasn't the laugh she used when she was humoring someone, the small, polite thing I'd heard before. This one was unguarded—sharp and warm all at once, like the first taste of spiced cider after weeks of water gone stale.

She spun with the children, skirts fanning out, the hem skimming the dirt in a rhythm that made the shadows cling and slide across her. The firelight caught in her hair like it had been waiting for her to step into its reach, every turn catching some new glint, every movement setting it free again.

Her hands were quick but gentle, catching little wrists before they tumbled, guiding steps without slowing them. Even when she stumbled—one of the older boys darting too close—she didn't break stride, only laughed harder, the sound melting something in the air I hadn't realized had gone tight.

I told myself I was watching to make sure nothing happened. That my eyes tracked her because someone needed to be the one to notice if the shadows around the edges of the square shifted the wrong way.
But that wasn't the whole truth.

It was the way her movements fit the space without trying to own it— how she shifted like she knew both the pull of the fire and the cool press of the dark beyond. Most people picked one or the other. She didn't. She let the light kiss her while the shadows curled at her edges, neither fully claiming her.

It was... unsettling.

I'd seen beauty before. I'd seen strength. But she carried both like they weren't separate things, like they'd been born in the same place inside her and refused to let go of each other.

A small girl looped her arms around Elara's waist mid-step, and instead of breaking free, Elara scooped her up, spinning her through the air until the child's laughter peeled out like chimes in the wind. The firelight caught in Elara's amber eyes when she turned, bright enough that for a moment, I forgot to look anywhere else.

And I hated that.
I hated how easy it was to forget.
I hated that I didn't have a name for the pull at the base of my ribs. I dragged my gaze away, jaw tightening, forcing myself to track the edges of the square again. Shadows, not her. Threats, not the way her skirt brushed her knees when she turned.

It didn't work.

Every time she crossed my vision, that pull tightened. I told myself it was wariness. That I was reading her the same way I would any stranger whose choices might put others in danger. But wariness didn't make my chest feel too tight. Wariness didn't make my hands want to move in time with hers.

"Come on."

Her voice yanked me out of my own head, and I blinked to find her in front of me, cheeks flushed from the fire and the cold, a strand of hair clinging to her skin. She held out a hand, expectant.

"I'm fine here," I muttered.

She didn't move. "That wasn't a request."

I almost laughed at the sheer audacity. "You're not dragging me into that."

"Oh, I absolutely am."

Before I could answer, her fingers closed around mine. Warm. Steady. Stronger than I expected. She tugged, and for some reason I didn't resist.

The music wrapped around us as she pulled me into the circle, the children parting like the tide. I kept my steps small at first, awkward, but she didn't let me hide in the rhythm. Her grip shifted, her palm sliding into mine, her other hand guiding my shoulder until I was matching her movements without realizing it.

For a minute—just a minute—the square narrowed to her. The way her eyes met mine when the steps brought us close. The faint smile that wasn't mockery, wasn't pity, wasn't anything I knew how to read.

And then the now reopened wound on my side reminded me it was still there. The heat flared sharp along my ribs, stealing my breath. I slowed, trying not to wince, but her gaze caught it. Concern flickered in her eyes before I pulled back, breaking the circle.

I turned—intending to retreat—and that's when I saw him.

Solari stood near the fire, a mug in hand, but he wasn't watching the children. His eyes were on us. On her. There was something in his expression—tight around the mouth, too still in the eyes—that I recognized instantly. It was gone in the space of a heartbeat, replaced with his usual sunlit composure.

But I'd seen it.

I backed away from the fire, the music dulling with each step until it was nothing but a hum behind me. My ribs throbbed in time with my pulse, the warmth from the dance already fading into the cold. I found an empty bench near the edge of the square, half-shadowed, and sank down with a slow exhale.

From here, I could see everything. The children darting in and out of the firelight. The banners snapping in the breeze. Solari laughing with a cluster of villagers, his attention pointedly not on me now. And—always—her.

Elara moved like she'd been born to it. Light on her feet, sure in every step, her hair catching the firelight in ribbons of molten gold. Shadows curled and broke across her skirts with every turn, the dark and the light dancing over her like they couldn't decide which owned her.

I told myself I was watching because someone needed to keep an eye on the perimeter. That was half a lie.

When she finally slowed, breath clouding in the cold, she glanced toward me. Whatever she saw must have been enough—she started weaving her way through the crowd until she was standing in front of me again, one hand planted on her hip.

"You're holding your side again," she said, matter-of-fact.

"I'm fine."

"You're not." Her tone left no room for argument. "Come on. Let me check it before you tear something open."

I considered refusing—my pride almost demanded it—but she was already holding out a hand again, waiting. I let her pull me to my feet, the warmth of her palm bleeding into mine, and followed her to a quieter corner away from the noise.

She crouched beside me, peeling back the edge of my coat with careful fingers. Her touch was gentle, but every brush sent heat crawling under my skin in ways that had nothing to do with the wound.

"You've strained it," she murmured, brows knitting. "You need to stop moving like you're invincible."

"Old habit."

Her lips pressed together, the smallest crease appearing between her brows. She didn't answer, just reached for the strip of cloth she'd been carrying and began re-wrapping the bandage. I caught myself watching her face more than her hands—how her focus sharpened, how the firelight drew shadows under her lashes.

When she finished, she sat back on her heels, her eyes lifting to mine for a fraction of a second before she looked away. The edges of her expression had shifted—less open, more... guarded.

"Let's get you inside," she said quietly.

The hall was warm when we stepped in, the smell of baking bread and wood-smoke settling around us. She didn't speak again as we crossed the threshold, just released my arm and moved toward her corner of the room.

I watched her go, that faint shadow in her eyes following her like a second skin.

The hall had gone still, save for the soft crackle of the hearth as its last embers dimmed. Shadows pooled in the corners, long and soft-edged, curling over the sleeping shapes of the children. I'd taken a seat near the door, the cold seeping into my back from the wall.

My wound throbbed in time with my heartbeat, but I kept still, watching her.

Elara lay on her side, hair fanned out over her blanket. She was too still — the kind of still that isn't sleep. I caught the shift of her breathing, the faint tightening of her jaw.

Then she moved.

Her braid slid forward over her shoulder as she sat up, her fingers pausing at the ties on her boots like she was making sure she hadn't woken anyone. The children didn't stir as she rose, weaving between them with steps so light they barely stirred the dust.

She didn't take a cloak. Just pushed the door open with care and slipped into the night.

I waited long enough to make sure she wasn't coming back, then followed.

The air bit colder than I expected, a sharp reminder in my ribs where the arrow had been. Frost glittered under the moonlight, crunching faintly beneath my boots. She moved ahead of me with purpose, never glancing back.

The further we went, the quieter the world became. The faint hum of the village faded, swallowed by the trees to the east.

Her pace never faltered.

The path narrowed to little more than a deer trail. Branches snagged my sleeves. Then the trees broke, and the sight hit me like a cold hand to the chest.

A house stood — or rather, what was left of one. The roof had caved in, the blackened beams clawing at the night sky like broken ribs. The stone walls leaned inward, ready to give way with the next heavy frost.

But it wasn't the house she went to.

It was the row of graves in front of it.

Five, side by side, their markers, simple planks of wood weathered gray by the years. The names were carved shallow, the edges softened by rain and snow. The surrounding earth was bare, swept clean of frost — a detail that told me someone still cared enough to tend to them.

Elara knelt at the first grave, brushing her fingers over the name. Her voice wavered as she reached the final lines of a lullaby, barely more than breath carried on the night air. The sound cracked on the last note, breaking into silence.

Behind her, I stilled. Even without looking, she felt the sharpness of my attention, the tension coiling tight.

"It was a song my mother used to sing to me," Elara said softly, brushing her fingers over the cold earth. "She said it kept the shadows away."

She cleared the frost from the next marker, her fingers lingering on the grooves. "It was the Autumn Solstice. I was eight. The raiders came after sundown. Moon-elves." Her voice caught, just barely. "I woke up under my parents' bodies. They thought I was dead too."

I stepped closer but didn't speak.

She moved to the third grave and rested her hand flat against it. "My father, Kaelen. He smelled of cedar and smoke. He wasn't... gentle. But he built this house with his own hands." She let her hand slide to the grave beside it. "My mother, Serinyà," The name was familiar, sticking with me more than it should. "She used to hum while she worked in the garden. The herbs always grew sweeter if they knew you loved them," he said.

Her breath trembled, and she turned to the smaller graves. "Ava," she said softly, brushing the smallest marker. "He was only three. He used to follow me everywhere, even when he could barely keep his balance."

The next one earned a faint, aching smile. "Mira. She'd steal my bread and hide it under her pillow because she thought I'd starve if I didn't eat in the morning."

Finally, her fingers settled on the last. "And Rowan... he was the fastest runner in the village. We'd race to the stream. I never won." She gave a shaky breath. "He was eleven."

Her hands stayed on that last grave a long moment.

"It doesn't get easier," she murmured.

"No," I said, my voice low, rough. "It doesn't."

Her eyes flicked to me, then away again. "The apothecary from Solavend found me the next morning. Took me in. I haven't been back here in years."

We stayed there in the cold, the wind moving softly through the skeletal trees, before she finally straightened. Her gaze swept over each grave again, deliberate, as though memorizing them all over.

When she stepped away, I fell into step beside her. We didn't speak on the walk back, but she walked closer this time, her arm brushing mine once in a while.

The graves vanished behind us, swallowed by frost and shadow — but the weight of them clung to her like it had just happened.

The village sleeps, but it's the kind of sleep that's too thin to be trusted. I can hear it in the way the shutters twitch in the wind, in the hollow knock of a loose latch against warped wood. The air holds the crisp bite of late autumn—cold enough to make the lungs sting on the inhale, but not yet winter's knife.

I linger in the shadow of a leaning wall, watching the loft window of the hall. A low light spills out—faint, steady. She's up there. Awake, maybe. Or lying still, eyes fixed on the dark the way they were fixed on those graves.

Her hands had trembled when she brushed the dirt from their stones. She'd hidden them in her skirts like she thought no one would notice. But I did. I notice too much where she's concerned. Five graves, each etched with names the rest of the village has learned to avoid. I'd been close enough to feel the silence pressing down on her, to hear the weight of it in her breath.

The moon hangs thin and high, its pale light barely catching on the rooftops. It's not enough to see by, but it still stirs something deep in me, something I've spent years refusing to name.

I push away from the wall, moving down the hall and out the door quietly, moving down the empty street. My steps are soundless, the packed earth not daring to give me away, heading for the far edge of the village where the buildings sag and crumble in quiet surrender. Frames splintered, roofs caved in, walls leaning like they've grown tired of holding their own weight. No one would call them salvageable. But no one ever asks the right questions.

I step into the first ruin. The air is heavy with dust and the faint musk of old timber. I press my hand to a beam that's blackened and soft with rot. Shadows curl out from beneath my palm, stretching slow at first, then swallowing the beam whole. Not a sound. Not a splinter. The structure folds inward on itself, as neat as if it had been dismantled by careful hands. The dust settles in moments, leaving nothing but what I choose to keep—sturdy planks, a handful of unbent nails, stones uncracked by frost.

One by one, I move through the rest. Each building gives up its pieces willingly, as though the night itself has whispered that it's time to let go. My hands work without tools—timber stacking itself at my side, nails slipping free without force, hinges loosening without rust protesting. The rest—the splintered wood, the warped stone—crumbles into nothing, carried off on the wind as if it had never stood here at all.

When I have enough, I pick my ground. A wide stretch, shielded from the worst of the wind by an old grove of ash trees. The air here is quieter, like it's holding its breath for what's about to happen.

I start with the frame. Shadows spill from my fingertips, stretching into lines and angles before drawing the salvaged timber into place. Walls rise straight and clean, grain catching in the dim moonlight. A roof seals tight over them without the groan of nails or the scrape of hammer.

Inside, I carve space for them. Ten rooms—small, but enough for each of them to have their own door, their own bed. A wide hall at the center, with a hearth big enough to draw the chill from every corner. A kitchen with shelves that won't bow, a table long enough to seat them all at once. Floors that won't shiver under the weight of a child's step.

It takes hours, but time doesn't press on me here. The night stretches, holding me in its palm until I'm finished. When I finally step back, the place stands solid and unyielding. No drafts in the walls. No gaps in the roof. I stand in the doorway, the smell of fresh wood still warm in the air, and think of her waking to this. She'll never believe it just appeared overnight. She'll try to find the reason, the trick. But it doesn't matter if she guesses right.

What matters is that tomorrow, she won't have to pretend that a broken hall is enough.

Chapter Fifteen

The old hall was never quiet. Even at dawn, when the frost still clung to the corners of the windowpanes and the hearth burned low, it breathed and creaked like some tired, half-broken animal.

The roof groaned when the wind slipped in through the gaps. Floorboards whispered beneath shifting mats. Somewhere in the corner, someone always coughed, a dry, persistent sound that blended into the faint rustle of blankets and the scrape of bare heels on splintered wood.

I lay there for a while, curled under my shawl, my toes stiff with cold, counting each sound like I could stack them into order. Then came the shouting.

It was not the sharp, frightened kind that twisted my stomach. This was high and breathless in the way only children's voices could manage, excitement that did not care who it woke.

I sat up, every joint protesting after another night on the uneven boards. The air was damp enough to cling to my hair, heavy with the smell of old ash and mildew. I rubbed my eyes, blinked against the dim light creeping through the warped shutters, and listened.

More voices joined in, followed by laughter, a squeal, and the muffled thud of feet pounding toward the door.

"All of you, slow down!" I called, but I knew better than to expect obedience.

By the time I reached the doorway, most of the children had already spilled into the square, their bare feet leaving quick ghost-breaths in the cold.

I stepped outside, the chill nipping at my ankles. The sky was pale and brittle-looking, the kind of light that came before the sun really woke. I could see them, a darting, tumbling flock racing toward the far edge of the village, to the place where the abandoned cottages had been collapsing in on themselves since before the festival.

"Stay where I can see you!" I called again, but the wind stole my words before they reached them.

I gathered my shawl tighter and followed.

Halfway there, I slowed. My steps faltered.

The cottages, the sagging beams and walls bowed from years of neglect, were gone.

In their place stood something that should not have been possible.

A building rose from the frost-hardened ground, solid and whole. The walls were fitted timber, every plank straight and smooth. The roof had no sag, no gaps, no patches of daylight showing through. Fresh pitch glistened at the seams. A single chimney breathed a slow ribbon of smoke into the sky.

The children swarmed the front steps, their voices bouncing off the clean lines of the walls.

I moved closer, my breath a white curl in the air.

"Salvage from the east side," a voice said behind me.

I turned.

Kael leaned against a fencepost like he had been there all morning, arms folded, sleeves rolled up. There was sawdust at the edge of his cuff, like an afterthought.

"You did this?" My voice came out thinner than I meant, the cold catching at my throat.

He tilted his head, not bothering to look at the building. "Figured you all deserved better than the drafty hall."

Better. As if this was just a step up from the warped boards and the chimney that smoked more than it drew.

"This isn't better, Kael." I took another step, my eyes dragging over every precise join and fitted seam. "This is new."

His mouth curved faintly, but his gaze stayed steady. "Patchwork. Bit of luck with the beams."

Patchwork did not explain how he had straightened walls without the help of half the village, or how every plank seemed cut to fit with impossible precision.

The first of the children broke through the doorway with a gasp so loud it carried back to us. More followed, spilling inside in a flurry of boots and skirts.

I followed, one hand trailing over the frame. No splinters. The wood was smooth, the grain warm under my fingers.

The hearth was already set with kindling, the stonework so clean it looked like it had never seen smoke. A sturdy table stood in the kitchen space, flanked by shelves and a proper cupboard with working hinges. Along each side of the hall were doors, eight of them, and behind each one I glimpsed beds. Actual beds. The kind you did not have to roll up and push aside every morning.

My chest felt tight.

And then I nearly walked straight into him.

Solari stood in the shadow of the doorway, sunlight spilling around his boots and pooling at his heels. He was not watching the children tumble through their new rooms, and he was not watching me.

His gaze was on Kael, as if he was seeing something in him that I couldn't.

The children, though, scattered into the new rooms like they had been waiting their whole lives for this door to open. Bare feet padded over fresh boards, little hands testing the springs of mattresses, voices rising in wonder at simple things: a window that latched, a blanket without holes, shelves that didn't sag.

I trailed after them, my fingertips brushing every surface. The air smelled faintly of pine and smoke, clean in a way nothing else in Solavend ever did.

In the kitchen space, a pot already hung over the hearth, hooks lined the wall for pans that had not yet been brought over. A real pantry—empty now, but solid and dry—waited behind a small door.

Kael had thought of everything.

I glanced toward the far corner where two boys stood frozen in the doorway of their new room. Beds, two of them, with frames that didn't wobble, each with a quilt folded at the foot. The quilts didn't match, but both were clean and mended with care.

"Go on," I said, nodding them inside.

They grinned and bolted for the beds, bouncing once before sprawling out like they meant to never get up.

When I turned back, Kael was leaning against the wall, watching me watch the children. There was a strange stillness in him, as though he was waiting for something I might say.

Before I could speak, Solari moved.

He stepped further into the room, the sunlight sliding with him. His gaze swept the space with the same precision I'd used a moment ago, but where my eyes caught on the comforts, his caught on the seams, the joints, the places where timber met stone.

"This was not the work of a single night," Solari said quietly.

Kael's head tipped, his smile edged. "You'd be surprised what a long night can do."

Something passed between them, something I couldn't name but could feel. Solari didn't look away.

"You've hidden yourself well," he said, the words so soft I almost thought I'd imagined them.

Kael pushed off the wall, stepping closer, his shadow stretching long over the fresh boards. "And you're still here," he murmured. "Why?"

For a heartbeat, neither of them moved. The air in the room seemed to draw tight. Then Solari's eyes flicked to me, quick but unreadable, before he turned and walked back toward the door. Kael's jaw tightened. His hand flexed once before smoothing it against his thigh, as if wiping away something invisible. When the door shut behind Solari, the noise of the children flooded back in.

Kael straightened, pulling his sleeves back down, and crossed the room to a girl struggling to lift her mattress. "Let me help you with that," he said, his tone easy again. I watched him tug the mattress into place like it weighed nothing, then adjust the blanket so it fell neatly to the floor. The girl thanked him and darted off, her face bright. Kael moved to the hearth next, checking the flue and stacking the kindling like someone who'd done it a hundred times before. If I hadn't seen that look pass between him and Solari, I might have believed this was simply kindness. But I had seen it. And it was still in the room, even if Kael pretended it wasn't.

When the children finished scrambling to their chosen rooms, the noise shifted from a roar to a steady hum. Doors thudded open and shut as they explored, calling out to each other over discoveries that seemed small to anyone else—a window that latched without sticking, a shelf high enough to keep treasures from younger hands, a bed wide enough to roll over twice without hitting the wall.

I lingered in the main hall, letting the sound wash over me. It was the kind of noise we hadn't had in weeks. Not the restless shuffling of too many bodies in one space, but something warmer, lighter.

Kael was at the hearth, crouched low, adjusting a piece of iron into a hook. His sleeves were pushed up, exposing the cord of his forearms, the skin faintly dusted with sawdust and ash. He worked without fuss, like he had done this a thousand times before.

"You worked fast," I said.

He didn't look up right away. "I didn't want to waste time. The weather will turn soon."

"That's an understatement," I replied. "But even with help, this would have taken weeks."

He gave a low hum, almost as if the thought didn't deserve words. "Found good beams. Most of the east-side rubble was sound once you stripped the rot. And the rest..." His mouth quirked faintly. "I made do with what I had."

"Making do," I said slowly, "doesn't usually look like this." I turned in place, sweeping my gaze over the straight walls, the even joins, the solid doorframes. "This is... more than shelter."

Kael leaned one shoulder against the mantel, the faintest trace of a smile tugging at his mouth. "You're welcome."

"That's not what I meant."

"Then you'll have to be clearer," he said, his voice smooth but not sharp.

I stepped closer, enough to catch the faint mix of pine and smoke clinging to him. "Who are you, Kael?"

The smile didn't falter, but something in his eyes shifted, like the ground under snow when the first thaw came. "A man who builds roofs over children's heads." He pushed off the mantle, straightening to his full height. "That's enough, isn't it?"

It wasn't. We both knew it.

Before I could speak, two of the younger boys skidded into the hall, their feet slapping against the fresh boards. "Kael! Come see our room!" one shouted, tugging on his arm. The other joined in, both talking over each other about the blankets and the shelf that didn't wobble. Kael let them pull him toward the far hallway without another glance in my direction.

I stayed where I was, the warmth of the hearth at my back, the cold knot of questions tightening in my chest. By the time I mustered the will to follow them down the hall, Kael was already in the boys' room, fixing the tilt on a shelf with a small wedge of wood he must have carved in advance. He didn't measure, didn't pause to think—just tapped it in place and stepped back, the shelf now perfectly level.

The boys clapped like it was magic. Maybe it was.

I moved on to the next room, where a pair of girls were showing off their quilts. "He put a hook for my satchel right here," one said proudly, pointing to the wall beside her bed. The hook looked as if it had always been there, the wood stained to match the rest.

In the kitchen, he was already stoking the hearth, laying the kindling in a pattern that caught the flame on the first strike. It burned evenly, without the smoky hiccups our fires usually had. He adjusted the pot hooks, so they hung level, then stepped back as if to check his work—though his gaze flicked briefly toward me before he turned away, heading back for the kitchen.

Everything he touched seemed to fit, to work exactly as it should. No trial and error, no second attempts. I'd grown up watching people build things in this village, and nothing ever came together like that.

The smell of wood-smoke and simmering stew wrapped around the hall like a blanket, pulling everyone toward the long table. Steam curled up from the pot, carrying the scent of carrots, onions, and whatever Kael had managed to salvage from the larder.

Bowls scraped and spoons clinked as the children settled in, shoulders brushing, heads bent over the steam. They ate with the kind of single-minded focus that comes after too many hungry days. A sharp laugh broke the quiet, and then another, until the whole room felt lighter.

I took a seat near the end, the fire's heat at my back, and watched Kael move among them. He topped off bowls, refilled cups, crouched to listen when one of the younger boys wanted to show him a loose tooth. Every movement was fluid, efficient, as though he'd been doing this here for years instead of hours.

When the pot was empty, he disappeared briefly, returning with small rounds of bread he must have baked in the kitchen's side oven while the stew cooked. The crust cracked perfectly under eager hands, releasing a warm, yeasty scent.

I caught myself wondering when he'd had time to make it.

Afterward, the older children cleared the table while the younger ones sprawled on the floor near the hearth. Kael joined them, showing two girls how to twist scraps of yarn into braided cord. They leaned in close, small fingers fumbling until he guided them with patient, unhurried hands.

When the last dish was washed and set on the drying rack, the children's chatter had faded to soft murmurs. They drifted off toward their rooms, quilts trailing behind them.

The hall felt bigger with them gone, the quiet pressing against the fresh walls.

Kael was by the far wall, wiping his hands on a rag. The room smelled faintly of smoke and pine, a warm, clean scent that didn't belong in this village. He moved slowly now, like someone finally letting the weight of a long day settle in his shoulders.

I let my eyes wander over the space—the straight beams overhead, the even joints where wood met stone, the solid doors that didn't stick in their frames. Not a single floorboard creaked under my step. No drafts sneaked through the seams. Every nail, every hinge, every line felt... deliberate. It shouldn't have been possible. Not in one night. Not with the scraps we had left after the festival.

I glanced toward the children's hallway. Hooks for their satchels, beds that didn't groan, quilts folded neatly at the foot. The shelves were level, the shutters closed without a fight, the pantry door didn't sag on its hinges.

And he'd done it all without ever looking hurried.

Kael caught me watching him and gave a small nod, the kind you give when a job is done. I returned it, unsure if I should say anything at all. "Get some rest, Elara," he said, his voice easy, almost warm. "Tomorrow's another long day."

I left him there in the firelight, but when I glanced back from the doorway, he was still watching me, before shifting uncomfortably and heading up to his own room, shutting the door. I stepped outside to breathe. The hall loomed behind me—solid, warm, a miracle built in a single night. Kael's work. Not mine.

"You admire it."

The voice slid from the dark. My chest tightened.

Kura emerged, shadows trailing him like smoke. Those crimson eyes locked on me as if I were the only thing worth seeing.

"You again," I said flatly.

"Still not glad to see me." His tone was amused, but there was an edge to it.

"I told you before. I don't want you here."

He stepped closer, shadows curling over the cobbles. "And yet, here I am."

I crossed my arms. "What do you want this time?"

"To see what he left behind." His gaze flicked toward the hall. "And what you've made of it."

"I didn't make it," I snapped. "Kael did."

His mouth curved, not quite a smile. "Does it matter whose hands raised the beams? You're still standing under it."

The shadows stretched, brushing lightly against my skin like a chill breeze. My fists clenched, but I held my ground.

"Stop that."

"I barely touched you," he murmured. "But you noticed."

I glared. "I notice vipers too. Doesn't mean I want them near me."

His laugh was soft, without humor. "And yet you keep surviving them."

"Why did you come back?" I asked, voice low with heat. "To remind me what you took? To twist the knife?"

"Perhaps," he said, tilting his head. "Or perhaps to see if you'll still look me in the eye."

"I don't fear you." The words left before I could stop them.

"Don't you?" His shadows flickered, curling higher—then stilled. He studied me a long moment, something unreadable slipping across his features. Not pity. Not remorse. Something heavier. Then it was gone.

He stepped back, the darkness folding around him. "You hate me. That's good. Hate keeps you strong."

I let out a harsh breath. "You don't get to tell me what keeps me strong."

His smile cracked, faint, fleeting. "No. I don't."

And just before he vanished, I could've sworn the mask slipped—a flicker in his eyes, a weight in his voice.

I swear... he almost looked sad.

Chapter Sixteen

The hall settles the way a body does after a long cry—hiccuping once, twice, then easing into a softer quiet. Doors click shut down the corridor. A late giggle gets swallowed by a shushing whisper. Someone turns over and the new bedframe gives a brief, satisfied sigh, like even the wood can't believe it isn't expected to carry the whole village anymore.

The fire has slumped to embers. I rake a log closer with the poker and watch a tongue of flame lick up, testing the air. Heat pushes against my face. Ash lifts and settles back like a breath taken and released. The room smells of stew and smoke and pine soap that Elara insisted on using even though the water was near cold. The scent clings to my cuffs. It shouldn't, but it does.

I sit until the warmth turns thick. Until the hum of sleeping bodies behind these new doors feels like it might press me flat. I don't belong inside this kind of quiet. The latch is cool beneath my palm when I take it, cooler still when it slips free. The night has been waiting.

Outside, autumn has taken the edges of things and made them sharp. The air finds the spaces between my coat and skin with unkind precision. Overhead, the moon is thin and stubborn, drifting between slow cloud. The square bares its bones under that light—ruts in hard-packed earth, a scatter of tools I told the boys to collect and knew they'd forget, the slick dark line where someone spilled broth and tried to wipe it away with a sleeve. The new walls hold the glow from the windows like cupped hands. Every seam is where it's supposed to be. Every board sits true. As if that should matter.

He's already here.

I see him first as refusal: a stillness at the far post where the path slides toward the trees, hands folded behind his back, head tipped slightly, as if listening to something the rest of the world forgot how to hear. The moon glances off him and loses nerve. Without the sun to crown him he is less spectacle, more gravity. The square seems to tilt a fraction toward where he stands.

"Could have told her," he says, not bothering to face me yet. It isn't a question. It's a judgment he has tried to keep out of his voice and failed.

Boot soles whisper against grit as I descend the stairs. "You could have stayed out of it."

He turns then. The practiced serenity is in place, but it strains. "She deserves the truth."

"She deserves sleep." I stop a few paces off, keeping the post between us. "She deserves a morning that isn't heavier than the night before. If the truth can't give her that, it can wait."

"That's not your call to make."

"It's the only one I have."

The wind hacks through the square once and drops, as if deciding there's nothing here it can take that hasn't already been taken. He moves into it and the edges of his coat lift, then settle, precise as ceremony. This is the game he prefers: measured steps, clean hands, power misnamed as restraint.

"I see what you're doing," he says. "The small comforts. The food, the beds, the walls that don't groan. All of it meant to make her softer toward you." His gaze drops to my hands, then back up. "She is not another thing you are allowed to destroy. Whatever game you are playing needs to stop."

"You don't know her." I shouldn't give him anything he can use, and still: "Not the way this place has taught her to carry what it asks. You think the truth is something you drop like a stone, it's not. Not this truth."

"I think you're afraid."

"Of you?" The smile I show him is a thin cut. "You should hope that's the thing I fear."

A breath, not quite a laugh. "You mistake me on purpose." He takes a step closer, the post no longer between us. "You're afraid of what she will be when she knows. Not because it will break her, but because it won't."

That's an old pattern between us—he steps nearer and names a fear, I stand still and pretend it belongs to someone else. I let my shoulders loosen as if the night has finally earned me. "You think she'll thank you for it? Truth as charity? Truth as coin you toss at her feet so you can watch her pick it up?"

"She isn't your project."

"She isn't your possession."

Silence runs between us like wire. Somewhere behind me a shutter ticks as wood adjusts to cold. A stray dog yips twice, decides to better, and is gone. I look past him to the dark smear of the trees and picture the path out of the square curving into their black. It would be simple to take it. Step off the road three paces, step sideways four more, and the night would fold its hands over me like a priest with a prayer he doesn't entirely believe in.

He narrows his eyes, a brief flash of heat under that well-schooled calm. "You built this," he says, chin tipping toward the new walls. "And you think that makes you necessary."

"I didn't build it to be necessary. I built it because the old boards were going to kill a child if one more wind got under them."

"You could have asked for help. You could have told someone what you meant to do."

"I did," I say. "I told the dark, and it agreed."

His mouth tightens. The words have flirted too close to where I live. I know it; he knows it. The moon slides free of clouds and paints a line along the edge of his cheekbone; the effect is almost merciful. He looks less like an indictment and more like a man who hasn't slept.

"She deserves the truth," he says again, quieter. "Not the version that makes your life easier. The kind that makes her free to decide."

"She has decided," I say. "Every day since the festival. She decided to get up. To cook when the larder was nearly empty. To bend her back and lift what the dead left. I didn't take choice from her. I took a burden she didn't need to carry yet."

"You took the weight of your guilt," he answers, barely above a whisper, "and wrapped it in kindness until you could pretend it wasn't yours."

The first anger arrives not as heat, but as focus. The world simplifies. The wind becomes a single thread pulled across my skin. The dirt remembers it is ground and not a road. I let my hands hang loose, imagining the night poured into them like water I could hold if I was careful.

"You speak as if you haven't rehearsed that line in your head for days," I say. "You're too pleased with how it sounds."

"It's true."

"Is it?" I let my gaze drop to the ground between us. The shadows there thicken of their own accord, tugged by thought, not will. I smooth them with effort. "Or is it easier to call it guilt because you can't stand that my kindness did what your light didn't?"

That finds the seam. His breath shifts—too subtle for anyone but someone who has been measuring him for years. "If you cared about her choice," he says, throat hard on the word, "you wouldn't be hiding."

"If you cared about her choice," I say, "you wouldn't be here."

We both look toward the hall at the same time. The square angles the noise toward us: a soft cough, a bedframe settling, the brief scrape of a latch. Then nothing. He tracks the sound and comes back to me with the same thought I didn't bother to hide—this conversation can't enter that light.

"You can keep playing at this," he says. "You can keep your polite voice and your wrapped hands and your borrowed name. It won't change what you are. It won't change that the thing you're keeping from her is the only thing that matters."

"Only to you."

"To her," he says, and the word is a dare.

"She didn't ask." The admission tastes like ash and truth both. "If she had, I would have—" I stop. I don't finish lies I can't stand in.

He hears that, too. "No," he says, very soft, almost pleased. "You wouldn't."

I want to step forward. Not to threaten, not even to shorten the distance, but because the urge to be closer to him when I break something in his composure is an old and terrible habit. Instead, I look past his shoulder toward the trees again, and imagine the way the trunks take moonlight and make it a secret. When I come back to him, his face has settled into the expression he wore the first time he learned any kind of gentleness can be used as a blade.

"You don't get to hold her future in your teeth and pretend it's mercy," he says.

"You don't get to use her past as a leash and pretend it's love."

He flinches. Not back—never back—but inward, like the word found an old bruise and pressed down.

We let the quiet stand there and show us both. Clouds drag across the moon and the square grows smaller; the dark finds its corners and sits in them. Somewhere an owl takes a mouse and the night thanks it by not caring.

When he speaks again, the ritual polish is gone. "No matter how you dress it up, you don't belong here—and we both know it."

There it is: not a name, but an exile. The old truth laid down like a boundary stone. It does what he wants; it finds purchase under the ribs, the way any accurate cut does. The shadows at my heels show their teeth. I school them, then put patience in my mouth and pretend it's humor.

"Then stop circling," I say. "If I don't belong, send me away."

"You know that's not how this works."

"It is," I say. "It's exactly how this works. You come into places like this with the sun at your back and everyone remembers how to kneel. If you wanted me gone, I would be gone."

He studies me as if the right angle might reveal a seam. "I don't want you gone."

"Then what?" I ask, and the question isn't rhetorical. I'm tired of pretending it is. "To stand at opposite ends of a square and speak like this until the moon forgets it has any pull left? To measure whose restraint is more virtuous? To set her between us like a field marker and call the distance respect?"

"I want her safe," he says.

"So do I."

His breath leaves him, brief and hard, like the admission took something he was saving. "Then stop lying."

"Stop asking."

His laugh is humorless and low. "You're better at evasion than I gave you credit for."

"You always were generous with me."

We have reached the point in the fight where everything loops unless one of us tears the fabric. He knows it. I do too. He takes one step nearer, not enough to crowd, enough to test. The instinct moves through me—answers him with a shift of weight, a change in balance, the small preparations a body makes when it has decided it may need to be a weapon again. There's a quick flash of something like satisfaction in his eyes that I refuse to reward.

"You're not one of them," he says, each word neat, placed. "No matter the meals you serve or the roofs you raise. No matter how long you stand in the doorway and pretend a good night's sleep can buy you absolution. You don't belong here. And we both know it."

"I don't belong anywhere," I say, and the truth of it is so old it's quiet.

He doesn't expect that. His mouth opens, then closes around whatever answer he had ready. The silence that follows is new. Not the strained silence of barely bridled anger, but the kind that enters a room and looks around for where it might sit.

In that space, a small thing betrays me. The post he leaned on throws a shadow I didn't invite it to throw; the lines of it pull toward me a fraction when the moon slips free again. He sees the change without quite seeing it, the way a man senses a loose stone underfoot but never looks down to find it. His gaze narrows anyway.

"You're running out of corners," he says. "Some truths don't fit in them."

"You've always liked to say that from the center of things."

"Come to the center, then."

"I have work," I answer. "Beds that won't collapse when a child rolls over in the night. A roof that doesn't drum panic every time the wind remembers it has hands. A woman who has been asked to shoulder too much while men argue air."

His jaw hardens on the last words. "You talk like I'm a man who enjoys arguments."

"You are a man who enjoys being right."

"And you are a man who enjoys being necessary."

The corner of my mouth lifts. "Then we are both badly made."

We look at each other as if there is anything new to see. There isn't—or at least, there shouldn't be. And yet the pause lingers a breath too long, heavy in a way I can't name.

The square breathes once. A door inside the hall gives a soft click as the wood cools. My hands have gone cold. I curl them into fists and uncurl them again until the sting loosens.

"This won't hold," he says, finally, and I can't tell if he means the building or the lie or me. "You can't stand on two names forever."

"I only need to stand long enough," I say. "There are things that can be finished in the dark if you keep your voice down."

He shakes his head. The gesture is too human to be entirely comforting. He steps back, not in retreat, but because leaving requires the same kind of will as staying and he's never been careless with will.

"Someday," he says, and I know he hates the word even as he uses it, "she'll ask you, anyway."

"She might," I say. "And I'll answer her."

He tips his head. There's curiosity in it, but no faith. "You won't."

"Watch me."

He turns then, cloak catching and settling in a single motion he has practiced longer than anyone here has been alive. His boots make careful noise on the hard ground. "There's something different about her thread—on the loom. Someone a long time ago tampered with it, possibly before they died since the resonant magic has long faded. She's stronger than you think." He takes the path toward the trees without glancing back. The darkness accepts him with a familiarity I am petty enough to resent.

I stay where I am until his shape becomes suggestion and then nothing. The square, relieved of him, seems to remember it is only a square. The wind comes back to see what it missed. From the hall, a sliver of light cuts across the step like a promise that hopes it won't be asked to grow into more.

The cold finds the seam between coat and shirt and runs a finger along it. I let it. The sky is clean for a moment, the moon unimpressed with both of us. If I draw the dark up now, if I let it braid through the grain of the new posts and write strength where there was only joinery, no one will be the wiser. If I smooth the dirt where our words scuffed it, the morning will never know we stood here and failed to move each other.

I don't. Not yet. I let the night sit as it is and bear witness.

From inside, a soft sound—someone turning over—reminds me why I built what I built and why I will keep doing it, whether it buys me anything or not. I roll my shoulders against the cold and go back up the steps. The latch is colder than before and bites my palm. The hinges keep their promise and don't complain.

The hall greets me like a held breath released. I pause, letting my eyes adjust to the smaller light. The embers have steadied. The new boards keep their counsel. Down the corridor, a door has been left a thumb's width open and throws a thin line across the floor. I don't close it. Not everything needs to be shut to be safe.

I cross to the hearth and crouch, careful with the poker. The coal I choose isn't the brightest, but it's the one most likely to catch. I lay it where it will do the most good and watch a filament of flame test it, retreat, then try again with better luck.

"Someday," Maybe. Or maybe not. The night has room for both.

The flame decides it is a flame and behaves accordingly. I sit back on my heels and let the warmth hit my face. My hands stink of smoke and stew and clean wood. There are worse things to carry.

Outside, the wind lifts once more, half-hearted now, as if it has remembered somewhere else it was meant to be. The hall listens, and then, satisfied, returns to sleep. I keep the watch he won't admit I'm keeping. I let the dark set its quiet shoulder against the door and stand there with me.

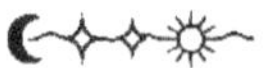

Chapter Seventeen

I woke to the sound of a door closing softly and the smell of something warm on the hearth. For a few long breaths I lay still, trying to place the hush. It wasn't the hollow quiet of the old hall, where every draft had teeth. This was the kind of quiet that collects when a building is full of sleeping bodies and there's nothing chasing them through their dreams. The surrounding walls didn't shiver. The floor under my toes was cool and clean when I swung my legs over the side of the bed.

The corridor beyond my room held a thread of morning. Light slanted low across the boards and dust moved through it like a slow tide. Two little ones darted past with quilts bundled under their arms, feet whispering over wood. Someone down the way laughed and tried to swallow it, which only made it spill into something brighter. I didn't shush them. The sound felt like a charm against whatever lingered outside.

In the main room the air was already warm, the hearth holding a steady glow. Kael stood at the cooking stones with his sleeves rolled, turning a ladle through a pot that smelled like onions and something meaty salvaged from last night's stew. He glanced over when I came in. It wasn't quite a greeting, but it was a recognition I could feel.

"You're up early," I said.

His mouth tilted. "Or late, depending on where you start counting."

Bowls lived in a neat stack now. I didn't ask who decided that. I set them out while he ladled, and the children came in waves, sleep-mussed and quick-eyed, taking seats where they liked along the long table. The new benches didn't complain, and the table didn't list toward any particular child as if choosing a favorite. We ate without ceremony. Someone spoke with their mouth full and got a look from Mira that would have peeled bark, which only made Darek snort into his bowl. Kael didn't raise his voice once, but when the littlest tried to trade a whole slice of bread for half a spoon more stew, he only tapped the rim of the bowl and shook his head. Order arrived in the room as if it had walked in with him and hung its cloak by the door.

When the bowls were empty and the last of the bread was torn into even pieces, he stepped back from the fire, rubbing his hands on a cloth.

"We'll need to start scavenging," he said, half to me and half to the air. "Warm clothes, tools, fasteners, anything that makes the walls hold and the doors stay shut."

"Food," I said. "Salt. Oil. Things that don't rot in a week."

"We'll get them," he said. "But we can't store food if the shutters don't close and the latch is a rumor." His tone wasn't sharp. It made its point anyway.

We divided the day without arguing over it. Mira stayed to mind the little ones and keep the kettle honest. Serin took three children to sort the heap of clothes by size. Kael and I would take Thalen and Gregor to the western edge of the village, where the houses were less torn open by wind.

The air outside had that clean bite that means autumn is sharpening its knife. We moved along the lane where the old thatch had collapsed and the stone stayed standing, careful about where we put our weight. I had walked these streets my whole life and never thought about the way a roof beam takes stress until it didn't anymore. Thalen tried to look bored and failed every time he found anything with a hinge.

We started with a cottage that still wore half its roof. The door leaned against a heap of broken wicker. Inside, it smelled of damp and smoke, like all that was left of a winter. Kael didn't stride in like a man used to being obeyed; he stepped as if the floor was listening. He ran a hand along a split board and moved past it, showing Thalen without explaining why. Gregor brought a basket to the light and held it up.

"That one will only carry promises," I said. He grinned and tossed it aside.

Behind a broken cupboard door we found jars still sealed with wax and rings of old twine. Most would be vinegar or pickles turned to something you don't invite to supper, but the glass alone was worth the trouble if we could scrub it clean. Kael bent to lift a fallen beam while I rolled a trunk toward him. He moved the wood like it weighed less than it did. I pretended not to notice.

"We should look for root cellars," I said, wiping my hands on my skirt. "If anything's lasted, it'll be there."

"We will," he said, tugging the hinge pins from a half-rotted door. "But I want proper latches for the rooms before night. And I need a longer length of chain for the well. If the bucket falls, we're finished."

"You and your latches," I muttered, not to pick a fight so much as to be honest.

"You and your pantry," he returned, a glance like the ghost of a smile.

We found two decent lengths of rope in another house under a fallen loft, and a wooden pulley so dry it nearly split in my hands. He took it from me and turned it to the firelight that sneaked through a gap, thoughtful, thumbs pressing gently at a crack until it decided to hold.

Thalen came back with a sack over his shoulder and triumph in his eyes. "Hooks," he said, lowering his voice like he expected someone to contest the claim. "And nails that aren't bent."

"Good," Kael said. "We need twenty more like that. Check the doorframes that still have doors. People leave their spare hooks under the lintel because they convince themselves they'll remember them later."

Thalen squinted. "How do you know that?"

"Because everyone thinks the same way when they're tired," Kael said. "Go."

We took a break on a stone step that had managed not to settle. The boys passed a skin between them like it was contraband. Kael was quiet, but it wasn't the quiet that tells you a man is measuring you. It was the kind that tells you he is counting the ways the wind talks to a wall.

"Which way first?" I asked, nodding toward the houses nearer the trees.

"Those," he said. "Less damage. And that one will have a cellar." He pointed to a low place where the earth humped slightly behind a broken railing.

"How can you tell?"

"Because whoever built it kept the kitchen on the cool side and left room in the slope. If you build for summer shade, you plan for storage. You know that."

"I do," I said. It came out softer than I meant.

We found the cellar. Half the shelves had fallen, and the jars that survived were new homes for the kind of life you don't choose. But at the back, under thick dust, three small crocks still wore wax that hadn't been gnawed by mice or time. I slid my fingers along the edges and felt the give. I willed them to be honey. When I cracked one and breathed in that familiar sweetness, it felt like a story I used to love. We set it carefully at the top of the steps for Gregor to carry.

We didn't speak much on the way back. The boys were tired in that good way and hadn't decided whether to admit it. The hall's windows threw out a warm promise as we crossed the square. Mira had hung three small bundles of herbs near the hearth, and the room smelled cleaner for it. Serin had made piles of clothes by size and scolded anyone who tried to steal from a smaller stack. I put the jars on the table in a line, and the children looked at them as if I'd brought them stars.

Kael showed Thalen how to measure a frame twice and cut once. He didn't make a speech about it. He simply handed the boy the saw and watched him miss the line the first time, then steadied his wrist and nodded when he found it on the second. Gregor sorted nails into a wooden bowl by length like he'd found religion. The space felt busy without turning frantic. When someone tripped, someone else steadied them. When a door didn't catch, Kael showed them where to plane and when to stop. He didn't have to be everywhere at once. He simply was where he needed to be.

The sun went down without ceremony and the cold came in low along the floor. We ate while the last of the light forgot us. I shared bread and a smear of honey from the precious jar. Serin pronounced it too sweet and tried to hide her second piece. No one pretended not to notice. We let her have it.

After dinner I took stock of our shelves. The room at the back that we were calling a pantry had walls that didn't mind a shelf being pressed against them. I made a list because a list pretends to be a plan. Salt. Oil. Soap. Needles. Thread. A length of canvas for a ground cloth. A hinge that won't shrug after a week. If someone had handed me a ledger and told me to keep this house running, I would have done it out of spite. Now I did it because the children had started to put their treasures on the hooks by their doors and call them theirs.

Kael moved to the far corner near the back door, where a cabinet leaned. He set the pulley we'd found on the table with the kind of care you give fragile things. He didn't touch it for a moment. He stood looking at it like a man deciding whether a thing wanted to be used or displayed. Then he gathered a short length of chain and a pin, and sat with one knee raised to bring his work closer to his hands.

"Why that first?" I asked.

"If the well gives us trouble when it gets colder, I want a way to take the weight without a second pair of hands," he said. "If the rope freezes, the pulley does the thinking."

He spoke like a man who had waited for water alone in a dark place. I didn't ask where.

Mira came by and set a cup near him. "For your stubbornness," she said. He accepted the cup as if that was the proper name for tea.

The evening slid into that hour when the fire is willing and the body begins to remember its own weight. Children drifted toward their rooms with blankets over their shoulders. Gregor carried a candle high and pretended it was a torch. Thalen had a few fresh, thin cuts along his palms that said he'd learned something. I touched one with salve. He bore it as if it were proof.

Kael worked on quietly where he sat. No flash of anything unnatural. Just measured strength and patience that had teeth. When he set the pulley aside and took up the broken chair, I watched the way he found the old glue line and scraped it clean. His hands are not the kind you expect to be gentle. They were gentle anyway. He fitted the joint once without pressure, tested the angle, changed it by a hair, and only then reached for the glue.

"Why do it by hand?" I asked, because I wanted to hear what he'd say.

"Because if I do it any other way, the room will expect it of me," he said, not looking up. "And then no one will believe in what their hands can do."

I didn't say what rose to my tongue—that I'm not sure belief has ever kept winter out. But I tucked the answer away. Some seeds need to sit in the dark before they're useful.

Mira shooed me toward the fire when she saw I was standing again. The bench knew me now. It didn't try to send me elsewhere. I stretched my hands to the heat and let it pull the ache from my forearms. Kael finished the joint, bound it with cloth until morning, and settled into the chair near the hearth. He had that way of taking up space while pretending not to. The shadows made a map over his cheekbones and jaw and then changed their mind.

We didn't speak for a while. The new building had learned how to make night sounds without sounding like a threat. Someone turned over in the first room off the hall. A door clicked softly where a latch made up its mind. The wind tested the shutters and found them sure.

Kael glanced toward the back door once, then back to the fire. It was the kind of look you cast when you don't trust the dark not to send a message. He didn't move to meet it.

"You'll teach Thalen to plane tomorrow," I said, more statement than question.

"If he still has fingers," he said, and the ghost of a grin arrived and left before it could be rude.

"He will," I said. "Serin will make sure. She's become the kind of tyrant we needed."

"She was always that," he said. "Now she's permitted."

I let myself lean into the warmth a little more. It felt earned.

By the time the last candle had been pinched out in the children's rooms, the fire had settled into a generous bed of coals. The building breathed, and I could breathe with it. I stared at the list I'd written and told myself it was possible. All of it. Even the parts that depended on a world that had always been stingy with us.

I turned my head to say as much to Kael and found him watching me. Not in the way men watch to see whether you're paying attention, but in the way someone looks when they are paying attention and didn't mean to be caught at it. I felt the look like I felt the fire—without needing to think about where it came from. The night slipped its hands into the room and made itself at home. I should have pushed myself up then and told my bones to go be dutiful in a bed that didn't remember other people's sleep. I didn't. I stood instead and gathered the last few bowls from the table, stacking them until they clicked together gently. I carried them toward the washbasin and put them down more carefully than I had to, so I'd have an excuse to stay in the pool of light by the hearth.

The fire was still warm, but most of the children had already drifted off, their chatter replaced by soft breathing and the occasional creak from the rafters. The new walls didn't groan like the old ones had, but the wind outside still whispered along their edges, reminding me the season was turning.

I rose, careful not to step on the blanket sprawled out at my feet, and started clearing the table. A few mismatched bowls clinked together in my hands as I stacked them, listening to the faint crackle of the hearth. Kael was still sitting in the chair by the fire, the shadows playing across his face in a way that made it impossible to tell what he was thinking.

When the last bowl was set aside, I caught him watching me.

He didn't speak. Just got up from the chair, the sound of his boots on the floorboards pulling my gaze up to him. He moved with deliberate ease, closing the space between us one step at a time. My pulse tripped over itself.

His hand lifted, fingers brushing through my hair with a touch so light I might've doubted it if not for the faint scrape of his nail against my scalp. He plucked something free—a stray thread, maybe—and let it fall.

But his hand didn't leave. It lingered there, warm and still, his fingers curling slightly like they weren't quite ready to let go. The air thickened between us, and for a heartbeat I forgot about the fire, the cold beyond the walls, even the way the boards creaked under his weight.

I looked up. His eyes weren't soft—never soft—but there was something in them, some shadowed pull that made me want to lean in instead of away. His jaw tightened, and I thought he might say something... or close the distance entirely.

The moment stretched, his fingers twitching once before he slowly lowered his hand.

"Better," he murmured, voice low. The word sounded incomplete, like he'd bitten off the rest of it.

He stepped back—but hesitated. His shoulders tensed, squaring again as though part of him wanted to stay closer. The flicker of conflict was gone almost as quickly as it appeared, replaced by the cool mask I was starting to recognize.

He turned, sinking back into the chair with measured care. "Don't stay up too late," he said, eyes flicking back to the fire.

I sat again, pretending to focus on the flames, but his gaze lingered for a fraction longer than necessary before he finally looked away. My skin still hummed where his fingers had been, and I didn't know whether to be grateful or disappointed that he'd walked away when he did.

The crackle of the fire filled the silence between us, neither of us speaking as the minutes stretched on. Outside, the wind picked up, carrying the scent of damp earth through the cracks in the shutters.

When the flames had burned low, I rose and banked them for the night. Kael didn't move until I reached for my blanket, and even then, it was only to glance up once before letting his eyes close.

I lay down facing the hearth, but my mind didn't quiet. Every time I closed my eyes, I saw that moment again—his hand in my hair, the way he'd almost leaned closer, and the sharp pull in my chest when he'd stepped away.

Sleep came eventually, but not before I caught myself wondering, not for the first time, if there was more to him than he wanted anyone to see.

Chapter Eighteen

Morning eased in quietly, a pale stripe of light skimming the floorboards and the faint hiss of the hearth remembering itself. I lay there long enough to count a few slow breaths, waiting for the building to complain. It didn't. The new walls settled like a satisfied cat.

Out in the corridor, small feet pattered. Someone laughed and tried to swallow it. The air smelled of porridge coaxed from very little and a hint of soap. When I stepped into the main hall, three of the children were already at the table, shoulders hunched in their coats. Kael leaned against the hearth as if he'd been born there, one hand around a steaming mug, the other braced on the mantel. He glanced over, gave the tiniest nod, and went back to whatever he was thinking.

"You're up late," he said.

"Sun's barely up," I told him, stealing a corner of bread.

"Still late."

He didn't smile, but it didn't sound like scolding. The morning found its rhythm quickly—bowls, spoons, Mira counting heads, Serin bossing a line of smaller ones with a string of mismatched buttons. Kael rarely raised his voice. He didn't have to. A look, a nod, a shifted bench, and somehow the room did what it needed to.

By midmorning he'd tapped two older boys—Thalen and Gregor— and handed me an empty sack. He didn't say "you're coming," just started toward the broken row of houses near the old square and trusted I'd fall in beside him. I did.

The frost underfoot was brittle, the air clean and sharp. We moved in a loose line, the boys ranging ahead and doubling back, Kael stopping to pry things from rubble: a dented tin plate, a mangled ladle, a lantern with most of its teeth. The slow, methodical way he worked made my jaw itch.

"You're ignoring the food stores," I said after the third house.

"We'll get to them."

"You grabbed lanterns over latches?" I held up the warped metal. "Light doesn't keep wind out."

"Light keeps people from burning the place down when they panic," he said, still crouched. "Locks come after they can see."

"Not when the gaps are big enough for a wolf to walk through."

He finally looked at me, eyes narrowing just a shade. "You want darkness and calm? Pick one. People don't panic in rooms that feel safe."

"Rooms feel safe when they're warm," I said, stepping closer. The frost cracked under my boot and the sound felt loud. "Start with warmth."

His gaze flicked to my mouth and back, quick and involuntary. "Structure keeps them alive."

"Heat keeps them human."

The wind threaded between us. For a breath the argument wasn't about lanterns or latches at all. I broke eye contact first, shoved the lantern into my sack, and kept moving.

The next cottage slumped into itself like a tired ox. Inside, a shelf had folded to the floor and pinned the lower half of a pantry door. Kael tested the frame with a knuckle, then shifted the fallen shelf just enough to make the door give an inch. A black sliver of space yawned beyond. You could smell earth and old vinegar.

"There'll be jars behind it," I said. "If the mice left anything."

"Board above your head looks honest," he said, eyeing the cracked joist. "The one at your back doesn't."

"I'll be quick."

"Elara—"

But I was already sliding in sideways. The door scraped my shoulder as I wedged through, cold wood catching at my coat. It was tighter than I liked. I got one arm into the dark space and felt along a tilted shelf until my fingers found the cool belly of a jar. Wax seal, give under my thumb. I grinned and reached for another. Something shifted above me, a tired groan from the shelf wedged across the door. I stilled.

"Hold," Kael said, voice low and close. He'd knelt without me hearing him. His hand came under the top shelf, his shoulder taking the weight. The wood creaked and settled. His other hand found my forearm, steadying me as I eased the first jar out and passed it back. The calluses against my skin were a shock of warmth in the cold pocket of space.

"One more," I murmured. "Maybe two."

"You get greedy when you're right," he said, breath a rough thread. "Be greedy fast."

I reached farther. My palm slid over a splinter and sliced open. I bit back a curse, found the jar, and wriggled it free. Kael took it with a gentle twist, then kept his hand on me a heartbeat too long—steadying, anchoring—before letting go.

"Out," he said.

"Two more," I said. "There's a small one behind the—"

"Elara."

The shelf above us complained again. I swallowed the argument, wiggled backward, and felt the door's edge scrape my ribs as I squeezed through. Kael held the weight until I cleared, then eased the shelf back down without cracking it. When I straightened, my palm was slick with blood.

"Told you," he said.

"About what?"

"Being greedy."

He tore a strip from the inside of his coat hem without blinking and wrapped my hand. He wasn't rough, just efficient. His thumb pressed the cloth tight, then eased when my breath hitched. He didn't look at my face. I didn't look at his.

We found a cellar two houses later half-swallowed by mud. The ladder was rotten, and the rungs broke under a test pole. The opening wasn't wide enough for Kael's shoulders.

"I'll go," I said.

"You'll fall," he said, already crouching. He braced one knee under the lip and laced his fingers. "Left boot here. I'll take your weight."

"You're sure?"

"Left boot," he repeated, voice even.

I set my foot in his palms and felt him rise a fraction, strong and careful. His other hand slid to my ankle to guide me. He looked away quickly, as if to give me privacy in a space without any. I ducked into the square mouth of the cellar, my shoulder scraping stone. The air inside was colder, damp with the memory of water. At the back, three low shelves held stout crocks and a tin whose lid had been tarred.

"I've got oil," I called softly, prying at the edge. "Maybe tallow. And something that smells like fennel."

"Pass what you can."

"I'll hand it to you," I said, and when I felt for his hand, it was already there—steady, warm, the grip careful. We found a rhythm: reach, lift, pass; his fingers closing over the weight, setting it aside, returning open and sure. A short, sharp skitter and a rustle from the corner made my heart kick, but the sound died. Mouse, nothing worse.

When there was nothing left worth the crawl, I turned to wriggle back toward the square of gray light. The lip was higher than I remembered going in. I reached. Couldn't quite catch it.

"Here," Kael said, and then his hands were at my waist, firm and unhesitating, lifting. The contact jolted through me like stepping from shade into sunlight. I grabbed the edge, shoved with my knees, and scraped out onto the floorboards, breath short.

His hands stayed a fraction too long at my waist. Not possessive. Reluctant to let go. When they did, he stepped back as if remembering himself.

"Thanks," I said, trying to pretend my voice hadn't gone quiet.

"Don't break my ladder," he said, deadpan. "I just decided it's mine."

"It's a hole in the ground."

"It's mine now," he said, and the corner of his mouth betrayed him for half a breath.

We loaded the sack with the oil, two crocks, and a tin of fat that would keep the pans honest for a month if we were careful. Thalen came in with a coil of wire he'd found under a lintel, looking like a king. Gregor had three clay mugs uncracked and a pride too large for his arms. We told them they'd done enough—half lie, half truth—and set off for the next row.

Past the mill stump, a low outbuilding still wore most of a roof. The door stuck halfway; Kael nudged it with his shoulder and it gave. Inside, a smell of damp straw and old leather, a scatter of tools on a bench, and a trunk with a strap that hadn't rotted through. He went for the bench. I went for the trunk.

"Careful," he said.

"Always," I said, which wasn't true and we both knew it.

The strap groaned, then broke in my hands and the trunk flopped open like a mouth. Inside—miracle—two wool blankets, moth-eaten at the edges but salvageable, a bundle of thick thread and three dull needles, and a small wooden box that chimed when I shook it. I glanced at Kael. He shook his head once: save surprises for later. I tucked the box away.

We were nearly done when a shadow slid across the doorway and paused. The boys stiffened. I looked up, a hand finding the knife at my belt out of habit. A fox stood in the opening, coat thin and eyes too big for its face. It sniffed once, then flowed away into the brush as if we weren't worth the trouble.

Thalen laughed too loudly. Gregor tried to turn it into a story immediately. Kael gave them each a look that said they were not required to be brave, only useful. They nodded like they understood. They did.

On the road back the sacks bit into our shoulders in the good way. The boys raced the last stretch because they couldn't help themselves. The hall's windows threw a soft gold that felt like an open palm. Mira met us at the door with a cloth over one shoulder and a frown she forgot to wear once she saw the bundle of blankets and the crocks. She didn't say thank you. The loosening at the corners of her mouth said enough.

We sorted the haul on the long table—wire, hooks, the needles and thread, the oil, the tin of fat, the blankets, three mugs, and a handful of nails the boys insisted had been forged by saints. I let them have their story. Kael set the lantern and a handful of parts at the corner and rolled his sleeves to his elbows again. The muscles in his forearms flexed in that quiet way men's arms do when they have nothing to prove and everything to do.

"Lanterns over latches?" I asked, dropping the thread into Mira's outstretched hands. "Really?"

"Light first," he said, already unscrewing a cap with his thumb. "They won't say they're scared. Their feet will. The lantern fixes it."

"And the latches?"

"After," he said. "When they sleep."

"When will you sleep then?"

"When I remember how." He said it like a joke and not a confession. I let it pass like a joke and not a worry.

He cleaned the chimney glass with a clean cloth and vinegar, teased the little gears until they turned smoothly, set the wick straight, and lit it long enough to prove it would obey. A pooled circle of warm light spread over the table. The children clapped as if he'd pulled a star into the room. Maybe he had, in a way. He snuffed it and set it back, satisfied.

We ate with our sleeves pushed up and our backs unknotting. The honey from yesterday stretched across bread in thin gold lines, and Serin pretended she didn't want more while hovering close enough to breathe on it. The tin of fat made the stew honest. The room sighed at once and the sound almost made me laugh. I didn't.

After the bowls were washed and stacked, the hall slid into its evening shape. Kael did a slow walk of the perimeter, touching hinges and testing latches, listening to the iron the way you listen to an animal—careful, respectful. He came back to the hearth and sat with a plank across his knees, sanding the splinters down with long, even strokes. No showy tricks. Just a man and a problem and the tool between them.

"You don't have to hover," he said when he noticed me near the table collecting the last of the mugs.

"I'm not hovering," I said. "I'm making sure you don't work yourself into the ground."

"When will you sleep then?"

"I'll sleep when—don't turn that around on me."

One corner of his mouth lifted. "Then stop trying to turn it on me."

I put the mugs down a little harder than I meant to. "Ever think people would follow you without you pushing so hard?"

"Pushing keeps them moving."

"Or it makes them push back."

He leaned back slightly, setting the plank aside. The fire popped. The shadows shifted along his jaw. Neither of us moved. A draft found a crack and sighed through it.

"You're not wrong," he said finally, voice low. "But the last time I waited for people to move on their own, they never did."

"What happened?"

His eyes slid away. "They paid for it."

I swallowed the next question because I didn't want to know even though I very much did. We sat in the sound of the hearth and the house breathing.

Most of the children drifted to bed early, heavy-limbed and wide-eyed with the kind of contentment that looks like exhaustion. The building held the quiet gently. Mira tapped the clock like it owed her a favor and disappeared down the corridor with a candle and three yawning shadows.

Kael set the plank aside and rose. He crossed the space between us slowly, each step measured like he was testing a bridge one board at a time. When he stopped, the distance between us was small enough that the warmth of him edged the edge of the fire's heat. He reached up and brushed a strand of hair back from my face, not rushed, not hesitant, just deliberate enough that my breath caught before I could hide it.

"Better," he murmured, the word low and unfinished.

For a second, I thought he might stay. His jaw flexed. His hand hovered like it hadn't decided whether to fall or anchor. The air seemed ready to collapse. Then he stepped back, distance returning in a breath he had to choose to take.

"Don't stay up too late," he said, retreating to the chair. His eyes caught mine for one last heartbeat before he looked to the fire.

I didn't touch the mugs. The skin along my hairline still hummed where his fingers had been. The room sounded too loud all at once, the crackle of the hearth and the soft hiss of the banked coals and the shy tap of a loose shutter.

I banked the fire when the embers dimmed and stretched the blanket over the bench. When I lay down, the only thing keeping me awake was the memory of his hand in my hair and the way it felt when he made himself walk away. The building breathed. I matched it. Sleep came like a reluctant guest, late and tired, and the last thought I let myself have was the one I've been trying not to feed: there is more to him than he wants anyone to see.

The first hint something was wrong wasn't the sound—it was the silence. The steady, shallow breathing of the surrounding children had lulled me into a half-doze, but a faint shift in the air pulled me upright. I listened. Nothing. Then—footsteps. Fast, unsteady, scraping against the stone in a way that made my gut tighten.

I stood before the latch even rattled. The door swung inward and Corin stumbled through, his face pale beneath the streaks of dirt and ash. His chest heaved like he'd been running for hours.

"Corin?" My voice caught halfway, but I crossed the room to steady him before the name had even left my lips.

He looked up at me, and that's when I saw the wet shine in his eyes—not from the cold, but from tears he was trying and failing to swallow. His mouth opened, but nothing came out except a sob that bent him forward.

Kael was there in an instant, silent but solid, taking the boy's weight with one hand on his shoulder. "Close the door," he told me without looking back.

The latch clicked into place, but the sound seemed small against the rush of blood in my ears. "Where's Bram?" I asked, already bracing for the answer.

Corin shook his head hard, like the motion might erase whatever he'd seen. His voice cracked when he finally spoke. "They—they killed him. Vaelor... the one with the silver braid. He—he didn't even give him a chance. I tried to wake Bram, but they were—there were too many. He didn't move. I ran when they started shouting. They didn't see me."

The name hit me like a cold stone. Vaelor. I'd heard the others whisper about him before—always in the kind of tone you used for curses or bad omens.

The words were jagged, torn apart by the edges of panic, but the meaning was clear enough.

I felt my stomach hollow out. Bram's easy grin, the way he'd tried to lift everyone's spirits with a stupid joke when we'd been short on food—gone. Just like that.

Kael's jaw tightened, the muscle along it flexing once, twice. His hand stayed on Corin's shoulder, steadying, but his gaze had gone distant and sharp, as if he were already seeing something past these walls. "How far?" he asked.

Corin sniffed, swiping at his face with his sleeve. "Half a mile. Near the old riverbank camp. They had... I don't know, five? Six?"

Kael gave a single, short nod, then stepped back. The absence of his touch made Corin sway, but I caught him and guided him to the bench near the hearth.

"I'll get him water," I said, but Kael was already at the door, pulling his cloak from the hook.

"Where are you going?" I asked, sharper than I meant.

His eyes met mine for a moment, and there was nothing soft in them—only something cold and honed. "To make sure they didn't follow him back."

He didn't wait for my reply. The door shut behind him with a heavy finality that made the room seem smaller.

Corin sat hunched over, both hands cupped around the mug I pressed into them. He didn't drink right away, just stared into the steam like he was afraid of what he'd see if he looked anywhere else.

I pulled a blanket from the stack and draped it over his shoulders. "You're safe here," I told him, keeping my voice low, steady. I wasn't sure if it was a promise or just something I needed to believe myself.

The minutes stretched, marked only by the pop of the fire and Corin's quiet sniffling. My mind kept circling the same thought—Bram out there alone, his body left in the cold.

It was nearly an hour before Kael came back. His boots were damp, his cloak streaked with mud, but what struck me most was his expression. He didn't speak right away, just latched the door and stood there for a breath, scanning the room like he was cataloging every detail.

"Nothing," he said finally, though his tone carried no relief. He moved to the hearth, holding his hands out toward the flames, but I noticed how his fingers curled slightly, not from the cold but from something he was holding back.

His shoulders were stiff, the kind of tension that came from rage kept on a short leash. His gaze flicked toward Corin—quick, assessing—and then away again. I wanted to ask him what he'd seen, what he planned to do next, but something in his stance told me the answers wouldn't be for me tonight. Instead, I sank back onto the bench beside Corin, offering him another mug of water. Across the room, Kael stared into the fire like it was the only thing keeping him from shattering.

Chapter Nineteen

The hall was warm when I stepped back inside, but it didn't touch me. I shut the door quietly, the weight of it sinking into the hinges with a dull finality. In my pocket, the folded scrap of paper pressed against my thigh like it wanted to etch itself into me — his handwriting sharp and deliberate, the crescent moon at the bottom drawn with a precision that made it feel like a blade.

Elara sat with Corin near the hearth, her arm stretched across the back of his chair, her voice low. He was small and hollow-eyed, clutching the mug she'd given him as if letting go would take away the only thing keeping him anchored. The firelight caught in her hair, weaving copper and gold through the strands, and for a moment I just stood there, letting the sound of the crackling wood carry between us.

The note burned in my pocket, louder in my head than the surrounding room. His handwriting. That mark. An invitation I hadn't asked for.

One by one, the others drifted from the table to the sleeping quarters I'd built, doors closing with soft clicks. Elara rose to guide Corin to his room, her hand gentle against his back. Whatever she murmured made his shoulders ease, even if only for a moment. She turned back toward the hearth and caught my gaze.

"You're not sleeping?" she asked.

"Not yet."

Her eyes lingered like she might press for a reason, but instead she let it go, returning to the chair without another word.

The silence settled heavy. The kind of quiet that thickens when everyone else is behind closed doors, when the only light left is from the fire. That was when I moved.

The night bit at me the second I stepped outside, cold gnawing through the seams of my coat. I didn't take the road. I let the trees swallow me, my magic already curling low under my skin, ready to be loose.

The first sentry didn't even get his hand to his weapon. Steel punched up under his ribs and out through his spine, his breath breaking on the way down.

The second tried to shout, but the shadows answered faster, closing over his mouth and nose. His panic flared in his eyes before my grip twisted his neck hard enough to splinter bone.

The camp erupted in shouts, but they were jagged, chaotic — too late to be organized. My magic tore weapons from their hands, dragged them into the dirt before the blade finished what it started. I didn't stop to see who they were, didn't care. They were here. They'd chosen this side.

A boy, barely past adolescence, froze when our eyes met. Someone older stepped in front of him. It made no difference. Steel didn't pause.

By the time I reached the largest tent, my hands, my shirt, even the edge of my vision felt steeped in red. The air was thick with iron and smoke.

Vaelor was waiting. His silver hair was loose, falling across his shoulders, and that smirk — gods, I'd seen it before.

"I heard you were still breathing," he said, circling slowly, his voice low and taunting. "Could've sworn you learned your place after last time. But then again..." He tilted his head, eyes narrowing. "Maybe you've forgotten what it's like to fail the people you love."

The words slid under my skin, finding the place I'd buried them.

"You didn't see her, did you?" he went on. "You were facedown in the dirt when it happened. Didn't even get to watch your sister beg. She lasted longer than the rest, though. I'll give her that." His smile sharpened. "Her eyes looked just like yours when she realized no one was coming."

Something in me broke loose, my voice came out cool and collected, charged with a rage I had no way to explain. "Do me a favor?"

"Oh-" He smirked at me, his ego dripping out with every elongated word. "And what exactly would that favor be bo-"

"Say hello to Mēnô for me."

The blade drove forward before his smirk could falter. Steel ripped through his throat, hot spray hitting my face. He choked, staggered, but my second strike buried deep at the base of his skull, cutting off the sound entirely.

I stood there, breathing hard, the night pressing close. Then I stepped over him and back into the camp, making sure there was nothing left alive but me, me and the note that reminded me my secret's time was running out.

The hall was silent when I stepped inside, shadows stretching long over the new stone floor. The kids were already gone to the back rooms I'd built, the door to their sleeping quarters shut tight. Only the low light spilling from the kitchen broke the dark, a soft gold that pulled me toward it despite the weight of the note in my hand.

I could still see the handwriting burned into my mind, the jagged moon symbol slashed at the bottom like a promise. I'd read it more times than I should have since finding it outside, my thumb rubbing over the crease until the paper felt thin. I knew exactly what it meant—what it wanted me to feel. And it worked. My chest still felt too tight. My skin still felt too hot.

The fight replayed in my head with every step I took, vivid and sharp. The snap of bone when I broke a raider's arm. The wet sound of my blade cutting deep. The way Vaelor's last breath sprayed warm across my face when I opened his throat. None of it felt finished. The rush still coiled in me like it was looking for somewhere else to go.

That's when I saw her.

Elara was standing at the counter, sleeves pushed up, her hair tumbling loose down her back. She was cutting bread, her shoulders relaxing with the easy rhythm of it. My eyes traced her shape in the light — the way her hips shifted slightly when she leaned forward, the faint curve of her neck when she tilted her head. Something in my chest pulled tight enough to hurt.

I didn't remember moving at first. One moment I was standing in the doorway, the next I was closing the distance, the fight still pounding in my veins.

She looked up just as I reached her, surprise flickering in her eyes. "Kael—"

I caught her waist and lifted her onto the counter before she could say more. The knife clattered from her hand, forgotten. My body moved on instinct, stepping between her knees, my palms braced against the counter on either side of her hips. She smelled faintly of sun-warmed bread and the faint trace of lavender from the soap she used, but under it all, I still tasted blood in my mouth.

Her breath hitched when my hands slid to her thighs, fingers curling into the fabric of her skirt. I didn't stop to think. I didn't want to. The same heat that had driven my blade through Vaelor's chest pushed me forward, and I caught her mouth with mine.

She kissed me back immediately — soft at first, then deeper, harder, like she'd been waiting for this as much as I had. My hand slid up her side, under the hem of her shirt, my thumb brushing bare skin. She trembled beneath me, her hands finding my shoulders, then the back of my neck, pulling me closer.

The taste of her pushed the fight further into my blood until I wasn't sure which one of us was breathing harder. I caught her lower lip between my teeth, not gentle, and she let out a small, breathless sound that made my control slip another inch. My other hand slid to the small of her back, pressing her against me until there was no space left between us.

Her skirt bunched higher under my hands, the fabric soft against my knuckles, her thighs warm and tense. One of her hands tangled in my hair while the other gripped my shirt, dragging me down until my mouth found the curve of her throat. I kissed there, slow, then harder, my teeth grazing skin until she gasped.

Clothes started to shift — her shirt tugging loose under my hands, my own half-untucked from my waistband where her fingers gripped it. Every inch of skin I touched made it harder to think, harder to remember why I couldn't have this.

I pressed my forehead to hers, our breathing ragged, my hands still resting high on her thighs. If I kept going, there wouldn't be a way to stop. And as much as I wanted to claim her right here, I knew once I crossed that line, I wouldn't give her the choice to turn back.

"This—" My voice came rough, low. "This is a mistake."

Her lips parted, confusion flickering there, but I didn't give her time to speak. I stepped back, forcing the space between us, the loss of her warmth hitting me like cold water.

The note burned in my pocket, the moon symbol heavy in my mind. I didn't look back at her when I left the kitchen, the sound of my boots against the floor was the only thing breaking the silence, the door of the hall closing behind me. I sat down on the front steps, digging the paper out of my pocket, hoping the cool air would cool the fire burning inside me, convince me to leave and never turn back to keep them safe, the pull of just knowing she's inside makes it impossible. I thumbed open the note, the words etched in what feels like prophecy.

The sunlings can't hide you forever. I know where you are.

Chapter Twenty

Morning knocks softly and waits for someone polite enough to answer. I light a taper from the last honest orange in the hearth and coax flame into the kindling until it remembers how. The boards have kept a little of the night's warmth; the doors to the sleeping rooms breathe with the small rhythms behind them. I straighten the boots by the entry, turn the latch twice just to feel it catch clean, and tip the kettle to listen to what water we have left from yesterday. Enough for tea and the first wash. Not enough for the second. There rarely is.

Kael stands at the narrow window with a cup he hasn't touched, watching the ridge admit the light in thin strips. He doesn't move for the room, only for the world beyond it—the way animals do when they hear what we don't. The cup warms and cools in his hand. Whatever lives in his pocket lives there still. He hasn't looked at it this morning, not with his eyes.

"Boots," I whisper when Corin's hair appears first, then the rest of him in a blanket-twisted shirt. I set his pair where his feet will find them and tilt my head toward the table. "And porridge before it forgets itself."

He makes the face he always makes—as if porridge is a concept designed to offend him—and then eats because my hand finds the back of his neck and his body remembers what anchor feels like. Loryn drifts in behind him, humming the tail end of a song that was probably meant to be happier than she makes it sound. She lays out the bowls in a straight line, nudges one into place until the line is true, steps back and nods at her own work. Miran arrives last, small swagger loaded with more hope than sense, and tries to take the door without taking breakfast. Kael catches his hood without looking, transfers a bundle of kindling into his hands, and tips his chin at the fence line.

"Three posts," he says. "Then back."

Miran tries for a sigh that implies deep tragedy and only gets halfway there. "Fine," he says, and then to me, with a grin he thinks I don't see: "I'll be fast."

"Be steady," I answer. "The fence keeps better company than speed."

He salutes with the kindling and goes.

I pour tea for my hands as much as my mouth and test the kettle's temper by the handle. Not too hot; good. I set a cup near Kael's elbow on the window ledge. He doesn't startle. He doesn't thank me, either, which is fine. Some courtesies shrink when you make them too loud.

The knife I use for peeling has decided to retire. I reach for the better one—the one sharp enough to split hairs and arguments—and slide it under a folded towel when I'm done. The children don't need to stare at a blade hungry for the wrong work. I gather onions from the bin. The light off their skins is the kind that makes you think about summer too long and forget where you are.

I cut the first one in half and lay the flat side down to make the board safer. My hands remember the rhythm. Heel, push, scoop, pile. The smell opens my eyes and my chest both; I don't wince. I think while I cut. If I keep the blade moving, my thoughts will flow around the edge and not straight into it.

The first thought is the children. It's always the children. Loryn's humming has gotten louder—she does that when she's making peace with a task—and if I don't remind her to breathe while she concentrates, she'll hold her breath and pretend she didn't. "In through your nose," I say without looking up. She inhales obediently, then grins because she knows I know.

Corin's bowl has taken the shape of his spoon and looks offended. I slide him another half-scoop when he isn't watching, and he accepts it like a man dealing with fate. "Story tonight?" he asks around a mouth too full for questions.

"If the chores are done, and the salt doesn't sulk," I say, wiping my knife clean between onions. "The fish that wasn't a fish?"

He nods, cheeks round with porridge, satisfied by the certainty of a story that ends the same way every time. Certainty is a precious metal around here. You portion it carefully.

The second thought is the village. Not just ours—ours is a hall stitched together from other people's losses and our insistence—but the wider circle of huts and doors that were doors and the good fences that had to be taken down and hauled here when we decided to stop pretending to be temporary. The roof tarps will need checking before the day tilts; yesterday's wind set its teeth in the canvas and shook. Pegs will have loosened. Ropes will have argued with knots and lost. I'll need Miran's hands on a ladder and Loryn's eyes on the seams and Corin's patience with buckets. We'll need more wood by night. We'll need to salt meat before the weather decides to mean it.

The third thought is a mouth, and it isn't mine. I don't let that thought get all the way formed. I put another onion under the blade and counted three strokes to steady it. The corner of my lip stings suddenly and I wish it didn't remind me why.

"Your sleeves," I say aloud to no one in particular because the sleeves on small bodies are perpetually near stew and flame. Loryn rolls hers before I finish the sentence, eyes never leaving the thread she's worrying into a proper line. "Already," she says. Corin tugs at his and forgets what the second arm is for halfway through; I do the rest and kiss the crown of his head before I can think better of it. He pretends not to like that. He leans into it anyway.

I cut the last onion thin and lay it in the pan with a slow handful of salt. The sound the sizzle makes is the sound of things agreeing. Kael turns from the window like the light finally moved somewhere new. He tests the door latch, turns the bar, nods once at its clean glide, then lays the mechanism out again like he's listening for a complaint in the metal that only he can hear.

"You oiled the pins?" I ask, cracking dry sage into the pan, the scent leaping up like it's been waiting for company.

"Three drops," he says. "Too much and grit loves you."

"Grit loves me anyway." I stir the onions and the sage until they stop arguing. My mind wanders, because it wants to, because last night still sits on my skin like a print that didn't lift. The moment keeps replaying without my permission—hands on my waist, the counter's edge at the backs of my thighs, his mouth, the way the room forgot everything that wasn't either of us. The way I forgot, too. Then the way he pulled away, and the way his breath sounded when he called it a mistake.

A good pan tells you the truth about your heat. I take it off the flame for a moment to bring it back into the range where food becomes itself and not a cautionary story. He glances over like he approves that I didn't scorch anything in a mood.

"We'll bring the racks around midafternoon," I say into the space between us that isn't as wide as it looks. "If the wind shifts, the smoke will sulk."

"It'll shift." He sets the latch back in the door and turns it slow, testing the tongue, every tooth of the plate. When it clicks, he lets himself be pleased for a heartbeat before he remembers not to show it.

Miran returns, lighter in the bundle, heavier in pride. "The fence liked me," he announces, hair wet at the ends, rain having found him in only the places he forgot to hide. "It told me so."

"Did it," I say. "What else did it say?"

"That I should bring it more wood."

"A wise fence," I say, and tip my chin toward the stack by the shed. "Go make it happy. And watch your feet on the back step. It's thinking about being slippery."

He's halfway out the door when he stops and looks at Kael with too much bravado and not enough man to wear it. "Can I tie knots later?"

"When your hands aren't trying to outrun your head," Kael says, which is his way of saying sooner than you think and longer than you want. Miran nods like he's just been entrusted with a dynasty and runs.

Loryn puts the bowls in a neat row where the heat is less likely to get ideas. "Can I take the left side for the tarps," she asks without looking up, "or do you want me to fetch pegs?"

"Left side," I say, because she's good with lines. "Miran can fetch pegs when he's done making the fence feel admired."

Corin has decided the spoon now belongs in his pocket. "Not a terrible idea," I say. "But we'll need it to be a spoon in a minute. Where do spoons live?"

"In my pocket," he says.

"Try again."

"In the bowl." He scowls, returns it, and looks very pleased with himself for obeying.

By the time the onions go translucent and sweet, my eyes have stopped watering, and the morning has decided to be gray. I add water, barley, last night's rabbit, a handful of dried mushrooms crumbled between my fingers, and the promise of thyme. The pot accepts all of it like it has been hungry for exactly these things. It isn't stew yet. It will be if the day lets it.

Kael wipes his hands on a clean cloth without noticing the old red that still insists on living in the seams near his knuckles. He scrubs and the color holds. He notices. I hand him the finer soap without saying anything, and he takes it without refusing what it is.

He doesn't mention last night. I don't, either. But the space where the mention would go feels like a door that's been left ajar; air moves through whether you want it or not.

"Would you check the small hinge on the pantry," I ask, not because I can't but because I want his hands on something that admits his touch makes it better. "It complained last night when I opened it wrong."

He crosses the room with that quiet the boards respect and kneels at the lowest hinge with his ear close, like hinges confess to him. The line of his neck under his collar remembers my mouth. I look away hard enough to feel it in my jaw.

Loryn steps onto the bench to reach the hooks for the tarps. "Hand," she says, and I give her mine without thinking, supporting her shin just above the boot while she leans and tests the cord. She's steady. She always has been. She learned to be when the world stopped offering steadiness in her size. "Left first," she says, and the words feel good on her tongue. She's always loved directions. Directions mean control. Control means safety. Or the promise of it.

Corin has discovered that barley swells into interesting shapes. He talks to the pot in a whisper. "We're friends," he says. "But you can't jump." The pot agrees by steaming politely.

When the first spit of rain kisses the panes, I put half the bread under a cloth and half on the board. "We'll need hands," I say, and the small hands attached to the small bodies present themselves immediately. I set them to tasks with names: Ladler. Carrier. Filler. Taster. Namer is the last job; Loryn gives the stew a name so it will behave for us. She calls it "Good Enough." She's wicked when she wants to be.

Kael looks up at that, mouth almost smiling before his eyes remind it not to. He pretends to test the hinge again. The hinge behaves better than it deserves.

We eat on benches that learned our weight last month and learned our grief the month before that. Corin asks for the fish story and gets it with the same number of pauses and the same wrong voice for the fish, which is how he knows he's safe enough to get angry about a fish. Miran asks when he'll be allowed to use the good knife. "In spring," I say, which means not yet and not no. Loryn asks no questions at all. She watches Kael's hands while he talks and learns the shapes of things instead.

When the bowls are empty, I scold them into washing and scold myself into letting them be loud while they do it. Loud is good. Loud means nothing outside the door is loudly disagreeing with our existence.

The rain makes the air taste like tin and leaf. We fetch the tarps and climb the ladder in turns. My sleeves soak through at the elbow and my hair escapes its pin exactly when it always does—when I've convinced myself it won't. Kael resets the ties with the patience of a man who would rather do something once correctly than twice, almost. When I misjudge the last rung and my heel slips, his hand is on my waist before the floor becomes an idea. The touch is practical. The touch is anything but. I feel it in my teeth.

"Thanks," I say to my collar, because that's where my voice stopped.

"Watch the rung," he says.

"It wasn't the rung," I answered.

He files it away. I can tell by the way his shoulder softens and then doesn't.

By midafternoon the room smells like stew and wet wool. The stove hums contentedly, proud of itself. I fish for the bone in the pot and find it clean; the stew is ready to be told to wait. I set it on the back, wipe the ladle, count bowls, and catch myself counting occupants twice, the way I do when my hands are busy and my head is somewhere I don't want it to go. Everyone is here who should be. That should always be enough. It almost is.

I carry the bucket to the stores and find the hinge ready to tell me it resents being ignored. I open the door a little to keep the pitch from building, and Kael appears behind me like he's been listening to the same complaint. "I'll take it," he says, and puts a hand over mine to move the door half an inch right. We both freeze. The air does, too. He removes his hand first, slow, like he's taking a bandage off something that might bleed if he's cruel. The hinge, traitor, stops complaining as if pleased to have caused a scene.

"I'd thank you," I say, attempting a smile that belongs to lighter rooms, "but I don't want to encourage the furniture."

"It needs no encouragement," he says, and for a heartbeat we are two people who can speak easily about nothing without getting swallowed by everything sitting between us.

"Racks," I say, rescuing myself from that precipice. "If we set them now, the salt can go on before the light sulks."

"I'll bring them round," he says, and takes his coat even though the rain has decided to be merely insistent now instead of cruel.

When he lifts the first rack from the shed, I can see the old notches where a different village wore these before we did. He sets the legs in the grooves we carved yesterday; I test the sway and find it acceptable. We work in silence so companionable I nearly forget that last night's heat still lives in my skin. Nearly.

The salt is the good kind, hoarded and wrapped and kept from damp with rituals Loryn invented and we all respect. We lay thin layers, pat them like infants, tell them what job they have. Children listen better when you tell them the job and the purpose; salt is the same. Miran sneaks a pinch like its candy. He puckers and pretends he didn't learn anything. Corin watches the crystals melt and then not melt, disappointed. "It's slow," he says, scandalized.

"Most good things are," I say. "Now fetch me the short peg."

He fetches the wrong one and then the right one after I look at him. Loryn ties the last knot with the kind of pride a small queen wears when her kingdom is straight and square. Kael checks the corner posts with the same focus he uses on enemies and tools. He approves with a tidy nod. Approval from him feels like weather: it doesn't ask permission before it lands.

When we're done, the rain has decided to pretend it never had opinions about us. The light goes to a gray that can't make up its mind. I send the children to the back with clean shirts and promises about stories. Miran asks how many chores count toward a story; I say "enough," and he accepts the answer because it's today.

I wash my hands in water gone cloudy with onion and barley and a little of my stubbornness. I wipe them on my apron and then on nothing for good measure. The room is quieter when the small doors shut, but it's not empty; it's like a chest with something valuable inside it, waiting to be opened.

Kael sits in his place between here and the world. He is not a guard, and he is not a guest; he is a fact. I stand by the stove longer than I need to, turning the spoon once, twice, listening to how the stew sounds when it thinks it's alone. Everything around us makes the noise it knows: hinge, rope, stove, wood. We're the only things pretending we can be silent.

He looks at me and away. I look at him and don't. The mark he left at the corner of my mouth this time yesterday is gone; my fingers go there anyway and find only skin that remembers more than it shows. I'm not sure if I'm relieved or disappointed. I settle on both and put them on the same shelf.

"Your hands," I say finally, because something has to go first. "Hold them out."

He does. The cuts on his knuckles have been scrubbed raw. I take the fine salve and set a careful fingertip to each place, smoothing the skin where it's tried to pull together too fast and will only tear if you make it hurry. He watches my mouth while I work. I don't let that stop me. When I'm done, I wrap a clean strip of linen around the worst of it and tie it neat, knot set to the side so it won't rub while he holds a blade. I press my thumb to the inside of his wrist to seat the cloth. His pulse meets mine there and for one stretched second neither of us pretends we're only talking about bandages.

"That'll hold," I say. "Don't pick at it."

"I won't," he says, and then—because some part of him can't quite help itself— "unless it needs picking."

The laugh that leaves me is small and traitorous. It warms the room enough that the stove sighs like it takes credit.

We feed ourselves after we feed the fire. Loryn eats standing because she's reading a scrap she found under the bench and refuses to be parted from it; I let her. Miran negotiates for seconds with a seriousness that would do well at court. Corin insists his bowl is the same size as mine and triumphs when I admit defeat. Kael eats like a man who remembers hunger too clearly and distrusts the idea of fullness. I let him take the last ladle. I pretend I didn't.

When bowls are stacked and small bodies washed and bedtime declared a fact, I pass from door to door and settle things that ask to be settled: blanket edges, lamp wicks, arguments that thought they could grow in the dark. Loryn tucks a wooden bird under her pillow and pretends she isn't scared of what sleeps in trees. Corin turns onto his side and his brow smooths. Miran asks if knots can be learned in dreams. "Yes," I say. He grins like he knew it.

Back in the hall, I close the last door and lean my shoulder against the frame for one breath longer than necessary. Kael watches because that's what he does. He stands when I step away like he's decided the room requires it.

Outside is the part of the evening that belongs to him. He takes his coat, checks the latch with the smallest, fondest tug, and opens the door like you open a mouth you're not sure will forgive you for what you put in it. The world smells like wet leaf and wood and the kind of cold that clarifies. He pauses on the threshold—not for me; he doesn't ask—more as if he's measuring the distance between the room and the line of trees. He goes.

I sit and don't. The quiet between us swells until it becomes something I could hold if I were foolish enough to try. I sew three stitches into a loose hem and tie two knots that would embarrass me earlier in the day. I stand and wipe a place on the table that isn't dirty. I sit again because the chair expects me to. I tell myself I'm not waiting and then wait, anyway.

He comes back with rain tucked into the hem of his coat and night leaning against his shoulder. He doesn't say if the shadows said anything worth repeating. I don't ask. He takes the chair near the door and settles with that posture that looks like a promise to a room. It is a promise to me, too, though I don't say that aloud. We hold the quiet together without letting it break.

I blow the lamp when the coals say they have enough light left to be kind. In the glow, his profile softens into something I might have let myself believe in once—if the world hadn't done such a thorough job of making belief look foolish. I lie down on the bunk behind the curtain and shut my eyes and listen. To the small doors breathing. To the hinge that has decided to behave. To the rain deciding not to. To the steady measure of his presence between us and everything else.

When sleep comes, it takes my hand like an old friend who still owes me. My last thought is of onions going soft in a pan and the way his pulse felt under my thumb, both of them small answers to a day that has asked too many questions.

Chapter Twenty-One

Rain took the sky and did not give it back. It came in honest and steady, a quiet hand pressing on the canvas eaves and a soft hiss through the pines, turning the clearing into a single held breath. The hall kept its own rhythm—stove ticking, rope humming, the small doors along the back opening and closing with the whisper of children moving through their morning.

Loryn took the bench beside me and counted knots out loud, the way she does when she needs the world to agree to order. "One... two... three..." She tightened each tie like the weather was keeping score.

"The left side will pull if the wind turns," I told her. "Double that one."

She did, neat and sure, her fingers quick as my mother's had been. Miran tramped past with two buckets brimming like a challenge.

"Stop filling like you're proving something," I said, taking one before the water taught him about elbows. "Half-full means twice as many trips and twice as useful."

"Twice as useful," he repeated, liking the taste of it, and tipped half back without sulking. He flashed a grin at Kael that was all hero-in-training.

Kael moved through the room like a shadow with a spine—rope over one shoulder, attention pointed at the door even when his hands were doing something else. He glanced up at the tarp seam Loryn had just tied and I caught the small nod he tried to hide. Approval, quiet and unspent.

"Fence line first," he said to Miran without breaking stride. "Keep to the path. No shortcuts."

"I know the path," Miran said, which is eight-year-old for Watch me, anyway.

"Good," Kael answered. "Keep it company."

The kettle breathed into a low rattle. I poured hot water over mint for him without asking, set the cup on the window ledge where his hand would find it when it remembered to. He didn't look; he still said, "Thank you," in that low way of his that made the room go as attentive as a dog.

By midmorning, the light had gone flat and cool. The forest beyond the fence blurred into one piece of dark. I took stock: racks ready for salt, pegs cut and stacked, hinges behaving. The firewood pile, though—still wearing yesterday's hurry. Uncovered, neat, getting wet by the minute.

Kael saw it the same moment I did. "Firewood's getting soaked," he said, already reaching for his coat. "If we let this go, we'll be looking at cold suppers for a week."

"I'll help," I said. It wasn't a question.

His mouth did that almost-smile that wasn't for anyone else. "Come on."

The rain prickled my skin as we stepped out; the kind that settles everywhere, even under clothes. The woodpile sat along the hall's lee, squared off and proud and very obviously damp. The tarp had slipped halfway, the wind worrying one corner like it had a grudge.

Kael tossed me one edge. "Hold this."

I caught it; our fingers brushed, a clean, brief spark that didn't pretend to be anything else. The wind snapped the tarp, and I had to lean into it with my whole weight. He stepped in behind me, chest close to my back, his arm coming around to catch the high corner.

"Higher," he said, voice near my ear. The word went straight down my spine.

I reached up, rain soaking my sleeves, and felt his hand cover mine for half a beat while he adjusted the angle. Warm, even in the wet. My breath jumped. He felt it. His fingers flexed once before he let go.

"You're freezing," he murmured, attention still on the tarp, like it would be less dangerous if he aimed the concern somewhere practical.

"You're dripping," I said, which wasn't an answer and still was.

He huffed something that might have been a laugh if it had remembered how. The tarp bucked in a gust; we rode it down together, edges slithering across the stacked rounds until the fabric lay where it should. He anchored corners with split logs and his neat, fast knots. I mirrored him on the other side, ignoring the way my hands wanted to shake.

"Good," he said finally, scanning the cover like it had to pass a test to stay. He raked wet hair back with his fingers, and his eyes found mine and held a fraction too long. Something unguarded sat there for just a moment—then he shut it. "Inside," he said, softer than he meant to.

We went back in with rain stitched into the hems of our coats. The hall felt warmer by comparison. Loryn had moved to the ladder to the loft and was counting rungs. "Rope length," she explained when I looked at her. "In case one breaks."

"It won't," Kael said—and then, catching the look I gave him, "Count anyway."

She smiled, quick and private.

I put the kettle back on to hush it. I could feel him in the room the way you feel a storm in your teeth. Every time I moved, he was one step to the side of where I expected him to be—out of the way, close enough to catch if I slipped. He checked the pantry hinge like he'd promised, seating the tiny screw with his knife tip, testing, adjusting. The hinge sighed, pleased with itself. Ridiculous to feel that same small warmth in my chest at a piece of metal doing exactly what it should.

He came around the table just as I did. His hip brushed mine. Nothing in it—except plenty. He stopped, heat and rain and him, and didn't pretend it hadn't happened.

"Don't," he said, not unkind.

"Don't what," I asked, too fast.

"Pretend you didn't feel that." He picked up two pegs and a crooked one with the casual attention of a man choosing where not to place his focus. "It's worse."

"You're the one pretending," I said, softer. "Every time."

This time he did smile, a bare, dangerous flash that went through me like someone had pulled tight on a tie-down. "Probably."

Miran blew back in, half-drowned and very proud. "Three posts," he reported, salute and all. "I checked twice."

"With your eyes or your head," I asked, handing him a dry cloth.

"Eyes," he said, offended. Then, grudgingly: "Mostly."

"Mostly counts." I pointed at the twine. "Tie me six lengths. Elbow to fist."

He unfolded his elbow grandly and measured like a merchant, cutting with grave attention. Kael glanced over, approved. The room settled around the work the way a body settles around breath.

We ate early, because we've learned to put food in before moods turn. Bread, stew, steam making the windows ghosts. Loryn asked if the creek would be too high to visit later; I told her yes if the rain kept on. Kael said, "It will," and then gave her a small apology with his eyebrows for telling the sky what it would do.

He stayed near the door after, watching the yard like he expected it to misbehave. I fetched pitch from the shed and nearly went out without saying; caught myself and said anyway, "Shed," because promises only work if someone hears them. He didn't turn. He still said, "Back in three," like the door understood numbers.

The step down to the shed had grown slick with a thin stain of moss; my heel found it. My body tipped an inch farther than it should have. His hand closed on my waist from nowhere, firm and unquestioning, and put me back where gravity meant me to be.

"You alright," he asked, the words plain. His thumb stayed at my hip a beat longer than necessary, a heat brand through wet cloth. The rest of me pretended to belong to me.

"I was," I said, sharper than I intended. He didn't flinch, didn't apologize, just took his hand away with that quiet, ruthless care of his.

"Hold the lid," he said, and I did, because the lid needed holding and because my temper needed work more than it needed words.

We brought the pitch back, set the brace, checked the line of the shelves. He wiped his knuckles on a clean cloth; the red that had dried in the seams didn't obey. I reached for the salve without asking. He didn't pull away when my fingers found his wrist. His pulse met mine like it recognized me. I smoothed the salve over each cut, tied the linen neat, pressed my thumb into the inside of his wrist to seat the knot. He watched my mouth while I worked. I pretended not to notice.

"Don't go out there today," I said, tying off. "Inner ring only."

He studied me, like a man weighing a map against weather. "Why?"

"Because it's wet," I said, hearing how foolish it sounded. Then, more honest: "Because you didn't sleep."

"I do fine without it."

"You do," I said. "Until you don't."

He breathed out. "Inner ring," he said. "Twice."

"Twice," I echoed, hearing more relief in it than I liked. He heard it too. He didn't make me pay for it.

The afternoon stretched long and damp. We set the new brace, tightened the ropes on the wood cover again when a gust tried to take it, and moved around each other with that practiced near-miss of people who have either learned from each other or refuse to admit they have. Loryn studied Kael's throw with a length of string and a peg; he corrected the angle of her wrist with two fingers, light. Miran counted the drip of the one honest leak like it was a race. Corin lined wooden soldiers under the bench and informed them—sternly—not to do anything stupid.

"Like what," I asked him.

"Like be loud," he whispered, as if the hall could be tricked into quiet by telling toys not to misbehave.

Rain softened to a finer thread near evening. The hall held a pocket of gold around the stove. I carried a bag of scraps to the bin by the shed; the foxes that pretended not to be ours would come later with their sly, hopeful bodies. Something in the line of trees flickered. Not a person. A suggestion of one. I stayed half a heartbeat too long, trying to turn a shape into a fact.

Footsteps crossed the yard, quiet and sure. Kael arrived like he always did when the world changed its mind a degree—just ahead of the problem and entirely too close to me. "Inside," he said, not harsh.

"I'm feeding something besides us," I said. "Hardly a crime."

"It is if it brings the wrong company." He took my elbow and guided me toward the door with pressure that wasn't negotiable. I could have yanked my arm back. I didn't. His body placed itself between mine and the trees by reflex. The part of me that hates being handled and the part that likes waking up both shouted. Survival won; it usually does.

"Don't wander out of my reach again," he said at the threshold, and it wasn't a request or an order. It was older.

"Since when is your reach a map," I asked, stepping in first so we used ground I chose.

"Since someone decided we were worth finding," he said. He didn't raise his voice. He didn't have to.

I warmed my hands at the stove for the principle of it. He kept his attention aimed at the yard, like the trees owed him an apology.

"You see someone," I asked.

"No," he said. Then added, "Not yet."

"Not yet doesn't count," I said.

"It does to me."

I left the argument there because all I'd win was the sound of my own voice.

We cleaned up early for once, not because there was less to do but because the day felt like a song, you'd rather not hear the last verse of. The children ate too fast, went to their beds without having to be asked twice. Loryn tucked a wooden bird under her pillow and asked for the quiet story; I told it and watched her eyes stay open with trust. Miran asked if knots could be learned in dreams. "Yes," I said. "Better there, sometimes." Corin fell asleep mid-argument with his second spoon, stubborn even in surrender.

On my way back through the hall, I caught myself in the small mirror propped by the door: hair damp, mouth set, eyes doing that thing where they tell too much and dare you to name it. I looked like a person doing fine. I looked like a liar. Both were true.

Kael stood at the door with his coat. I stepped into his path like I meant to.

"You promised the inner ring," I said.

"I did."

“Twice.”

“Twice,” he agreed.

“And then you stay.”

He studied me like there was print on my face. “And if I don’t.”

“Then I follow you,” I said, sick of begging myself not to be this person and deciding to be her, anyway. “And you’ll spend an hour pretending not to mind.”

“I don’t pretend,” he said, flat.

“You do,” I said, just as plain. “You pretend you don’t want and you pretend you don’t worry. You pretend last night was a mistake like the word makes it smaller.”

His hands didn’t move, and that was the loudest thing in the room. “Don’t start this now.”

“Why not now. When? When you don’t come back? When I have to tell the children the door is what keeps them safe because the man behind it couldn’t be bothered to carry his body home?”

“I always come back,” he said.

“Always is a big promise,” I answered.

He breathed in, steady, as if his ribs needed the order. “Inner ring,” he said. “Twice. Then I stay.”

“Good,” I said, and hated how relief felt like a bruise easing.

He went. The hinge made a small pleased sound; I hated it for helping him leave easier. I sat in his chair and learned immediately why he preferred it: the room arranged itself from that corner. Everything is visible. Not everything reachable. It comforted and infuriated me in equal measure.

He took longer than he should have for one slow circle and not long enough to break the promise. When the hinge sighed and his shoulder came through the door with the rain stretched thin across it, my anger had nowhere useful to go. It settled under my ribs and sulked.

"Twice," he said, answering the question I hadn't let myself ask out loud.

"Good," I said, staying in his chair just to prove a point small enough to hide.

We finished the small things. I rinsed bowls; he tested the bar across the door, fingers reading each pin like braille. The way he touched the latch wasn't the way he'd touched me. I didn't know how to feel about that.

When the lamplight fell to a modest circle and the room found its lower voice, I brought the mending basket close and chose the smallest job— Corin's sock with the honest hole. Thread, needle, the repetition of fixing what declared itself broken. Sometimes the only way to keep from breaking something big is to mend something small.

Kael sat nearer than last night. Not next to me. Not across from me. A middle distance that told on him more than any admission would: I'll bend my own rules to be close without calling it that. I didn't thank him for the kindness; he wouldn't like it.

We were quiet long enough to call it peace, if not the easy kind. Then he said, without looking, "Elara."

"Mm."

"Don't take scraps past the shed alone again."

"I wasn't alone," I said.

"You were."

"I wasn't," I insisted. "You were watching."

"That's not the same thing," he said, which is exactly what I'd told him when he claimed to know where he was. It would have been funny if it hadn't landed where it did. "Promise me," he added, and the words came carefully—expensive.

I finished my stitch, turned the sock, and looked at him. He'd angled himself to see both me and the door, ruinously polite to danger. "Fine. I promise. If you do something for me."

One of his eyebrows showed up, economy of expression. "What."

"Tell me if you see something I should be afraid of. Not the weather. Not the usual. The other thing."

He weighed the request, the way he weighs whether to draw steel. "You'll know," he said at last.

"That's not telling," I said.

"It is the truth."

"I want both."

He nodded once, twice, each like a small paper folded in half. "If I see him," he said, and neither of us needed a name for the crescent we both saw when we closed our eyes, "I'll tell you."

"Good," I said. The room let me breathe differently by a hair.

He leaned forward, elbows on his knees, hands loose for once. "Elara."

"Yes."

"Don't ask me 'why then' tonight."

It landed perfectly. Gentle, final. My teeth found the inside of my cheek before my temper did. "What if I want to?"

"Want later," he said. "I want something else now."

"Like what," I asked, too curious for my own survival.

He turned his head just enough that the lamplight shaved one edge of his mouth and left the other in shadow. "Quiet," he said. "The feeling of you not walking into the trees alone. Ending the day without breaking something I can't fix in the morning."

We let the quiet be what we wanted, for once. I stitched. He listened to a world I couldn't hear. The rain eased to almost nothing. The stove sighed and became red instead of flame. My eyes got heavy. His didn't.

"Go," he said finally, softer than the hour before could have coaxed from him. "Sleep."

"You," I said.

"I will," he answered, and I accepted the half-truth because it was made honestly.

I stood, and he watched the movement without flinching from it. At the curtain, I paused. He had turned his chair a fraction more toward the little doorways and me at the same time, posture like a promise he hadn't found a language for.

"Kael," I said.

"Elara."

"If you're going to watch me," I said, keeping my voice even so the room wouldn't take sides, "say what you're looking for."

"Trouble," he said immediately.

"Try honesty next time," I told him.

He considered, and for once, didn't fight the instinct to give me the thing I'd asked for. "Want," he said, barely above the lamp's breath. "And trouble."

It should have made me angry. It made something in my chest light and hurt at the same time. I went before he saw both.

Behind the curtain, the small room was the size of one steady breath. I lay down and made myself take it. The hall spoke in small noises I knew by heart now: hinge, rope, the soft settling of shelves, the easing of the stove. His chair creaked when he shifted. I almost slept.

A knock that wasn't a knock woke me—the sound a choice makes when it hits wood. I eased the curtain back. The hall lay in a low wash of coal-light. Kael stood by the door, head tilted like he could hear a whisper under the rain's last quiet. He didn't turn; he didn't need to. He knows when I'm looking.

"Inner ring," he said into the dark, as if the promise wanted checking.

"Twice," I answered, not much louder than my breath.

"Twice," he echoed.

I could have let the curtain fall and closed my eyes. I didn't. Something about the slope of his shoulders—less stone, more man—held me there. "Kael," I said, and at his name the set of him changed, almost like relief.

"What."

The question I meant to ask—what did you hear—died in my mouth. What came out was smaller and, somehow, heavier. "Do you sleep at all when I don't?"

He was quiet long enough to make me think he wouldn't give me anything. Then, without turning, he said, "I count your steps until I can't hear them. Then I count the ones you would take if you got up."

It broke something soft and necessary in me. Not a bad break. A reset. "That's not sleeping."

"No," he said. "It isn't."

"Kael."

"Elara."

"Thank you," I said, because there are courtesies that grow larger when you speak them quietly.

He set his hand on the doorframe like it was my shoulder. "Stay where I can reach you," he said, and for the first time since the note, a single word slid out unarmored. "Please." The crack was small. It was enough. The room changed shape around it. I let the curtain fall and lay back down, heart louder than sense. Outside, the rain finally forgot about us. Inside, the hinge decided not to complain. Between them, the man by the door kept the dark where it belonged.

Chapter Twenty-Two

The rain softened overnight until it was just a breath on the canvas eaves, and by morning it had stopped pretending to matter. The air smelled rinsed. Pines shook themselves off with a sound like someone settling a cloak. Inside, the hall held that light, gray calm that makes you think the day might behave if you don't startle it.

I ladled porridge into bowls and tried not to look at the place by the door where Kael likes to stand when he isn't standing anywhere. He was there anyway, shoulder to the frame, eyes on the line where the fence gives way to trees. The hinge he fixed yesterday swung clean when I nudged it to test, and he glanced back, the smallest flicker of satisfaction passing over his mouth before it remembered not to.

"Boots," I said, and Corin's feet found them, heel-toe, heel-toe, like a game he'd played a thousand times when the ground was more trustworthy. Loryn brought a bundle of dried thyme and set it near the stove without being asked. Miran came in with the kind of pride that announces itself in the way his chin sits and nothing else.

"Fence line's fine," he told Kael, before he told me anything.

Kael nodded once. "Keep it company again after breakfast."

"Why," Miran said, offended by what he heard as repetition.

"Because fences like being admired," Kael said, deadpan. Miran lit up as if this confirmed everything he suspected about wood.

We ate without hurry. I kept my eyes on spoons and elbows and the level of the kettle because it was easier than keeping them off the corner of the room where last night's promise still sat—small and heavy and bright. When the bowls were empty, I set the children to tasks with names that sounded important on purpose: Keeper of Buckets, String-Measurer, Door-Guard, Corin always took that one too seriously.

Kael drifted toward the table with the neat slope of a man who doesn't drift. He checked the pegs we'd cut two days ago, ran his thumb along a few and put them aside as not worth trusting. He didn't ask me to sharpen the good knife. I sharpened it anyway, long, steady strokes, the rasp a metronome for thought. By the time the blade returned to proper behavior, I was ready for conversation that wasn't about weather.

"You said 'please' last night," I said, light, like we were discussing whether a thing needed salting.

He didn't look at me. He didn't have to. "You make that sound like a rare animal."

"It is." I set the knife down and wiped the blade with a dry cloth because I needed an excuse to keep my hands busy. "I wanted to make sure I heard it."

"You did." He picked up a peg and put it down because it wasn't good enough. "Don't make me regret it."

"Then don't make it a loan."

That got me a glance, quick and sharp. "And what would you like it to be?"

"A habit." The word came out braver than I felt. "Like sleeping. Or telling me what you hear when you pretend you don't hear anything at all."

He made a sound in his throat that wasn't quite a laugh and wasn't meant to be. "You want too much."

"Only from people who've given themselves the job of keeping us alive," I said, and we both knew I wasn't talking about me.

He went quiet long enough that Loryn filled the space on accident by dragging a bench across the floor to reach the loft rung she'd decided needed counting again. The bench squealed. Kael flinched so small I almost missed it.

"Rope length," she announced, because the world is easier if you can measure it.

"It'll hold," he said, like he couldn't help himself, then saw the face I made and added, "Count anyway."

We worked through the useful middle of the day. He brought the last of the split wood under the cover we'd fixed; I stacked it with my back to him so I wouldn't ask questions with my face. Miran practiced the throw, tongue between his teeth, posture set in earnestness. Kael corrected his wrist with two fingers. "Don't muscle it," he said. "Let the line do the work." Miran nodded like this applied to everything.

By midday the light had the thinner quality it gets in fall when the sun is there and not there and the trees are the strongest thing in the room. Corin asked if the fox had come for the scraps. "Not yet," I told him, and watched Kael not watch the trees.

"Quick walk," Loryn asked, tapping a peg against her palm in a rhythm that meant she needed air more than she needed distance. "Just along the inside of the fence."

"Together," I said, already reaching for my shawl.

"I'll go," Kael said, as if the sentence had been his idea first.

"We don't need a guard for the fence," Loryn muttered.

"You won't have one," he said. "You'll have company."

She tried not to smile. She failed in a way that made my chest ache.

We took the inner path, boots scraping the damp earth where the rain had offered softness and the day had taken it. Kael didn't lead, and he didn't follow. He placed himself where he could touch either of us if we made a mistake and pretended not to be doing that math. Loryn counted fence posts out loud until the order of it worked on her mood and left her lighter.

"How many today," I asked when she stopped counting just to hear the quiet.

"Enough," she said, stealing my word and using it back on me like a mirror. "Can we pick the yarrow by the stump on the way back?"

"Yes," I said. "Not the small ones."

She nodded like a queen accepting a treaty.

At the far corner we stopped because that's what you do even when there's nothing to see: you check the horizon and pretend it listens. There was only the forest, arranged as it always is—darker where the spruce stand close, lighter where the birch insist on being friendly. A squirrel stole a cone and told lies about who it belonged to. The fence post at the corner leaned like an old man. Loryn pushed it back upright with her whole body and declared victory. Kael said, "Good," in that low tone he uses when approval is a tool.

On the way in, he fell half a step behind me and I could feel the shape of him at my back. His shadow sat on mine like it fit. It made my hands want to do something foolish. I kept them in my pockets until the feeling passed.

We ate bread and apples and a stew that had taken on the personalities of everything we put in it and become something calmer. The children argued about nothing, happily. Kael sat across from me and didn't watch my mouth. He watched my hands instead and pretended it meant less. When Miran asked if knots could be learned with your eyes closed, Kael said, "Better," and tied one without looking to prove it. Corin applauded as if magic had been performed. Loryn tried and tied her hair to the bench. We undid the mistake carefully, together, laughing.

Afterwards, I washed bowls while Kael set a new brace under the top shelf of the stores. The shelf had given up a fraction to the weight of jars and winter. He drove the peg home in two clean strikes. The sound was satisfying enough to make me close my eyes for a heartbeat.

"Alright," I said, not turning, "I can't keep pretending this is nothing just because you like being stone."

He paused. The room paused with him. "Elara," he said, and the way he said my name wasn't a warning. It was a hand on a door that wasn't latched yet.

"I'm not picking a fight," I said, and that was only half true. "I'm picking the moment."

"What are you asking?"

"I think you know."

He didn't move for a long second, then set the mallet down gently, the way he sets sharp things when small people are within reach. "Not here," he said, with a quick glance toward the little doors along the back.

"Outside, then." I dried my hands on my apron and walked toward the wood cover because the trees are less judgmental when you embarrass yourself.

He followed. The light was thinner now, the kind that makes edges important. The tarp over the wood hummed gently in a breeze that had finally decided on a direction. I pressed my palms against the rough canvas like I needed the friction. He stopped close enough that I could feel his heat along my left side, then took half a step back because he's cruel in the kind way.

"Why?" I asked, and the question came easier than I'd expected. "In the kitchen. After you looked at me like you were choosing not to breathe until you didn't."

He tipped his head, slow, as if he was measuring how hard the answer would land. "Because I was alive," he said, and I almost laughed because it was a line and not an answer and he knew it.

"Try again."

He was quiet. Birds moved through the lower branches with the quick, private sounds they use when they aren't performing for sky. Somewhere, water ticked off a rock. The fence creaked in a way that told me nothing was wrong and everything was old.

"You don't want me," I said when the silence made me brave and stupid. "You want the idea of me. Something to hold when you're tired. Something that doesn't need anything back."

The look he gave me was almost anger and almost pity and stopped in a place I couldn't name. "Don't tell me what I want," he said, and the words touched my skin like a hand that knows where the nerves live.

"Then tell me," I said, and stepped closer, because if this was going to bruise it might as well be from truth. "You won't even look at me when I say it."

He looked. He looked everywhere. "Elara," he said again, softer, "You think I don't want you?" He laughed once, and the sound cut. "That isn't the problem."

I hated that I loved the way he said it. "Then what is."

"If I start," he said, and his voice went low enough to warm the cold edge of the day, "I won't stop."

I swallowed, because my body had an answer to that sentence and it wasn't language. "You think I can't stop you."

"That isn't the game," he said. "I won't let you."

"Because you're in control." I said it like a joke so it wouldn't be.

"Because I won't be." He took a small step in, like a tide testing a shore it means to take later. The heat of him made the air between us thin. "And because the children sleep twenty paces from where you taste like something that would end me."

"Don't bring them into this," I said, softer than I meant. "Don't make them your excuse to not answer me."

He flinched, and it wasn't a man's flinch. It was something older. "You want an answer you won't like."

"I asked for the truth."

He dragged a hand down his face, scraping yesterday's stubble into attention. "I kissed you because I had blood under my nails and nothing in my mouth that wasn't rage, and I needed... something that reminded me people aren't just jobs." He looked away, jaw tight. "And because I wanted to," he added, like the admission cost something he'd been hoarding.

The honesty made me dizzy. "And then you called it a mistake."

"Because it was the wrong room," he said. "And the wrong hour. And because I don't get to take without telling you what I am."

"Then tell me."

He smiled without humor. "Not like this."

I hated him for that. I did. I hated that he could land a sentence and leave it sitting in my ribs. I leaned back against the covered wood and felt the steady hum of the wind through the tarp. "What am I supposed to do with that."

"Wait," he said.

"Now you're cruel."

"I'm careful," he said. "You call it cruelty because you're brave and I'm not."

"You're not allowed to say that," I snapped, stung. "You're not allowed to pretend you're the only person here who is deciding to do hard things."

He took it, the way he takes weather, shoulders set against it. "Fine. You're brave. I'm careful. We still end up at the same door."

"Which is?"

He stepped in, and there was nowhere to put my hands that wasn't him. "If I walk through you," he said softly, "I won't come back out." His breath hit the place where my jaw meets my throat. "And you won't be able to lock it again."

I closed my eyes because looking at him and breathing and choosing not to grab his coat were three things too many. The sound the tarp made in the wind was suddenly obscene.

"Say you don't want me," I said, because I was done being the only one to put soft parts on a table. "Say it and I'll leave it, Kael. I'll be your doorstop. I'll be your hallway. I'll be nothing and something useful and I'll make the soup and I'll pretend that night didn't happen. But say it."

He didn't. He came so close I felt the shape of the word he didn't say at my mouth. His hand lifted, hesitated, closed into a fist like he'd caught himself reaching for fire. "I can't," he said, raw.

"Then don't tell me to wait."

"I'm telling you to live," he said, and the anger in it wasn't at me. "I'm telling you that if I take you into my mouth in that hall again I won't leave the room until the world notices and knocks the door off the hinges to see why we stopped."

I laughed then, not because it was funny but because my body needed somewhere to put what it felt and laughter was less dangerous than the alternative. He looked at me like I'd surprised him. "It's not your job to save me from want," I said, wiping my eyes with the heel of my hand. "I carry want just fine."

"You carry everything," he said, and the admiration in it wouldn't be disguised by tone. "I'm asking you to let me not break the parts of this that keep the children asleep."

The children. The hall. The fence. The hinge that didn't complain anymore. I looked at him and saw every reason I should be careful. I looked at him and saw every reason I wasn't.

"Fine," I said, the word a little ugly because I didn't sand it. "We won't break the hall." I let myself take one step into his space because I am not made to leave a fight with my hands empty. "But don't call me a mistake again."

He didn't move back. He didn't touch me. "I won't," he said, like an oath. Then, quieter: "It wasn't."

We stood there until the wind decided to look elsewhere for entertainment. When I finally moved, it was because I remembered we had a life to tend and adults don't get to drift into corners and think about mouths all afternoon. I pushed off the tarp, and it pushed back, and that little absurdity helped.

"Truce," I said, offering him my hand because I needed something that looked like a ritual.

He looked at it like a man looks at a rope he knows will hold and hates, anyway. He took it. His palm was warm. He didn't let go quickly, and I didn't ask him to.

Back inside, the room felt changed. The children emerged from the little doors because silence makes them suspicious. Loryn wanted to show me the knot she finally got right without tying her hair to the bench. Miran wanted to be congratulated for the extraordinary work of refilling the water bucket. Corin wanted to be carried even though he was much too big for it. I carried him anyway.

Kael cut bread with the good knife and didn't look at me while he did. He tipped a slice a fraction thicker onto my plate because habits are courtesies when you don't admit them.

We ate, we finished the small work that makes a day end properly. The sky decided to be colorless in a way that makes the evening slip in slyly. I checked blankets and wicks and small foreheads with the back of my hand. I told a story that had no wolves in it because the world had enough. When the last door closed behind the last set of small arguments, I came back to the hall and found him where he always is, between us and everything else.

The lamp made a clean circle on the table. I brought the mending and didn't touch it. He watched the door and didn't pretend he was doing anything else. For a while, that was enough.

"Teach Loryn the anchor hitch tomorrow," I said finally, because I am made of ambition and lists when I don't know what to do with my heart. "She's ready."

He nodded. "And Miran the half-hitch. No knots with names that make him feel like a king. He doesn't need help with that."

"Corin can keep being a Door-Guard," I said.

"The door approves," he said, and the hinge decided to agree by behaving.

We let the silence sit down with us like a friend. The stove ticked as if remembering a different house. My hands found the sock and threaded the needle, more to keep the evening company than because fabric doesn't forgive delay.

"Elara," he said into the quiet.

"Mm."

"You were right," he said. He didn't look at me. "I pretend, sometimes."

"I know," I said, very gently, because gloating is a sport I'm not interested in with him.

He breathed once, and it wasn't steady. "Not about want," he added, and that was the crack, clean and precise, the kind that lets light in.

I didn't answer because I didn't trust what would come out if I did. I tied off the thread and smoothed the tiny mend with my thumb and looked at the door instead of at the man sitting next to it and let the room keep the rest for us.

The lamp burned lower. The night took its place at the windows without ceremony. I rose when my eyes asked me to and he said, "Sleep," like he had been waiting for the chance to grant permission.

"Will you," I asked, not mean.

He smiled a little, tired and true. "I'll count your steps," he said. "And then the ones you'd take if you got up."

"That isn't sleeping."

"No," he said. "It isn't."

At the curtain, I stopped because I am a creature of the last word whether I should be or not. "Not a mistake," I said, without turning.

"No," he said. "Not that."

"Goodnight, Kael."

"Elara." He said it like thanks and warning and something else I would not make him name. "Goodnight." I let the curtain fall, lay down, and listened to the hall—rope, hinge, stove, breath—until the dark became kind enough to cover me. Outside, a fox spoke to the night like it had every right to. Inside, a man sat by a door and counted the steps I wasn't taking, and that was enough for now.

Chapter Twenty-Three

Sleep refused me.

I lay on my side and counted the breaths I could hear through the wall—Loryn's even, Miran's pretending not to snore, Corin's little stop-start rhythm like a bird landing—until the counting turned into its own kind of noise. I turned the other way. The blanket warmed, cooled, warmed again. The quiet did that trick it does at night where it starts to feel like a presence. I tried the trick back, the one where you tell yourself, If I lie still enough, my mind will give up. It didn't.

I pushed the blanket back and swung my legs over the side. The floor was cool under my feet. I stood for a moment with my hand on the latch, listening for any small sound from the rooms along the hall—nothing but the wood settling, the soft whisper of banked coals turning in on themselves. When I eased my door open the hinge gave a faint, guilty creak. No one stirred.

The main hall breathed low. Firelight from the hearth washed the long table and died in the rafters. The kitchen to the right held a cooler darkness, orderly shapes of shelves and worktop and hung iron. The doors to the children's rooms were closed along the far wall—small, square shadows with the comfort of names behind them. The air smelled like pine smoke, dried thyme, and that clean resin note that still lives in new wood.

He was there, of course. Near the door. Not sitting. Not exactly standing at ease, either. He'd taken up that position he does when he means to be part of the room and not in it: shoulder near the frame, arms folded, attention arranged on the outside world as if the night had said something he didn't like and he'd told it to repeat itself. In the low light, his features were angles and shadow. When I stepped out, he didn't turn, but the part of him that registers movement... did. I felt it like the tug of a thread around my ribs.

"Couldn't sleep?" My voice tried to be casual and landed somewhere between soft and a little annoyed with myself.

"No." He didn't make me ask the next question. "You?"

"No." I rubbed my thumb along the inside of my wrist, a habit I keep meaning to break. "Tea would be loud."

"Mm." The sound lived somewhere deep in his chest. He kept his eyes on the seam where the door met the frame. "You shouldn't be up alone."

"You're here."

"That's not the same thing." He breathed, slow and measured. "You were sleeping."

"I was pretending." I crossed the hall, not toward him, not away—just along the long table, fingers straightening a cloth that was already straight. The fire popped, the spark skating up into the flue. "You're going to wear a path in that spot."

"Good." He shifted his weight. The floor answered with a small, familiar groan. "We'll know where to stand when we need to."

Something small in me eased at that—how practical he could make worry sound. Another part tightened because he had said we, and I liked it too much. "You always know where to stand," I said, and meant it, and then wished I hadn't, because his head tilted a fraction and the heat that poured through my face was both ridiculous and unhelpful.

He didn't tease. He never does. He let it sit there and be true. For a few breaths the only sounds were the little sounds a room makes when it prefers you to listen: a soft drip as snowmelt from earlier found its way along a seam outside and decided against coming in; the tiny complaint of a board relaxing; the sigh of the fire.

"I'm going outside," I said, more to the door than to him. "Just to the step. It smells like rain that changed its mind."

"Don't." He said it like a man placing his hand on a hot iron so someone else won't.

"I'm not a child, Kael." I walked anyway, because the whole day had been made of not going anywhere I wanted to go, and I needed three breaths that belonged to me.

He moved before I did. Not fast—just decisive. One step and he was there, turning into the doorway as I reached it, one palm braced high on the frame beside my head, the other catching the latch, easing it back down before it lifted. He didn't touch me. He didn't have to. The door was a waist-wide slice of cold and he was the whole edge.

"Not alone," he said. Quiet. Not a command. A line.

"I'm not alone." I heard my own stubbornness and wanted to kick it under the table. "You're here."

"That's the problem."

I looked up. He was close enough that the light from the hearth found the cut of his cheekbone and the line of his throat, close enough that I could see where a nick on his lower lip had not quite finished healing. His eyes were the dark that eats light and gives none back. It wasn't a metaphor in that moment. It was a fact.

"What is?" My voice came out steadier than I felt.

"You asking me to stand here." He cocked his head a little, and something like humor flickered at the corner of his mouth, then died. "You walking toward the door like it hasn't been waiting all night for the chance to take you. You looking at me when you say my name."

"I didn't say your name."

"You did." He let go of the latch and set his hand against the frame on the other side of me. The heat coming off him felt like he carried his own weather and hadn't decided yet if he'd share. "You said it inside your mouth."

The sensible part of me lined up all the correct replies: The children. The hour. The way the outside looked like the inside of a held breath. I didn't pick any of them. I took one small step forward until the front of my body met the front of his coat and the smell of smoke and night and him closed over everything else.

He didn't back up.

"That's not smart," he said. The words were a warning. His voice wasn't.

"I know." My hand lifted—traitor that it is—and found the edge of his collar. The cloth was cool. The skin beneath it wasn't. "You think I don't know."

"Don't." He said it on an exhale, eyes dropping to my mouth for the barest beat.

I did. I rose on my toes just enough that my mouth lined up with his, just enough that he could have turned his face and I'd have kissed his jaw instead and pretended that had been the plan all along. He didn't turn. That tiny tilt of his head was an answer and a surrender and a problem and I felt all of it as clearly as I felt the frame at my back and the strength in his shoulders holding the world where he wanted it.

When his mouth met mine, it wasn't careful. He kissed like a man who had been holding a door shut against a storm and changed his mind. Heat jumped through me like I'd touched a wire. He made a sound low in his throat that I swear woke up the hair at the nape of my neck. His hand left the frame and landed at my waist, fingers firm, dragging me one inch closer. The other stayed braced above me, the muscle along his forearm tight under my palm as I reached to steady myself.

The hall narrowed to this. The feel of him. The heavy, steady thud of his heart under my hand where my fingers had closed without permission over the front of his coat. The rasp of his stubble against the corner of my mouth when he angled the kiss to take more. The way breath turned into something else when he took it from me and I took it back.

Around us, the light seemed to lean. The fire didn't so much dim as bow. Along the floorboards at his boots the shadow thickened, too dark for the room, like ink catching that didn't belong to the paper. It slid and stilled—no wind to move it, and yet it moved. If I'd had more sense, I would have been afraid. If I'd had less, I wouldn't have noticed. I noticed and didn't stop.

"Close the—" The word door got lost between our mouths. He didn't reach for the latch. He pressed me back with his hip just enough that the wood kissed my shoulders, and the small sound I made when the cool of it met warm skin earned me his hand lifting from my waist to the side of my throat, thumb resting in the soft just below my jaw, not squeezing, just there, grounding and impossible to ignore.

My own hands had a life. One curled in the hair at the back of his head, feeling the damp left by evening air that hadn't decided to freeze. The other flattened against his chest and slid, slower than was wise, to the seam of buttons, to the edge where coat gave to shirt. Cloth shifted. Heat climbed. When my fingers brushed skin at the open V his breath faltered. He didn't move my hand. He moved into it.

"Elara." He said my name like it was the first thing he'd spoken all day that mattered. It landed low, worked its way through me and made a home.

"Don't stop," I said, and hated how honest it sounded.

He didn't. Not for a handful of heartbeats that felt like more. The kiss went ragged and real. His mouth learned me. Mine answered like it had been waiting for this exact set of angles and pressure since the minute he stepped into our ruined life and decided to put his body between ours and the next bad thing. The shadows at our feet twitched, gathered, then thinned, as if breath had a color and his was leaking into the room.

Something inside him slipped then—not his control, not exactly. More like a weight he'd been carrying shifted and bared an edge. He made a small, vicious sound and stepped even closer, the doorframe taking part of the impact. His hand left my throat and found my waist again, fingers splaying, hauling me that last impossible bit until I felt the solid line of his thigh between mine and the room spun in a way that had nothing to do with balance.

I would have let it take me. All of it. Right there with the door cold at my back and the heat of him making everything else in the hall a memory. My body said yes in a language older than any promise. I tipped my head to take him deeper and he—

He stopped.

It wasn't a clean stop. It was that jolt a horse gives when it hears a snake in the grass. Every muscle along his arm went iron under my palm. The hand at my waist tightened hard enough to make a sound catch in my throat. His mouth left mine by one aching inch and he dragged air in like a drowning man breaking water.

He didn't put his forehead to mine. He didn't soften it. He tore himself back two inches, three, his eyes still on my mouth as if they didn't trust it to stay where it was. He lifted his hand and covered his own, not gentle, fingers digging into his lower lip like he had to physically hold himself back from reaching for me again. His shoulders shook once, barely there, like something ugly and old had rattled its cage inside him and reminded him of its teeth.

"Not—" He swallowed. The word scraped. "Not like this."

The hall rushed in on a cold wind that hadn't opened a door. I stood with my hands caught mid-reach, stupid with want, the imprint of him heat-branded along my front, the sting of his lip on mine telling me, True, true, this happened. A small part of my brain that still did its job noticed the fire flare as if whatever had touched its light had let go.

I found my voice. It didn't behave. "What did I—"

"This is me." He tapped his knuckles once against his mouth, a correction, like he didn't want the next word to come out wrong. "Stopping." He studied my face like a man memorizing a map he expects to lose. "If I don't, I won't." His gaze flicked to the row of doors down the hall, all those tiny rooms, all those small breaths. He looked back at me and the battle on his face was not with me. It was with the part of himself that stands between bad things and the door, even when the bad thing is his own hunger. "And I won't do that here."

Every answer I had lined up to throw died in the level way he said here. It held too much. The children asleep. The table that had fed us. The walls that had finally learned our names. I hated him for making me love him for that.

"You think this—" I didn't point between us because that would have been ridiculous and also accurate. "You think this stops because the room remembers it in the morning?"

"No." He dropped his hand, jaw tight, a white marking where he'd pressed skin too hard. He didn't try to hide the way he looked at my mouth again. "It doesn't stop."

"Then—"

"Then I go outside," he said, and it sounded like a punishment and a prayer. He reached past me for the latch and I felt the heat of his forearm along my shoulder and had to bite down on the inside of my lip to keep from leaning into it.

He opened the door a hand's width. Cold night slipped in, clean and damp, bringing the smell of wet cedar and earth. The darkness beyond looked ordinary, and it wasn't. It looked like any night and it wasn't. On the threshold, his shadow shouldn't have fallen forward. It did. It stretched too far, as if the light behind us couldn't keep its grip on him when the dark asked for more.

"Lock it," he said. "After me."

I should have argued. I wanted to bite him for the order like it had teeth. What I did was nod, because even angry I am not foolish.

He didn't leave. Not immediately. He stared past me into the hall we had made ours and his eyes did that narrow thing they do when he's measuring a distance only he can see. "Stay where I can reach you." It should have been the same line it was last night. It wasn't. The please was there without the word. It made something low in me go soft and lit at once.

"Don't be long," I said. I hated how much I meant it.

His mouth twitched like he wanted to say something better and didn't trust himself with more shape than that. He stepped into the gap. Night took him the way water takes a stone—it made room and then it owned him. For a heartbeat he was the tall, solid line in the doorway, a fact in the world. Then his outline thinned into the dark like ink in cold water.

The shadows that had been curled at his boots leaked forward as he went, a smear against the threshold that had no business moving that way. It slid over the sill and down the step like it knew where it was going. I watched until I couldn't see anything but night, and only then did I push the door shut with both hands and set the bar. The latch clicked. The sound was too loud.

I stood there braced against the wood, breathing with my mouth open like the air had gotten smaller. The hall looked normal. The fire gathered itself with that little rising sigh it makes when it has finally decided to behave for its keepers. The long table was an honest length of wood holding its own quiet. From behind the doors came nothing but the good silence of sleep.

I set my forehead against the back of the door, then thought better of it—not giving the door that satisfaction—and pressed my palm there instead. My other hand found my mouth and hovered and didn't quite touch because if I put my fingers to my lips I wasn't sure whether I'd steady or shake.

I didn't cry. Not out of pride. Just because there was no room for it and also because nothing about what had just happened felt like loss. It felt like the opposite, which is its own problem.

Down the hall, a little click, the comforting kind—the sound of Loryn rolling over and checking the small knife under her pillow before she forgot it again; she would put it farther from her head in the morning and feel very responsible about it. Another door shifted; Miran's foot probably had gotten out from under his blanket and decided the world should hear about it. Corin mumbled a word that sounded like ship and definitely wasn't.

I moved. Not quickly. Just enough to give my hands something that wasn't my own mouth. I went to the hearth and took the small poker and coaxed the coals into a more sensible shape. I laid one more split at the far edge so the room would stay kind until morning. I wiped a clean spot on the table that didn't need wiping and straightened a bench that didn't need straightening and told myself I was not waiting.

The bar on the door sat like a line I could touch. I did, once, fingers to the grain, as if that would translate into knowing where he was. It didn't. It never does. But I could feel, as surely as I can feel weather, the way the night seemed to pull in the direction he'd gone, the way the dark outside the windows leaned a hair closer and then thought better of it.

He hadn't taken his coat from the peg. I stood there and stared at it like that meant something. It didn't. Or it did, and I wasn't ready to read it. A sliver of dead leaf had hitched a ride on his sleeve earlier and was still caught in the seam. I plucked it free and put it on the shelf by the door because people keep foolish little altars to the things that make them feel like the world is connected, and apparently I am people.

The room settled. My heart didn't. I went to the kitchen and drew a cup of water and drank half and then the rest because my body was trying to be practical about blood and air and the fact that my hands wouldn't stop remembering the shape of him. On the way back, I passed the row of doors and set my ear to each, because habit is its own god. Enough breath. Enough silence. Enough.

At the main door, I stood again and told myself I was checking the bar a second time like any sensible person would. My palm found the wood. Through it, cold. Through the cold, a steady nothing. I closed my eyes and counted three slow breaths and there he was, on the far edge of my listening: that odd sense I get of him when he is very near and very far at the same time— the way the room feels when he is outside it but still holding it in his sights, the way the dark seems to slow down around him, like even night is careful.

I left the bar where it was. I didn't go back to bed. I sat at the end of the long table closest to the door, where I could see the hearth and the row of small doors and the latch that keeps what is ours inside and what isn't out. I folded my hands so they would stop making a map of my mouth on the table. I stared at the hinge until it blurred.

When the night breathed in a little colder, the fire answered. When it breathed out, the rafters creaked a reply. We held, the hall and I. We waited without calling it waiting. And I let the ache he'd left under my skin sit there and be the truth of the hour, a heat that wasn't kind and wasn't cruel, exactly—just honest.

The next time the wind worried the edges of the roof and the hearth snapped sharp, I told myself it was the kind of sound you hear when a man steps back in from the dark. I almost rose. I didn't. The latch stayed quiet. The door stayed a line I wasn't going to cross. The shadows along the sill looked ordinary again, and I told myself that meant nothing either way.

I didn't fall asleep in the chair. I wasn't that foolish. I sat there and let my body settle around the fact that he had put his hand over his own mouth rather than be cruel, that he had said not like this and meant it, that he had asked me to lock the door and that I had, and that nothing about that changed the simple, impossible truth of how his name sounds when I say it inside my mouth.

When the coals dipped and I rose to feed them, I caught my reflection in the small piece of polished copper we used to check our faces for soot before we scare the children with our foreheads. My mouth was swollen. My hair had done what it always does in heat and trouble—escaped. I looked like a person who had been kissed against a door by a man made of patience and hunger and bad history. I didn't look sorry.

I set another split on the far side of the hearth and turned it so it would catch the slow way and sat again within reach of the door, where the night's cold couldn't quite touch me, and let the hour keep its shape without softening. The dark had steadied. The hall had, too. Only I hadn't. That would be tomorrow's problem. For now there was only the bar under my hand, the heat at my lips that refused to fade, and the knowledge—clear as the line of the door—that when he came back, I would hear him before the door cracked open.

Chapter Twenty-Four

The night clung to me like damp wool, heavy and sour with the day's rain. I hadn't gone far—just to the edge of the yard, where the grass broke into pine needles and shadow. The hall still glowed faintly behind me, its hearth throwing out a light I couldn't bear to look at, not with her face still burning in my mind.

My hand was pressed over my mouth like it could hold back what I'd almost let loose. Elara. The taste of her still lingered, and the pull in my chest hadn't settled—it raged, clawing for more.

The shadows at my boots stirred, restless things that answered me too easily. I ordered them down, but they hesitated, quivering like hounds on the leash. The air bit cold, though sweat slid down my spine, and I tried to breathe slow, steady, human. But memory has its own teeth.

The scream bled into a ragged gasp, my lungs burning, my hands shaking with the force of it. Ash rained down, slow and silent, as if the world itself had paused to watch. And in that silence, I made a promise, not to the gods, not to the dead, but to myself.

I would not forgive.

I would not forget.

And I would never, ever be powerless again.

The promise hadn't even finished echoing in my skull before the shadows moved. They slithered out from the wreckage, curling through the smoke like they'd been waiting, like they'd been listening. They didn't feel foreign—not exactly. More like an extension of the rage that was already splitting me open, the grief that had nowhere else to go.

The first tendril brushed against my hand. Cold. Alive. It twined around my wrist, pulsing like it had a heartbeat of its own. I should've recoiled. I didn't. I wanted more.

My teeth ground together, jaw aching, as the darkness crawled higher. Across my arms. My chest. Into my lungs until I was breathing shadow instead of air. The firelight dimmed, swallowed whole, leaving only the silver-gray glow of the moonlight above, cold and merciless.

The shadows did not simply guide me. They demanded.

I hunted.

The first I found was a deserter, half-drunk on sour ale, stumbling through a backwater tavern. I dragged him into the night, shadows coiling around his throat until his face purple. He begged. He lied. But shadows cut the lies from his tongue, tearing them into scraps of truth. He told me of garrisons, of outposts where moon-elf banners still flew. When his voice broke, I let the shadows fill him until his body was nothing but a husk.

The second thought he was brave. He spat in my face when I pulled him from his saddle, silver armor gleaming in the torchlight. My fist shattered his jaw. The shadows whispered through his broken teeth, spilling his secrets in a wet, gurgling mess. I left him hanging from a tree, the crows circling before his last breath rattled out.

With every kill, the trail sharpened. With every truth torn from unwilling throats, I saw more clearly the path to the man who had ordered it all.

Days bled into weeks. My hands were blackened with soot and blood, my cloak stiff with the filth of travel. Villages whispered of me—of a shadow-wraith that hunted moon elves and left no survivors. Mothers barred their children indoors, soldiers doubled their patrols. I found them anyway.

One I pinned to the ground with spears of shadow, each thrust sinking deeper as he screamed names of commanders, whispered of palaces carved in white stone. I listened only long enough to know which road to take. His eyes were still wide when the darkness folded him into silence.

Another I cornered by the river. He tried to pray to the Moon God, silver words bubbling on his lips. I broke his prayer with my hand, crushed against his throat until he confessed what I already knew—that all roads led back to the same throne.

It became less about information, more about the breaking. I no longer cared how many throats it took to wring out the truth. I wanted them to suffer as my people had suffered. I wanted their children to choke on grief as mine had.

At last, the trail converged on a city carved into the hillside, marble and silver gleaming in the night. The palace rose above it all, smug and untouchable.

The guards at the gate laughed when they saw me. They weren't laughing when their shadows rose up and strangled them from behind.

I left their bodies where they fell. Let them be a warning.

Inside, the halls glimmered with torchlight. Music floated from somewhere deeper, laughter spilling from courtiers who feasted while ashes still smoldered over the graves of my kin. Each sound stoked the fire inside me until it burned so hot I thought my bones would split.

I moved like a phantom through the corridors. Servants screamed when they saw me, silver plates clattering to the floor. I let them run. I wanted them to tell the story. I wanted the whole palace to know what was coming for their god.

And then I found him.

Mēnô. Draped in silk, silver hair falling loose over his shoulders, a chalice of wine in his hand. He looked at me as though I were dirt dragged in from the road.

"You've come far," he said, his voice calm, amused. "For a corpse that refuses to lie still."

The shadows tightened around me, writhing, clawing, desperate for his blood. My lips curled into something that might have been a smile, though it felt more like a wound.

"You killed them," I said, my voice raw, jagged. "Every last one."

He tilted his head, sipping his wine as if I were no more threat than a stray dog. "I ordered a balance. Villages fall, others rise. That is the way of gods." His eyes gleamed with disdain. "But you... you are no god. You are an abomination. A night without day. A shadow without flame. Power without tether. You should not exist."

His words slashed through me sharper than any blade, but they didn't slow me. If anything, they made the shadows surge, eager, hungry.

"I'll show you what I am."

I lunged. The chalice shattered when my hand closed around Mēnô's throat. His body slammed against the marble wall with a crack that echoed through the chamber. His smirk faltered then, lips peeling back to reveal teeth clenched against the crushing weight of my grip.

"You think grief makes you strong?" he rasped. His voice broke as the shadows pressed tighter. "It makes you blind."

I threw him across the chamber. The silver god skidded, stone splintering beneath his fall. He rose slowly, straightening his robes, silver light kindling in his hands.

"Power without balance devours itself." His voice rang, not just in the hall, but in my skull. "And you will devour yourself, boy."

The word burned hotter than fire. Boy. As if I were still the trembling moon elf who'd buried his sister in ash.

"I buried my people because of you," I snarled. "So now—" the shadows coiled, thick and writhing around me, "—I'll bury you."

Mēnô struck first. Light speared the darkness, sharp and blinding, lancing through my ribs. I staggered, a snarl ripping from my throat. But the shadows didn't retreat. They thickened, fed on the pain.

I let them.

I hurled them back at him in a tidal wave, a storm of smoke and claws that shredded his silks and tore gouges into the marble floor. He raised a shield of moonlight, but it cracked under the weight, spiderwebs of darkness splitting its glow.

"You cannot last," he hissed, voice strained. "You are hollow—nothing but rage and ruin."

"Then ruin will be enough."

I dove into him, shadows tearing, biting, rending like wolves starved too long. His blood stained the stone, silver-gold pooling beneath us. His screams shook the palace walls, his light flaring bright enough to sear the edges of my vision— then dimming as the shadows devoured it.

He fought like a god. But I killed him like a man.

I pinned him against the throne, the same seat from which he'd ordered my family's death. My hand closed over his chest, shadows stabbing through bone and flesh. His body convulsed, the last dregs of power spilling into the dark.

"Abomination," he croaked, blood flecking his lips. "The world will never suffer you to rule."

I leaned closer, my voice low, guttural. "The world doesn't get a choice."

The shadows crushed his heart.

The light in his eyes flickered, guttered, and went out.

For a moment, silence. Then the chamber quaked, a deep, earth-born groan that rattled the stone. His body crumbled into ash beneath my hand, his divine spark bursting free—wild, untethered, a torrent of silver fire.

The shadows seized it. Drank it. Twisted it.

I screamed as it tore through me, fire and darkness warring in my veins, every nerve set alight. My vision went black, then white, then something beyond sight altogether. My bones cracked, my skin burned, my blood sang with something greater than mortal, greater than elf.

When it ended, I was on my knees, the throne room in ruin, the stench of charred stone thick in the air. The shadows no longer whispered. They obeyed. They bowed.

I was no longer Kael, the boy who had lost everything.

I was something else.

The doors burst open. Courtiers fled, their screams piercing the wreckage. A woman stumbled inside, her hair loose, her gown torn—her eyes wide with horror as they found the ash where her god had stood.

She screamed a name, raw and desperate.

"Hima!"

A small boy darted from behind the broken throne, no more than six or seven, tears streaking his face. He ran to her, burying his face against her skirts. Her hands clutched him tight as she backed away, eyes locked on me with terror that carved deeper than any blade. The shadows surged forward, eager, reaching for them. My breath caught—my body ready to unleash—but the boy's cry cut through the haze. Not words, just the broken, keening sob of a child who had just lost his father. For one heartbeat, I saw Mayli's face in his. I turned away.

The woman fled with the boy clutched in her arms. Their screams echoed through the hall until they were gone, swallowed by the night. And I was alone.

The throne sat shattered behind me, the world changed before me, and the shadows inside whispered a name.

*Eclipse. **Kura.***

Chapter Twenty-Five

The first crack of the axe woke me before the light did, a hard report that traveled through the floorboards and up into my ribs. The second came a breath later, then a third, each blow a clean, merciless answer to a question no one had asked out loud.

I rolled onto my back and stared at the ceiling beam above my bed, counting the strikes until the rhythm settled into something like a pulse. The room held the thin blue of pre-dawn; my breath fogged faintly in the sliver of cold near the window, the place the frame never liked to seal unless Kael leaned his weight into it and swore under it like he meant to reason with the wood. I should have slept—should have let the night swallow what it could—but sleep had never felt farther. My mouth still burned with the memory of him. My hands remembered what they had grabbed. My spine remembered the door at my back and the heat of his body closing the world to a single point where yes was the only language left.

The axe answered again. I sat up.

By the time I tied my hair back and eased my door open, the hall had begun to breathe its morning—coals ticking into the first low flame, the smell of ash and old thyme—and a hush that wasn't quite quiet, because the house knows how to listen. Loryn's door made the small sound it makes when she turns over with a hand under the pillow where she keeps what she calls a knife and what Kael calls a poor excuse. Miran snored once, surprised at himself, as if even in sleep he didn't expect to be that loud. Corin murmured a word that wasn't a word and then sighed, as if that solved something.

I crossed the hall, lit a taper from the ember and coaxed the hearth, set the kettle where it could consider boiling, and stood for a moment with my palms to the stone, taking the warmth into my fingers like I could hold it for later. The axe struck again. Outside, the air answered with that small metal ring it makes when cold doesn't want to let go of sound.

"Is he going to split the whole forest?" Miran's voice came from the doorway behind me, sleep-heavy and already dramatic.

"He'll stop when it asks nicely," I said, and kept the smile out of my mouth because I didn't trust it.

Miran yawned like a cat and leaned his shoulder to the frame, hair a tangle that would require a wet comb and bribes. "It's early."

"It is." I found the cups with a hand that knew where everything lived now and set three out because we don't drink alone if we can help it. The kettle considered the request and did not hurry. "Go back to bed."

"I'm not tired." He yawned again. "Is he mad?"

"Yes," I said, because there was no use lying about gravity. "And he's working."

Miran made a thoughtful noise that was not thoughtful. "The wood didn't do anything."

"Mm," I said, which is the sound adults make when children have the right of it and there's nothing useful to do with the fact.

The next strike landed harder. Loryn's door opened, soft. She peered out, braid already tight, eyes sharper than the light. "It smells like smoke," she said.

"From the hearth," I said, on instinct.

"Not that kind." She wrinkled her nose and tilted her head like birds do when they've decided to be smarter than they have to be. "From outside."

I went to the window and set my palm to the glass. Cool. A faint breath of air slipped through the seam and brought with it a taste that wasn't ours. Not resin, not home-fire. A thin, bitter edge that sits on the back of the tongue like a warning.

"Stay inside," I said, too quickly. "Both of you."

Miran folded his arms. "Are we in trouble?"

"No." I put my hand on his hair and flattened a wayward curl; it sprang back up like it had principles. "We're being careful."

He made a show of being very brave about something he didn't yet understand. Loryn was already pulling on her boots, because if trouble is coming she plans to meet it with her feet ready. I let her. There are fights I pick and fights I save for when they matter.

The kettle reached its peak. I poured a little hot water to warm the cups and left the rest on the stone lip to keep thinking. Then I went to the door.

The morning had that hard, colorless look that happens when the sun considers work and decides to be late. The yard was a skin of frost over yesterday's mud, shining where the axe had thrown chips of wood like pale birds across the ground. Kael stood near the pile, coat off, shirt sleeves rolled, his breath a steady cloud that didn't match the violence of his arms.

He wasn't chopping. He was breaking. Each split was precise but not gentle: blade raised, pause, strike, a clean crack that ran the length of the log like a decision, his hands sliding down the haft to catch the finish and bring it back up in one motion. He worked through a stack that would have taken two men three mornings in a single hour like the world had asked for proof and he'd decided to give it. Wood dusted his shoulders, clung to his hair. A vein in his forearm jumped with the rhythm. The muscles around his jaw had set into that line they take when he is arguing with a part of himself he will not introduce me to.

I stepped out onto the porch. The chill went through me like a polite knife. He didn't look up, which is how I knew he knew I was there.

"You're going to frighten the trees," I said, because the first thing out of my mouth needed teeth and humor both or I was going to say something we could not afford to say this early in the day.

"They started it," he said, and brought the axe down again. The split answered like a shout.

"It's barely dawn."

"I noticed."

"You'll dull the blade."

He set the axe head on the chopping block and leaned on the haft, breath steady but too loud in the quiet. He looked at the line of fence, at the rim of the trees, at everything but me. "I can sharpen it."

"I could help," I said, and hated that it sounded like a question.

He glanced at me then. The look was quick; it still read my throat, my mouth, the way my hands had settled into fists and then reminded themselves how to unclench. "No."

"You're not the only person in this house who knows how to split a piece of wood." I took the step down from the porch to make the ground between us honest. "Or use an axe."

"You're the person who needs all her fingers to braid Miran's hair into something that won't attract crows," he said, which would have been funny if it hadn't been a retreat disguised in a joke.

"You can be a coward later," I said, soft. "Right now you're going to talk to me."

The axe moved—just a fraction. He didn't lift it. The shadows at his boots flexed once and then lay flat like they remembered the lesson. "About what."

"About last night." There. The ground was set. The words sat between us like a bowl of water we were both going to have to put our faces into. "About what you do every time I move close."

He lowered his eyes to the grain of the chopping block like it had asked a difficult question. "I told you—"

"You told me 'not like this,'" I said, and the words tasted like the edge of a blade I'd been carrying in my mouth. "Which is not the same as no. So I'm asking you what you need. When? Where? How far you intend to drag me up to a line and leave me staring at it."

His throat worked. "You think I like leaving."

"I think you like control."

"I think you like pretending you don't."

"Don't do that," I said, and stepped closer, because the cold made honesty easier. "Don't throw my stubbornness at me and call it equal to your secrets. You kissed me, Kael. Then you put your hand over your mouth like you didn't trust it. And you walked into the night like the world had offered you an out and you were going to take it before you did something you couldn't talk your way around in the morning."

He closed his hand on the axe haft like he meant to break it. "I walked away, so I didn't burn the house down."

"Then don't set it on fire," I said, and felt my voice go steady in a way that surprised us both. "Tell me the shape of the flame and let me decide if I'm willing to stand near it."

Wind came down off the trees and shifted the line of his hair across his forehead. He watched me the way men watch ropes before they decide whether to pull. The yard held its breath.

Loryn came to the doorway and didn't step over the threshold. Her eyes flicked to me, then to him, then out past the fence. "It's not just hearth smoke," she said. "It's east."

He lifted his head. The shift was small and absolute. "How far."

"Far-far," she said, because she's ten and honest. "But the line's too straight to be a house."

I turned. There it was if you knew how to look: not a column, not yet, just a thread laying dark against the pale sky where the hills flatten. The wind wasn't blowing toward us. The taste still rode it.

Kael breathed in and out like a man setting something heavy down where it won't crush small feet. "Inside," he told Loryn. The word wasn't loud. She moved like he'd pulled a string. "Wake the rest. Boots. Warm layers. Pack the small bags with the dry bread and the hard cheese. No arguments."

Loryn nodded once and disappeared. Miran reappeared and then re-disappeared because he knew enough not to be seen until he had done as told. Corin's door clicked shut very softly; he would be making sure the laces on his boots weren't knotted like snakes the way they always are until someone is watching.

Kael didn't move for a heartbeat. Then he set the axe upright and began to stack, hands sure, the shape of his motion too efficient to be about anger anymore. "We'll need the seasoned wood under the lean-to if we have to bank the fire low for smoke," he said, as if we had already stepped from argument into a list. "Wet wood will call the valley."

"We," I repeated, because my mouth wanted it.

He nodded, not looking up. "Take the leather sacks from the bottom shelf. Fill them with water. If the wind shifts, we soak the roofline—thin spread, not a sheet. It needs to look like dew if anyone is looking. Not a shine."

"That's a lot of ifs," I said.

"That's how you live," he answered.

He finished a stack and lifted the axe again, not to strike, to test the handle for a crack only he could feel. "If it's raiders they're burning line for cover," he said, thinking aloud now, that low cadence he uses when he is building a map in his head. "If it's patrol, they're marking distance. If it's neither, it's a village, and we mind our own heartbreak."

"And if it is raiders." I put my hands in my sleeves to keep them from going to my throat, to my mouth, to the place where last night was still living.

"Then they'll come quiet first," he said. "Check the timber, look for animals, watch the air." His eyes flicked to the tree line again. "They won't expect a hall to be standing."

"Because it shouldn't be," I said, and tasted the edge of what we do not say about the way wood can look new under old hands.

The axe head shone dull and honest. He set it down again. "Get them inside," he said. "In the main room for now. Not the cellar. We don't hide until hiding is the only thing left."

"And you?"

"I finish this." He motioned his head to the pile of wood, as if that was the most important thing right now.

"You could finish it later." I heard the plea in it and let it stand. "We could make a plan that doesn't require you to pretend you're fine."

He looked at me then. Really looked. There was an apology in it, and hunger, and the thing that keeps him from setting his mouth to mine in daylight. "We are making a plan," he said. "You're part of it."

"That's not what I meant."

"It's what I have," he said, and that was the end of it because the wind shifted a fraction and the taste of the smoke came clearer and he went very still.

A flock of dark birds cut low across the far field and turned sharply, all at once, the way they do when something they don't like draws a line where it shouldn't be. The hair along my arms rose. The sound from the trees thinned, as if every small thing with sense had opened its eyes and decided to be quiet.

I took a step toward the porch. "I'll get the bags."

"Take the small ones," he said. "If we have to run, I'll carry the rest."

"I can carry my share," I bit out. "You don't have to carry it alone."

"I know." The words were plain. "You'll be carrying them." He tilted his chin toward the doors along the hall.

That was answer enough for me. "Then I'll need a list."

He nodded once, the smallest ghost of a smile for the way I always will ask for one. "Bread. Cheese. The dried pears. The short knives that live under the table—yes, I know about them," he added when I raised my eyebrows. "The flint. The small pot with the good lid. Blankets. Not the wool ones—the woven ones that dry quickly."

"And your coat," I said, because it was still on the peg where it had been when he stepped out last night and didn't take it.

He glanced at it like he'd forgotten he owned anything that wasn't a blade. "If there's time."

"There will be," I said, and made it a law.

Inside, the house changed shape the way good houses do when asked. The children moved through their rooms with that new, brittle competence they've learned, the one that lives where childhood used to. Loryn stacked the little loaves into a sack with methodical care and checked the knots twice. Miran rolled blankets and then re-rolled them tighter because he has decided being useful is a thing he can practice. Corin, who tells me he is not afraid whenever fear is in the room, set his jaw and cleaned the soot from the small pot like it mattered whether it shone. I took the short knives from their hiding place and laid them in a loaf of bread like stories do when they want to make a point. Loryn saw me and didn't blink. Good.

Between tasks, I went to the window and watched the line of smoke draw itself a little darker against the light. Not a plume. A smear. Too smooth. Not a house. Not by itself. My stomach hollowed and set.

When I stepped back onto the porch with the first armful, Kael had moved through the rest of the stack and into a state that looks calm, but is not calm. Sweat had cut dark lines down his temples. The skin at his throat was flushed where the collar rubbed. He had that look men get when they're listening for something they prefer not to hear and already know they will.

"Do you want me to ring the small bell?" I asked, because we don't ring it unless we must.

"No." He shook his head once. "Not yet."

"Because it will carry."

"Because it means panic," he said, and then softer, for me, "and because I want them to hear it from your voice, not a piece of metal that can't tell them where to put their feet."

I went back in and told them where to put their feet. Miran asked one question—Are we running?—and I told him the only true thing while lying as little as I could. "We are ready," I said. "That's what we're doing."

He set his chin. "Ready is fine."

"Ready is better than fine," Loryn said, because she has decided to be in charge of wisdom until someone else volunteers.

The house finished packing itself. I hid the last of the coins in the seam under the bench where no one sits because it wobbles and we haven't had time to fix it. I put the smallest knife in the pocket inside my coat and said hello to its weight. I checked the bucket by the door and topped it with the water that had come off the kettle after it decided to be useful.

When I went out again, I put the water at Kael's feet without being told. He took the cup and drained it and didn't do something stupid like thank me. The shadows near his boots flexed once, like dogs asking if they could be bad yet. His jaw ticked. Not yet, he told them, without moving his mouth.

"Talk to me," I whispered, careful to keep my voice low. Inside the hall, the muffled sounds of the children carried—footsteps, a short burst of laughter. Too close. Too innocent.

"About the smoke?" His axe halted mid-swing, wood cracking beneath the half-finished cut.

"About last night."

His jaw clenched, eyes fixed on the split log as if he could bury the memory in it. For a moment, he was stone. Then he lifted his gaze to mine, and it was like staring into a storm about to break. "Not here."

I glanced toward the hall, shadows flickering against the shuttered windows. "And if here is all we have?"

His hand tightened on the axe, knuckles pale. When he spoke, his voice was raw, dangerous. "Then I'll hold my tongue until their eyes are shut. Because if I say the wrong word now, Elara—if I let it out—it won't just be you that hears. They'll feel it. Every last one of them."

The wind shifted again. A thin ash flake—too small to be honest ash, the kind that drifts from brush lit at the far edge of a field—made a soundless landing on the back of my hand. I rubbed it away with my thumb. It left a gray kiss.

Loryn stepped out with a sack that was too heavy for her and planned to argue about it when I told her so. I took it and handed her a lighter one and didn't explain. She didn't ask. Miran came behind with two rolled blankets he held like baby animals. Corin followed, arms around the pot like he'd been given a crown to carry and did not intend to drop it even if the house caught fire under him.

Kael's back straightened. His voice changed shape. "Inside," he said to them, and it wasn't louder, it was larger. "Now."

They went. No one asked why. No one ran. The door took them and closed softly as if it had been told a secret.

Kael looked at me and I felt that stupid, serious thing that happens when two people decide without speaking who will do which part of the work. "If it's nothing," I said, "we eat pears and you pretend you meant to chop enough wood for a week because you like a neat stack."

"If it's nothing," he said, "I still meant it."

"And if it's something."

"Then you keep them where I put them and you don't open the door unless I tell you with my mouth."

"You don't like bells," I said, trying for humor and landing on plea.

"I like doors that know the names of the people who walk through them," he said, and there it was again: the promise he won't say where children can hear it. I will stand in it. I will be it. I will hold.

I should have left it there. I should have gone inside and told them three true things and one useful lie. I stepped closer instead and touched the inside of his wrist where the skin is always warmer. He didn't flinch. His eyes closed for one breath as if that one square inch of my hand against one square inch of him had the power to change the weather. His pulse under my fingertips was a faster drum than he would have liked me to know.

"Not like this," I said, and made the words gentler than last night had been. "I heard you."

He opened his eyes. The look in them was a held door. "Elara."

"Yes."

"Later." He took a breath like he was lifting something. "I want there to be."

I let my hand fall. "Then don't get yourself killed trying to prove you can't be."

He huffed something that might have been a laugh if the day had been kinder. "I'll do my best to disappoint you."

From the fence line, a sound like a branch snapping under a foot that doesn't belong to the forest. It was far. It was the kind of far that turns into near without telling you when it crosses the line.

Kael reached for his coat at last and didn't put it on; he threw it over the chopping block, lifted the axe, and set it against the wall. He took up the shorter blade he keeps where a man who doesn't think would think to look last.

The shadows near his boots lifted their heads and smiled with all the teeth shadows own.

"Inside," he said again, this time to me.

"I have to—"

"You have to be where they will run first," he said. Not a correction. A truth. "Go."

I went, because we have made it a rule that when he says that word in that voice, I do. I barred the door and turned to find three small faces looking at me like I was going to make the weather change. I did the only thing that ever works. I gave them work with edges.

"Loryn, lay those blankets under the table and make a lane from the hearth to the back wall we can crawl through if we have to. Miran, fill the little lamp and check the wicks—no spills. Corin, bring me the pot and the bread and put the knives where I can reach them without looking." I kept my voice steady. They moved steady. The house changed shape again. The hearth breathed low and even because I told it to.

Through the window I could see the yard in slices—the edge of the woodpile, the mark in the mud where Kael's boots had gone back and forth, the slice of the world beyond the fence where the morning had finally decided to show its face and was already sorry. The smoke line was darker now. Two more threads had joined it, finer, the kind patrols lay when they want to mark a grid. The birds had gone somewhere they hadn't told us about.

Miran set the lamp down and tried not to look out the window and failed and looked, anyway. "Is he going to fix it?" he asked, in that voice children use when they're trying to make a question sound like a statement.

"He's going to keep you safe," I said, which was not the same sentence and we both knew it. "And I'm going to help."

"How," he said, reasonable and small.

"By keeping you where he needs you," I said. "Which is exactly where you are."

He nodded, brave by force. Loryn shot me a look that was almost a woman's, sharp and measuring. Corin hugged the pot and whispered something to it like it was a person he liked.

The bar on the door felt like a living thing under my hand. I stood with my palm on it and listened. The house listened with me. The morning narrowed.

Outside, far and nearer than I liked, wood cracked that wasn't on our block. Then a holler, not loud, not raider-loud—testing-loud. Seeing-who-answers-loud. The kind of sound men make when they want the world to raise its head.

"Under the table," I said, before fear could choose a voice for me. "Now. It's a game. The kind where being still is the only way to win."

Loryn grabbed Corin's arm and the three of them went without making it an argument. I knelt and set the lamp where it would be useful if we needed it and a bad idea if we didn't. I set the knives where my hands would know them in the dark. I breathed and then remembered how to keep doing it.

The door stayed a line I could touch. The house stayed our name. The smoke drew its threads. The world tried to make me small. I refused. I set my mouth and waited for the knock that would make me a liar or a promise-keeper.

And somewhere just beyond the fence, a voice I didn't know said a word I couldn't hear, and the morning tipped.

The word beyond the fence snapped something in the morning that hadn't decided yet what it wanted to be. I didn't catch it—just the shape of a man's mouth forming a sound that doesn't belong to greeting. Not loud. Not asking for bread or directions. Testing.

Outside, something brushed the fence—the whisper of a sleeve against a post—and then the very faint, very specific sound of a boot sole testing for creak. Careful. Practiced. Not a hunter. Not a neighbor.

Kael's shadow crossed the slice of my window for the briefest heartbeat: a darker dark against the day, a shoulder where a man belongs when he intends to make himself between.

Another voice answered the first, lower, with a slant to the vowels I don't hear in these hills. Moon-elf words cut clean; these were softer at the edges, someone schooling his tongue to pass where he didn't grow. A quiet clink: metal touched metal and then was told to hush.

"Wolves?" Miran breathed, trying to make his fear small.

"Men," Loryn breathed back, correcting him not because she wanted to be brave, but because she wanted fear to name the right thing.

Kael came into my sight line again, but lower now, a shadow among shadows as he moved along the side of the hall toward the corner. He didn't look in; he knew I was looking. He lifted two fingers: wait. Then he was gone, swallowed by the angle where the wall meets the small lean-to we use for seasoned wood.

From the far side of the fence, the testing voice tried politeness. "Hall there! You got water to share?"

The accent did its best. The pitch was wrong. Men who need water use more please.

I didn't move. Didn't answer. The bar under my palm had a pulse.

Silence, like a smile that doesn't reach eyes. Then a second line tossed light: "We're three. Not looking for trouble."

Not looking for trouble is a thing people say when they're counting yours.

Kael lifted his head above the corner of the wall the way foxes do, no wasted motion. He looked long at the line of pines to the east, then at the place where the fence makes its turn. His hand not holding steel made a small motion: two, then three—numbers? No. Angles. The way he marks positions when he's building a map under his skin.

The men outside stepped closer. I felt it in the floor—just the smallest tremor in the boards, as if their weight wanted to come through by itself and ask me to open. The hall had learned us. It settled around the children like a dog lying down across feet. I wished I could pull it tighter.

"Strong hall," one of them said, with admiration he hadn't earned. "New wood."

That did something to Kael's mouth. Not a smile. A bare show of teeth, the kind wolves give branches they intend to move through.

"Keep your heads down," I whispered. Corin pressed his forehead to the mat and nodded against the weave like he could press the word into his skull. Miran had the small knife in his hand under the blanket, not to use—just to remember it existed. Loryn wasn't looking at me at all; she was looking past me, at the door, with eyes so wide and dark they made promises I didn't want to have to keep.

I eased to the window and pressed my cheek to the cold pane to get the right angle. Two men stood at the fence, breath in little clouds, one with a hand on the top rail as if testing the grain might tell him whether the hand that built it was the kind that sleeps hard. Their coats were wrong for the valley—cut like city work—and their boots were too new. One wore his scarf like a man who learned it from watching others. The third wasn't at the fence. He was ten paces back, pretending to look at the trees, doing the counting he thought no one saw.

Kael slid into my peripheral again. He had the short blade. He didn't hold it like a threat. He held it like an answer to a question he hadn't yet been asked. The shadows near his boots did that ripple I've learned to pretend not to see when the world is sane. This wasn't a sane morning. They lifted like breath and then lay obedient again, as if they understood the difference between keeping and spending.

One of the men at the fence leaned in, eyes on the yard. "Pretty chopping," he observed, as if praising a pie. "Mind if we borrow a block?"

Kael stepped into full view at last, not from where they guessed—he'd circled. He stood inside the fence line to the left, where the light made him fact instead of threat. He kept his hands low, palms empty to the eye that doesn't know where to look. "You'll use your own block," he said. Calm. As if he were discussing weather. "Farther from my door."

The men twitched. They hadn't liked not placing him. The one with his hand on the rail pasted a smile onto his face. It didn't fit. "We're friendly."

"You are strangers," Kael said. "Friendly is for after."

The third one at the back turned his head just enough that I saw the profile of his cheek, the cut of his ear. Younger. Nervous. The kind who overcorrect. He made a little gesture low at his side that was supposed to be secret and wasn't. The man at the fence shifted his weight in answer and put both hands up like he was offering a blessing. "No harm meant."

"Good," Kael said. "Keep it that way."

The younger one said something I couldn't hear. The older one kept the smile. "You got a well?"

"Not for you," Kael said.

The smile dropped. The polite voice did, too. "You turn us away? After a night this cold?"

"You don't look cold," Kael said. "You look like men trying a door."

The younger one bristled. "We're not thieves."

"Then you won't mind moving on," Kael said, very mild. "Plenty of road. Plenty of trees. No shortage of air."

"Funny," the older one said, voice going flat. "You sound like a man who doesn't want company. Like you've got something inside worth keeping."

"Breakfast," Kael said. "And poor manners. You've met both."

The younger one took one step forward, hand on the rail. Kael's head tilted a degree. He didn't move otherwise. "That's your line," he said, and the way he said it made the boy's palm flatten, then lift, as if the wood had grown hot. He stepped back.

"Now we're going to be neighborly," the older one said, and gave a small nod to the third, who shifted again, intending to come around for a better look at the back of the hall.

Kael didn't look at him. He didn't have to. "Don't," he said, voice soft as cloth. The third man froze like someone had pressed a thumb to the base of his neck. Kael let him breathe and added, to the first two, "You see that smoke?"

They turned their heads like men who think they're hiding the way their ears move. The east smudge had darkened a tone, drawn itself finer. "Looks like brush," the older one offered.

"Looks like trouble," Kael returned. "If you're smart, you'll put your backs to it. If you're stupid, you'll stand here and ask me more questions." He gave them a bright, hard smile that didn't touch anything that could be wounded. "Sometimes I enjoy stupid. Not today."

They didn't like that. They also didn't like the way he didn't blink.

The younger one blurted, too quick, "You alone?"

Kael's mouth curled a fraction. "You tell me."

The boy's eyes flicked toward the windows. I didn't move. The children didn't breathe. The hall made itself heavy over us like a hand.

A long beat. The older one's jaw worked. He had hoped for a simple mark or a fight where numbers would do the work. This wasn't that. He put his hand to the rail again, lighter, not to test it—because not touching would have admitted he'd been afraid. "We'll move along," he said at last, with a sneer like a punctuation mark. "Keep your precious breakfast."

"I intend to," Kael said.

They backed off—slow, like men who are leaving a room without turning their backs on a dog. The third one at the rear took two steps more than the others, then turned as if he'd forgotten something. He wanted to see how the gate latched. He wanted to know if the hinge sang. His eyes took in the line of the house, the lean-to, the stack, the places a man could put a ladder. He filed it. He would tell someone with a better smile.

They went. Out of sight, not gone. I knew that because the air didn't stand down. The line of smoke drew a second breath and let it out dark.

Kael didn't come to the door. He stayed where he was until the stillness loosened its teeth. Then he walked the fence, not showy, checking slats, touching posts, making the kind of noise you make when you want a listening ear to think you're thinking about wood. He came to the lean-to and lifted his coat finally and shrugged into it with a small, violent motion like putting a lid on boiling water that has no intention of obeying.

I unbarred the door and stepped out because not going to him was something I had no interest in practicing. He turned before my boots hit the step.

"They'll circle back," I said, not asking.

"Yes." He looked at the tree line again, measuring, mapping, shoulders loose the way he makes them when he is about to ask his body for things it shouldn't do in daylight.

"Scouts?" I asked.

"Not good ones," he said, "but not vagrants. They know what they're doing with their hands." He made a small gesture with his thumb and forefinger—placement of a trigger, the way a man rests a finger when he intends to lie about not wanting to pull. "They were looking for signs."

"Of what."

"Of who lives here," he said, which wasn't the answer and was.

"You're going after them," I said, because I know the shape of a leaving when I see it put itself in a man's shoulders.

"I'm going to see where they sleep," he said. "If they're making marks for men with more nerve, I want to know how many of those men plan to be."

"You intend to count them with your knife," I said.

He didn't pretend not to hear the accusation. "I intend to make sure they don't count us."

"Then take me," I said, and it came out too fast, too bright, because there's a part of me that would rather be in the story than read it in the room after.

He stood very still. "No."

"Don't do that," I said, and stepped close enough that my breath made a ghost in the morning air between us. "Don't tell me my work is inside because my hands are smaller."

"I'm telling you your work is inside because their hands are dirty," he said, and he didn't raise his voice but everything in it raised hackles. "Because if they circle back while I'm gone and you've left the door to come keep me brave, the three people under your roof will learn what bravery tastes like when it turns to ash. Do you want that lesson for them? Do you want to teach it today?"

The words landed. I hated them for being true. I hated the way truth sometimes wears a man's voice like that. "You think I can't fight," I said anyway, because anger likes other clothes.

"I think you can," he said, and stepped one pace into me until his shadow darkened the pale skin above my collar. "I think you will. I think you'll do everything I would do and half of what I won't, if it means their mouths still open at noon and say the stupid things children say. And that is why you're not coming with me."

He smelled like pine and sweat and the clean iron of a man who hasn't bled yet and intends to if the day asks. I put my hand flat on his chest to stop both of us from more movement. His heart ran hard. "You don't get to kiss me and then make me smaller by leaving," I said, and felt the tremor in my fingers give me away.

He closed his eyes once, hard, as if the inside of his lids had teeth. When he opened them the look, there was not a plea; it was a held line. "You think I don't want you," he said, quiet, like a knife laid on a table. "You think I walked out because I don't. You think that because it keeps the world in shapes, you can fight. You're wrong." His hand lifted and hovered near my jaw and didn't touch, because he had learned the cost of that when the door was behind me. "I walked out because if I had stayed I would have put you on the floor and I would not have stopped. Not because I don't want you—because I do. And because they sleep with their doors cracked, and because this house carries sound like a church, and because I don't get to take what I want when the people we keep are listening for the footsteps that tell them morning came."

My breath left me in a rough sound that wasn't a sob and wasn't a laugh and was something humiliatingly honest. "Say that again," I said, because I am greedy for the things that hurt and heal at once.

"I want you," he said, and didn't dress it. "I want you in ways that make me look at my hands and count my fingers to keep them on this side of decent. I want you in ways that take the names off doors. But if I make you the way to quiet the other part of me—the part that is a problem the world won't stop having—we won't be standing here arguing. We'll be something else. And I don't trust that something to be kind to them."

He didn't whisper. He didn't need to. The children couldn't hear that tone. It was built for one room only.

"And you think going alone to pick a fight with three men who are pretending they aren't what they are is kind to them?" I asked, achingly reasonable. "You think coming back soaked in someone else's blood is the lesson they need?"

His mouth went flat. "I think not coming back is worse."

"You can't promise that," I said, and felt the raw edge of it open inside me. "You can't promise any part of this and you know it."

"I can promise you my intent," he said. "I can promise you I will make the road shorter for the next bad thing before it finds our door. I can promise you I will put the bad thing in a ditch if it's only three men and a bad idea. And I can promise you if it's more, I won't be heroic about it. I will come back with the number and the direction and we will decide how to make them sorry they woke up." He leaned in, not to touch—just to press the air. "I can promise you I won't let them walk into our yard and find you not looking at them."

He didn't say please. He didn't say trust me. He didn't use any of the soft words men reach for when they want you to do the hard thing for them. He gave me the truth and waited for my hands to bruise on it.

"Fine," I said, because I am not soft and I am also not stupid. "Two knocks, then one. If it's not you, I won't open."

"No knocks," he said. "They'll try." His eyes flicked to the seam of the door. "I'll say your name twice. You'll answer with the right lie."

"The right lie," I repeated, because we tell each other things that sound like jokes, and later we use them for door codes. "Which one?"

He almost smiled. He almost didn't. "You'll say you burned the stew."

"I never burn the stew," I said, indignant on principle.

"Exactly," he said. "So I'll know it's you."

"And if I forget—"

"You won't." He looked past me into the room where three children were being still on purpose. The look on his face made my mouth tilt against my will. "And if you do, I'll keep talking until you remember you're stubborn."

"Go, then," I said, and caught the sleeve of his coat as he turned. The fabric was cold. Under it, heat. "Come back."

He nodded once. It wasn't an agreement. It was a re-stating of the law.

He stepped around me and took the path along the side of the hall that keeps a man out of sight of the road until the last breath, boots whispering over frost that didn't dare crunch. At the corner he paused and turned his head a fraction, the way men do when they plan to say something and decide against it. He said it anyway. "Keep them breathing."

"I will," I said. "And I'll keep the door."

His mouth softened for half a heartbeat. Then he was gone, into the slice of world between the lean-to and the first saplings, hat pulled low, coat shadowing the line of his shoulders. The air where he'd been felt like someone had lifted weight off it and the plank underneath had sprung back into place too fast.

I barred the door and put my back to it until my heart remembered how not to beat like a rabbit. The children had their faces half out of the blanket lane and didn't ask with their mouths. Loryn asked with her eyes, which is sharper. I answered with my hands, which is kinder.

"Show me your boots," I said. They stuck their feet out like little horses at a fair. Laces. Knots. Good. I had them crawl farther back—not to make them smaller, to make the room bigger around them—and set the lamp where the light would look like a question if it leaked and not an invitation.

Outside, the morning put a second thread beside the first on the horizon, then a third, thin as a hair. Not a village. Not a farmer's panic. Grid fire—distance marks. Whoever they were, they wanted to see what moved inside the lines. The birds had vanished in the direction of the ravine; even the crows were pretending they had appointments.

I stood at the window and watched the fence do its job of being a line. I listened hard enough to hear the frost lifting off the weeds. My hands itched for work my body had already done, so I did the work you do when you have to tell your mind you're not useless: I moved cups where they would be closer to small mouths, re-laid the poker where my hand would find it without looking, checked the knot on the cord that holds the little bag of tinder. Small things. Blades hidden in bread. Lies ready to be told.

Something moved at the edge of sight—a gray shape that could have been fog if fog wore boots. Closer than I liked. A glint—not sunlight; steel—then gone. I swallowed and kept my face calm when Miran's eyes snapped to mine to use it as a mirror.

The house breathed with me. The hearth kept its small, steady promise because I had made it do so. The bar held. The wood remembered who asked it to stay.

Far to the east, a new sound rolled in the thin air, not loud but dense: not hoofbeats. Wheels. A cart or two. Supply or trap. Men who mean to stay awhile bring wheels. Men who mean to take children bring quiet first and then sound that can carry fear faster than feet.

I put my palm flat to the door again and told myself three truths: he went because it needed doing; he would not pick a fight he didn't have to; he knows the path between anger and fool and doesn't like walking it in daylight. The lie I chose for myself tasted like iron and onion skin. He will come back before the kettle boils.

Minutes pulled their stupid strengths. Behind me, Corin, who has always needed his hands full, began to stack the cups and unstack them in patterns that made sense to him. Loryn counted under her breath, making numbers march because it makes fear sit. Miran whispered words into his sleeve he would deny later, prayers to no one he knows, just syllables that feel like walls when you stack them enough times.

The yard stayed empty. The fence stayed a line. The smoke wrote its message: we are working.

I didn't hear him come back. I felt it—the air shifted, the way it does when a door in a different room opens. Then a brush of knuckles on the wood—no knocks, not a pattern—just an agreement being kept in another dialect. I didn't move. I waited.

"Elara," his voice said through the seam. Not loud. The kind of voice that makes muscles quit bracing and starts other problems. Then again, deliberate: "Elara."

"You burned the stew," I said to the door, because sometimes the stupid code is the one that saves you.

"Good," he said, and I unbarred and pulled, and he was already moving past me as I latched it again, already shedding the cold and the slick of frost off his boots, already counting where we had put things.

He looked like a man who had gone to the edge of the field and put his eyes under the grass. He didn't look bloody. That was both relief and its opposite. His coat had a smear of mud at the hem, a darker line along the sleeve where he'd leaned on something that had leaned back. His hair had collected a burr. He didn't notice me brush it out of the curl.

"Three camps," he said, no preface. "Not big. Not meant to be. One at the cut below the ridge. One at the old birch stand where the creek does that mean little bend. One farther east, out of sense—bait or a place to run to if the first two tip. They've got children with them."

My eyes snapped to his. "As in—"

"As in not small," he said. He caught himself. "Teen boys. Not fighters. Runners. Messengers. If they see anything they like, they'll run it to a mouth with more teeth."

"Uniform?" I asked, because I need facts to keep my throat open.

"Mixed," he said. "Moon straps, yes. City leather, yes. Nothing that looks like the palace. No banners. They want to look like men looking for work. They'll smell like orders if you get close enough."

"You got close enough," I said, sharp without meaning to, because the idea of him near any of it made the hand inside my ribs twist.

He looked at my mouth and away. "Close enough to hear the way they say the word hall," he said. "Like it's a thing they get to own if they put their boot on the right part of the floor."

I felt the burn crawl into my face. "So we—"

"We behave like nothing they want lives here," he said. "We keep the smoke honest. We don't send any more sound into the trees than the trees make by themselves. We don't give them a flinch or a shout they can taste. When they come back to try the rail again, I meet them farther from the door."

"You're not going alone," I said.

"I am not bringing them to the porch," he said, which wasn't the sentence I asked for and was the only one I would be getting.

"Kael," I said, and put my hand on his sleeve because it's the only thing that sometimes changes shape. He went still under it, the way a horse does when a bird lands on its withers and it decides not to shake. "If you don't come back—"

"Then you do what you already know," he said, and there it was, the cold iron in him. "You take them down the back gully to the split rock. You keep them on the shale until your feet hate you. You don't light anything that has the nerve to call itself fire. You don't tell them stories to make them forget. You tell them truths to make them move." His eyes sharpened. "And you don't wait for me unless waiting will get you farther than running."

"I hate you," I said, honest as a knife.

"I know," he said, and something like a smile ghosted across his mouth. "It keeps us alive."

Loryn's face appeared at the edge of the table lane, white-blind with curiosity and fear. She held my look steady. She didn't hold his; she doesn't like seeing him like this. He sees too much back into people. He softened the edges of his face for her without making it show. "You three," he said, not loud, all authority, "are going to win the game where being still is the way you win until I say otherwise." He crouched, and it is always unnerving seeing a man like him make himself small on purpose. "What's the rule if you hear a man say your name from the door?"

Corin lifted his chin, proud to know something grown. "We don't open."

"What do you do?" Kael asked Miran, whose mouth was already three truths ahead.

"I bring the pot," Miran said, clinging, stubborn.

"And you?" he asked Loryn.

"I decide where we run," she said, not looking at me because she knew that would make me try to make a different rule.

"Good," he said, and put his knuckles very lightly to the floorboards between them like he was touching the skin of a sleeping dog. The hall approved. It eased another breath.

He stood. He looked at me like he planned to say one more thing that would ruin the argument we hadn't finished last night. He didn't. He knows when leaving makes a better promise than words do.

"Two hours," he said.

"No clocks," I said.

"Then by the way the light sits on the left fence post," he said, and that would have to be enough.

He pulled the door open the smallest amount and slipped through without letting the hinge notice. I set the bar and put both hands on it, not because it would make the wood stronger, because I wanted it to know I was there. His shadow slid across the seam and was gone.

The house listened to me again. I listened back. The children breathed in the lane like synchronized swimmers. The kettle, traitor that it is, chose that moment to say it had arrived at a boil. I almost laughed and didn't. I took it off and poured the water into a bowl just to have done something with it.

I went to the window and watched the world. The smoke threads held steady, not closer, not yet. A jay threw its opinion at the morning and then shut up fast. Far off, the same voice as before said the word I didn't catch. Closer, a pair of magpies leapt from the fence like a hand had swatted at them.

I waited.

The first sign was not a man. It was the quiet that follows after men have decided to be loud somewhere else. Then, in the cut below the ridge where the ground dips, a flash of movement that didn't match the wind. Then Kael, or the idea of him—a darker shape that moved like he'd been born with the map of this yard under his skin—ghosting along the far fence line, taking the low places, angling his body so anyone in the trees would think he was a log arguing with itself.

He reached the corner and vanished. My heart did the dumb bird thing and tried to fly out through bone. I swallowed it back down and made it perch.

Two beats. Ten. The length of time it takes to count Loryn's freckles. Then a shout—not at our door, farther, the wet bend of the creek. A single shout. Not pain. Surprise being taught manners.

Another. Closer to the birches. Short. Cut off.

Silence again, the kind you can sweep up and put in a jar.

He didn't come straight back. Of course he didn't. He isn't that man. He rounded the long way, like a hunter who doesn't trust snares you haven't set yourself. When he came into the slice of my window again, he was a silhouette that looked like any other shadow until you've learned the shape of his shoulders. He moved to the door and didn't touch it.

"Elara," he said through the seam, and the way he said my name turned my knees to something that needed furniture. "You ruined the stew."

"I never ruin anything," I said through my teeth, unbarring. "Get in."

He slid through. He wasn't covered in blood. His coat had acquired a second smear and a tear near the hem, as if the world had tried to keep him and failed. His knuckles were raw. There was a leaf stuck to the side of his throat that I plucked without asking, and he took the liberty of existing while I fussed over a thing that didn't matter because it let us both breathe like people again for three breaths.

"Two," he said. "Won't be three." His eyes were on the door, not me. "One at the creek won't be talking. The other went to find his friends who aren't there anymore."

My stomach went hot and then cold. "You—"

"I told him a story," he said. He must have seen my face because he added, "With my hands. He'll remember it when he breathes. If he breathes."

I tried to be angry that he was joking with that frost on his breath. I failed. "So we have—"

"Time," he said. "Not much. Enough for me to get eyes on the ridge and make sure what's coming isn't bigger than a lie can handle."

"You're going again," I said. Of course he was.

"Yes."

"This is the part where I say don't and you say you will and we pretend that's a conversation," I said. "Let's skip it."

"Thank you," he said, and my temper had the decency to laugh at me in my own head.

He put his hand on the door. He didn't open it. He turned his head and looked at me like he was memorizing my mouth in case the day got ideas it didn't need to have. "If I'm not back by the time the light moves off the top of the post," he said, "you take them to the split rock. If there's a crow that follows, don't kill it. If there's a man that follows, don't warn him. He'll think he's invisible. He isn't. The gully will do the work."

"I hate you," I said again, because sometimes the only thing that keeps a thing from breaking is saying the wrong sentence at the right time.

"I'll bring you something to hate better," he said, and then he was gone, into the white edge of the morning, coat snapping once like it had its own spine, boots whispering to the frost like they shared a secret.

I set the bar and didn't move for a long breath. Then I did everything he'd told me to do already, because the body needs work when the mind is gnawing itself. I checked the loop on the little bag again. I moved the pot two inches because my hand told me it would be easier to find there. I took the lamp to the corner and drew the wick lower because dark is a friend if you teach it your name.

The children stayed still until stillness turned into fidgeting and the fidgeting turned into a game they made up to trick themselves into not thinking about the door. I let them. Loryn caught my eye, and I gave her the smallest nod that means: yes, I see you trying; yes, it counts.

The smoke threads out east thickened and then lay flat. Somewhere a branch snapped the way it does under boots that belong to men who think neither branches nor women will mind. The house settled its shoulders. The hall breathed. The bar did its job. The world lined up to try to take something it couldn't have unless we let it.

I stood with my palm against the wood and listened for his voice. When it didn't come, I listened harder. When that didn't help, I did what he told me. I kept them breathing. I kept the door. And I let the fear sit in my mouth without chewing it to pieces, because it tastes worse that way and makes your tongue useless when it's time to say the right lie.

The morning stretched thin. Somewhere beyond the fence a crow called once and then again, and this time its note sounded like laughter that had been taught better manners. I smiled in spite of myself and hoped the world didn't notice.

He didn't return before the light slid off the top of the post. He returned when it kissed the nail head below, which is exactly the kind of lusty bargain he makes with time because he's never liked being told how to behave.

"Elara," he said from the seam, dry as frosted leaves. "You burned the stew."

I opened, and this time there was blood on him. Not much. Enough to mean the morning had answered back. It speckled the side of his cheek in a constellation, dried at his collar. His eyes were brighter than I like and his mouth had that set that goes with his hands being steadier than good sense.

"Tell me," I said, because I am done being kept stupid for my own good.

"Line patrol west of the creek," he said. "They thought three was clever. They have five." He dropped the short blade on the table and it didn't sound like a blade when it hit; it sounded like a bell. "There won't be a knock today. There'll be a test. Maybe two. They want to know if we're worth the trouble of a night."

"And are we," I said, because I am cruel when fear has both hands on my ribs.

His look to me was the only kindness the morning had. "Yes," he said. "We are."

He reached for me then, not to kiss—he isn't that man when children can hear—but to put his hand at the back of my neck for one second and tell my skin what his mouth would wreck. It steadied me more than any word could have. It also set me on fire. He felt it; of course he did. He took his hand away with a care that would have been tenderness in any other life.

"I'll be the one who answers them," he said, and turned, and this time when he took the treeline he didn't look back. He didn't storm—storming is for men who want to be seen. He went like a shadow choosing a place to lie down and become part of the ground. The wood took him. The smoke threads kept writing. The morning finally made up its mind and decided to be a day that would require all the names we had for each other and a few we hadn't learned to say yet.

I barred the door and set my hands flat on it and let the heat in my face cool into something I could use. Under the table, three pairs of eyes watched me for the weather. I showed them my good one.

"We'll eat," I said, because we are not soldiers yet and hunger makes cowards of children. "Quiet. No crumbs. Then we'll beat Kael at the stillness game so badly he'll refuse to play it ever again."

Miran grinned like a boy who wants to win more than he wants to breathe. Loryn allowed herself three bites of bread and one of cheese and then began to drill the others in silent chewing, because her way of being brave is to copy me until she's better. Corin set the pot exactly where I'd already put it and announced he had helped. I kissed the top of his head because I am not above buying courage with nonsense.

Outside, in the trees, a different kind of quiet took hold—the one that knows a man like Kael is in it and has decided to learn his name the hard way. I kept my promises. He kept his. And the line between our yard and their day held, for now, because he had gone to draw it farther out with the edge of himself, and I had stayed to make it a wall.

Chapter Twenty-Six

I couldn't sleep.

Kael had left hours ago, his broad silhouette swallowed by the dark just beyond the treeline, and every second since had stretched thin, taut as a bowstring. The smoke was gone from the horizon now, swallowed by the night, but I could still taste it when I breathed. Ash. Burnt wood. Flesh.

The children had settled in their rooms, though none of them had slipped into true sleep. Their whispers carried through the new hall's walls, questions they didn't dare speak where I might hear. Was Kael coming back? Were the raiders coming here next? If the gods really cared, why hadn't they stopped any of this?

I sat at the long table, the wood polished smooth by Kael's hands and magic, my candle guttering low. Shadows jumped and swayed on the walls, stretching long fingers across the hearth where the fire had burned down to embers. The silence pressed close, thick, unnatural. Even the crickets had gone quiet.

I tried to steady myself with small, meaningless tasks. Checking the doors. Stacking the bowls. Laying out more wood for the morning. Anything to trick my mind into believing I had control. But my hands shook, betraying me. Each time I glanced at the door, expecting him to walk through it, my heart kicked hard against my ribs.

He wasn't just gone. He was gone into *that*.

Smoke that carried the stench of death. Raiders who gutted villages without pause. Raiders who had left us all with nothing.

I closed my eyes and tried to slow my breathing, to remind myself who he was. Kael wasn't like anyone else. He had walked through fire and shadow, carried burdens older than I could comprehend. He could hold his own. I had seen it. I had felt it.

But the silence gnawed holes in my faith.

The door groaned before dawn, low and slow. My body jerked upright so hard the chair scraped against the stone floor.

Kael filled the doorway, bent under the frame, shadows curling at his shoulders like smoke desperate to follow him inside. His cloak hung in tatters, one sleeve torn nearly to the shoulder. Blood streaked his cheek, drying black where it had seeped from a shallow cut. His jaw was set like stone, but his eyes—his eyes were worse.

Flat.

Empty. Dead in a way that terrified me more than any wound could.

"Kael," I breathed.

He said nothing. Just shut the door behind him, slow and careful, as if even the sound of it might splinter the night further than it already had. The shadows trailed after him as he crossed to the hearth, kneeling to rake at the embers until flame licked back to life. His movements were too precise, too clean, as if the only thing holding him together was the act of *doing*.

The firelight showed more than his face. Blood not his own. Caked thick under his nails. Spattered across his chest, his boots.

I forced my legs to move. "What did you—what did you find?"

His hand stilled over the poker. For a moment, he just stared into the fire, its crackle filling the silence. Then he spoke, voice low, shredded around the edges.

"They weren't hiding."

I blinked. "What?"

"They weren't hiding," he repeated, and the words came like shards. "They wanted to be seen."

He looked at me then, and the emptiness in his gaze turned sharp. A knife meant for me, though he didn't mean it.

"They left them strung in the trees," he said. "Bodies. Men, women. Children." His throat worked. "Hung up like banners. Their throats carved open. Their insides torn out and left for the crows."

My stomach lurched, bile burning hot up my throat. I pressed a hand to my mouth.

"They painted symbols in the blood," he continued, relentless now, like if he stopped the weight would crush him. "On doors, on stones. Moon marks. Not random. Not wild. This wasn't chaos."

He turned back to the fire. His voice dropped lower, harsher.

"This was a message."

I swallowed hard, my legs trembling beneath me. "A message to who?"

His jaw tightened. He didn't look at me when he answered.

"To us. To me."

The fire cracked, sparks leaping. I wrapped my arms around myself, suddenly cold despite the heat.

He leaned forward, bracing his forearms against his knees. The shadows behind him shifted, restless, drawn toward the flames like they wanted to burn too.

"They're being led," he said. "By Hima. The Moon God. He doesn't seem to like what we have here." The reasoning felt stretched, drawn out like he had rehearsed it the entire journey home.

The words settled heavy between us, a weight I couldn't move, couldn't breathe around. Led. Organized. Purposeful. Raiders weren't supposed to be that. They were supposed to be hunger and chaos, teeth snapping in every direction until they tore themselves apart.

But Kael's voice was certain, iron under ash.

"They're not hunting food anymore. Not supplies." His hand closed into a fist. "They're hunting us."

I realized, too late, that my candle had burned down to nothing. That we sat together in a hall lit only by the fire and the shadows it cast, his face cut in half by flame and dark.

And the worst part wasn't the blood on him.

It was that his emptiness was gone now—replaced by something sharper, colder. Something that looked a lot like hunger.

I moved without thinking, found the basin, poured water that steamed faintly in the cold. He didn't reach for it. His hands were still—too still for a man who'd been moving through night. I took one in mine anyway and turned it over. Skin split across the knuckles. Blood ground into the lines like dirt. He let me work—no flinch, no protest—while the fire caught and made the shadows step back a little. The water went red; I changed it without comment. He didn't thank me. I didn't need him to.

"What else?" My voice came out level. "If they wanted us to see the bodies and the marks, they wanted us to read something. What's the rest of the sentence?"

He cut a look at the door, then the windows, then the corridor where the children slept behind their new doors with the crooked handles Miran had insisted on helping set. "The rest says they aren't finished," he said. "And they're keeping score." He reached into his torn cloak and set something on the table between us: a small disk of wood with a crescent carved clean through, the cut rubbed with ash to make it look old when it wasn't. "Boundary markers. Lines strung across the woods with these at the knots. They've laid a grid from the ridge down to the creek. Not tight. Loose enough to move. Tight enough to catch anything that thinks it's clever."

I touched the edge of the disk. It was warm from his body. "So they're counting where people move."

"And how," he said. "Where the earth gives up tracks, where it keeps them. The bodies were placed at the edges of the grid, not the center. You're supposed to stumble first and then learn how far wrong you've already walked."

"And the children?"

He understood what I meant and answered the question I hadn't given words. "Taken before. Not left with the... messages. This was about fear, not theft."

I swallowed. It scratched going down. "And you?"

He lifted his hand, and the motion stopped halfway, like he meant to show me something and decided against it. "I followed two lines. Broke one. The other... I let run so I could see where it told its friends to look." His mouth flattened. "He didn't finish his sentence."

"He," I repeated, because people become smaller when you call them a pronoun in a story.

"Boy," Kael said. "Young. Too proud to be good at being careful yet." He looked at his raw knuckles, at the way the skin had split. "He wanted to be important."

"And you let him."

"I let him think he was," he said and looked back at the fire.

The house made a settling sound, wood easing into a warmer breath. I realized my hands had stilled and forced them back to moving, dabbing at a cut along his cheek I hadn't noticed until the light made it a line. "And the organization—you're certain?"

He reached into his cloak again and produced a second thing: a bone whistle, small enough to hide in a fist, carved with the same crescent and two slashes beneath. He set it down beside the disk. "Three notes," he said. "Descending. Patrol calls it to test an edge. One long note means sweep. You won't hear two rising unless a group is calling the cart."

"The cart?"

"They bring wheels when they want to stay." He looked at me so I would understand he had seen this before in lives I didn't own. "They'll want to stay."

The candle had guttered to a stub; the fire took over, a low, steady burn. My hands had gone cold around his and I hadn't noticed. I let them go and reached for the towel, drying him with care I didn't try to hide. "You're shaking."

"Not from cold." He said it like a joke and let it be one for half a breath. Then: "I can hold it here. With you."

"Then do." I tried for steel and found something softer that was somehow stronger. "Hold it. I need you to be the man who makes lists and draws lines. I'll be the one who keeps the children from reading your face."

His mouth tipped, not a smile, an acknowledgment. "You're better at that than I am."

"I know." I set the towel aside. "Eat."

"I can't."

"You will," I said, and in another life that tone would have belonged to a different room. He took the bowl. He didn't argue. Two bites, three. Enough to lie to your body that the world is ordinary while you plan a war.

The hall door down the corridor creaked. Loryn appeared first, hair mussed out of its braid, boots on the wrong feet because she'd put them on fast and in the dark. Miran hovered behind her with the lamp, his mouth set in a line so serious it made my heart hurt. Corin clutched the small pot to his chest again, because rituals mean we're the same people as we were last time we did them.

Kael set the bowl down and stood before I could speak. He didn't harden his face this time; he softened it. "It's early," he told them. "And I'm sorry."

No one asked what for. They know what men say sorry for in houses like ours.

"Are we running?" Miran asked. The lamp shook in his hand once and then was still.

"Not unless we have to." Kael's voice was calm. He tapped the bone whistle on the table with a knuckle. "You're going to listen for three notes going down. If you hear them, you stay where your feet are unless Elara or I tell you to move. If you hear one long note, you go to where we practiced and put your mouths on the quiet." He looked at Loryn. "What do you do if someone says your name through the door?"

"We don't open," she said, fierce. "We don't speak. We don't cry."

"You can cry," I said, because I won't have them making rules that make them less human. "You just do it quiet."

Corin's chin wobbled and fixed itself. "Will there be... bodies?" His voice was very small. "Like before?"

The air hitched in my chest. Kael didn't blink. "No," he said, in that way he has of making the word heavy enough to become true by sheer weight. "There won't be bodies here."

Loryn's eyes cut to me; she measured that answer and found a place to set it inside herself. "What do you need us to do now?"

"Eat," I said. "Boots right way 'round, Loryn. Lamp on the low flame, Miran. Corin, put the pot down before your arms fall off and bring me the small knives."

Kael gave me a quick look that said thank you without saying anything. We moved. The hall became a machine that knows what each part is for. The children obeyed like it was a game we played too often to fail at. I kept glancing at the door without meaning to do it. Kael saw me do it and said nothing because he does not waste words on things I can't change.

He went to the window, slid two fingers along the seam, and leaned in as if he could hear the morning thinking. "They'll test," he said, almost to himself. "Not a knock. A brush. A voice that sounds like a neighbor from two roads over. Someone will say a name wrong and pretend it's the wind."

"You taught me the right lie," I said.

"Say it," he told me.

"I burned the stew."

"You never burn—"

"—anything," I finished, because if you survive long enough, even the dark jokes become a talisman.

He lifted his hand and traced something in the air before the door seam—nothing I could see, but the shadows there seemed to remember it. He did the same to the window latch, then the back door, then the small hatch we used to pass wood in when the wind is mean and we don't want to let it in to make points. The hall felt it. It settled its weight differently, like a big dog rolling closer to lay across your feet when thunder begins to talk itself into becoming a storm.

"Did you see anyone follow?" I asked, because fear has to be fed facts or it eats everything else.

"I didn't lead anyone," he said. "But there was a watcher at the birches who thought he was a tree. He isn't anymore." He washed the sentence clean of anything the children shouldn't take into their pockets.

I poured more water. He drank. That small domestic sound—swallow, breath—did more to steady the room than anything else I could've done.

"What do you need from me?" I asked, because if I didn't ask, I'd start to fill the silence with the wrong things.

"Count," he said. "People. Steps. Heartbeats if you have to. Keep numbers in your mouth. It helps."

I knew what he meant. "And you?"

"I go to the fence," he said. "Not to be seen. To be the thing that sees first."

I wanted to grab him by the front of his shirt and keep him, because I am not a saint and I am tired of watching the world take men like him out into its bad air. I didn't. I'm not a child anymore. "If you hear me curse your name," I said, "that means come back faster."

He huffed half a laugh. "You curse my name when there's no danger at all."

"Practice," I said.

He reached out and touched the back of my neck like he had earlier, just once, like he was lighting a candle there he planned to find again in the dark. "If I don't come back—"

"You will," I said.

"If I don't," he said, because he won't let me make easy laws, "you take them to the gully and you don't stop until the split rock decides it likes you. You don't wait three breaths for me and call it love."

I looked up at him. "I know the difference between love and waiting." It came out sharper than I intended; good. He respects sharp.

"Good," he said, and then—to the children, lighter— "Loryn, your boots."

She looked down, swore under her breath in a way she thought I wouldn't hear, and fixed them. Miran adjusted the lamp wick with a surgeon's care. Corin finally, finally set the pot on the table and sagged with the relief of a man who's carried treasure across a desert.

Kael took the bone whistle and tucked it into the torn edge of his sleeve where he could get to it fast. He didn't look at me for the goodbye. He looked at the door. "Elara."

"Yes."

"Stew."

I rolled my eyes at him, and he took that with him like a luck charm. Then he slipped through the seam he'd soothed, a shadow sliding out to join a morning that had not yet decided what kind of day it wanted to be.

The door settled. The house listened to me again. I listened back. I went to the window and watched the thin gray of pre-dawn decide to turn blue. In that color, the world looks like it's holding its breath, deciding whether to be kind or correct. I stacked bowls for hands that would want them if there was time to eat. I tucked knives under bread. I set the little bag of tinder where my fingers would find it blind.

From the far grove, a crow called once. Another answered from nearer. Then the kind of quiet that isn't quiet at all—just every living thing deciding to listen with you.

Time became the stupid animal it is when you need it to be tame. Loryn practiced her knots. Miran counted with the lamp wick—thirty, blow, relight, thirty, blow. Corin whispered to the pot like the two of them had an understanding and the pot had agreed to be brave if he would.

I ran the numbers like Kael told me. Steps from the table to the door: eight. From the door to the back hatch: six. From the hatch to the small window with the view to the east: eleven. From the window back to the table: nine. I mouthed them and let them become a rope. Eight, six, eleven, nine. Eight, six, eleven, nine.

When the first sound came, it didn't sound like a sound anyone made. A soft brush against the fence, like fabric deciding to misbehave. Then the whisper of a post taking a breath it shouldn't. Loryn's head lifted. Miran's counting stalled on twenty-three. Corin's hand found my sleeve without asking permission. I put my palm over his and pressed once. He pressed back twice. We kept breathing.

A voice, far at first, then closer, trying on a neighbor's cadence like a coat that didn't fit.

Miran's eyes jumped to mine. I shook my head. The voice tried friendliness. "Got water to spare?"

He had better practice than the boy at dawn yesterday. He'd gotten the valley's lazy vowels almost right. He hadn't gotten the way we leave the ends of sentences on the ground like seeds to be planted later. He clipped them. A man from here doesn't cut words like that; we save our sharp for other things.

Boots in the frost. The soft clink of metal making a point and being told to hush. The fence making the smallest complaint, as if the hand on it was heavier than it had planned to be. The house held. The bar breathed. My palm stayed on it and didn't sweat.

I waited for the code that would break me gladly. I didn't get it. What I got instead was silence that began to taste like decision.

"Elara," Miran whispered, and I put my finger to my mouth without looking at him.

The voice spoke again, closer. "Hall there," it said in a tone that had stopped pretending it was from here. "We won't ask twice."

I felt something in the wood under my hand change like a muscle tightening. That would be Kael, I thought—some trick I can't see making itself ready to be useful. I didn't look for him. Looking for him would make him easier to see for the wrong eyes.

The first note came so soft I might have called it wind if I hadn't had the whistle on my table imprinting shapes in my palm. High, then lower, then lower again. Three descending, just like he'd said. The hair on my arms stood up.

"Still," I breathed, so quiet the word barely left my lips. Loryn's lids slid half down. Miran's mouth stopped being a question. Corin turned his face into my sleeve and let his breath warm my skin.

The three notes came again, closer, sure of themselves this time, as if the man who blew them liked that his breath made the world answer back. I could hear the smile he thought he was hiding. I pictured Kael hearing it from the trees and making himself thinner than bark. I pictured the shadow of him spanning the ground between the fence posts.

The whistle fell silent. The voice didn't. "We know you're in there," it called, bright now, as if this were a joke between acquaintances. "We'd hate to bother your breakfast."

"You'll choke on it," I muttered to the door, and Loryn's mouth twitched the way mine did when Kael tried his worst jokes.

Silence again. Then wood creaked—three steps along the fence line, then one backward. Measuring. The man with the whistle wanted to know how the sound carried, where the gaps in the grain were, how deep the posts ran before they forgot their roots.

The whistle again—this time one long note that poured itself into the morning like a line of hot tar. Sweep.

My mouth went dry. My hand tightened on the bar. I set my foot behind me to make my body a different kind of wall. Behind my knee, Corin tucked closer without making a sound. Miran's lips moved soundless over numbers. Loryn's eyes were knives. The house pressed its weight into the ground and decided to be a fact no one had counted on having to swallow.

Something tapped the window glass so gently I almost missed it. Not a knock. A test. Another tap. Then a third, sharper, as if the patience had run out. I smiled without humor. Men who get paid by the hour don't like waiting.

I didn't turn my head toward the noise. I looked at the door seam and let my mouth shape the lie Kael had given me. My lips barely moved. "I burned the stew."

Outside, distant, a crow laughed like it had finally learned a proper joke.

Then, from the edge of the trees where we had our first argument with the morning, another sound answered the whistle. Not three notes. Not one long. A sharp, clean crack followed by a cut-off breath that wasn't a word and wasn't a scream. The kind of sound men make when they learn too late that a line they thought they drew belongs to someone else.

Silence. Heavy. Full of decision.

I didn't move. Neither did the children. The hall didn't sigh. Even the fire forgot to crackle for a heartbeat.

Then the whistle blew again—two hard notes rising, urgent, shaking. Cart. The wrong time for it. Panic where there hadn't been any. Good.

I let myself breathe once, slow, careful, and didn't let it look like relief. This wasn't over. This was never over. But the shape of the day had changed, and not because of the men at our fence.

I pressed my palm more firmly to the wood and felt, through the grain and the iron and the old bones of this house that had been made new, the faintest hum. A signal I couldn't name. A promise I could. He was out there. He was doing the work only he could do. I would do mine.

Another long note wailed, farther now, picked up by someone who didn't know what else to do but blow air through bone and hope it made sense of the morning. The birds came back to themselves in a stuttering burst. The wind shifted and brought me a thread of ash that wasn't ours.

I kept my hand on the door until the tremor left it. I didn't let go of Corin. I didn't try to be brave in a way the children could not copy. I stood and did the simplest, hardest thing in the world: I waited for the man I loved to come back to me after making other men regret learning to breathe, and I made sure that when he did, there would be a house to walk into and a set of eyes that knew the right lie and the right truth when they heard them.

The whistle broke once more, a ragged little call that sounded like it had forgotten its own notes. Then the woods swallowed it. The morning listened. So did I. And in that held-breath space, just before the light came clean through the shutters, I heard the small, unshowy sound of a man's boots moving exactly where he meant them to go. The sounds faded, boots stepping off into the distance.

Kael returned later and took his place at the door watching. Like always.

Chapter Twenty-Seven

I couldn't sleep. The hall was too quiet, too heavy, the silence pressing against my ribs until I felt like I'd suffocate. Kael hadn't returned to his bed. I told myself it didn't matter, told myself I didn't care—but the restless ache in me didn't listen. My feet moved on their own, slipping from the thin blanket, carrying me toward the front of the hall.

The door was cracked, the night spilling through in thin ribbons. And there he was—leaning against the frame, shoulders tense, as if holding the weight of the darkness outside on his back. Shadows clung to him like a second skin, coiling and twitching, restless with every breath.

He didn't turn as I approached, but I knew he heard me. He always did. "You should be sleeping," he said, voice low, roughened by something I couldn't place.

"So should you." My arms crossed before I realized what I was doing. Brave, foolish words for someone who couldn't seem to stop looking at him, at the sharp line of his jaw and the way the moonlight turned the strands of his black hair silver.

That was when the shadows stirred. Slow at first, like smoke catching a current. They slipped along the floorboards, curling around my ankles before I could step back. I froze, pulse hammering. His head tilted, just enough for me to see the tension in his mouth.

"Kael," I whispered.

He didn't answer. The shadows tightened, smooth as silk but firm as rope, binding me in place. My breath hitched as they slid higher, up my calves, coiling around my thighs. My skin prickled where they touched, a heat sparking low in my belly that left me dizzy.

He finally looked at me then. And gods, the hunger in his eyes made my knees weaken.

"You don't know what you're asking for," he said.

"I didn't ask for anything," I managed, though the words were unsteady.

"Didn't you?" His voice was a challenge, but softer than I expected, as if he hated himself for every word. One hand rose, brushing over his mouth like he wanted to hide it—hide the way his lips parted, the way his breath shuddered out.

The shadows pulled me, inch by inch, until the doorframe pressed cold against my back. My hands went up instinctively, but the shadows caught my wrists and pinned them above my head.

My chest heaved. "This isn't fair."

His mouth curved, but there was no humor in it. "Nothing about me is fair."

The first touch came like lightning. Not his hand, not yet—but the brush of shadow slipping between my thighs, feather-light and devastating. I gasped, my body arching before I could stop it. He swallowed hard, and the shadows stilled.

"Tell me to stop." The words were ragged, torn from him like they hurt.

I should've said it. Should've forced the shadows back, turned away, fled. But the word refused to come. My lips parted, and instead of saying stop, what fell out was a broken whisper, "Don't you dare."

Something snapped in him then. The shadows surged, spreading over me like a tide. My wrists pressed harder against the wood above me, pinned so tightly I couldn't move. A second tendril traced the line of my throat, curling there as though waiting for his command.

His voice was a rasp, dark and trembling with restraint. "You don't know what I'll do to you."

"I don't care." My breath shivered out, but my gaze didn't leave his. "I want—" The words tangled in my throat, but he understood. He always did.

The shadows obeyed before I could say more. One coiled firmly around my waist, the other tracing the inside of my thigh, slow enough to torment. I writhed against them, my head knocking back against the frame. He groaned low in his chest, stepping closer, so close I could feel the heat of him through the night air.

"Gods, Elara." His hand hovered near my face, trembling, before he dragged it away and clenched it at his side. "You'll ruin me."

The shadows slid higher, grazing the edge of my pussy, My breath broke into a ragged cry, and that sound undid him. He leaned in, his forehead nearly touching mine, his mouth so close I could taste the heat of his breath.

"Say it," he demanded, voice sharp as glass. "Say you want this."

My answer tore free without thought. "I want you."

The shadows tightened, and he looked up at me, a strained, half-restrained look was plastered on his face. "Last warning, Tell me to stop."

"I can't." The words tore out of me, a desperate plea in each syllable for him not to pull away from me again.

"Good-" A tendril of shadow finally slipped under the thin layer of silk, grazing over my clit in slow, teasing motions. "I don't think I could even if I wanted to now." His smile curved, and he stepped back, the shadows tightening around my thighs stuck, and lifted, spreading my legs apart as the shadows binding my hands kept me in the air, leaving me fully suspended. Kael leaned against the frame like he had all the time in the world, his chest rising slow, eyes black with hunger. He wasn't touching me with his hands. He didn't need to. The shadows moved like they *were* his hands, his mouth, his breath.

The first rush of pleasure hit quick, startling, a slow spiral, the tendril of shadow that had been teasing my core finally making it's way to my clit, covering it at every angle, the sensation of it was burning and warm, as it circulated itself around it. Finding every sensitivity, my back arched, urging myself forward to try to feel more, throbbing with every stroke, just as the lights in my eyes turned blinding the tendril pulled away.

A ragged sound tore out of me. "Kael—"

"Not yet." His voice was low, iron–clad, almost cruel. "You'll wait until I decide."

The next wave was sharper, almost punishing. The shadows toyed with me, solidifying against my pussy, grinding back and forth, teasing my entrance like it was a door they didn't know if they should go through or not, the shadows wrapped their way up my chest and around my breasts, teasing over my nipples. His glare only intensified on me as he watched his shadows toy with my body like it was a show for him, his eyes full of hunger as he stepped close enough to lean over me, watching the shadows from a better angle, leaning to kiss and bite down my neck, the burning sensation was back, climbing and climbing until- Nothing.

When they stilled again, I nearly sobbed. "Please—don't stop—"

His lips curved, but it wasn't kind. It was power, sharp as a blade. "You begged me to stay," he murmured. "So I'm here. But *I* say when."

The third cycle was worse. He pushed me to the edge faster, the shadows stroking me in perfect rhythm, relentless, until I was certain I'd fall apart. My body tightened, breath breaking into shallow gasps, and then— emptiness.

I cried out, voice breaking on his name. My legs trembling in the grip of the shadows, my whole body burning and begging for more that he wasn't allowing me. "Kael, please," I begged, not caring how pathetic I sounded. My throat burned from the strain, tears pricking my eyes.

His shadows shifted, one curling under my chin, forcing my gaze up to his. "Do you feel it?" he asked softly, as if he wasn't tearing me apart on purpose. "The ache. The want. That's mine now."

I shook my head, half-sobbing, half-laughing at the cruelty of it. "You're—you're a monster."

"And still you beg." His words cut through me, dark and steady. He pushed off the frame at last, coming closer, though the shadows did not relent. They coiled tighter around me, dragging another broken gasp from my throat. "And I'm not just a monster. I'm your monster. The one you've been begging for since the first night I kissed you in the kitchen. Can you picture it? How my shadows could have made a mess of you on the kitchen counter. Or how I could have ruined you the last time my lips were here—" He pressed his thumb to my lips. "Or here—" He moved his mouth down my neck again, gently biting at my shoulder, before he crouched down in front of me, his breath brushing my inner thigh as he bit down gently.

"What—?"

"Say what you want."

Heat scalded my face, shame and need tangling in a way that left me trembling. The shadows stroked again, slow, patient, as if waiting for my confession.

"I—" My voice cracked. The denial had unraveled me; there was nothing left to shield myself with. "I want you. Please, Kael. Don't—don't stop again."

For a heartbeat, his control faltered. I saw it in the way his jaw clenched, in the shadows tightening reflexively, betraying him. His hand came up to cover his mouth, as if holding something back, his eyes burning into mine like he was at war with himself. "Then I'm yours. But first- I think you deserve a little gratification."

The shadows pressed inward, the larger tendril thrusting into me, just enough to feel the burning sensation again, the rest of the shadows tightening their grip on me, some snaking around my waist to keep me perfectly pinned in place, the shadow inside me quickening its pace just enough to keep me right at the edge of climax, slowing down anytime I get too close, all while Kael kneels in front of me, watching my pussy like it's the last thing he ever wants to see.

I shook in their grip, sobbing with the intensity of it. "Kael—*please*—"

"You think you want release." His voice was softer now, but no less ruthless. "But what you really want—" His fingers brushed over my thigh, slow and deliberate. "—is to know you're mine."

I couldn't argue. I couldn't think. Every nerve in my body was tuned to him, every heartbeat waiting for his next command. The shadows thrusted a little deeper into me, curling and twisting, hitting every nerve possible, the sensation was too much, the burning, the pulsing, the warm cold that was coming from the shadows inside me.

I collapsed against the tendrils, sobbing openly now. "Please," I whispered. "I can't—I can't take it anymore."

Kael's hand slid from his mouth at last. He looked wrecked, his control fraying. "Cum for me," he said hoarsely, his voice breaking in a way I'd never heard. "And then I'll give you everything."

The shadows stirred faster now, thrusting as deep as I can physically handle, my back arching against the wood, my nails reaching for grip when there was no grip to be had, every muscle in my body tightened sending a burning sensation of pleasure ripping through my body, leaving me trembling against the shadowy restraints keeping me pinned to this gods forsaken door, I need him. I need to feel the cool-warmth of his skin, the feel of *his* cock filling me. Not his shadows. My cry was swallowed by the dark, my body collapsing against the shadows that still held me like threads spun from his will.

"Kael—" It came out fractured, a plea and a prayer all at once.

His name stilled the magic. The tendrils loosened their grip, slipping away like smoke, and for the first time I felt the ground beneath me again. My legs buckled, but he was already there, catching me before I could fall.

I pressed into him, chest heaving, sweat cooling on my skin. His heartbeat was a hammer against my ear, too fast, too wild for someone who looked so composed. He tipped my face up with rough fingers, his eyes still dark with the power he hadn't let fully go.

"You don't know what you do to me," he murmured, voice raw, as if it hurt him to say it.

I could only shake my head, too wrung out to answer. The word *please* still burned in my throat, though I no longer knew what I was begging for.

His mouth brushed my temple, then my jaw, a fleeting mercy compared to the cruelty of before. And then, without warning, he swept me into his arms. I gasped, clutching at his shoulders.

"Kael—"

"I'm not finished with you." The promise in his tone was dark, final. "Not here," His gaze flicked past me, toward the hearth still glowing with embers. "There."

Each step toward the fire was slow, deliberate, like he wanted me to feel the shift in the air, the change in battleground. The doorway had been his shadow–domain, his stage for control. The hearth would be something else entirely—closer, hotter, no shadows between us.

He lowered me to the rug before the firelight, his hands braced on either side of me, his shadow–dark hair falling loose around his face. The flames painted him in gold and crimson, making him look less like the dark broody moon elf I know and more like a god.

The firelight flickered across his face, cutting hard lines of shadow along his jaw, gilding his mouth in molten red. I lay beneath him, the rug scratching my back, the air still thrumming with the memory of the shadows he'd used to unravel me. My body hummed, trembling with the echo of it, but Kael wasn't satisfied. Not even close. He lowered himself slowly, the weight of him sinking over me, caging me in with nothing but fire on one side and his body on every other. His hair brushed against my cheek, a dark curtain that smelled of smoke and pine.

"I can stop." he said again, his voice low and rough, but the fire in his eyes made the words meaningless. A dare. A threat. A prayer.

My lips parted, the protest I should've given lost somewhere in the raw edges of my throat. "Don't."

A shadow of a smile touched his mouth. Dangerous. Satisfied. "Good, I won't."

His hand traced down my side, not gentle—possessive. His fingers grazed down my hips, over the curve of my thighs, gently teasing around my pussy, until his fingers found my clit, gently teasing, circling around the overstimulated nerve endings. He leaned his head down, kissing down my neck, rough, needy kisses, the kind that leaves marks. "Tell me what you want." The first push of his fingers inside me made it impossible to answer as he let out a low growl into my neck.

"Kael—" His name tore out of me again, half-choked, half-sobbed.

"Say what you want." His voice was a growl, the command rumbling through his chest into mine. His fingers stretch apart inside me, stretching my already abused core further, forcing a what felt like more of a whine from my lips.

"You," I stuttered out, struggling to breathe when his fingers were moving inside of me like that. "I need you to fuck me. Make me yours."

"You'll remember this," he said against my throat, biting down just enough to leave heat behind. "Every time you close your eyes. Every time you dream. You'll remember who made you fall apart." The words clawed through me, as sharp as the edge of his teeth. His pants were off in what felt like a fumbled instant, grinding his cock against me, pressing it warm and hard against the warmth of my core.

"Fuck Kael—" The sound that came out of me was involuntary as I moved my hips up to meet him. "Please," the beg came out more desperate than intended.

The sound that came out of him was nothing short of matching the desperation in my plea. He had waited for this just as long as I had. Maybe even longer. I felt him slowly thrust himself into me, stretching my pussy just slightly enough that I felt every inch of his cock filling me. The groan that came out of him was pure relief and ecstasy.

"Shit Elara—" I could feel him struggle to keep control, by the gentle movements of his hips while he decided how far he wanted to go.

"Don't hold back." I breathed out, grinding my hips around him, granting me another low groan from his lips. "I want you—, I want all of you."

He watched me at first, before letting himself unravel, thrusting relentlessly into me, gripping onto my hip with one hand, his other pinned next to me, gripping the furs like it was the only thing keeping him here. With me.

"Don't stop," I gasped, fingers tangling in his hair, dragging his mouth back to mine. The kiss was nothing like the ones before, this one was bruising, hungry, all and fire and desperation. He swallowed my plea with his mouth, his body answering the command before his words did. The rug burned against my skin with every thrust, the fire searing my vision until there was nothing but him, him, *him*.

The rhythm built, unstoppable. My voice broke against the sound of his breathing, rough and ragged in my ear. My nails scored down his back, a match for the dark marks he'd left on me.

"Kael—"

He caught my cry with his kiss, his own body trembling above mine as if he'd been holding himself on the edge for too long. He pressed into me once more, deep enough that I thought he'd split me open, and then he stilled, shuddering against my skin.

For a long moment, there was nothing but firelight and the frantic beat of our hearts, loud enough to drown the silence.

When he finally pulled back just enough to look at me, his face was shadowed and unreadable, but his thumb brushed across my jaw in a touch that almost felt gentle.

Almost.

"You begged me not to leave," he rasped, chest rising hard against mine. "But now you see why I should."

I held his gaze, my own breath still shaky. "All I see," I whispered, "is a man who stayed when no one else did."

His eyes flickered, shadows twitching low at his back. "You don't know me, Elara. Not really. Not enough to understand the danger I bring."

"I know what you've shown me." My fingers trailed down to his wrist, steadying him even as he tried to pull away. "You built these walls to keep the children warm. You hunted so they wouldn't starve. You fight so they can sleep through the night. If that's not knowing you, then tell me what is."

His jaw clenched, a storm rising in his face. "That's not the whole of me. There are pieces you'd never forgive."

"Then let me decide," I breathed, softer than a prayer. "Let me see all of you, not just the parts you think I can bear."

The words cracked something in him. His shadows recoiled, curling tighter around the stones as if trying to shield him from me. His forehead dropped to mine, breath shuddering, every line of him taut with conflict.

"You'll ruin me," he whispered, voice breaking.

My hand slid to the back of his neck, holding him close. "You're not ruined," I murmured. "You're the reason we're still alive."

For a moment, silence hung heavy, broken only by the crackle of the fire and the distant murmur of wind outside the hall. His thumb rested on the base of my chin, as if he was contemplating getting up and leaving again, but he opened his mouth to talk.

He wasn't pushing me away—he was unraveling.

"I left my sister to check the traps," he began, voice distant, like he was walking those woods again. "It was only supposed to be a moment. I remember the air was sharp, the kind that bites your lungs, and I thought we'd eat well that night. Then I saw it—smoke, curling above the trees. Too much smoke." His jaw tightened. "I ran. Faster than I ever had. And when I broke through the treeline..."

His voice cracked. He swallowed hard, staring past me. "The village was gone. Fire had taken everything, everyone. My parents were in the square, on their knees, and Vaelor—" The name cut from him like glass. "He cut them down while I watched. I tried to reach them. I didn't even make it two steps before something struck me from behind. I woke in the ash, alone. My sister's voice was gone. Everyone was gone."

The silence that followed felt heavier than the shadows themselves. My chest ached like the loss was my own.

"What was the name of your village?" I asked softly.

He hesitated, then gave it, Valledel. The sound of it was like hearing a ghost. My brows furrowed—I knew that name. From whispered tales of ruins swallowed by the forest centuries ago. A village that should have been nothing but stone and overgrowth long before my lifetime.

"That village has been gone for ages," I whispered.

Something unreadable flickered in his eyes. "I wandered after that. For years, maybe longer. I don't know how time passed. I only know that grief doesn't measure in seasons. It just stays. And then...the Eclipse found me." He exhaled like the words burned. "He gave me purpose. He gave me power. And I worked for him, because what else was left for me to be?" The surrounding shadows shivered, restless, as if even they remembered the ash. "Now you know more of me."

His words still hung between us, raw and frayed, and I could see the storm of it in his eyes—how much it cost him to say any of it. Before he could look away, I lifted my hand and cupped his cheek, the rough stubble scraping against my palm.

"Thank you," I whispered.

His brow furrowed, as though the gratitude puzzled him more than the pain.

"For staying," I breathed, leaning closer so he couldn't mistake it, "and for trusting me with that part of you." My thumb brushed across his cheekbone, slow, reverent. "You didn't have to—but you did."

His lashes lowered, and for a heartbeat he just pressed into my touch like he didn't know what to do with it, like the warmth itself might undo him. The shadows that always curled so restlessly at his back were still now, quiet.

I smiled, small and earnest. "Whatever comes, you won't carry it alone. Not anymore." He let out a low exhale, and though he didn't answer, his hand covered mine at his face, holding it there as though anchoring himself.

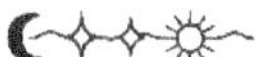

Chapter Twenty-Eight

The first thing I noticed when I woke was not the cold of the floor beneath the rug, nor the ache low in my hips, but the quiet. Real quiet—the kind that feels earned. The kind that settles after storms.

The hall lay washed in thin morning light, soft as milk through the high slats, dust drifting in the beams like slow snow. The embers in the hearth still glowed, breathing red, and the air held the faint scent of banked ash and old thyme. For once there was no crying in some corner, no bad dream, no rolled cup clattering across the boards. Just warmth at my back and an arm heavy over my waist.

Kael's.

I stayed still, greedy. His breath ghosted the curve of my neck; when I shifted the smallest bit, his hold tightened by instinct, gathering me as if sleep had left him no choice but to keep me. Shadows had sprawled around us sometime in the night—thin and loose, like spill-black silk tossed across the boards. They rose and fell with his breathing. I felt the beat of his heart against my spine and, for a fragile breath, let myself believe in the simplest truth: he stayed.

I turned just enough to see him. The firelight had softened his face, easing the hard lines I'd learned to navigate, the edges that had cut me so often when he'd used silence like a blade. There were things I still didn't know— things he couldn't give me yet, things he might never—but last night had cracked something open. He'd let me see the boy who woke in ash. He'd let me see the man who decided to stay, anyway.

My fingertips found his jaw. Stubble rasped against my skin, real and ordinary in a way that undid me. He stirred, lashes lifting, eyes finding mine without the usual distance. He looked like a man startled by the sight of an unguarded morning.

"You stayed," I whispered.

His voice was sleep-rough, a scrape of stone. "For now."

I made a face at him because if I didn't, I might cry. "You're infuriating."

"And yet." His arm tightened around my waist, a dry amusement touching his mouth, as if my insult only confirmed something that pleased him.

We lay like that for a few breaths more, pressed close on the rug where we'd fallen, the wood warm under us where the banked coals had fed the stones all night. Somewhere across the hall a small body turned in a nest of blankets, then another; a cough chirped and stilled. I felt the moment the house woke—tiny shifts, quiet murmurs, a held breath becoming many.

Kael felt it too. He drew back an inch. The shadows at the edge of my vision quivered like watchdogs lifting their heads. He didn't move to leave. He only looked down at me, studying, as if committing the exact shape of the light on my cheek to the same hidden place he keeps every knife and secret.

"Morning," I said, because if I didn't say something simple, I'd say something foolish.

"Morning," he answered, softer than I expected, and it did something unhelpful to my ribs.

A snicker popped from the children's alcove. Then the whisper that follows every forbidden thing.

"Is he—"
"He is."
"With Elara?"
"On the floor."

Heat shot up my throat so fast I nearly choked on it. I started to sit, to gather the blanket up and pretend I'd meant to do it all along, but Kael didn't even lift his head. He only flicked two fingers, a lazy bit of magic like a man pushing a curtain aside—except the curtain rose from the floor itself. Shadows slid and thickened around us in a smooth sweep, black as spilled ink, opaque as cloth. They draped over my hips and shoulders without touching my skin, a modesty screen sculpted of night.

I glared up at him from behind it. "Really."

He made a thoughtful sound. "You said you like the hall neat."

"That isn't what I—"

He raised his voice a shade—not loud, just large. "Good morning."

The whispers died like someone had pinched them shut. A beat of awed silence. Then the small, scandalized voice of Miran, who has never successfully whispered in his life, "They were naked."

"Miran," Loryn hissed, scandalized and delighted.

"I didn't look!" he lied brightly. "I looked at the ceiling."

I pressed a hand over my mouth. It didn't help. Laughter wanted out. Kael, the traitor, didn't look the slightest bit chastened. He tipped his head, and the shadows wrapped tighter around my shoulders—scandal-proof now—then unrolled in a second curl toward his own hip where the blanket had slipped low. A second screen rose, dark and sleek, giving him cover as he reached for his shirt.

"Kind," I muttered, though the corner of my mouth betrayed me.

"Efficient," he corrected, and because he's insufferable, he let just a sliver of darkness fall for half a heartbeat, enough that the older boys saw the line of his stomach before the shadows closed again. Their collective hiss—half envy, half hero worship—was not subtle.

"Buckets," I said briskly, capturing their attention before they could stage a commentary. "We need water for porridge. The well won't draw itself."

Miran saluted me with a serious face he did not deserve. "Yes, Commander."

"Don't call me Commander," I said, and he grinned and bolted for the door with Corin at his heels, their bare feet soft on the planks. Loryn stood slower, eyes tracking the edges of Kael's magic with the same suspicion she saves for eels and strangers. She drifted near enough to aim a look at him that translated, in her sensible language, too *if you hurt her, I will stab you with something I sharpened myself.*

Kael didn't blink. "Don't slip on the steps," he said, as if that were an answer.

Loryn sniffed. "I never slip," she declared, and left like a general who's decided to allow a truce she doesn't believe in.

The shadows loosened. I wriggled into my dress behind them, tugged ties, smoothed skirts. When I was decent, they peeled away from me like soot washing off in a stream and flattened back into the ordinary morning gloom. Kael let his own cover fall a breath later, pulling his shirt over his head with that infuriating ease. The fabric skimmed his scars, silvered lines catching the light before vanishing under linen. I swallowed. He pretended not to notice.

"How's your back?" he asked, deadpan enough to be a joke only if I let it.

"Fine," I lied with the dignity of a woman who refuses to admit to rug burn.

His mouth twitched. "I'll sand the boards smoother."

"If you start sanding because of this," I said, pinning him with a look, "I will never forgive you."

"Noted."

The smaller ones had sat up now, blinking, hair standing in directions that defied gravity and sense. I did a quick count. All here. Safe. The coil in my stomach loosened another degree, and I moved through them the way I always do—hands straightening blankets, tucking stray toes back into warmth, getting a murmur here, a pat there. Kael watched me with that sharp, intent focus that often reads like judgment. Today it only felt like attention. He was building a map again, the quiet kind—the one that lives in who smiles and who winces and which cup is chipped and who always picks it anyway so someone else won't have to.

"Go on," I told the older girls, tipping my chin toward the hearth. "Fill the pot. Small ladle first. Slow pour."

They moved, efficient as any army when given the right orders and a pot they've decided is a friend. The hall breathed with them. Somewhere, a tiny carved horse that had seen better years made its faithful clack-clack-clack across the floor as Corin claimed it for his morning patrol. Routine knit itself into the bones of the day.

Kael stood, rolling his shoulders once like a man trying not to wince, and the shadows gathered along his spine in a ripple then settled. He scanned the windows, the seam of the door, the beam above the hearth where the wood is new and the old nail holes mean nothing now. Then, as if he'd heard the voice in my head, he looked down at me.

"You're flushed," he said, maddeningly mild.

"You're impossible," I returned, equally mild.

Something like a smile warmed the edge of his mouth and was gone. He reached past me for the poker and stirred the embers, coaxing flame. Sparks lifted, tiny stars. I watched his hand instead of them.

"Eat first," he said, like a man issuing a command to troops in the field. "Then chores. Then I check the fence line."

"You're going to rest," I said, equally commanding.

He didn't argue. He didn't agree. He glanced at the door again. The smallest muscle jumped in his jaw.

"Kael." I put my hand on his wrist. He went still. "You stayed."

He looked down at my fingers on his skin, up at my face, and whatever words he hadn't said last night, he didn't say now. He only nodded once, a bow you might miss if you didn't know him.

The door hinges gave a small complaint as Miran and Corin came back with the first sloshing bucket, damp footprints blooming in their wake. Cold air rode in behind them—crisp and clean, laced with the green of the trees and the wet metal scent of the well. I inhaled, content in the small way you can be when every larger thing is a question you've agreed not to ask until noon.

Then, feather-light under the good smell, something else slid in. Not ours.

A faint bite.

I frowned. "Do you smell—"

Kael's head snapped toward the door before I finished. Whatever ease had crept into him dropped off like a cloak. He took two quick strides, set the bucket out of little hands without looking, and stood with his palm hovering over the seam where light spills thin in the early morning. The shadows along the baseboards stirred, attention pricking like the lift of hackles.

Miran tilted his chin, trusting me to be the interpreter for things his throat wasn't ready to name. "What is it?"

"Nothing," I started, and the lie died in my mouth as the air shifted again. Harsher now. Acrid. The sting that lives at the back of your nose when something hot eats something green.

Fire.

Not ours.

"Inside," Kael said, not loud, but the word went through the room like a pulled string. The older children hustled the little ones up onto benches; the girls at the hearth stilled their hands, eyes going wide. Loryn, who had been halfway to the door to prove she doesn't slip, changed direction mid-step and went to bar the back shutters, her face set.

I crossed to Kael. He didn't look at me. He didn't need to. The faintest crackle had reached us—the brittle pop of twigs giving up, the greedy murmur of flame sucking close to bark. Beneath it, there—men's voices, not the ones I know, not neighbor low or traveler high. Shouts sharp with joy that has teeth.

Every muscle in Kael's body drew tight. The shadows lifted in a smooth wave and stood at his shoulders, taller than a man, lean and black and ready.

"Stay with them," he said, and if I had been a different woman on a different day, I might have argued. Today I nodded and turned as if I hadn't noticed the way his mouth had gone thin, the way the light through the seam had stopped flickering and started to pulse.

The kettle hummed, absurd and loyal to its only job. I took it off the hook and set it safe, because doing something small with your hands sometimes keeps your mind from making you stupid. Then I went to the table, laid out cups, not for tea—for water, if smoke came. For mouths that would need wetting when fear dried them out. I put the small knife where I could find it without looking. Loryn met my eyes and put her hand on the back of the smallest child's neck, a steady weight.

Outside, the crackle thickened, grew teeth. A whoop cut the air—too bright, too pleased. Through the seam of the door, a thin curl of alien smoke pushed a fingertip into our good morning and smeared it.

Kael set his palm flat to the wood. The shadows at his back leaned into him like dogs ready to run.

"Whatever happens," he said, low for me alone, "you keep them where I put them."

I lifted my chin. "And you?"

His mouth curved with no humor at all. "I put the fire out."

He looked down at my hand, at the place I hadn't realized I was still holding his sleeve. I let go. He stepped back, rolled his shoulders once, and then the dark rose around him like a cloak thrown by an invisible hand.

The fragile peace of dawn broke clean down the middle.

He unbarred the door in a single, silent motion and slipped through like he'd been made for doorways—half in, half out, deciding which world he would belong to today.

Smoke bit the edge of the air, sharp and wild, and the first true snap of burning wood carried across the yard.

I set my palms to the table to stop their shaking and drew a breath that tasted like ash and old fear. The children watched my face the way sailors watch the horizon. I gave them the steadiness I could.

"Under the table lane," I said, calm as bread. "Now. Quiet feet."

They moved. The hall shifted shape around them, practiced now, ready in the ways we'd prayed we wouldn't need to be.

Outside, voices rose. The shadows in the seam flinched and surged. The forest, our forest, crackled like something hungry.

I lifted my eyes to the door and did not blink.

The door shivered in its frame. Not wind—weight. Something heavy slamming a shoulder into the wood, testing. I held my breath, and the room held it with me.

A scream tore across the yard—raw, short, cut off like a rope pulled taut and severed. Not a child's voice. A man's. The children flinched as one. Loryn's fingers tightened at the nape of the littlest girl's neck until the child went still under her hand. I didn't tell her to loosen her grip.

Through the thin seam of light, the shadow moved fast and sure— Kael's shape and the other shapes he carried with him—then vanished into smoke. The crackle outside stuttered and dimmed, flames smothered the way a hand kills a candle. Something else hit the door, higher this time, a boot trying the latch like it owned the right. It held.

"Miran," I murmured without turning my head, "under the table, left side. You can watch, but your hands stay on the floor."

He slid where I pointed, jaw set, eyes huge and dark. Corin flattened beside him, the carved horse clenched so hard his knuckles went white. The older girls stayed at the hearth on the balls of their feet, ladle and poker in their hands like weapons they wished were something else.

The air changed. The smoke pushing under the sill took on an edge like metal. Voices came closer, rounder, wrong—tasting the yard with their words. A laugh too bright. Boots on the step that had only ever known bare feet.

I took the small knife from the table and felt its poor weight, its sharp honesty. "Loryn," I said without looking away from the door, "if I say down, you drop. If I say run, you don't ask where."

"I won't need you to say it," she muttered back, but I heard her shift her stance.

Another scream. Another wet silence.

I wanted to look out. I did not. I kept my hand on the table to stop its tremor, and I listened.

Out beyond the door, fire spat and went quiet again—smothered, smothered, smothered. In the gap between crackles, I caught the sound of a man choking like the air had turned to pitch in his lungs. A blade rang once on stone. The shadows that clung to the seam like curtain fringe thickened, then thinned, like breath.

The back shutter banged hard.

My head snapped toward the sound. Once. Twice. The latch juddered against wood I had sworn last week we would reinforce after breakfast. We had not. The third strike splintered the old brace. The shutter flew open, banging against the outer wall. Cold air and smoke shoved in with a man behind them.

He was bigger than the doorway made him seem, wide through the chest, a smear of someone else's blood at his jaw, and an excitement in his eyes I recognized and hated. He grinned at the sight of me like I was a thing you grab. His blade flashed. Behind me, Miran moved, too brave, too fast—both hands on the poker, swinging up.

The raider caught it, jerked, and Miran lurched toward him, almost lost to the pull.

I didn't think. I drove the knife up and in, angling for soft between ribs. The man bellowed and backhanded me without looking. A spray of light burst behind my eyes and the wall caught my shoulder as I stumbled. He dragged Miran closer by the poker. The boy planted his feet and shoved and made a high sound at the back of his throat he didn't mean to, but he didn't let go.

"Down!" I snapped.

The girls dropped. The blade that would have found one of their throats met air, and Miran, shocked loose by the sudden lack of target, slammed the poker down at the man's knee with a crack. The raider shouted and folded half a foot, just enough. I stepped in again and drove the knife higher, felt the bite of cartilage, the awful give. His breath went out of him in a sound like a sob. He grabbed for me, missed, grabbed again; I twisted hard, and his grip met air where my shoulder had been.

He went to one knee, then the other, then face-first to the boards, a heavy, graceless collapse that rattled what lived in my chest.

For a stretched heartbeat, there was only the wet scrape of my breath and the kettle ticking on the hearth like it had opinions about timing.

Then Miran sucked air through his teeth. Blood striped his forearm in a line where the raider's blade had kissed him too close while we fought over the poker. Not deep enough to take him, too deep to be nothing. His face had gone paper-white. He didn't cry. He looked at me to learn how bad it was.

"Here," I said, my voice too thin. I tore a strip from the hem of my dress and pressed it to the cut, firm. He gasped and nodded and stared at the dead man like he'd keep staring until the shape of him made sense.

Loryn stood, slow, and planted herself like a post between the shutter and the small ones. Her hands shook once and then decided not to. "They'll keep coming," she said, not a question.

"Not through him." My words came from somewhere lower than my throat. I checked Miran's arm again, adjusted the cloth. My hands left fingerprints in his blood. I pressed harder. He made a small noise and then was ferociously silent, eyes on my face.

The front door shifted—the weight on it easing, then loading again. A shadow split clean across the seam and scattered over the wall, long and thin like a crack. Something outside screamed once and stopped mid-sound as if a hand had closed over its mouth and taken the voice with it.

Silence. Then another man shouted to his friend and did not get an answer. The crackle at the edge of the yard died entirely. The smoke thinned, changed, as if the fire didn't want to be here anymore.

I realized I was shaking when the knife handle tapped the floorboards. I set it on the table where my hand could find it without looking. I met Loryn's eyes. She met mine without flinching. We understood each other.

"We can't wait for him to save us," I said, and my voice came out steadier than my bones. "If they find their way in again, we don't give them time to be clever."

In the hall's dim, the older children shifted. The word *older* didn't feel like the right measure anymore. Corin tucked the little horse under the edge of the bench so he could use both hands if he had to. Miran stared at the blood on his arm and then at the door and squared his shoulders because that is what boys do when they can't square the world. Loryn lifted her chin that brutal inch.

"Next time," she said, "we hit first."

"Next time," I returned, "we don't have a next time because they don't get through the door."

The latch lifted. The door swung open a hand's width, then all the way as if pushed by wind. Kael came through with smoke stuck to his skin and sweat in the hollows of his throat and darkness following him like a tide.

He didn't need to ask what had happened. He saw it in a single sweep: the dead man at our feet, the blood drying on my hand, the cloth tied too tight around Miran's arm, Loryn holding the poker like she'd inlaid it into herself.

"You let one in," he said, not accusing, just naming the thing so it would stop pretending it was anything else.

"We killed him," I said, and the words made me want to sit because saying them out loud put weight on them I hadn't felt until that instant.

He dropped his gaze to the raider, caught the collar, and dragged the body out with a clean, practiced motion. The shadows went with him, slicking across the floor like oil. Outside, a thump and a scrape, then the heavy sliding sound of a body being moved where children wouldn't see it. He came back in the same breath he'd left, already scanning, counting, mapping.

"Arm," he said, and by the time I turned back he had the water I'd left by the hearth, clean cloth, the small tin of salve that lives under the table leg where Miran once hid it from himself to see if he could find it again in a hurry.

"It's fine," Miran lied, fiercely.

Kael sat on his haunches in front of him. "Good," he said without humor. "Then hold still while I make it finer." He rinsed the cut, not gentle, not cruel, and when Miran flinched, Kael's voice didn't soften—his eyes did. "That sound you didn't make just saved your fingers," he said. "Noise tells a man where to put his knife next."

Miran swallowed and nodded like he'd been told something sacred.

Kael worked quick, hands steady, and tied the cloth true this time, snug but not strangling. "You'll keep it clean," he said. "You'll keep it dry. If it weeps yellow, you'll tell Elara before it gets ideas about killing you."

"It won't," Miran said, because he intended to make that true by force of will.

Kael's mouth ticked. He straightened, looked me over once—blood, not mine; bruising at my cheekbone; hands that wouldn't stop their small tremor—and didn't say be careful, didn't say what were you thinking. He only nodded, like accounting for me on a list, and let out a breath that sounded like a blade sheathing.

"The fires?" I asked.

"Out." He glanced toward the windows. The smoke rolling past them had gone from black to a tired gray. "They tried to use heat as cover. Shadows don't burn."

"You did that," Loryn said, not asking.

"I did," he said, and didn't reach for pride. He walked the room without seeming to move, touched the back shutter where the brace had split, pressed the board, tested the hinge. "We fix that today." He turned back to us. "And we don't pretend our luck will keep."

I met him half a step closer than you do when you don't intend to argue. "We won't. I'm done keeping them soft because I want them to have something left of childhood. It's gone. We make them dangerous."

The room listened to that sentence and made space for it.

Kael's gaze moved to the older ones again, measuring not their height but their steadiness. "If you're going to put steel in their hands," he said, "you do it my way or not at all. I won't bury any of you because you think bravery is noise."

Loryn lifted the poker a hair. "What's your way?"

He didn't take the bait. "We start with feet," he said. "Then with hands. Then with eyes. Steel last. A blade is the easiest part. The rest is work."

Miran's head bobbed too fast. "I can work."

"You'll learn to be quiet first," Kael said. "Then you'll learn to see. Then to move where the seeing tells you to. Today you found out how heavy a body is when it stops arguing. You'll learn to move around that truth, not through it like you have something to prove."

The children went solemn, even the ones who didn't fully understand. The hall changed shape again, not into fear this time, but into a place that had decided to do something about it.

"Eat first," I said, because routine is scaffolding you climb to do hard things. "Everyone with a cup, slow, no spills." I set the pot on the trivet and poured water along the edge to keep the porridge from sticking because today of all days the last thing we needed was smoke we made ourselves.

While they ate, Kael and I barred the back shutter with a length of sound wood he pulled from the stores, his fingers moving with a carpenter's certainty that made something complicated twist in my chest. He set a new brace, tested it with his weight, nodded. "Better," he said. "Not perfect."

"Perfect is a lie," I said. "Better keeps breath moving."

He set the hammer down. "Then better."

When bowls were scraped clean and there was nothing left to distract their hands, Kael turned the big table sideways and pushed it back against the wall to clear space on the floor. He didn't tell anyone to move. They moved anyway, drawn by the gravity of something that made more sense than waiting.

"We fight in a house," he said, standing where the light found him and made the shadows at his back look like wings, "not a field. That means we don't swing wide. We don't show off. We don't let our arms take us where our feet didn't agree to go." He tapped his boot heel to the boards. "Everything starts here."

He had them mimic his stance—knees soft, weight balanced, toes pointed the way they meant to live. He pushed Miran's shoulder lightly until the boy found the lean that would let him move forward without falling. He nudged Loryn's ankle with the side of his boot and said, "Less proud," and when she bristled he added, "Proud is taller. Tall gets cut." She lowered an inch and looked more dangerous for it.

"Hands," he said next. He showed them where to put their palms if someone grabbed their wrists, how to turn the thumb, not the whole arm. He let each of them catch his forearm and try to hold it. He slipped out of their grips like water and had them do it back to him until they learned that strength is sometimes only a trick of angles and a decision not to panic.

"Eyes," he said. "What do you look at?"

"His weapon," Corin piped.

"No," Kael said. "You look at his middle. The weapon lies. The middle doesn't." He pointed to his own sternum. "You watch this. It tells you where the rest will go."

He walked Loryn through a simple shoulder-check that would take a man off his feet if he'd been foolish enough to underestimate her. He taught Miran how to use a doorway as an ally, how to keep his back to a wall so no one could put a knife where he couldn't see it. He showed the older boys how to step *past* a reaching arm so the arm belonged to them for a heartbeat and then belonged to the floor.

The shadows slid along the edges of the room, quiet, attentive, keeping the boundary as if it were their own lesson. When someone's heel squeaked on the board, they winced and lifted their foot and set it down smoother the next time. Kael said little, only what couldn't go wrong. I filled the space between his curt corrections with the kind of encouragement that doesn't make a person soft— "Yes, like that," and "Again," and "Hold your breath for two and then let it go."

"Steel," Loryn said at last, breathless and hungry. "When do we get steel?"

"When your feet know how not to trip over it," Kael said without blinking. Then, because he read the stubborn tilt of her chin and didn't want it wasted, he added, "Soon."

I brought the short knives from their hiding place in the bread bin and laid them on the table one by one. Kael checked each with a thumb along the edge and set aside the one with the nick that might fail them. He handed Loryn a blade with a plain wooden grip, not the prettiest, the one that would not slip. He handed Miran nothing but the stick he'd used earlier.

Miran flushed. "I killed a man," he blurted, too loud, too proud, trying to swallow fear with bravado.

Kael's look cut that talk clean in two. "You helped keep your family alive," he said. "The man killed himself when he brought a knife into your house. You don't take pride in that. You take notes."

Miran's throat bobbed. He nodded. He held the stick like it mattered.

Kael sets them in pairs, slow at first—reach, turn, step, press; the small violence of a wrist twist; the safer violence of a shove that puts a body into a table instead of a knife. He made them swap partners, so they learned different weights, different tempers. He made them switch which hand they favored. He made them say "enough" when they meant stop and honored it like a law, and in that way he taught them the word has teeth if you give it any.

I worked the edges—tying Miran's bandage cleaner, taking a look at a bruised knuckle here, smoothing fear with tasks there: "You—fetch more water. You—fold those blankets tight. You—bring me the cord from the shelf; no, not that one, the stronger one we saved from the old tent." Busy children are braver children. Braver children make fewer mistakes.

By the time the light had turned from thin to honest morning, sweat had broken across Kael's temples. He didn't slow. He took Loryn through a drill again and again until her feet found the place they belonged without a thought. When she finally nailed it, smooth as breathing, he didn't praise her. He nodded once like they had both agreed on a truth. It put steel in her spine better than sugar ever could.

We stopped only when the little ones began to drift—eyes heavy, mouths slack, the exhaustion after fright catching up. I released them to nap in the small rooms, two to a bed, older ones posting themselves at doorways like dogs who had decided their bodies were worth something after all. The hall quieted into the hard kind of peace. The dead man was no longer in the corner to make a lie of it.

Kael leaned his hands on the table and rolled his neck once, the movement pulling at the torn shoulder of his shirt. A line of red tracked there were something sharp had tried for him and failed. I reached for the salve tin without asking. He let me dab at the scrape; the skin there went hot under my fingers. His shadows lay flat, dozing, but they kept an eye on the seams, anyway.

"Again after we eat," he said, not to the room, not to me—just to the day. "Short drills. No flourishes. Lines and exits. Where to put your back. Where not to put your feet."

"And if they come again before then?" Loryn asked, blade at her side, pointing down like he'd told her.

Kael's mouth pressed into something that wasn't a smile. "Then you use your feet and your eyes and your hands exactly like you did without knowing how. Only sharper. And you don't wait to be brave."

She nodded, solemn. Miran lifted his stick like it was a promise. Corin tucked his carved horse back into the corner, just so, as if it were his job to convince the room nothing had changed when everything had.

I met Kael's gaze across the table. The hall held our look, and in it was a conversation we didn't have time to have.

"We train," I said.

"We train," he agreed. He tipped his head toward the windows where the smoke had thinned to a ghost and the sky beyond them had settled into a pale, bruised blue. "And we don't pretend the day is done with us."

He was right. Even the quiet felt like a held breath. I put my palm to the beam above the hearth, feeling the warmth there, the life we'd managed to stitch together between burns. Under my hand, the wood hummed like a thing that wanted to last.

From the far edge of the yard, a sound rose—not fire, not men. Something lower, stranger. The hair lifted along my arms.

Kael's head turned, slow. The shadows at his back pricked their ears.

Out beyond the smoldering treeline, a light bled through the smoke. Not a firelight. Gold. Blinding, pure, too steady for flame. It spread in long rays like spears cast over the blackened ground.

The air shifted. Heat rolled across the clearing, pushing against the cool night air like an invisible hand. The children behind me went silent all at once, every breath caught, as if even they knew something older than them all had stepped into the world.

Kael's stance didn't move, but his shoulders tightened. His shadows fanned out across the ground, trembling faintly like a pack of wolves sensing the alpha they could never defy.

The gold light resolved into a figure—tall, broad, his presence eclipsing even the surrounding flames. Solari. The Sun God. His gilded hair caught the blaze like it was born from it. His armor glowed faintly as though hammered from the heart of a star. His eyes found Kael first, and I swear the night bent to make room for his gaze.

I wanted to believe—just for a breath—that he was here to save us. That he'd come for the children, for me. But the weight in his stare wasn't salvation. It was judgment.

Then another light stirred the smoke—this one colder. Silver sliding along the ash, pale as a blade under moonlight. From the opposite side of the treeline, Hima descended with a grace that cut sharper than any flame. The Moon God. His pale hair shimmered like frost, his expression calm, almost curious, though the legion behind him was anything but.

Shadows shifted in the haze. Dozens—no, hundreds—of figures poured from the treeline, their armor glinting with lunar sigils. Moon-elf warriors. An army.

My breath snapped against my ribs. This wasn't a rescue. It was a reckoning.

Kael stepped forward, one pace only, his shadows lashing the dirt behind him. "Inside," he said, low, the word meant for me alone.

I didn't move. My hands were braced on the wood of the window frame, nails biting into it. The hall behind me quivered with fear.

"Elara." His voice cut sharper, shadows spiking at the edges of the yard. "Go inside. Now."

I flinched but couldn't tear my eyes away—not from Solari's unwavering stare, not from Hima's calm cruelty, not from the lines of soldiers flanking them both.

Kael's shadows wrapped around him, pooling and tightening as if preparing for a storm. Solari's light flared brighter in answer, Hima's silver rising to meet it, and for a heartbeat the entire yard seemed to split between day and night. The air thrummed. The ground vibrated beneath my feet. And as the three of them faced one another—sun, moon, and shadow—the world itself seemed to hold its breath. And I made my way inside. Anchoring myself at the window.

Chapter Twenty-Nine

The moment the words left my mouth—*Go inside*—I caught the flicker of hesitation in her eyes. But this time, she obeyed.

The door shut with a muffled thud, cutting her from view. For a breath, relief eased the coil in my chest. At least she was safe behind the walls. At least she listened.

But then—movement. From the corner of my vision, I saw her silhouette framed in the narrow hall window. Her face pressed to the glass, pale in the firelight, her gaze locked on me. She hadn't truly left.

And somehow, knowing she was still there—watching, seeing—steadied and shattered me all at once.

The clearing emptied of breath. Then Solari stepped forward. His presence made the air itself glow, a burn along my skin, like the sky was trying to peel me open. He had left the heavens to stand in the dirt. For this. For me.

"I knew the moment I saw the hall," Solari said, voice carrying like a verdict. "No elf builds like that—not with stone and shadow woven into its bones. You left your mark. I should have destroyed it before it grew into this lie."

Behind him, Hima walked lightly, all cold moonlight and contempt. His legion of moon-elves flared out in a line, their silver armor catching the firelight from the forest edge. A wall of spears and bows. A reminder that this wasn't just a reckoning—it was an execution.

"You speak of lies," I snarled, shadows hissing from my palms, "but your line began in blood. Do you remember what your father did Solari? What he allowed?" His question was met with a hesitated silence from Solari. "Or how about your father? Slaughtering innocent families and children all for the sake of territory and sacrifice? Your father—"

Hima's smile was thin as he cut me off. "My father is ash. You, however, are not. That's the problem."

The first blow was Solari's—a lance of light, sharp and fast. I dragged the shadows up into a wall. The impact ripped the ground, throwing sparks of white and black into the night. My chest jolted with the force, but I stayed standing.

The moon warriors tightened their ring, but none came forward. This was between gods.

I drove the shadows forward, tendrils striking like vipers at Solari. He cut through them, golden arcs scattering them like smoke. Hima darted in with silver fire, a slash of light that cracked across my shoulder, searing through fabric and skin.

I staggered, teeth grinding. My body screamed for release. This false form—this elf's skin I'd worn like armor—was fraying. Every time I threw the shadows, my strength bled faster.

Don't. Not yet. If she sees—

Another strike from Solari hammered me to one knee. My vision blurred, edges glowing red. Shadows swarmed, desperate, wild. My heart pounded too fast, too heavy, and then it broke.

The change ripped through me.

Black hair lengthened, sweeping past my shoulders like liquid night. Tattoos burned up my arms, over my chest, curling up my throat in jagged lines of red and black. My muscles strained and stretched, strength flooding every vein as if the earth itself poured into me. When my eyes snapped open, the world blazed in scarlet.

The shadows at my back screamed like old friends finally unchained.

Hima's face hardened. "There he is. The abomination."

Solari's jaw clenched, but he didn't look surprised—only grim, as if the world had proved him right. "Kura."

The name hung in the clearing like a curse.

I forced air into my lungs. "Kael," I rasped. My voice came rougher, deeper, edged with something no longer mortal. "My name is Kael." Solari's light surged, but I met it with shadows, the collision thunderous enough to shake the trees. Each strike tore more of me loose, unraveling what little disguise I'd clung to.

And then—The sound of the door opening. The scuff of her bare feet on stone. I twisted too fast, my chest clenching tight. She stood just outside the hall, framed by firelight, her hand white-knuckled on the doorframe. Her eyes found me—not Kael, not the stranger who had built the hall and carried water, but the thing beneath.

Her breath caught, and mine broke.

"**No**." The word tore out of me, guttural, raw. Not at Solari, not at Hima, but at her.

The word broke something inside me.

No.

It wasn't the sound of refusal—it was grief, as if he'd known this moment was coming, as if he'd prayed it never would. And yet here it was. The man before me wasn't Kael. Not the weary stranger who had carried stone with bare hands, who had knelt in ash to build the hall the children now slept in,

who had listened to me rage and weep and laugh until I thought maybe—
maybe—I was allowed to live again.

This was someone else.

His shoulders broadened beyond anything mortal, black hair spilling
like ink, his skin alive with blood-red markings that seared up his arms and
across his throat. His eyes—gods, his eyes—were no longer night but furnace,
molten red that cut through me like blades.

And I knew him. Not by name, but by ruin.

The clearing blurred. My breath hitched as if the air itself turned to ash
in my lungs. Images rose, unbidden, cruel: the night the eclipse blotted out the
sky, the roar of flames, the shadows tearing through my village, my mother's
scream cut short. The hand that had dragged me beneath broken beams, the
silence after.

That was him. That was *this*.

My legs trembled, refusing to move forward, refusing to retreat. I
clutched the doorframe until my knuckles ached, nails splitting against wood.

"No…" The word escaped me, ragged. "No. You—"

Kael—Kura—whatever he was, flinched at the sound, like my voice
hurt worse than Solari's fire.

Behind him, Solari stood taller, righteous light haloing his frame. He
didn't need to name what I already saw. Hima didn't hesitate to.

"The abomination," the Moon God sneered, his silver fire dripping
with contempt. "You let him crawl inside your walls, sun-child? Let him curl
his lies around you?" His voice sliced like a blade. "You let the butcher of your
kind lay his hands on you?"

I couldn't answer. My throat had sealed shut.

My heart screamed yes. My soul screamed no.

Kael's—*Kura's*—gaze clung to mine, desperate, wild. His chest heaved, shadows trembling at his back as if they mirrored his panic. "Elara," he rasped, reaching as though he could cross the distance with a single word. "It's still me."

I shook my head, tears streaking hot down my cheeks. "You... you killed them. My family. My village. Everything." My voice broke. "You left me with nothing."

His hand dropped. The fight faltered in him, only for a breath, but enough that Solari's next blow sent him staggering back. The light splintered across his tattoos, searing red against red.

He didn't fall. He refused. But every line of him seemed carved open. Not just from their magic—mine too.

I should have hidden inside. I should have shut the door and let the gods tear each other apart. But I couldn't move. Not when the truth stood so plainly before me. Not when the man who had rebuilt my world turned out to be the same one who had burned it down.

The children's laughter in the hall echoed faintly behind me, oblivious. They still believed in him. In us. In what we'd built together.

And I—

I had to watch it shatter.

"Why?" The word tore from me, thin and broken. "Why come here? Why pretend?"

His face twisted. Not with anger, not with cruelty, but with something far worse—shame. His mouth opened, then closed, like every truth he wanted to give me would only damn him further.

Solari's voice cut the silence. "Because that's what he does. He takes. He lies. He destroys." His eyes flicked toward me, golden and unyielding. "You see it now, don't you?"

I did. Gods help me, I did.

And yet when Kael stumbled again, shadows coiling protectively around him, my body lurched forward before my mind caught up—as if instinct still wanted to shield him.

The man I loved.
The god I feared.
One and the same.

I didn't know if I wanted to run to him or strike him down.

The ground split beneath them as light and shadow collided, thunderous blasts ringing through the clearing. Yet I couldn't hear them. Not really. All I heard was his voice, raw and broken—*Elara.*

And I couldn't move.

Every strike that landed on him rattled in my chest, every flicker of his eyes searching for me carved deeper into my ribs. He should have been watching them. He should have been fighting. But instead, every blow landed easier because of me.

"Pathetic," Hima spat, voice sharp with scorn. "Look at him—eyes off the battle, begging a mortal child for forgiveness." Silver light flared from his hands, searing into Kura's side. The god staggered, gritting his teeth, but his gaze didn't leave mine.

"Elara," he rasped again, chest heaving, "please—go inside."

I couldn't. I wouldn't.

"You should listen," Hima mocked, prowling forward, his soldiers shifting like shadows behind him. "Your god wears a mask, and it's cracking. Do you like what you see underneath?"

My stomach turned. His words lanced through the raw wound splitting me open.

Kael—Kura—straightened, blood running dark along his ribs, shadows pulling tighter to shield him. His voice shook but didn't falter. "Leave her out of this."

Solari's golden light lashed across his back. He roared, staggering but holding. "You dragged her in the moment you stepped foot in that village," Solari said, his voice taut with anger—and something else, something that made my heart twist further.

"She doesn't belong to you," Kura spat, throwing a wall of shadow against the searing tide of sunlight. The ground hissed where the two forces collided. "None of them do."

"And yet you keep them," Hima sneered, circling like a predator. "The little ones, the helpless ones. Do they know what kind of beast shelters them? Or do you hide that, too?"

The smirk he cast at me made bile rise in my throat. He *wanted* me here. He *wanted* to twist every knife, to force me to look.

I swallowed, shaking, nails biting into the wood of the doorway until splinters dug into my skin. "Stop it," I whispered, but no one listened.

Kael—Kura—lifted a hand, shadows rising to block the next barrage, his body heaving with the strain. He looked at me through the darkness. *Go back inside.*

I shook my head, tears streaming. "Not without you."

The hesitation cost him—Hima's silver strike slammed across his chest, ripping a cry from his throat. He staggered, knees nearly buckling, but his shadows surged again, slamming the Moon God back a pace.

"Stupid girl," Hima hissed at me, eyes gleaming. "Do you think he hasn't done this before? Do you think your pretty little village was his first? How many women cried your same tears while he stood over the ruins?"

"No!" The word tore from my lungs before I could stop it. "He's not—"

"Not what?" Hima cut me off, voice cold. "Not the butcher who painted your people's bodies across the dirt? Not the monster who stands here now, red-eyed and branded by shadow?" His smirk widened. "Look closer, sun-child. You already know the truth."

The shadows around Kura flickered, his jaw tight with fury—but his eyes... gods, his eyes never stopped clinging to me. Even as Solari's light hammered down. Even as Hima's jeers ripped through my resolve.

"Elara—" he choked, staggering under the twin assault. "Please."

But I wouldn't move. Couldn't.

Because even as the gods bore down on him, even as his body broke under their light, I could see it: the man who had built a hall with his hands, who had carried children on his shoulders, who had cut bread into pieces so no one would go hungry. The man who had sat beside me in silence until silence no longer felt so heavy.

Kael.

Kura.

Both.

And my heart was being split in two with every breath.

Moonlight ran along the length of his spear as he lifted it a fraction, just enough to let the silver bite the air. "The ember who lived. Tell me, little sun-elf, do you remember the night your village learned to be quiet? The sky went wrong, the houses breathed smoke, and your people discovered how quickly a throat forgets how to scream."

The words hit where they were meant to. My mouth went dry. The ash that never really leaves the back of my tongue rose like it had been waiting. For a heartbeat I was under splintered beams again, tasting soot, counting heartbeats to the shape of boots outside that never turned into rescue.

Hima stepped closer. "You were there when your mother stopped," he added, voice soft as if he were telling me my own history. "You were there when the light ran out of the faces you loved. And now—" he looked past me, to the shadowed figure bleeding and breathing hard in the yard "—now you cling to the thing that finished the work."

My hand found the doorframe without thinking. The wood bit into my palm. Inside the hall, a floorboard creaked the way it only does when small feet forget which plank complains. I didn't look back. I didn't dare.

Across the yard, Kael—Kura, and there was no use pretending anymore—shifted like a man forcing his bones to stay where he needs them. His chest heaved. The tattoos that climbed his arms and throat pulsed like embers when he moved. His eyes found mine, hot and red. The look there wasn't apology. It was a warning. It was *please*.

"Inside," he said. His voice was wrecked. "Elara. Inside."

I stepped out instead, just beyond the threshold.

It wasn't bravery. It wasn't defiance for its own sake. It was something simpler, stubborn and honest as a nail: I wasn't going to let Hima speak *for* me.

"You think you know me?" I asked. It surprised me how steady I sounded, considering how hard my heart was beating. Heat was already crawling under my skin, rising, hard to contain. "You know nothing."

Hima's smile sharpened. "Oh? Enlighten a god."

"You're not here to be enlightened," I said. "You're here to make noise and call it judgment. You talk about what I lost like you were a witness, like you offered a hand and watched me refuse it. But you weren't there to help. You were there to *hurt*. You and yours came to take. You keep calling him a monster, but when we had nothing he raised walls. When children were hungry, he cut the bread smaller so everyone ate. When fear made the room too small, he sat on the floor and made it big again. He stood in front of us when no one else would, including you."

A crease formed between Hima's brows. It wasn't confusion. It was irritation at being contradicted.

"You mistake shelter for virtue," he said lightly. "An abomination can build a box as easily as a temple. That doesn't make it sacred. It only makes the prison more comfortable."

"You mistake power for worth," I shot back, the heat in my chest pushing the words out before I could smooth them. "You think standing on a hill and calling yourself god is the same as being one. It isn't. It's just height and noise. You haven't built anything you didn't plan to own. He has. And you hate him for it."

The smile fell away. "Careful," Hima said, and the warning in it wasn't about etiquette. "Your tongue is making purchase it can't afford"

"Then come try to collect," I said, and the heat finally broke loose.

Fire jumped from my hands.

It wasn't neat. It wasn't shaped. It flew the way a breath does when your body remembers it wants air—sudden, hungry, too strong. The air between us warped. The grass hissed, curled, blackened. Hima pivoted aside, spear flashing as he knocked the blast into the dirt where it carved a dark scar the length of a cart.

He laughed, low and delighted. "Oh, she *bites*."

I didn't stop. The next burst came hotter. He deflected that one, too, but not with the same lazy grace—his wrist firmed, his footing sharpened. I threw again—left, then right, then high, so he had to lift the spear and leave his middle open. He flowed around each strike, but the smirk thinned at the edges.

"Good," he said, circling. "Let's see how bright the ember burns."

On my left, Solari's light dimmed a fraction; his head turned. He shouldn't have been watching me. He should have kept hammering at the man of shadow in front of him. But his eyes found me anyway—gold hardening, focus tightening, the smallest flicker crossing his face that read to me as *concern* before he killed it.

Kael's—Kura's—shadows tangled with a sheet of sunlight and shredded at the edges. He didn't grunt. He never does. He simply took the hit and kept his feet and cut his gaze back to me like he could physically push me backward with a look. "Inside," he said again, teeth bared. "Please."

"I'm not leaving," I said, and I didn't shout. I just put it into the air like a law I intended to enforce.

Hima's grin twitched. "Sweet. Suicidal, but sweet." He slid to the side, spear lazy, eyes not. "Tell me, girl—when he broke your village, did you hide in a cellar and pretend you were brave then, too? Or did you only find this tongue once he taught you how to like the hand that took everything from you?"

My vision whitened at the edges. I wasn't careful. I didn't plan. I threw what I had. The next blast flared so bright the night reeled back. Hima batted it aside but had to plant his feet, shoulders bracing. The silver around his weapon thickened. The silver around his hands brightened. The lazy amusement dropped away for the first time.

"She's holding," Solari said under his breath. It wasn't praise. It wasn't condemnation. It was the thing a general says when he corrects a bad assumption. His gaze never left me now.

Hima's eyes narrowed. "Stronger than you should be," he murmured. His head tilted, predator recalculating. "Too strong for an elf without training."

I didn't answer. I couldn't without losing the air I needed. The heat kept climbing, too much, the way a fever climbs when you convince yourself you don't have one. My hands hurt. My forearms trembled. The world tunneled down to Hima and the clean silver line of his spear.

"Enough," he said.

I threw again.

His spear met it with a crack that traveled down my bones. He slid back half a step, not much, but I saw it and so did he. The silver along the haft flickered. His lip curled.

"This isn't a lesson," he said, and the pleasant tone was gone. "It's an irritation."

Solari lifted his hand as if to speak— "Hima—"—but Hima ignored him. He turned his wrist. The light around his fingers condensed, packed tight until it went too-white, the kind that makes your eyes water. The spear in his hand sharpened, the edge taking on a chill even across the yard.

"This game," he said quietly, "is over."

My stomach went hollow. I knew I couldn't move fast enough. I knew it the way you know water is wet and grief is heavy.

Across the yard, Kael—Kura—straightened as if hauled by a rope. He used what was left of his body like leverage and his shadows like a brace. He looked at Hima, and then at me, and then at the distance between us like he meant to unmake it.

"Don't," he said, and there was a plea in it I'd never heard from him before.

Hima didn't look at him. He looked at me, and lifted the spear, and pointed it at my chest like he was choosing where to hang a painting.

"Last chance, little ember," he said. "Bow. Crawl. Beg. Or go out like the rest of your village did—too proud to understand what was killing them."

I didn't bow. I didn't beg. I tilted my chin up, keeping my eyes locked onto him. "I don't bow or beg to a god scared of an elf."

It was reckless. It was true. His eyes flared—a tiny, involuntary betrayal of the calm he was wearing.

He threw.

For a heartbeat, the world snapped into the cleanest, sharpest focus it has ever had. The silver line between Hima's hand and my sternum was bright enough to carve sight itself. I got my hands up—useless, too slow—and then the shadows cracked like a whip across the yard.

"K—" I didn't finish his name.

He was there.

He didn't blur. He didn't have grace left. He *moved*, the way men do when they decide their body will obey the order even if it breaks. He cut the distance, twisted his torso in front of mine so the spear would have to go through him first, and for an instant I saw him the way the world must: bigger than any lie he'd worn, hair down his back like spilled ink, tattoos lit from inside, all the strength I've felt under my palms in a doorway turned toward one purpose.

The spear met flesh.

It sounded like a bone splitting under an axe. The silver drove in deep at his side and stopped there—not clean through, not for lack of trying. His shadows swarmed the wound and hissed, recoiling and then forcing themselves back in, smothering the light. Heat hit my face. Blood hit my hands. He took one staggering step back into me and dropped to a knee, using my body and the doorframe to keep himself upright because he refused to fall in front of me.

The yard went silent.

Not the forest—the trees still popped and the far fire still cracked—but the line of moon-elves didn't breathe loud enough to be heard, and Solari's light drew in tight, and Hima's arm sank by inches, surprise sneaking over the edge of his anger like foam on a black wave.

I went down with him without choosing to. My knees hit the threshold. One hand found his face. The other found his shoulder and then slid to the haft of the spear and then jerked back because the heat there was too much.

Chapter Thirty

I went down with him without choosing to. My knees hit the threshold. One hand found his face. The other found his shoulder and then slid to the haft of the spear and then jerked back because the heat there was too much.

"Hey," I said, stupidly, like we were in the kitchen and he'd nicked a finger on a blade. "Hey. Look at me."

He forced his head up as if the air were heavy. The red of his eyes locked to mine and held. Up close the tattoos at his throat and along his jaw pulsed like banked coals. Blood slicked under my palm, hot as a stove, and ran in a steady patter off the lip of the step.

"Breathe," he rasped. "Elara. Breathe."

"Don't tell me to be calm," I said, and bit the end off because it was going to turn into a noise that would make the children panic.

Leather creaked out in the yard; the faint, deadly soft shift of armor when someone squares for orders. Solari's voice cut through the smoke—low, controlled, barely leashed.

"Hima," he said, "you had no right. This isn't judgment. This is cruelty."

Hima's reply came bright and careless. "Law is not cruelty, Sun. You clutch at words so you don't have to clutch at the truth."

"Law doesn't permit torture," Solari snapped.

Kura's mouth twitched like he'd warn me not to spend myself on rage I couldn't afford. He turned his face until his stubble rasped my palm and the line of his cheek fit my hand like it was supposed to live there. He found my eyes and held them steady, anchoring both of us in the middle of a field that had decided to become an ocean.

"Listen," he said, and I heard the effort it took him to make each word gentle. "I need you to hear me. I have walked in the shadows for longer than any man should. I thought I would live and die inside it. I didn't know there was anything else." A breath. A flinch he couldn't hide. "Then I found your hall. I found your laugh when you were too tired to make it. I found Miran's stubborn jaw and Loryn's blade of a look and Corin's hands that wanted to help even when they shook. And you." His lids lowered, then lifted, like the weight of everything wanted to shut him and he refused it. "You were the light in my endless shadows."

The words landed everywhere at once—bones, throat, the place behind the heart that makes a person stay or run. I shook my head because there was too much in it and not enough room to hold it all. "Don't," I whispered. "Don't make it sound like a goodbye."

A dry, wrecked laugh escaped him. "It isn't. It's a truth. One you keep if I can't." The corner of his mouth tried to turn up and failed. "You turned me into a man who wanted more than anger. That doesn't leave."

Behind him, steel hissed against wood. Boots hit our porch. Hima didn't raise his voice; he didn't have to. "Bring them out," he said. "All of them."

"No," Solari barked, real heat in it. "You have no right to punish mortals for what he is."

Hima didn't glance at him. "They live under his roof. They are part of his stain." A tilt of his chin at the hall. "You felt it the moment you stepped across the threshold."

"You mistake what you fear for a stain," Solari said, and there was an edge in it that made me look up because I'd never heard it from him. "Enough. This ends with him."

"You will help me seal him," Hima said, calm as a closed door, "or you will explain to the Celestial Council why you refused."

Solari's light flared and dimmed. A long breath. "This isn't justice."

"It doesn't need to be pretty," Hima said. "It needs to be done."

The inner doors slammed open. The sound of children's feet and panic hit in a wave. Loryn's snarl, high and defiant. Miran's "don't you touch him!" broken in the middle by a hit I didn't see. Corin's thin, furious cry. Another door. Another crash.

Kura tried to rise. The spear shifted. The shadows went tight around it, smothering the bright, and he stifled a sound that split me. He failed at standing. He caught my sleeve instead, fingers slick and strong.

"Go," he said. "Elara. Keep them breathing."

"I'm not leaving you."

"I know," he said. "But go anyway."

I shoved up before my fear could decide for me. I made it a single step. Two soldiers cut across the doorway. One caught my wrist, the other my upper arm, and the third came from the side and hooked my elbows back so hard I saw white. I went to bite and took a gauntlet to the mouth that filled my tongue with coin-taste.

"Let me go," I said, and didn't recognize my voice. "Let me go."

"Restrain her," Hima said, idly.

Leather cinched my chest. A strap bit under my ribs. Someone put a knee in my back and made the ground complain. It didn't matter. I saw everything from the ground.

They hauled the children onto the porch and then into the yard. Loryn went for a wrist, then a knee, then a throat; she got a chin with the crown of her head and made the man swear and bleed. Miran threw all his weight into one leg and took a soldier staggering two steps before a hand caught the back of his collar and wrenched him off balance. Corin clutched the soot-black pot like it was a person; when a man pried it out of his hands he screamed a sound I've never heard from him in his small life and launched himself at the thief's shin as if he planned to break it with his teeth.

"Miran," I called, and the boy's head snapped toward me like a tether had yanked it. "Dead fish—now." He went limp on command; the man holding him cursed and almost dropped him. "Loryn—crown, not bite." She aimed higher. Connection. Blood. She bolted, quick as a fox, two strides of freedom before a spear shaft caught her stomach and folded her into a soldier's arms.

"Enough," Hima said, impatient as a prince delayed by rain.

Solari's light flared. "You will not hurt them," he said, and when men with god-light in their chests speak like that, even soldiers look twice at their own hands.

"We are not hurting them," Hima replied. "We are containing a problem you were too squeamish to confront."

He lifted his palm. Silver built along his fingers, bright and merciless, and hung there. Solari raised his, and sun-fire gathered between them, the sigils sharp as cuts. Where the two lights met, the air went white.

The ground under Kura darkened.

His shadows flinched like animals. They tried to hold him. Then the spell settled like a net and they learned to listen to a different voice. They coiled around his wrists, his ankles, his ribs, and began to pull.

He didn't cry out right away. He set his teeth and bowed into it as if he could make his body into a shape that would slip the drag. Then the pull deepened. The boards under him creaked. The breath tore out of him in a sound I will never forget as long as I live, and I have lived through a village burning.

"Kura," I said, and I didn't even know what I was asking.

He fought for air. He found my face like a man feeling for the one solid thing in a flood. "Elara," he said, and forced the words through his lungs as if he could carry them to me like bricks. "Listen. You are the bravest thing I have ever seen. You love like a law. If I had a hundred lives, I would spend every one to stand between you and what wants to devour you."

Tears burned my eyes and didn't fall. He saw the shock of that on my face—the betrayal of even my body refusing me the relief—and his gaze gentled in a way that hurt worse than the rest.

"Tell them I'm sorry," he said, and his eyes shifted past me, past every soldier and every god, to where three small faces shook and shone with salt. "For everything."

Loryn's mouth opened and closed, furious with words that wouldn't come. Miran's chin trembled, and he locked it down hard because he'd decided crying would make it worse for me. Corin's "Dad!" came raw and ripped, like the boy had torn it out of his chest.

"Do not do this," Solari said—at Hima, at the spell, at fate; I couldn't tell. "Hima—"

"Finish it," Hima said.

The sigils tightened. The shadows obeyed. They took Kura by the hips and dragged, slow and unkind, like a man pulled under by a river he had tried to cross after a flood. He clawed for purchase; his nails split on wood. His spine bowed. He bit back the first scream, failed at the second, and the sound made even the soldier with his knee in my back flinch.

"Don't let them win," Kura forced out, and we both heard what he didn't say with it: Not your grief. Not your rage. Not your memory of me.

I wrenched against the straps with everything I had left. Leather burned. Something in my shoulder shifted wrong, and I didn't care. Heat rose under my skin until the hands on me hissed and someone swore and tried to hold me anyway because orders were orders.

He went down to his elbows. He dragged his head up by will alone and found me one last time. The set of his mouth was a lesson I understood: I am terrified. I am not afraid. He tried to say my name and managed only the vowel. It felt like a prayer.

"I love you," I said, because I wasn't leaving it unsaid in a world that would do this with or without me.

He exhaled like a door being opened. "Good," he whispered, with that ridiculous, battered almost-smile. And then— "I'm sorry—for everything."

The shadows took him.

He didn't vanish so much as he was swallowed. The ground didn't open. They accepted. The last of his breath ghosted my face, hot and iron, and then there was nothing where there had been a man who had rebuilt a hall with the stubborn certainty of a tide.

"Get her," Hima said, as if he were tired of a game.

My scream tore itself out of me before I could choose it. I didn't know I could make a sound like that. The air recoiled. The hall went silent as if it were listening. The soldiers' grips faltered a fraction because no human throat should be able to sound like that and still belong to someone breathing.

Something gave.

Not outside—inside me. The pressure that grief makes, the one I'd been holding since the first night Kael refused to sleep, since the first time Loryn set her jaw the way I do, since the first time I realized I would kill to keep a child from learning what ash tastes like—it broke. The world did not rush in. Something in me reached out and took from it.

Moisture. Everywhere at once.

The sting at the corner of my eyes dried into heat. The damp along my hairline crisped away. The grass at the threshold dulled to a flat, tired green; then a harsher shade. The packed earth under my knees lost its dark and went pale. The River's voice, always there if you knew how to listen for it, thinned.

Stuttered. Failed. The air pulled tight in my chest like I'd been running for miles, except I hadn't run; I'd been emptied and something else was filling the space.

"Solari," Hima said. Not quite a question. Not quite alarm.

Solari moved before his mind had words. His head jerked toward me, all the sun in him narrowing to a single, bright line of attention. He took a step—then another—expression reshaping from command into that rare, deadly thing: recognition.

"Elara," he said, and this time it wasn't an order. It wasn't even a warning. It was a name spoken in the presence of a truth arriving.

Blue light pricked across my forearms like frost. It stung, then burned; I watched it write itself into me in clean, sure lines—whorls and bars and arcs that knew where they belonged without asking. The marks wrapped my wrists and climbed, etched the inside of my elbows and curled over the biceps and shouldered on, racing for my collarbones. They weren't painted. They weren't glamorous. They were as real as breath, as permanent as scars, as undeniable as thirst. I smelled steam and realized it was my tears searing off my cheeks before they could fall.

The soldiers tried to keep their hands where they were and failed. The one gripping my left arm let go with a curse, palms blistering. The one behind me lost his nerve and his balance at the same time and fell back. The leather strap across my chest slackened. I shoved up and men skidded backward in dry dust as I stood, my feet carrying me forward to the gods in front of me with a weight I didn't recognize.

"Stop," Hima barked, but he was looking at the wrong person. His gaze flicked from me to Solari and back with the offended confusion of a predator who has never seen prey turn into weather.

"Leave me alone," I said, hoarse, and the words scraped the inside of my throat raw. They still hit the air like a thrown weight. "All of you. Leave me."

The ground cracked in a hairline at my feet. It spidered outward toward the fence, faint at first and then truer as the dirt dried and split. The blue along my arms flared. I felt the river again—felt its shape as a lack, the empty of it, the way it wanted to run and couldn't. Panicked birds lifted from the ravine, went silent mid-flight, and veered. Solari closed the last yards in three long steps. For a heartbeat he didn't reach for me; he only stared, his mouth pressed into a line torn between awe and dread. I lifted my eyes to meet him, glaring at him with a look I didn't even recognize. Then he lifted his hand—open, fingers spread, as if he were keeping me at bay. "You don't even know what you are," he said, the words gentle and terrible at once. "But I do."

Hima's head snapped toward him. "Solari—" He ignored him. He never broke my eyes as he took my forearm in both hands.

"Don't touch me," I said, and would have knocked him flat if anything had been left in me that was only anger. The children's cries ripping from their throats screaming my name, screaming *Mom*, as if I deserve the title. The world went silent around me. Their cries fading into distant waves crashing against a barren beach.

Light took the rest

Epilogue

The world was water and ash when I closed my eyes. When they opened again, I was on a shore that couldn't exist.

The sand beneath me was pale as bone, washed smooth by waves that broke in silence. The sea stretched endless and dark, but when the foam curled at my feet, it glowed faintly blue, as if moonlight had been caught and scattered in every crest.

I didn't know how I had come here. I didn't know if I had died.

But the quiet was wrong. Too heavy. Too expectant.

A shape waited for me at the edge of the tide.

He wasn't Kael, not truly. He wasn't the god whose shadows had held me, nor the man who had smiled at me beneath the broken rafters of our hall. He was something in between—smoke and silhouette, carved from dusk. The sea bent toward him, and the shadows bent too, their edges licking at the waves like fire.

"Kura?" My voice cracked like the shore under lightning.

The figure tilted his head, but his face was featureless, blurred, as if the tide itself refused to remember him clearly. When he spoke, it wasn't his voice alone—it was the water, the sky, the pull of the undertow.

You were the light in my endless shadows.

The words struck deeper than any spear. My chest ached. My hands curled into the sand, though it sifted away like water between my fingers.

But light does not last. It changes. It bends. It becomes something new.

I shook my head. "I don't want new. I want—"

The tide surged, cutting me off. Spray touched my skin, cold as knives, and when I looked down, my arms weren't bare. Blue fire threaded through them, tattoos glowing like rivers mapped under my flesh. They climbed my shoulders, twined my throat, each line pulsing in rhythm with the waves.

My breath stuttered. The air grew damp, heavy, thick with storm.

"What's happening to me?"

The figure stepped closer. The shadows that draped him bent low, curling along the sand toward me. They didn't burn, not like fire. They wrapped soft as smoke, familiar as nightfall.

You are what comes after.

I couldn't breathe. The glow beneath my skin spread faster, rising up my neck, curling at the corners of my eyes. The sea seemed to lean forward with me, every wave holding its breath.

Daughter of flood. Vessel of vengeance. Power runs with you as rivers run to sea.

I pressed my hands to my face, but the light only seeped brighter between my fingers. My heart pounded against my ribs like a fist against a door.

"This isn't me," I whispered. "I'm not—"

They took. You will drown them.

The voice was not cruel. It was not kind. It was inevitable.

Images surged behind my eyes: my village burning, the hall splintering, children dragged screaming into the dirt. My mother at a loom, hands steady even as the walls shook. Her voice low, soft, a thread sliding through my own on the shuttle. Blue fire woven into me.

I staggered, the memory burning like the tattoos now crawling my skin. "She... she gave this to me," I breathed.

The shadows stilled. For the first time, Kura's blurred gaze lifted past me, toward the horizon. *Ask her.*

My blood ran cold. I turned, slow as the tide.

And there she was—my mother. Not as I remembered her, but more. Her eyes held sorrow and something vaster, as if she had been waiting all along.

"Elara," she said, her voice as soft as the threads she once wove. "I stitched it into you the day you were born. A thread no blade could sever. My gift. My warning. My hope."

My throat closed. "Why? Why me?"

"Because they would come for you." Her gaze flicked briefly to the shadow figure dissolving into the surf, then back to me. "Because I knew the tide would rise again. And when it did—you would not be swept away. You would *be* the tide." Her words sank into me like the sea itself, steady and relentless. My chest ached, caught between grief and fury, love and inevitability.

I reached for her, but already she was fading, light breaking her into threads, unraveling her into the glow of the waves.

The tide does not beg. The tide does not forgive.

The figure reached for me then, shadows brushing my cheek. For a heartbeat, I felt warmth—like the rough callused palm that had once cupped my face in firelight.

I looked up, desperate, but his features stayed blurred, his edges dissolving. He was not Kael, not fully. Not anymore.

Rise, Elara.

The whisper came from the sea, the sky, the blood in my veins. My tattoos flared brighter, my body shuddering with something vast and unstoppable. The water bent toward me, pulled by a will I hadn't chosen but could no longer deny.

Rise, and make them fear the tide.

The figure unraveled, dissolving into the surf. The sea swallowed him whole, and where he vanished, the water glowed brighter still, as if lit from within. I reached for him, but only foam met my fingers.

The whisper lingered, curling soft and sharp all at once: *Power is yours. Vengeance is yours.* The waves surged higher, sweeping around me, carrying me off my knees. They wrapped me in their cold embrace, filling my ears, my lungs, my veins.

I didn't choke. I didn't drown.

I breathed.
And the sea breathed with me.